LORDS OF DECEPTION

AN EARTHPILLAR NOVEL

Christopher C. Fuchs

LOREMARK
PUBLISHING

VIRGINIA

Cartography by Christopher C. Fuchs.

Ordering Information: Special discounts are available on quantity purchases by corporations, associations, and others. For details, please write to: contact@loremarkpublishing.com.

Lords of Deception / Christopher C. Fuchs – 1st edition
Paperback ISBN 978-1-946883-00-1
Hardback ISBN 978-1-946883-11-7
eBook ISBN 978-1-946883-01-8

www.loremarkpublishing.com

ALSO BY CHRISTOPHER C. FUCHS

EARTHPILLAR NOVELS

Coming Soon:
The Depths of Redemption
A Light in the Depths

EARTHPILLAR HALF-TALES

The Fourth Messenger
The Revolution Machine

Coming in 2020:
Arcodum
The Feuding Tower

CONTENTS

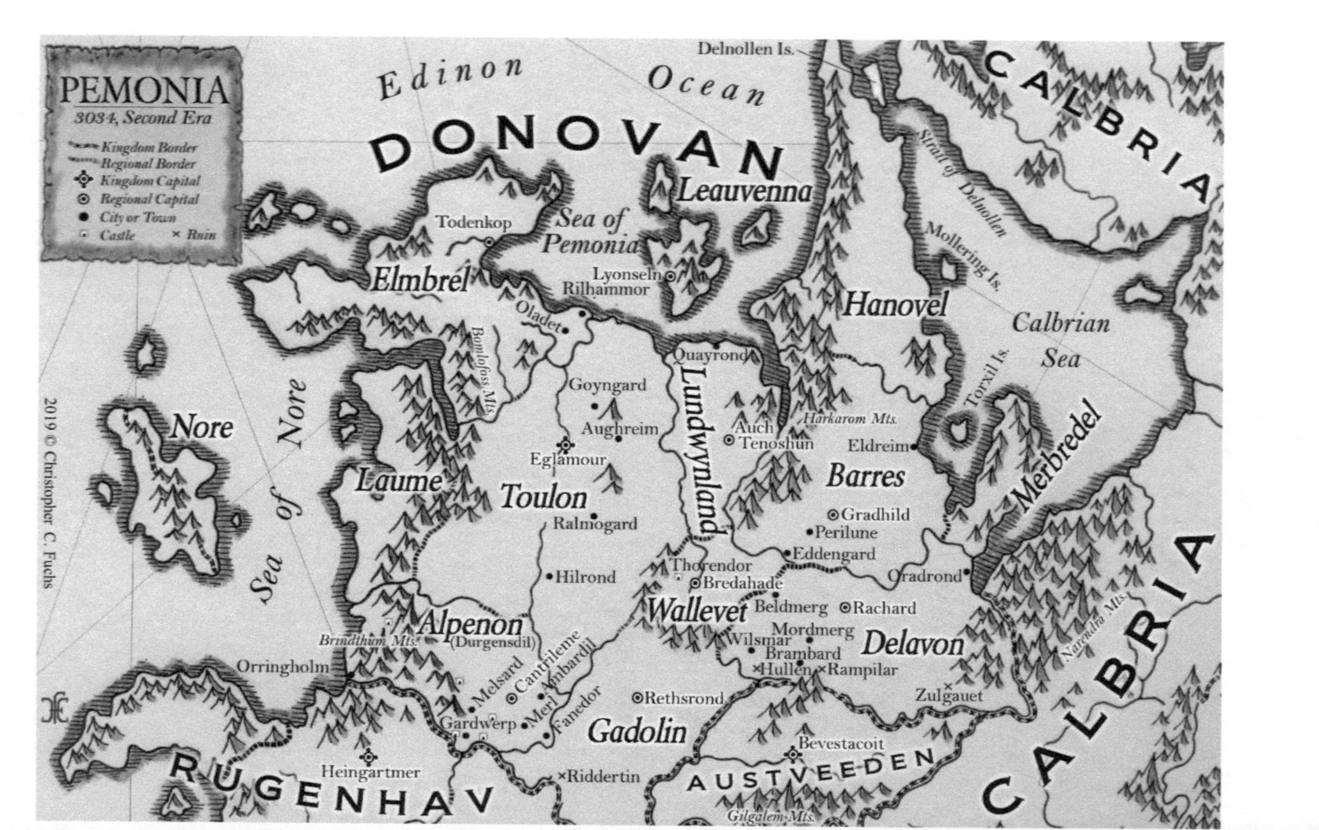

PEMONIA
3034, Second Era
Kingdom Border
Regional Border
Kingdom Capital
Regional Capital
City or Town
Castle
Ruin

Edinon Ocean
DONOVAN
Leauvenna
Delnollen Is.
CALBRIA
Strait of Delnollen
Mollering Is.
Todenkop
Sea of Pemonia
Elmbrel
Lyonseln
Rilhammor
Oladet
Hanovel
Torxil Is.
Calbrian Sea
Quayrond
Lundwynland
Goyngard
Aughreim
Auch
Tenoshun
Harkarom Mts.
Eldreim
Merbredel
Nore
Sea of Nore
Eglamour
Laume
Toulon
Ralmogard
Barres
Gradhild
Perilune
Eddengard
Thorendor
Bredahade
Oradrond
Hilrond
Wallevet
Beldmerg
Rachard
Alpenon
(Durgensdil)
Brindthium Mts.
Mordmerg
Wilsmar
Brambard
Delavon
Hullen
Rampilar
Narendra Mts.
Orringholm
Melsard
Cantrilene
Cambardil
Merl
Fanedor
Rethsrond
Zulgauet
2019 © Christopher C. Fuchs
Gardwerp
Gadolin
Bevestacoit
Heingartmer
Riddertin
AUSTVEEDEN
RUGENHAV
Gilgalem Mts.
CALBRIA

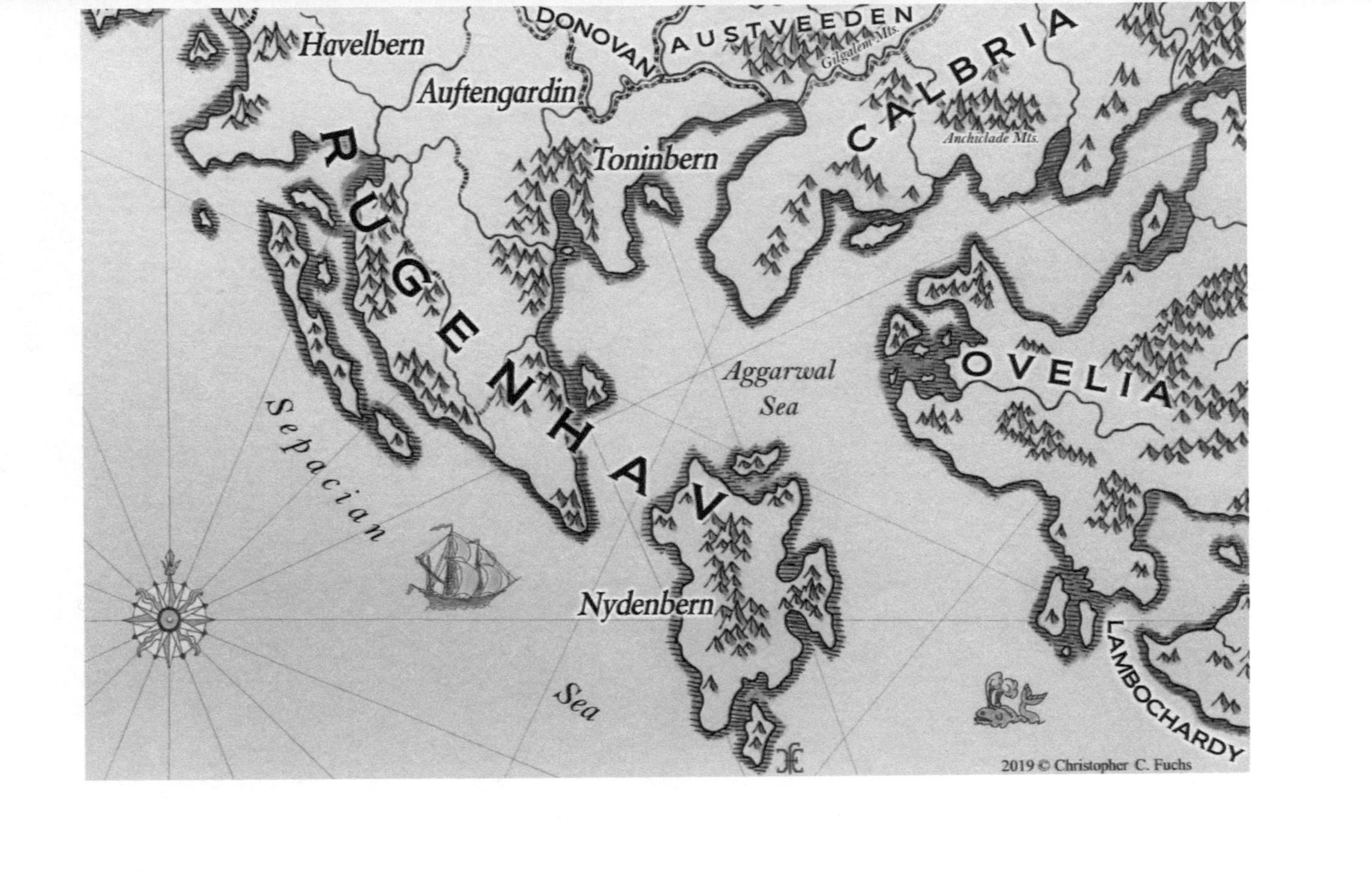

Havelbern
DONOVAN
AUSTVEEDEN
Gilgalem Mts.
CALBRIA
Auftengardin
Anchiclade Mts.
Toninbern
RUGENHAV
Aggarwal
Sea
OVELIA
Sepacian
Nydenbern
Sea
LAMBOCHARDY
2019 © Christopher C. Fuchs

PROLOGUE

Bredahade Castle, Wallevet Ministry
Midspring, 3034

"Are you all right, Lord Raymond?" The young man stared at the gray-haired lord minister until he looked up, blinking. "You look pale, sir. Perhaps you're not well enough to travel?"

"I'm fine, Gerold. Besides, no one else can broker the peace."

Gerold shook his head. "If only the Almerians would be more flexible in their demands. They've held territory in Pemonia for far too long."

"Many wars have failed to dislodge them," Lord Raymond answered. "But we have a chance to keep the Empire Alliance alive to stave off another war. If the king is still prepared to follow through, that is."

"He is, my lord, I assure you. King Erech doesn't want to see the Empire Alliance fall. Now that you have his letter in hand, you can travel back to Eglamour confident that he will support your plan to—"

"Surely you don't mean for me to travel back at this moment?" Raymond squinted at him.

Gerold knew the old man thought him too inexperienced to be a royal courier. "Yes, lord minister," he said. "If we leave tonight we'll be in Eglamour in two days. The Almerian ambassador is already th—"

"You brought no guards, Gerold!"

"My lord, I have two soldiers, and the armored carriage is—"

"Do you realize how many crowned heads would like to see my effort fail, Gerold? To say nothing of the surge in banditry. Yet you presume to take me at night without a guard force?"

"But we—"

"Silence! If the king didn't bother to send a proper escort to bring me to the capital then his heart is not in this. Just like all his other ill-conceived policies. Summons or no summons, I'll not expose myself on the road. I'll not risk my life to save an alliance no one wants."

"Many want it, my lord," Gerold said, his words straining for truth. "I've stood in King Erech's court and heard many nobles voice support for the Empire Alliance."

"That's not what I've heard . . ."

"If only you'd come, lord minister. Then you'd see."

"I had little faith left in this king, Gerold. And the last of it was just washed away by his light regard for my safety. He's the weakest king to sit on the throne of Donovan since Armagnon the Pocked. You are dismissed."

"Lord Raymond . . ."

"You may tell the king that, like the other lord ministers, I will fall in line behind whatever policy he chooses regarding the alliance. If he wants a war, so be it. But I'll not be killed for . . ."

Gerold noticed Raymond glance toward the door. As Gerold turned to look himself, he heard a faint swish. The candle between the two men flickered, and a shadow moved across the doorway.

Gerold was startled by what he heard next. Raymond was gurgling as blood surged out of his mouth. The lord minister clutched his neck, dark red oozing around his fingers. Gerold tumbled off his chair and drew his sword, but there was no one else in the room. For a moment he caught an indistinct movement of something coming toward Raymond, like an insect or blown leaf.

Gerold turned back to Raymond, whose face was now veiled by black mist. The courier smelled soot and putridity.

He stepped toward Raymond as the lord minister fell from his chair, his body limp.

The courier swiped wildly at the shadows in the room, deafened by the throb in his ears. He ran for the door and felt a soft touch on the back of his head. He caught another whiff of the rancid soot but kept moving. He vomited when he turned into the hallway, grasping for the walls as he staggered toward the exit.

"Help me!"

But no guards or servants came. Gerold felt another touch at the base of his head, this time a little sting that blacked out his left eye. He glanced behind him, but the hallway was dark and empty. He struggled for the door, then pushed out into the courtyard.

"Help me!" he shouted toward his waiting carriage.

The two guards came down from the driver's bench. One fell into the dirt, unmoving, as if struck by an invisible hand. The other cried out and bent to cradle his leg. Gerold found himself on the ground, too, his right eye suddenly blind as well.

"Who . . . Who are you?" he demanded as the remaining guard screamed.

"You have a message to deliver," a calm, muffled voice said.

Gerold heard a short whipping sound, like a crossbow, and the screaming guard was silenced. He tried to control his shaking. "Y-yes . . . What m-message?"

"Tell them what happened," said the muffled voice. "Your horses will lead you back."

"You are a Donovard . . ."

"I am an ancient flaming stone. Now go."

PART I

THE ROADS TO RUIN

1

ARTHAN

Rachard Castle, Delavon Ministry
Midspring, 3034

Arthan Valient ducked under the sword swipe. His counterstab was parried by his opponent, so he spun away, catching his second opponent wrong-footed. Arthan lifted his shield overhead, deflecting the first man's attack, then prepared for the second man's charge. But he missed what came next and landed on his back with his ears ringing inside his helm.

"We've been at this for a week now, Brother," came a young voice through the piercing ring.

Arthan unclasped his helmet and let it fall onto the matted grass. "Don't complain to me, Bardil," he said. "I've seen more real battles than you. How many times have you been surrounded?"

"Bardil is right," Pelinaud said. "This maneuver is critical to crusader swordcraft, and it matters not what he has experienced. This is your training, my lord. You can either learn it or learn to run."

"We Valients don't run," Bardil said as he pulled Arthan to his feet. The strength of his younger brother embarrassed Arthan despite it being just the three of them in the field.

"Why must we learn the ancient technique, Pelinaud?" Arthan asked. "Surely a master like yourself prefers the modern techniques. My prior fights did not use—"

"It's one thing to wield a sword—any peasant can do that," said the old master. "But learning the old ways gives you a

7

unique advantage over those of lower or foreign birth. If I had my way, your father would not have brought you into those battles until you had learned the crusader way. The fire in the blood of the Valients was born in the Second Crusade in wild Pemonia, but your skill must be honed."

"My brother prefers books about strategy, politics, and all the rest." Bardil smiled. "Maybe he'd prefer to learn Ovelian dagger dancing."

"I thought that was your desire, Bardil," Arthan said, raising his sword toward his brother. "How else would you attract a respectable ten Ovelian wives? Not with your looks."

"More honor in that than the builder's assistant you've had your eye on," Bardil answered with a grin. "Besides, no lord minister can juggle his duties to the king *and* ten womenfolk. You see, when you die for lack of crusader swordcraft, I'll be next in line to replace Father."

"You're forgetting Rowan," Arthan said. "You are the baby boy."

"The Rugens will get Rowan too . . ."

"Enough foolery," Pelinaud said. "I wish the two of you and Rowan had known your mother. You'd be the better for it. Now, let us begin again."

"Must I play the charging Hral again?" Bardil asked.

"At least I'm not making you run up into the trees," Pelinaud said. "Not that you could, but that's what our crusader ancestors faced back in colonial times, and much more . . ."

"Our enemies don't fight like the heathens of ancient Pemonia," Arthan said.

"Correct," Pelinaud said, "but crusader swordcraft remains relevant, for reasons you'll learn. On guard!"

Pelinaud nimbly lunged between the brothers, swiping at Bardil's and Arthan's breastplates and prompting them to restore their helmets to their heads. Bardil raised his sword at Arthan.

"Watch it!" Arthan pointed his sword behind Bardil.

His brother took the bait, glancing to his left for Pelinaud and lowering his sword. Arthan swiftly spun past the blade, pommeling Bardil's visor before disarming him. Arthan laughed as Bardil lost his balance and teetered backward into the grass.

"Trickery will only get you so far," Pelinaud said, moving to engage Arthan.

"Courtiers use trickery with every other breath," Arthan said.

"But your father and other lord ministers are above the rabble," Pelinaud said.

Before he could respond, Arthan found his vision blocked by a handkerchief thrown across his visor. He felt the crash of Pelinaud's sword on either side of his helmet, then in his backplate. When he regained his vision, he found himself facedown on the ground. Bardil struggled to rise nearby.

"Crusaders fight best as a pair or in a group," Pelinaud continued as he strolled between them. "Now that you've taken your falls, unite against me. Show me what you have learned . . . or have yet to learn."

Arthan felt a flutter in the left of his chest, a familiar tickle that had come and gone since he was a boy. He ignored it and stood first, offering his hand to Bardil, who lay like an ironclad turtle.

"Trick me, eh?" Bardil whispered, grinning through bloodied teeth.

Arthan shouted as Bardil snagged his hand in the crook of his armored elbow and rolled, pulling Arthan down. The two grappled as Pelinaud protested.

"This is not a befitting way to fight," the master said. "Get up, both of you."

Arthan struggled to free himself from Bardil's grip. Only when quick thuds echoed in the ground did Bardil release him. They came to their feet as three riders approached from the adjacent field, their father's magnificent city rising beyond. The brothers removed their helmets as they approached.

"Lord Arthan, you must come quickly," the lead rider said. "Your father sends for you."

"General Medoff, what has happened?"

"Please, my lord. It's urgent."

"We will continue this later," said Pelinaud. "Both of you are dismissed."

"His days of training may be at an end," Medoff said to Pelinaud, the general's dour face grayer than usual.

Arthan sheathed his sword and jogged to his grazing horse. His mind raced as he considered what could be so pressing. In sensing danger he could not help but think of Meriam, of her safety. Damn Bardil for trashing her tranquil beauty with "builder's assistant." Meriam was more than that even if Arthan could never say it. He mounted his horse, feeling the flutter in his chest again. Twice in one day was unusual, but he remained focused.

Medoff escorted Arthan across the fields and up to the gates of Rachard, with Bardil and Pelinaud following. Arthan watched his father's castle on the hill in the city center. The sun was pleasantly warm on his face. But inside he felt unwelcome change afoot.

&

"Sit down, both of you," Maillard said.

Arthan watched his father as he and his brother quietly sat at the table, joining General Medoff and Alfrem, the Alderman of Rachard. Maillard gathered his thoughts for a moment.

"Raymond Reimvick has been killed," Maillard said. "Murdered in his home."

"The Lord Minister of Wallevet?" Bardil asked.

"Most disturbing," Alfrem said with a nod.

"Raymond was found with a stone dart in his neck and poisonous dust on his face," Medoff said. "He had been meeting with a royal courier, Gerold, who barely escaped with his life."

"The killers?" Arthan asked.

"The survivors didn't see anyone," Maillard said. "But Gerold, blinded in the attack, said a man spoke to him. He called himself an 'ancient flaming stone.'"

"How odd," Alfrem said. "I hadn't heard that part . . ."

"What does it mean?" Bardil asked.

"It may—*may*—be a reference to an ancient tale, but we won't discuss that right now," Maillard said, waving his hand dismissively at Alfrem. "What's important right now is why.

Where to begin . . ." Maillard massaged his temples and gave a long sigh.

Arthan could not remember ever seeing his father so visibly shaken. He glanced at Bardil. His younger brother was excited but unaware of anything deeper. Arthan turned back to Maillard, silently urging him to continue.

"Raymond was a dear friend," his father said. "But his mysterious murder is more than personal for me, for all of us. His death could well mean the unraveling of the Empire Alliance, which has prevented a major war for a century and a half."

"My lord, the Almerians never let the alliance stand in the way of their robbing the Pemonian kingdoms," Medoff said.

"This is greater than that," Maillard continued. "Unfortunately, Raymond was the only one willing to risk his life to save the talks. He believed that the alliance, despite its faults, put an end to the broad conflicts that used to rage across this continent and the Middlesea. And he was right. Now that he's gone . . . My sons, you need to understand how the winds are changing. Many crowned heads will see this as an opportunity."

Alfrem jabbed his finger on the table. "And with a king as weak as Erech on the throne of Donovan, the buzzards are likely already circling Eglamour."

"Precisely," Maillard agreed.

"Father, why would such an important alliance rest on one man?" Arthan asked.

"Excellent question. Despite being mostly successful at preserving peace, the Empire Alliance has become unpopular because of how it froze the claims of the kingdoms. The Calbrians want their islands back, for example, as do we. The Rugens, with their burgeoning navy, have grown weary of an old clause in the treaty that limits where they can sail. The Austveedes grow tired of shipping half their electrum ores to the Almerians as protection payment. The list goes on . . .

"For his part, Raymond wanted to rewrite the founding treaty of the alliance to make it more favorable to the Pemonian kingdoms, given the failing power of faraway Almeria. Raymond ostensibly had King Erech's support and certainly mine. But he wrote to me of his fears, given the visceral attitude of many in various courts—especially Rugenhav—that it would be the end of him. In short, Raymond was the only one willing to lay his pride as a Donovard aside—to say nothing of the danger to his person—to negotiate with the Almerians. Many simply didn't want to negotiate with the weakening Almerians, especially if it meant extending the Empire Alliance."

"Your father was Raymond's staunchest supporter," Alfrem added, looking to Arthan and Bardil. "Unless the king ordered Raymond's death, he is likely to ask Maillard to continue Raymond's work, if only to save face with the Almerians—including that runt of a man, their ambassador in Eglamour."

"The king did not kill Raymond," Maillard said. "If Erech wanted to end the alliance, he would have ignored it and let it flounder, as he has other responsibilities."

"Forgive me, Father," Bardil said, "but if the king doesn't want the alliance, why should we bother?"

"He just told you the reason: war will come," Arthan said.

"Perhaps that is what the king wants," Medoff said.

"No one can know Erech's mind," Maillard said, "except perhaps those worms who have burrowed deep inside his head. The king is pushed and pulled by so many powers behind the throne, it is impossible to know his genuine desires.

"Alas, I must go to Eglamour to join the other lord ministers in advising the king on Raymond's replacement, likely to be his brother. While I'm in the capital I will try to help negotiate the Empire Alliance's fate. Arthan, you will remain here and watch over Delavon. Bardil, do as your brother asks. As for Rowan, he should stay in Gadolin for now."

"But Father, I wish to accompany you to the king's court, so I might learn."

"You have a lifetime of court politics and intrigue ahead of you, Arthan. Stay and consult with Medoff and Alfrem on what is best for our ministry while I'm away. As the bastion of the kingdom's eastern borders, Delavon must be kept in steady hands in the weeks and months ahead."

"Training is over," Medoff said, his face dour.

Maillard looked at the general, then around the table. "Only fools cease to learn. Arthan is young and Bardil younger still, but all of you will ably guide them in my absence."

"Father, what about Raymond's assassin?" Bardil asked. "I'm not the brightest by far, but the Reimvicks are the only lord minister family besides us Valients that are not relatives of the king. Could you be next?"

Arthan glanced at Bardil, surprised at his moment of intellect but lamenting his tactlessness.

"Peace is worth every risk, Bardil," his father answered. "Now—farewell."

Arthan watched Maillard depart before looking back at his father's counselors. He could see some doubt in their eyes as they prepared to go about their tasks. Alfrem noticed his stare and approached.

"Don't worry, my lord," he said, placing a comforting hand on Arthan's shoulder, "your father knows how to navigate the king's court, and Delavon is in our collective good hands."

"Thank you, Alfrem." Arthan nodded and took a deep breath, steeling himself for whatever was to come next.

2

FETZER

Perilune Academy, Barres Ministry
Midspring, 3034

Fetzer tapped his foot impatiently and looked around at the other young men and women on the benches. Fresh-faced sergeants all, hoping to hear their names called at the end. Fetzer's mind drifted to his journal entry prior to the assembly.

> . . . and if they don't, well, that will be it. I'm already twenty. Most make knighthood by now. I don't even have a squire badge. If Father were alive he'd have made this right. Uncle won't, so perhaps I must.

His thoughts were interrupted when everyone jumped to their feet and stood at attention. Fetzer did too. Headmaster Cabot entered the assembly hall, followed by Count Atilon's representative, Renz. Fetzer wrinkled his face in disgust. The count could not be bothered to greet his new knights.

"Be seated," Cabot said as he took the podium. "Today I have the honor of announcing the promotions to squire and knight for service in Count Atilon's army under Sigbert, Lord Minister of Barres and servant to our king. As you know, every year we . . ."

Fetzer's mind wandered again. He stared past the headmaster to the count's coat of arms, the lord minister's coat of arms above that, and the king's royal banner above that. He hated their ridiculous, overdone ornamentation. His own Sember family crest was a simple azure shield with thin bands of red and black. He had once written in his journal:

> The academy's crest is painted with boar heads that speak of decapitation, not vigor. The grain bundles of Atilon are reminders of famine, not plenty. And the wheels of Sigbert Wachot betray crushing oppression, not commerce . . .

"And now," continued the headmaster, "the count's representative will call the names of those promoted with these honors."

Renz stepped to the podium and began reading a list of names given to him by a scribe. The young men and women across the benches could not stifle their small celebrations upon hearing their names. It made Fetzer feel sick. To be placed at Perilune Academy was easy for low nobles like the Sembers. But to be personally chosen by Count Atilon was rare.

Fetzer kept his eyes fixed like ice on Renz as he spoke, anxiously thumbing the sapphire wist ring on his finger. He recalled his father giving it to him, and how his older brother sneered at Fetzer's pride at feeling like a Sember man. The longer Renz spoke, the more agitated Fetzer became and the harder he pinched the sapphire. Shame and anger burned like a red coal within him as he stared into the bland face of Renz.

"Report to the courtyard in the morning," Renz said. Fetzer watched him and Headmaster Cabot depart, leaving some sergeants elated and others hopeful for next time. He noticed a group of sergeants congratulating Gade and a few others. Before Fetzer could look away, Gade sent a glare his way that slowly turned into a smile.

"Another failure for Fetzer!" Gade shouted across the hall. "Tuck your tail and go home!"

Fetzer felt the burn swell within him. He made himself breathe and recalled his plan.

> . . . pass me over again. Then I'll abandon my post here. I don't need them. I don't need any of it . . .

Fetzer finally stood and yanked the yellow Perilune tunic up over his head and let it fall to the floor. The young man next to him picked it up.

"Fetzer, you dropped your—"

"Shut it! You can stop pretending to care." Fetzer glanced toward Gade again but he was gone. He felt a chill down his spine.

He leaped into the aisle and rushed straight to the barracks, expecting to find Gade ransacking his things. Everything seemed normal, so he gathered his few possessions and stuffed them into his travel sack. But there was something missing. He held his breath and looked again. His heart throbbed as his eyes darted across the room, looking for the worn binding of his journal. He overturned his bed in frustration. Then snickering bubbled up behind him.

"Looking for this?"

Fetzer turned to see Gade flipping roughly through his journal. Pages were tearing.

"Listen," Gade said to the group that had gathered before him. He cleared his throat as he prepared to quote: "'I do miss Fernon, though I wouldn't tell him so. My brother has followed in my father's footsteps better than I ever will. Fernon will have the barony. He will carry the Sember banner. I cannot share in his honors, his victories, or his loyalty . . .'"

"Who knew the bastard son of a dead baron and a leper whore could have a soft heart?" said one of Gade's friends. They all laughed.

"But you're right," Gade said to Fetzer. "You'll never be a knight, much less have any shred of honor or victory to speak of. Just another Sember swamp rat."

Fetzer kept calm, squared his shoulders, and stabbed Gade with his eyes. "I don't need the rank to prove I'm better with a sword than you. I've spent more time wielding my sword than you've sp—"

"This one?" Gade grabbed a sword from a nearby sergeant and held it up.

"That was my father's sword when he was at Perilune," Fetzer said. He felt a fire bubbling over within him.

Gade spit in Fetzer's journal before snapping it closed. He tossed the book toward Fetzer, then hacked at it with the sword, cleaving off a corner.

Fetzer wasted no time. He snatched up a woolen blanket and tossed it toward the group, then rushed Gade. He deftly dodged the point of his father's sword and punched Gade in the throat. Then he received a few blows from the other sergeants and new knights as they swatted the blanket away. But he managed to pluck the sword from Gade's hand.

Gade sputtered backward as the others fell upon Fetzer. Fetzer defended himself as best he could. They did not stop kicking and hitting when he fell. They grabbed for the sword, but he held fast.

Something sparked within him. Images of his dead father's body and his mother's leprosy flashed through his mind. His brother's absent stare, his uncle's cruel face, and Gade's sneer. As they pummeled him he turned his wrist to position the sword, then he thrust out repeatedly. Two sergeants screamed, and the others let up.

But Fetzer did not stop. He shoved and cut, bringing the blade up over his head and striking in every direction. He felt a hot rush in his veins as his hands and face dripped with crimson. When he stood alone, he slung his travel pack over his shoulder as the rest of the sergeants and new knights fled the barracks or took up arms.

Fetzer stepped toward Gade. He was slouched against the wall, still holding his throat and gasping. Fetzer was comforted by the fear in Gade's eyes, and remembered his own thoughts:

> . . . because fear is a curious thing. It arrives when
> we see our life leaving us, yet its shock can send
> us on our way to live again. Fear cannot be
> anything but the tool of a devious god who enjoys
> bending the wisps of our lives . . .

Fetzer stooped to pick up his damaged journal and level his eyes to Gade's. "You know, I'm certain you would have made a good knight . . ." The fear brightened in Gade's eyes as he struggled to breathe. "But I don't think you would have lasted long outside Perilune."

Fetzer stood and placed the journal in his pack. Then, without hesitation, he swept the blade across Gade's face. He stepped over the bodies toward the door. The remaining sergeants kept their swords up but made no attempt to stop him.

～

"What in God's name?"

Fetzer gave his puzzled uncle a cautious glance as he entered the house and locked the door. "What is God's name, Uncle Laval?"

"What have you done?" His uncle looked over his bloodstained clothes with wide eyes.

"We give ourselves many names, many titles," Fetzer said. "But God seems nameless, faceless, detached . . ."

"What are you talking about? Why this bloodshed?"

Fetzer quietly filled his pack with food from the pantry.

"I warned your father long ago," Laval said. "'This one,' I said, 'this one is trouble.' But he wouldn't listen. To his last dying day he wouldn't listen!"

The door shuddered as there was a sudden pounding from outside. "Open in the name of the count!"

"What trouble this time, Fetzer?" Laval asked as the shouting grew more intense. He grabbed a sword from above the mantel as Fetzer calmly approached him.

"They were no trouble, Uncle," Fetzer said. "Neither will you be . . . Put the sword down."

"Stand fast, little devil," Laval said, stepping toward the door. "I warned your parents. And I kept a place for you here after they died. I did what I could for you and Fernon . . ."

"You treated Fernon like a prince and neglected me at best. Step away from the door."

Laval lunged for the door as it shuddered amid the shouting. Fetzer drew his sword and lashed at Laval's wrist, then his knees. Then he walked away, gathering up additional supplies as Laval writhed in pain on the floor.

When he was done, Fetzer took a small burning log from the hearth. He walked around the house, touching the log to fabrics and furniture and Laval's clothing. Then he walked upstairs and exited out a back window.

3

TRONCHET

Eglamour Palace, Toulon Ministry
Midspring, 3034

"Ill news indeed," King Erech said, stroking his blond beard. "This is the worst time to lose Raymond . . ."

Tronchet stood in his customary place in the front row of court, but it was still difficult to hear the hushed voices of the king and the lord ministers who huddled around him. Like everyone else, Tronchet suspected the rumors were true.

"Aren't you glad Raymond was not in the capital?" whispered someone beside Tronchet. He turned to see Hamelin, commander of the Crownblades that protected His Majesty.

"Yes," Tronchet whispered back. "As a lawkeeper, such a brutal and mysterious murder would be embarrassing for me. And you."

The pair turned back toward the king and his cluster of whispering advisers. Then the quiet was interrupted by a loud, obnoxious voice.

"Can the Lord Ministers' Council offer a recommendation to His Majesty?"

Tronchet knew the voice well. Duke Brugarn walked out from behind Erech's throne, picking his teeth while glaring at the ministers.

"We do," Maillard Valient answered as the lord ministers finally stepped back from the throne. "The eldest of Raymond Reimvick's living brothers, Edmond, would be an able ruler for Wallevet. We recommend the king confirm him as Raymond's successor, in line with ministerial tradition and Edmond's abilities."

"What has he paid you to give his name?" Brugarn asked, his voice heavy with accusation.

Maillard ignored Brugarn's insult and kept his eyes on King Erech. But Tronchet noted that the king seemed detached. Erech simply stared back until Maillard responded.

"Your Majesty, it will not surprise you that we are also concerned that Raymond's death will cause the negotiations on the fate of the Empire Alliance to falter. A few of us are prepared to keep talking with the Almerians and the kings of Pemonia, should you wish it."

"Should I wish it . . ." Erech repeated absently.

Tronchet caught himself shaking his head and stopped. He had too often witnessed the king's indecision on important matters, but it was getting worse.

"Foolish talk with foul beasts is foolish indeed," Brugarn said.

Tronchet looked away. It was always a bit too much when the king's brother fancied himself a purveyor of wisdom.

"What need do we have for it now?" Erech finally asked.

"The Empire Alliance has been the foundation of relative peace between us and the other kingdoms and Almeria," Maillard said. "Well before any of us were born."

"Hasn't stopped the battles I've been required to fight my whole life," General Chaultion said.

"Small borderland battles were always understood not to jeopardize the broader peace," Maillard said. The general glared at him.

"And there are other repercussions to consider," said Sigbert Wachot, lord minister of Barres. "Even if we get the Almerians to withdraw from our islands, the Kingdom of Calbria claims those islands, too, and will surely fight us for them."

"To say nothing of their claims to my gold mines in Merbredel," said lord minister Rand Halevane.

"Then we attack first!" Brugarn shouted.

"Your Majesty, I also support attacking the islands," Chaultion said to Erech.

"We are not prepared to make war on two fronts," Maillard said. "Calbria can summon twice as many soldiers as we can, and the Almerians occupy heavily fortified positions on those islands. Furthermore, the Rugens on our southern border will suspect we plan to attack them as well, given their conspiracy-drunken leaders."

"We cannot afford to provoke war on three fronts," Sigbert agreed. "We must settle our demands over the table, not on the battlefield, if we can."

Tronchet could see the word *cowards* forming on Brugarn's lips. But the duke was cut off.

"So be it," the king said. "Then the Valients will host the talks. Rachard is a faster ride for the Calbrians, Austveedes, and Ovelians anyway. We can arrange for the Almerian and Rugen ambassadors to be escorted to your capital forthwith."

"Finally rid of them!" Brugarn blurted.

"But this will be the last attempt," Erech continued.

"And doomed to fail," Brugarn said.

"I'm honored to serve," Maillard said.

"Don't budge on our demands to the Almerians," Erech said. "I've grown weary of them."

"We could join forces with anyone on the continent to kick them off the islands," Chaultion said. "And if anyone else wants our islands, I'll meet them on the battlefield."

"If we provoke war," Maillard said, keeping his eyes on Erech, "we'll get it three- or fourfold."

"Then let it come," Brugarn said. "The Almerians probably killed Raymond to provoke us. We'll answer sword with sword!"

Tronchet noticed Sigbert straightening to his full towering height. "Cared for Raymond, did you?"

"Sniveling appeaser of Almerians," Brugarn said, "but he was still a Donovard."

"My lords," Maillard began, "these are grave issues that the king must—"

"My brother the duke has always been my wisest counselor," Erech interrupted. Tronchet wanted to vomit at the notion. "We are all aware of what is at stake. The Empire Alliance was broken years ago and merely limps along today. Do what you can, Maillard, and we will see who needs the alliance more. As for Raymond's successor, Edmond Reimvick will be satisfactory."

Waldemar, Steward of the Palace, called Tronchet's name as the lord ministers filed away from the throne. "Your Majesty, your next audience is with Sir Tronchet, Chief Magistrate of Eglamour."

"Not again . . ." Brugarn mumbled. Tronchet ignored him.

"My king, I'm aware of the many important issues that trouble your time. However, I bring to you another matter, one more personal to you . . ." Tronchet glanced at Brugarn's souring face.

"What could be more personal than the future of my brother's kingdom, you old fool?" Brugarn asked. Erech raised his hand to silence the duke.

"My king," Tronchet continued, lowering his voice to a whisper, "her thefts have continued. I don't know how much longer I can contain this. The victims demand your justice."

"Victims?" Brugarn chuckled. "Anyone who loses jewels to her is careless, brainless, or both."

"Your Majesty, she continues unabated," Tronchet said.

"One of his lord ministers was murdered and his favorite messenger blinded by an assassin from the shadows," Brugarn said. "The Empire Alliance will collapse any day now, and our treasury dwindles while your constables are too lenient with collecting taxes. Yet you continue to bother the king with this pestering mite of an issue?"

"Your Majesty, I only—"

"Speak to Her Mother the Queen, if you must," Erech said. "But don't bring this to me again."

Tronchet bowed his head low.

"If you bring this again," Brugarn said, "I'll piss in your pretty chief magistrate hat and you'll wear the new hat of chief of the chamber pot."

Tronchet kept his composure, adjusting the royal purple feather in his black magistrate cap. "Your Majesty . . . Duke Brugarn," he said with a bow as he departed.

Tronchet stopped himself before he came to Queen Andrilenne's outer chambers. He did not trust her judgment any more than he did the king's. The queen had become increasingly insular over the years as Erech lost the little respect he had previously commanded.

If only I could catch that girl red-handed, he thought to himself. Perhaps then the king or queen would listen. Probably not. But perhaps Tronchet could convince the girl to change her ways.

4

MARLAN

Thorendor Castle, Wallevet Ministry
Midspring, 3034

Marlan shook his head. "I could have done better, Master. I was careless."

"Nonsense" Arasemis said.

"I didn't intend to blind the king's courier. We're lucky he was well enough to make it to Eglamour to convey what happened."

"You went in and came out undetected. You eliminated Raymond. Nothing else matters. Concentrate on your studies and training again, until the next task."

Marlan wanted to ask what the next task would be, and when. But he had learned that Arasemis only provided details when everything was prepared. As Marlan sat down to eat, he noticed the place was too quiet. "Where are Bertwil and the others?"

Arasemis looked up from his scrolls. "They have begun a new task. It begins in Barres Ministry, and then they are bound for Leauvenna."

"Are they ready for a mission without me?"

"Individually they are not as talented as you, Marlan. But together they should be fine." Arasemis returned to his reading.

Marlan occupied himself with an ancient Naren-Dra alchemical text while he ate. He loved all the harvest charts and ingredient tables. The mixture sequences and formulas. And the peculiar glyph writing of the Naren-Dra. Marlan slipped a hand into his tunic, reaching for his alchemy belt. He pulled out a small, soot-dusted egg and held it up to the candlelight.

"I've told you before to empty your pouches and belt downstairs before coming up," Arasemis said without looking up. "Particularly the shroud eggs."

"I wanted to tell you that these did not work as quickly this time. The lord minister took at least a minute to choke. And he didn't vomit."

"If you shot a dart in his throat he likely wouldn't," Arasemis said. "Especially if you didn't mix in enough toad vinegar." The master stood and plucked an empty glass jar from a shelf. He filled it from the water pitcher and set it before Marlan. "Drop it in."

They watched the surface of the water cloud as the soot washed off the egg. Arasemis jabbed his knife into the egg, and black powder surged out into the water like webbed hands. Then it congealed and fell to the bottom of the jar while tiny white granules floated to the top.

"You see?"

"I needed more toad skins for the vinegar," Marlan said.

Arasemis nodded. "And be patient with the distilling. It is one of the most important conversion methods of chemina arcana. Slowly feed the powder into the hollow eggs when you're sure it's completely dry." Arasemis flipped through the Naren-Dra alchemy book. "There—'Death should occur within one minute or less. Good vomiting and itching should be shorter still.' Now, go down to the laboratory and empty your belts. Refill them and a second set with our standard poisons, incendiaries, and illusories. Put it all in the carriage, then come back so we can discuss the next task."

"Yes, Master Arasemis."

Marlan went down to the large room hidden beneath the floor of the great hall that served as the laboratory. Shelves from floor to ceiling were crammed with every size and shape of bottles, jars, alembics, canisters, and other vessels made of glass, ceramic, stone, iron, and wood. There were two large hearths hung with cauldrons and numerous workbenches strewn with tools and leftover raw ingredients.

He walked to his worktable and carefully removed the bottles from the belts under his tunic, then unstrapped the belts. He glanced at the barrel in the corner of the room. Unable to resist, he walked over and peered at the hilt of a sword resting on the lip of the open barrel. The whole blade was submerged in a shimmering solution.

"Unchanged, damn . . ." he muttered. It wouldn't be ready in time for the next task. He visually inspected the sachets of stones hanging in the solution. Particles were slowly melting out of the sachets, falling along the blade and resting on the barrel's bottom.

Marlan went back to the shelves and filled his belts with everything he would need. He did the same for Arasemis's belts, then stuffed it all into the pack. He carried the pack to the stables and placed it in the carriage, his mind still on the sword. When he returned to Arasemis he found the master poring over a map.

"You didn't touch it, did you?" Arasemis asked without looking up.

"No. But it looks the same as when we put it in."

"Patience. It's worth waiting for." Arasemis pointed at a small blot on the map, east of Thorendor Castle. "We leave tonight for Delavon Ministry, to a free city called Mordmerg."

"We?" Marlan was surprised. The master rarely left Thorendor.

"We'll go by carriage, disguised as merchants, to meet a group of criminals called the Blackhoods. They fancy themselves protectors of Mordmerg's free city status, which they think is threatened by Lord Minister Maillard Valient. But the Blackhoods rob their own people because there is no actual threat to the city . . . yet."

"I don't understand. We're going to meet with petty thieves in a neighboring ministry? I'm sure Vorrault has thieves if you want to hire—"

"Listen and try to follow. When you killed Raymond it disrupted his ongoing negotiations to preserve the Empire Alliance. Maillard is likely to continue those negotiations. The vast wealth and skilled soldiers of the Valients make doing a task against Maillard more difficult. We're not going to do things as we normally would."

"So the Lord Minister of Delavon is our next target." Marlan nodded with satisfaction. "Why don't you let me creep into his castle and do it myself? I can easily get past his—"

"He is not in Rachard, he's in Eglamour. He's too well protected, Marlan, even on the road. If Bertwil and the others were here, it would be possible. But it doesn't matter, because I have a better plan."

"What could be better than killing another lord minister?" Marlan asked.

"Quiet and follow what I'm saying. Instead of directly attacking Maillard, we'll encourage a revolt against him in Mordmerg, not too far from his capital in Rachard. Like all the free cities, Mordmerg is an enclave within Maillard's lands but under Almerian influence. The Blackhoods are there and itching for a fight, which we'll help arrange. After the revolt, the Donovards and Almerians will blame each other."

"I see," Marlan said. "Donovan and the Almerian Confederation will be at each other's throats, more than they already are. We'll exploit the weakness of the Empire Alliance."

Arasemis nodded. "If Maillard becomes the negotiator between alliance members, trouble in Mordmerg will put him in a difficult spot—if we can get the Blackhoods to do what we want. My hope is that they'll cause enough problems that Maillard himself will go to Mordmerg when he returns from Eglamour. I doubt he'd bring a large force so as not to provoke the Almerians in the city. That will give us an opening to assassinate him."

"Then the alliance falls and the Pemonian kings are at each other's throats, giving Candlestone room to thrive," Marlan said. "I like this plan. But can I kill Maillard myself, or at least manage the Blackhoods solo?"

Arasemis shook his head. "The leader of the Blackhoods, a man named Navarron, is a skittish fellow. I suspect he is an agent of the Almerians, but I can't be sure. I had some dealings with him years ago. Navarron will remember me, but he wouldn't trust you if I sent you alone. We'll meet him together, then you'll stay in Mordmerg to carry out the plan."

"If this works, will we do the same in the other free cities?"

"It probably wouldn't be difficult, especially if the alliance falls and the Donovards pillage the free cities. But we have too much to do. After Mordmerg, our focus must be on the king, his most powerful supporters, and the full resurrection of Candlestone."

"I'll ready the horses," Marlan said.

5

MILISEND

Near Eglamour Palace, Toulon Ministry
Midspring, 3034

"Then run away with me." He brushed the back of his hand across her cheek.

"You know I cannot."

"Oh, Mili. You live the life of a thief. You meet me in the woods like this. But you can't come away with me forever?"

Milisend pulled the soft blanket up to her chin. "Like your jewels, you'd lose interest in me once you have me to yourself, Regaume."

"You are a gem I would pocket for life," he said. "Come with me. We will steal anything you wish, from anyone. The tiaras of the hundred wives of the Ovelian Emperor. The scepter of the Martinus in Almeria. We could take an entire Austveede ship of electrum, if you wish."

She snugged the blanket up to her nose, considering the offer.

"Is that a yes?" Regaume asked.

"Silence is not a yes."

"My heart is but the plaything of a princess . . ." he said.

"No one has pity for such a lament." She smiled.

"Still, I must have your answer."

"Again, I cannot leave. You know Father has gotten worse. The stress upon his mind, the fitful indecision, the influence from many dark quarters . . ."

Regaume turned away from her with a theatrical sigh.

"He has the world on his shoulders . . ." she insisted.

30

"The world, Mili?"

"You know what happened to his lord minister in Wallevet. Father keeps a hard face in court, but privately he's depressed, downtrodden. Mother avoids him. Only I can—"

"Mili, if I were a spy, the king's poor health might be valuable information." Regaume grinned with eyebrow raised.

"Don't be ridiculous. Anyone who attends court can see it. His lengthy blank stares and bouts of anxiety. Uncle Brugarn speaks more and more on his behalf. The storm of intrigue and ill health that brews around the king is hardly a secret worth paying for."

"Then escape it all. Come with me."

"I want to, Regaume, but I must stay and help him."

"I admire your love for your father, though I am jealous of it. But I wish you would run away from the royal life. Find your freedom in the thrill of thievery. I haven't taught you everything yet, you know."

Milisend raised an eyebrow. "I've surpassed you, and you know it."

"Really? Then why is that pesky chief magistrate Tronchet on your trail, Mili?"

She laughed. "He has yet to catch me and I've always denied his accusations."

"Then hear my final plea, Thimblegloves . . ."

"Don't call me that."

"Every good thief needs a name. And . . . oh, what's this?"

She tried to hide her smile with the blanket. "Don't . . ."

Regaume reached for his jacket and pulled a silver thimble from the pocket. He held it up with a smile.

"I don't bother with thimbles anymore," she said. "I felt so guilty about those first thefts. I had to leave them a little something."

"I remember. Those poor, unfortunate, wealthiest of victims. Even Tronchet was amused with the swap. In truth, I thought it was brilliant. A symbol of your fearsomeness: stolen jewelry replaced by a humble thimble."

"Or the symbol of a courtly life I do not want?"

"Thimblegloves, if you come away with me I will teach you the advanced evasion techniques . . ." Regaume rolled over and gently pinned her to the moss-covered ground. "You see? You have much still to learn."

She smiled and pulled her hand up, dangling his coin purse. "Seems you need help in detection."

"Let me search around a bit . . ."

She giggled but the face of her distraught father returned to her mind.

Regaume sensed it. "Pick the locks and remove the chains that entangle your life," he said. "Abandon the life of a princess."

"It's my father that I cannot abandon, Regaume. Nor you. I must try to help him."

"Then I will wait until your answer changes. For now, I will keep the name of Thimblegloves a secret in my heart."

"Thank you."

6

ARTHAN

Rachard Castle, Delavon Ministry
Midspring, 3034

"What is it?" Arthan asked.

A letter from your father, Medoff said. "His messenger said he's already on the road by now." Arthan opened the letter.

> My son,
> I will return to Rachard much sooner than I expected. The king has ordered me to continue Raymond's negotiations in earnest. I am to host the foreign ambassadors in Rachard. A few of them will arrive with me. Ensure that we are prepared to receive what will be a large assembly, perhaps the last for the Empire Alliance.
> Have General Medoff introduce you to Serdot. It's time you put down the strategy books and practice real diplomacy and other, more discreet, methods of politics.
>
> Maillard Valient
> Eglamour

Arthan let the parchment fall from his hands. He leaned back in the chair with a heavy sigh.

"Reading it seems to have aged you," Medoff said. "What does he say?" Arthan handed him the letter. The general's bushy black mustache locked in a frown. "This will not be pleasant."

"How can this be anything but dangerous for Delavon?" Arthan asked.

"I will call up extra men from your father's vassals. The castle will be doubly secured and I'll increase the patrols in the city. We should inform Countess Iserenne so she may escort your father from the western border. And I recommend sending word to Count Dardanon in the east so he can watch the ports and inform us when new ships arrive."

"All of that sounds fine, Medoff. But why must Father remain so loyal to such a weak king?"

Alderman Alfrem cleared his throat and leaned up to the table. "As one of the twelve lord ministers, Maillard is oath-bound to serve the kingdom and advise the Crown. Most of the ministers do not favor King Erech but they must support his policies or forfeit their lands and titles."

"But the Valients were kings once," Arthan said. "Father does not talk about it much, but surely we did better than the House of Avaleau."

"That was a long time ago," Alfrem said with a nod. "Your father serves the king."

"Do you think the alliance will crumble?" Arthan asked, turning to Medoff.

"War and defense are my domain, my lord. I can only guess at the minds of politicians."

"It's all but a certainty," Alfrem said. "What's more, they'll blame your father for it, regardless of whether they supported the alliance in the first place."

"Then we must prepare Rachard for the worst," Arthan said, stroking his short beard. "Aside from marshalling more guards, how can we learn what to watch for?"

"We can secretly listen to the ambassadors in their private chambers," Medoff said.

"And thus aid your father's negotiations," Alfrem said.

"It's easily done," Medoff continued, glancing at Alfrem. "We have a company of special scouts, widsemers, skilled in such things. They can pose as servants and such. Serdot is among them."

"Good. If these ambassadors are soon to become our enemies, we'd do well to know them better. Tell me more about this Serdot fellow."

Medoff turned to the alderman. "Sir Alfrem, might I speak privately?"

"Of course," Alfrem said, excusing himself with a curt nod. When he was gone, Medoff continued.

"I'm glad your father mentioned Serdot. If he hadn't, I would have, given the sensitive situation we're about to find ourselves in."

"Well, go on. Who is he?"

"He is a servant of your father, only a little older than you. Our best widsemer. But whereas most widsemers prefer to work alone in the woods or on the road, Serdot has a knack for people. He's good at learning the secrets they hold so dear and persuading them to do things they normally wouldn't."

"A spymaster so young?"

"I will introduce you when he returns from . . . wherever he goes. He's not my sort, mind you. I prefer soldier to soldier on the battlefield. But your father's adept use of shadow men has proven to me that they have their place."

"Very well, I look forward to meeting Serdot. In the meantime, make our necessary preparations for the assembly. We don't have long."

"Of course, my lord."

The arrival of a courier interrupted Medoff's departure. "My lord, an urgent message from Count Golbane. Trouble in Mordmerg Free City."

"Mordmerg?" Medoff repeated in disbelief.

Arthan opened the letter.

> Cousin Arthan,
>
> I regret to inform you that there has been a disturbance in Mordmerg. My knights have secured the city but it has been difficult to determine what happened. Fires were set in a dozen places in the city over the past week, but they were put out before posing much threat to the city.

> I will write to you again when we've caught
> the culprits.
>
> > Count Golbane Valient
> > Mordmerg

"This cannot be coincidence," Arthan said, handing the letter to Medoff. As he waited for the general to read it, Arthan realized he did not know much about Mordmerg. It was only a day-and-a-half ride away from Rachard.

"It probably is merely coincidence," Medoff said. "Golbane will handle it. We should keep our focus on the arrival of the ambassadors."

"But what if it is related?"

"I don't see how it could be, given Mordmerg's own troubled past. If someone wanted to sabotage the Empire Alliance they would set the fires here in Rachard."

Arthan pursed his lips, but let it go.

ॐ

Arthan was up on the tallest ladder in the library, searching the forgotten volumes near the ceiling, when he heard her voice.

"Seems the world is coming to Rachard in mere days, yet you're searching for books to read?"

He turned to see her curling her chestnut hair behind her ear. She held a collection of old parchments against her chest.

"Good afternoon, Meriam." He climbed down, giving himself a moment to muster a stern, focused face. "Just looking for something . . . What are you doing in the library?"

"Bellumet sent me to look for the old drawings of the visitor quarters. He thinks there are hidden passages behind the walls. Do you know what that's all about?"

"I would have thought the old engineer kept such papers in his chambers."

She feigned sad eyes. "Not happy to see me?"

"Meriam . . ." He tore his eyes from hers. He always felt at peace looking into her deep brown eyes, but his father had entrusted him with preparing the city. He opened his mouth to give his excuses but found himself clutching a nearby chair as his breath was interrupted. Her playful gaze flashed with fear.

"Arthan, are you all right? Did you feel it again?"

"It's fine."

"You need to see the physician. You only have one heart. Even if it can't be mine, you must take care of yourself."

"I don't have time for that. It comes and goes. It's fine." He felt her glare but did not meet her eyes. He skimmed the upper shelves. "I was just looking for the Mordmerg survey. I was curious . . ." He knew she would take the lure.

"Digging up the past? I thought you didn't have time to waste."

"I'm not doing it because of Mother. There is new trouble in the free city that doesn't sit well with me. Medoff says it's nothing and Golbane is there, but . . ."

Meriam closed the distance as he spoke. She smelled like the chief engineer's chambers. Ink and paper, brass instruments, and old Bellumet's pipe. And lilac. Though a commoner, Meriam was more beautiful than any nobleman's daughter. Arthan physically shook the notion from his head.

"What?" she asked, her face close to his.

He knew she knew. "Meriam, I have work to do."

"A man does his duty better when a woman balances his life."

"We've been through this. Father would never—"

"You'll be lord minister one day. Maybe then you'll do as you desire."

"Is my love in secret not enough?"

"Do I have even that? The fortune of being the mistress of a young lord? Or am I merely an occasional entertainment for you?"

"Meriam . . ."

"You have work to do," she said, turning past him. "And so do I." She laid her parchments on the table, then searched the low shelf for the old castle drawings. "If I see the Mordmerg book I'll leave it out."

He turned to the door.

"Arthan . . ."

He looked back at her.

"You must see the physician about your heart."

He turned and departed from the library, struggling to focus his mind.

7

FETZER

Perilune, Barres Ministry
Midspring, 3034

Fetzer thought no more of the smoke and shouting behind him at his uncle's house. His mind was moving forward, leading him through the slums of Perilune that he knew so well. They had regularly served as an escape for him when the stuffy academy became too much. Despite his own arrogance, he preferred the plainspoken poor over the snotty-nosed cadets. And he knew exactly where to go this time.

"What do you want?" sneered the grouchy, round-faced man in the doorway.

"I want to work on one of your boats."

"Do I look like a merchant? Be gone!"

Fetzer put his foot in the door. "You look like Rilranef the Round."

"Maybe I am, maybe not. What makes you think I have a job for you?"

"I've seen your . . . sailors, let's call them, working down on the Elme River, at the Eddengard inland port. I want to go to sea."

"Forget about it. What else have you seen?"

"I've seen enough to know the money is good. Stolen goods move quickly and demand is high. I won't ask questions."

Rilranef's round face scrunched uneasily. "You're a petty noble . . . and I don't know you and no one sent you."

"I'm just a traveler. My name is Fetzer. Perhaps only my first name will suffice?"

"I won't hire you. Get out."

Fetzer flung his cloak and pulled his father's Perilune sword. Staggering back, Rilranef reached for a fish knife on the table. Fetzer slammed his sword on the knife and shoved Rilranef away. "I thieved this nobleman's sword from the academy. Worth ten lorins or more."

The man glanced at the sword. "I don't need a thief . . . Wouldn't sell anyway, not here in Perilune. No one would take the risk."

"I'll do whatever job you need on the boats."

Rilranef thought for a moment. "One of my captains needs a clerk. You read and write?" Fetzer nodded. "You'll write up the papers for the cargo, then," Rilranef continued, "to avoid the tax. If the ship is caught, you're caught. Follow me? The job pays four faits a day plus rations and a Calbrian silver penny if the job goes smoothly. Be at the Eddengard docks by sundown tomorrow."

"Who shall I ask for?"

"Talk to no one but Captain Renaud. The ship is the *Meurden.* Here." Rilranef pinched a quill and scratched on a scrap of paper for Fetzer.

"A triangle with a dot?"

"It's all you'll need. Don't lose it and don't ask questions."

৽

Fetzer found a crate in a quiet alley where he could write in his journal and sleep the day away. When night fell he ate from his pack, then started walking to Eddengard. He walked all night along the road, hiding in the bushes when riders approached. His mind drifted to his writings as he walked in the moonlight.

> . . . can finally escape. My only regret is not seeing
> Fernon one last time. I imagine he has identified
> the charred remains of Uncle Laval. And the dead
> at Perilune are wet with their mothers' tears . . .

Fetzer smiled to himself, proud of the manner in which he had exited. He whistled in the dark, thinking of what it would be like to be out on the open sea.

> I have often dreamed of vast stretches of sparking water. The towers of Perilune tumbled down by the salty winds. The surrounding hills melting into the lake. It widens until the earth is pushed away and only the waves remain . . .

When Fetzer grew tired he slept in the forest until late morning. He broke the night fast and continued walking, preferring the shadows of the woods. It was midday when he came within view of the river port. He crept to a hidden overlook, discovered years prior, and took out his journal.

> The port is not grand but it's a jewel to me. I see the docks near the bridge to Wallevet. There are three river boats, only one of which could rightly be called a ship. It must be the *Meurden*. Men are loading it with sacks, barrels and crates. It seems like they are taking their time, though I'm no sailor. Sundown is a while yet. I will sleep.

When Fetzer awoke, the sky was beginning to redden as the sun dipped between the peaks of the Harkarom Mountains. The sailors had finished loading and were lying about, waiting. The other boats were gone.

As Fetzer gathered up his things, something changed. A bell rang out and the crew of the *Meurden* unfurled her sails. Three figures ran toward the docks from the far side of the bridge. One of the figures was a lumbering hulk, the other two thin and nimble like women. They did not slow down until they were aboard the ship, where they disappeared belowdecks.

Fetzer scrambled down from the overlook, trying to keep his eye on the ship. The remaining sailors were boarding. He hurried down the road and trotted up to the ship as they were pulling the gangplank. The sailors glared at him.

"I have the triangle dot," he hissed, holding up the scrap of paper. The sailors paused, then extended the gangplank and he hopped aboard as the ship pulled away.

✑

"New clerk?" Renaud asked. Fetzer stared back at the captain's squinty eyes. "I didn't need a clerk."

Fetzer looked out across the river to the darkening banks, then out to the deck before them. When he glanced back at the captain, he spotted a half-corked bottle of Gromanese wine in Renaud's hand.

"Grom is my favorite," Fetzer said. "Unfortunately, the thieves of the Perilune slums can never steal enough from the nobles' tables to satisfy demand."

Renaud's scowl softened for a moment. "Yes, yes. A most fine wine . . . I'll wager smuggling is nothing new to you?"

"Newly rekindled, let's say. But I'm new to the sea for sure."

"Get belowdecks and make yourself useful clerking the cargo. Stay out of the way or silver pennies is the least you'll lose. And do your vomiting above or you'll swab the whole deck for a week."

Fetzer excused himself and descended into the nearest hatch. From the ladder he bumped into the walls and other smugglers as he tried to find his footing amid the rocking of the ship. When the *Meurden* lurched to starboard he spilled into the kitchen, where a sack of flour burst to break his fall.

"I'm the new clerk," he said, trying to gather up the pile.

The cook grinned. "Been on ship before?" Fetzer shook his head as the cook extended his hand. "I'm Greffid. Scoop it up like this. I won't say a word."

Fetzer stood when most of the flour was recovered. "I was looking for the quarters."

"Officers get the aft cabins near the captain's. I'm there too because Renaud likes to eat."

"I'm an officer?"

"On this ship you are. If as clerk you don't fake our papers properly, we're all in the brig. That's your job. Come, I'll show you the quarters."

Greffid stowed a few more supplies, then led Fetzer toward the rear of the ship. "Over there is the captain's chamber. This one is the first mate's, and a few others are down that corridor. You'll be with me in here. Five hammocks, four empty, so take your pick. Usually they'd be occupied but Renaud isn't keen on this crew for some reason. He makes them sleep toward the bow."

Fetzer remembered the three figures who hurried aboard ship before he did. He also remembered the warning from Rilranef the Round to not ask questions. "Thank you, Greffid."

"Clerks read and write. Might you teach me to read a bit before we get to Leauvenna?"

"Leauvenna?" Fetzer asked. "We aren't going to Middlesea?"

"No." Greffid smiled. "We'd need more food for that voyage. First we'll be on the rivers a bit, then to the island ministry."

Fetzer put his pack in a hammock. "Fine enough. Yes, Greffid, I can teach you to read."

❧

During rations Fetzer tried to ask Captain Renaud how he might make the cargo ledger forgeries. But the captain wanted to focus on his wine, not business. So Fetzer retired to his hammock. He found it difficult to sleep, so he pulled out his journal and wrote by the light of the tin lantern that swung from above.

> I'm not one day from Perilune and already the
> world is different. Ship life is cramped and
> difficult, but it's better than the academy. Despite
> making a mess of his kitchen, I've also found one
> who might be called a friend. But I remind myself
> that these men are thieves. Smugglers. Criminals.
> And a means to an end: escape . . .

8

MARLAN

Mordmerg Free City, Delavon Ministry
Midspring, 3034

"Didn't think I'd ever have to see you again."

Arasemis smiled. "Thank you for standing down your men, Navarron. It would have been a shame to have to kill them just to talk to you."

Marlan glanced at the Blackhoods who remained in the room. Most were younger than he, and he guessed they had no idea who Arasemis was. But the veteran Navarron clearly remembered exactly who he was dealing with.

"Send them out," Arasemis said, gesturing toward the young Blackhoods.

Navarron chaffed. "You don't come here and order me around."

"I'll do more than that. If you don't want my gold I'll dump it on your closest enemy. Get them out."

Navarron scowled but gestured to his men. Marlan was impressed with the Blackhoods' lair in the basement of a respectable tavern on a busy Mordmerg street. But the Blackhoods themselves were a bit soft to him.

"But your friend can stay?" Navarron asked. "Who is he?"

"We'll get to that," Arasemis said, reaching inside his cloak. Navarron jumped back from the table, overturning the candle. His sword was already out. Arasemis chuckled. "Settle down. If I wanted you dead would I do it like this? You've seen my work." Arasemis pulled a coin pouch from his cloak and tossed it into the spilled wax on the table. "Sit down."

Marlan watched as Navarron carefully returned to his seat, his eyes shifting between Marlan and Arasemis.

"If this is some trick, you won't get out of here with your lives," Navarron said.

"Which is why you know this isn't how I'd do you in." Arasemis smiled. "Now, if you can settle yourself long enough to talk business, I have a job for you. You've heard about the Empire Alliance Council that will be held in Rachard?"

"Just another way for the Donovards to make a grab for our city-state. What of it?"

"I've also heard about the fires in Mordmerg. Is that your idiotic way of warning them off the city?"

"Just cleaning up some of our former rivals," Navarron said. "We're united now, so tell your Donovard brothers not to try anything."

"You know me, Navarron. My loyalty is to myself."

"What do you want?"

"I want you to do more than fires."

"Destroy my own city? You're mad."

"The Empire Alliance is going to fall. Then, after the Almerians evacuate, the Donovards will come for Mordmerg and the other free cities, and you know it. Unless you demonstrate you're a snake that's not to be toyed with."

"What makes you think I need your help? Count Golbane is already here. We're dealing with it."

"Expel him by any means necessary. The more violent the better." Arasemis grinned.

"We plan to."

"And do you have a plan to deal with the lord minister when he comes?"

"Well, no, but we—"

"Once Maillard is no longer distracted with the Empire Alliance, and especially if it collapses, the Valients will come for your city. I don't think your Blackhoods are prepared for the Army of Delavon, are they?"

Marlan watched Navarron chew the inside of his lip. His silence answered the question.

"That is why I'm here," Arasemis said, smiling again.

"Why are you suddenly so concerned about our fate?"

Arasemis feigned surprise. "As a merchant with many interests in your city-state, I care deeply . . ."

"Then why not talk to the alderman about your interests, instead of coming to me?"

"You know my trade is not, how shall we say, in the light."

"How do you propose to help, then?"

"I want to finance your Blackhoods properly." Arasemis tossed a second coin purse onto the table. "We both know you'll need it."

"In return for what?"

"Killing Maillard's nephew."

"I told you we would take care of Golbane. We're waiting for—"

"Stop waiting. Kill him as soon as possible, then defend yourself when Maillard comes for his revenge. You'll have more than enough gold to pay your Blackhoods and anyone else you can recruit. Survive this and perhaps I'll have further use for you."

"You still haven't told me who this kid is."

"He's my liaison to you. Marlan has ensured many of my trading interests, if you will. Indispensable for this effort."

"I don't need him," Navarron said, glaring at Marlan.

"Yes, you do. He has inside knowledge of the Army of Delavon . . ."

Marlan looked at Arasemis but didn't dare act surprised. He quickly turned back to Navarron. The Blackhoods leader regarded him with suspicion.

"Marlan will help you find the weaknesses in their attack when it comes," Arasemis said.

"Just tell me what I need to know now," Navarron said.

"The knowledge is dependent on the circumstances of their attack," Marlan said, playing along with whatever ruse the master was building. "I'll not be in your way, I assure you."

"So, Navarron. You have some seed gold, more is coming, and you have the kid's secrets about the enemy. Kill Golbane and survive Maillard. Then be open to working more together when it's all done."

Navarron watched them for a moment.

Arasemis threw a third coin pouch on the table to prompt him. "Four hundred guldirs to start. Marlan has more and perhaps you'll get a bonus at the end."

Navarron's eyes finally dipped toward the bags. He reached out to take the gold. Arasemis leaned in and snatched his wrist. "We have an agreement?"

"Yes, agreed."

Arasemis stood. "Marlan, a word before I leave."

Marlan followed the master up to the tavern, feeling Navarron's eyes on the back of his head.

"Inside knowledge?" Marlan asked, strolling toward the tavern bar.

Arasemis grabbed him and jerked him close. "Silence. Keep to yourself and say as little as possible. Golbane's death will draw Maillard to Mordmerg. Then finish him, as we discussed."

"Do you want me to kill Navarron after?"

"Leave him be. We may have further use for the Blackhoods if they make it through this."

"Master, does Navarron know who we are?"

"Of course not. He thinks I'm a merchant. Bloodthirsty and willing to pay for anything, which is true. Don't let them see your alchemy or equipment until absolutely necessary. If it all goes wrong, remember your training and get out. If you can't, then take the name Candlestone to your grave. Don't disappoint me."

"I will not fail you, Master."

9

ARTHAN

Rachard Castle, Delavon Ministry
Midspring, 3034

"Have you seen the physician?" Meriam asked.

Arthan gazed around the room, feigning interest in all the building schematics and measuring instruments of the engineer's study. "Not yet."

Meriam glared at him, laying her quill down. "Why do you put it off?"

"He's never any help," Arthan said. "Besides, as the eldest son, I have more important things to do."

"As Maillard's heir, what can be more important than ensuring your health?"

"A flutter now and then is not unusual, Meriam. Perhaps my heart simply tremors when it's close to yours."

"This is not a jesting matter. What about the squeezing in your chest?"

Arthan waved his hand dismissively. "That's rare. It's nothing to—"

"You've convinced yourself that it's rare. What if it happens when you're in battle?"

"I won't let it distract me."

"It used to not be this often. How can I convince you to see the physician?"

Arthan tinkered with a tool hanging on the wall, unsure what to say.

"What if I stop annoying you about us?" Meriam said. "I would trade that for your health."

"It isn't an annoyance," Arthan said.

"You know what I mean."

"I cannot wed you, Meriam."

"But you can take me to bed? Hold me and talk with me as if we are wed? Is there another mistress, Arthan?"

"Of course not, Meriam."

She picked up her quill again and turned her eyes to the writing table. "Perhaps I am ungrateful," she said without looking up. "I should be thankful that a young commoner like me can apprentice under Chief Engineer Bellumet. And I should be satisfied with that."

"Don't be that way. We do have us. But I cannot give you what you want. Not now . . ."

"Then when?" She eyed him.

Arthan sighed. "I don't know, Meriam."

Meriam dipped her quill and made a notation on the castle schematic on the table. The silence between them made Arthan uncomfortable, but he was unsure how to fill it.

"I have work to do," Meriam said. "Please, see the physician."

Arthan left, feeling torn. If only Meriam could understand his responsibilities. He walked to Maillard's solar, her words echoing in his mind. He placed his hand on his chest, feeling the thump of his heart through his tunic. Nothing unusual. Bouts of pain were mild and infrequent, if startling. He wouldn't waste any more time talking about it.

As he approached the solar, he heard his father's voice.

"I asked you to find Serdot for Arthan," Maillard said. "And now I need him as well."

"Apologies, my lord," Medoff answered. "Serdot has not been in Rachard for more than a week. He does not tell me his comings and goings."

Arthan entered the solar.

"The Almerian and Rugen delegations are settling into their quarters and I expect the Calbrians, Austveedes, and Ovelians to arrive tomorrow," Maillard continued. "Your servant-garbed scouts are fine for chamber talk, Medoff, but I need Serdot for more complex matters."

"I'll send him to you straightaway if I see him, my lord."

"Father, what can I do?" Arthan asked.

"Stay at my side and observe. You'll learn more about diplomacy, trade, and war in the next few days than all your lessons hence. Where is Bardil?"

"Master Pelinaud has him practicing his crusader swordcraft."

"Not today," Maillard said. "Arthan, retrieve your brother. We need to discuss the protocol for the council."

Protocol rang through Arthan's ears as he exited the chamber and made his way down the corridors to the training hall. He was excited to have all these representatives of foreign kings and emperors in Rachard. But he was not looking forward to protocol. He heard footsteps behind him and turned.

"My lord." A man with shorn hair and a stubbly beard not unlike his own bowed before him. "I already sent someone to fetch Bardil."

"How did . . . Who are you?"

"Apologies, my lord. I am Serdot, ever at your service."

"Serdot? My father is looking for you."

"Yes, but it's you I wanted to speak to first. Will you walk this way with me?"

"Why didn't you just—"

"My lord, I've returned from Mordmerg." Serdot led Arthan into a side room, where a tapestry of the Pemonian continent hung on the wall. "I smelled a stench and followed it there. I trust your cousin Count Golbane told you of the fires?"

"Yes . . ."

"Here is Mordmerg," Serdot said, pointing to a city symbol just south of Rachard on the tapestry. "You don't go there because your family has a bad history with the place. Your enemies know this—perhaps this is something they know better than you."

"I know it's where criminals killed my mother years ago."

"Criminals . . . Yes, well it is a breeding ground for revolt, like all the free cities of Donovan. But this is different. Mordmerg will revolt again, soon. I'm still uncertain of the details, but there must be a new power behind it this time, one that remains hidden to me."

"Shouldn't you be reporting this to my father and Medoff?"

"Of course. I will. But Mordmerg will be your task."

"Mine?"

"With the foreign delegations here and the Empire Alliance hanging in the balance, your father will be quite busy. And the general will be preoccupied making sure the Rachard guards keep the rowdy foreigners from each other's throats. Yes, Mordmerg will be assigned to you, I'm certain. So I chose to tell you first so you can begin thinking about it."

"Why do you think Mordmerg is so important?"

"The Empire Alliance is doomed. It will be a calamity that shakes the foundations of power on two continents and on the seas between. Quick minds will see opportunities in that. But with the knife that is Mordmerg sticking out of our backs, we won't be quick enough to deal with the change. Mordmerg is an intelligently crafted distraction, though by whom remains unclear."

Arthan stared at him for a moment. "You're young to be a spymaster."

Serdot grinned. "Only two years, thirty-four days, and seven hours older than you. But I learned from your father's previous captain of the shadows: my father."

"What happened to him?"

"Dead, probably. No one knows. Just disappeared."

"I'm sorry."

"Don't be. It's the dark game we play so that life in the light can be brighter. That's the widsemer code."

"The world seems gray to me . . ."

Serdot smiled. "Spoken true, my lord."

"Thank you for the information. I will think on it. Shall we return to Father?"

"I suppose. I did enjoy seeing Medoff squirm when your father harangued him about me. The general has always been miffed that I don't report to him, especially since its Medoff that your father complains to when I'm out on a ride." Serdot grinned and led the way.

10

MILISEND

Eglamour Palace, Toulon Ministry
Midspring, 3034

Dearest Regaume,

I miss you terribly. I find myself longing to escape into your arms more frequently as the troubles at Father's court intensify. Uncle Brugarn speaks more and more on his behalf, while General Chaultion regularly proposes war as the cure-all for the kingdom's problems. He forgets the treasury is empty. Both are conniving, sinister men who too easily have father's ear.

I also wanted to warn you that Chief Magistrate Tronchet has grown more persistent. He sees it as his personal crusade to catch me thieving, but of course he won't. I look forward to our next job, perhaps a more challenging target. More than that, I yearn to be with you again.

Yours always,
Me

Milisend rolled up the letter and placed it carefully in the jewel-encrusted ceramic cylinder. She handed it to her handmaiden. "Do be more careful this time, Rosellen. I couldn't bear the thought that my silly letters cause harm to befall you."

"Don't worry, Princess. I will ride with a royal courier this time, and during the day."

"Good. It's sad that even the roads near Eglamour are plagued with bandits now."

Rosellen smiled. "If only all thieves were as gentle and discreet as you, my lady."

"Which courier? The new handsome one, what's his name?"

"No, I'll be with Gerold, the one who was attacked in Wallevet."

"Blind Gerold? They still send him?"

"They say he refused to give up the post. His scars make him more handsome though."

"So there are some who are still loyal to Father . . . Off with you, Rosellen. And be careful."

11

FETZER

Elme River, Barres Ministry
Midspring, 3034

Fetzer watched the river pass by from the railing as the sun set. He had spent most of the day belowdecks working and writing in his journal. It was good to finally breathe the fresh air.

The *Meurden* and her crew are bolstered by a stiff wind that carries us downriver faster than usual. Getting used to the movements of the ship has not been too difficult though. Greffid says the swells of the sea will be larger.

Worse is my disappointment to learn that we will not be venturing beyond the Sea of Pemonia, which lies between the mainland and Leauvenna Ministry. I had hoped that we would sail into the Middlesea, or perhaps even to the Old World. At least I will get a taste of Middlesea when we arrive in Port Lyonseln, the capital of Leauvenna. Greffid says the port is a gateway for the exotic spices and timber and other goods from the Middlesea archipelagos.

For now, Captain Renaud keeps me busy writing up false papers for our cargo, of which I've actually been told nothing. Judging by the papers I'm copying, it seems routine for these

smugglers to pass off their stolen goods as merely
sacks of oats and bundles of cotton cloth . . .

Fetzer scooted aside to let sailors pass and felt the
scabbard of his father's sword catch on the rail. It was stifling
and reminded him of Perilune. He unbuckled it and lifted it
over the railing, the blade pointing at the water. Then he let
it fall.

"Peculiar," said an old salt nearby. "I once heard told that
a man who casts away his sword has already cast away his
life."

Fetzer ignored him and thought about tossing his Sember
sapphire wist ring as well. But receiving it from his father
was his favorite memory, and he knew Fernon would always
wear his. Fetzer walked away from the railing, leaving the old
smuggler puzzled, and returned belowdecks to finish his
papers.

He found the state room locked. He put his ear to the
door and heard Captain Renaud.

". . . said before, I don't know who you are and I don't
care—so long as the pay is good. But I must be prepared to
defend my ship when we dock at Lyonseln."

"No need," said a young man's deep voice. Fetzer
detected an Almerian accent. "Your ship and crew will be
fine," continued the man, "and your pay will be as we agreed.
You won't have to see us again."

"No passage back to the mainland?" Renaud asked.

"That is none of your concern. The pay was for the
voyage to Leauvenna, then your job is done. Until then,
ensure that none of your crew be allowed near our quarters
below. Your cook has come down several times."

"He's a simpleton and no threat to you, and he's used to
seeing smuggled loot," Renaud said. "Your quarters share
space with our provisions, so surely the cook can—"

"I don't care what he's used to. I don't want him to see us.
Understand?"

"I will speak to him," Renaud said. "Perhaps he can come
down for provisions at specified hours. If there's no food for
the crew, there's no crew for the ship."

"Fine. Between the fourth and fifth bells. But not otherwise."

"Done."

Chair legs scooted across the decking. Fetzer froze, not knowing where to go. As boot steps neared the door he rushed back down the corridor and turned, as if he was just now approaching the state room. Renaud and the big man with the Almerian accent were surprised to see him.

"Afternoon, Captain," Fetzer said. "Shall I continue the cargo papers?"

"Yes," Renaud said, pushing past him. The big man regarded Fetzer carefully before following Renaud.

Fetzer worked on the papers until evening when Greffid served up a hot meal of cod stew and ship biscuits. Afterward they spent time in their quarters with their ration of grog, and Fetzer gave Greffid a reading lesson. But his mind soon turned to the three mysterious folk aboard the ship. He grew more curious as he replayed the conversation between Renaud and the Almerian in his mind.

"How long have you worked aboard this smuggling ship, Greffid?"

"Nigh on twelve years now. Been to every major port from Durrow to Nore, and down south past Lambochardy. Cold, strange waters there . . ."

"Ever been caught or seen battle?"

"We've been caught a few times, but nothing a bribe or good threat couldn't resolve. Our group is well connected, too, but that's beyond my duties to know. Battles? Mostly with pirates near Middlesea islands even the Almerian patrol ships won't sail near. But the captain and his first mate are expert at avoiding trouble wherever it is."

Fetzer almost asked Greffid about the three people hiding down in the hold. But he could not be sure Greffid would keep it to himself if he didn't already know. So he put aside his curiosity and slept.

❧

The state room was empty when Fetzer arrived the next morning. His mind wandered as he settled into his routine.

He turned and looked at the captain's writing table. It was cluttered with parchments and maps, heaped candle nubs, and frayed quills.

The corridor was quiet, so Fetzer pushed up from his slender table and stepped toward the captain's. He pretended to look out the windows at the stern, glancing down at various bits of correspondence on the table. He spotted Rilranef the Round's signature and what he assumed were references to various stolen cargos, but nothing unusual. With the state room door still open, he dared not touch any of it.

Fetzer walked to the door and quietly closed it, stopping short of turning the key to avoid suspicion. He quickly returned to Renaud's table and flipped through the parchments. More letters from smugglers in Perilune, Eldreim, Oradrond, and other places. Nothing about the secret passengers.

Fetzer opened the drawers but found nothing. The last one was locked, but he had not seen any keys. He looked toward the door and gritted his teeth as he listened. Silence, except for the lantern swaying on its nail above the table. He squinted up at it, then quickly pulled over a chair to stand on. He peeked inside the lantern and found a key resting at the bottom. He picked off a few dots of wax as he came down, then inserted the key into the lock.

Inside he found a gold-bladed knife, small coin pouches, and a few loose gemstones. There was also a stack of letters. Most of them were from a woman, except one. It was hastily scrawled on a scrap of wrinkled vellum.

> Captain Renaud,
> Thank you for your aid in our safe passage to Lyonseln. After giving the issue more thought, I'm certain it is a risk we cannot take. I prefer you dispose of the clerk, in case he did overhear us. I don't care when or how, so long as it is done before we reach port. I expect your cooperation in return for another purse of silver for your trouble.
> Bertwil

Fetzer swallowed hard and felt his brow bead with sweat. He looked at the door, then back to the drawer. He quickly pocketed the note and the gold-bladed knife. He returned the woman's letters and then stood on the chair to return the key to the lantern.

Footsteps came down the corridor. Fetzer rushed for his table, planting himself in the chair and picking up the quill just as Renaud opened the door. The captain gave him a peculiar look.

"Why is the door shut?"

"The men were getting loud, sir. I needed to concentrate."

"I see . . ." Renaud glanced up at the swaying lantern, then walked toward his writing table. Fetzer froze as he realized he had forgotten to relock the drawer. He dared not turn to see whether Renaud would notice. Renaud rummaged through the stacks on the table before returning to the door with a navigational chart in hand. He paused to regard Fetzer for a moment.

"Carry on," was all he said before departing.

Fetzer sat back in his chair and sighed. His mind quickly turned to Bertwil's letter. It occupied his thoughts until he could write in his journal later that night.

> . . . even if he doesn't act on Bertwil's order, it's only a matter of time before things turn bad. There is nowhere to hide on this ship. We're within view of the Sea of Pemonia, so five more days until Port Lyonseln. Perhaps the captain will have crewmen quietly take me from my hammock. Or have Greffid poison my food. Or send me to bump into Bertwil while fetching supplies down below.
>
> I must be cautious and think of something. I do not expect to survive for long . . .

"What's that?"

Fetzer turned to see Greffid peering down from his hammock. "What's what?"

"That book you're always pulling from your pack."

"My journal." There was no reason to hide it, since Greffid couldn't read.

"What's it for?"

"My thoughts. It's like talking with the pages . . ."

"That's what crewmates are for." Greffid smiled.

"I like talking to you too, Greffid. But today has exhausted me. Good night." Fetzer blew out the lantern and lay wide awake.

12

ARTHAN

Rachard Castle, Delavon Ministry
Midspring, 3034

"Surely there is no finer setting for an Empire Alliance Council," Arthan whispered as he looked around the great hall of the castle. Nearly every chair was full and many more people were standing.

"It will be ugly," Medoff whispered back.

"Even so, I've never seen such a collection of foreign dignitaries."

"A collection of windbags. You'll see many more in Eglamour, my lord."

"Quiet," Alfrem hissed.

Arthan was excited to see all the delegations settling in. Maillard presided over the assembly at one end of the hall on a raised dais. Ambassadors from the Almerian Confederation, Rugen Empire, Calbrian Empire, Kingdom of Austveeden, Kingdom of Donovan, and the Empire of Ovelia were seated at long tables, their translators and other members of their entourages clustered around them. Arthan, Bardil, Medoff, Alfrem, and more of his father's counselors were seated beside the dais with a perfect view of the speaking floor and the whole hall beyond.

"How long will it last?" Bardil asked.

"Days. Hours," Alfrem whispered. "Depends on who wants what and how desperately."

Arthan looked toward the Donovard delegation. "Why would the king choose Meltres to represent our kingdom?"

"Haughty, rude, witless," Alfrem whispered. "Exactly the emissary the king would choose if he cared nothing for the alliance. Officially, your father is mediator and host. But in truth, the task of saving the alliance—or at least averting war—is squarely on Maillard's shoulders."

Maillard opened the council by thanking the six ambassadors for traveling to Rachard. He gave each one the opportunity to make an opening speech. The Almerians went first. They wanted to keep the current state of the alliance, unstable though it was. This notion irked the other delegations, their faces already sour.

After some tense but cordial discussion, Maillard isolated one of the issues. "Regarding the islands," he began, "could the Almerian Confederation concede that they lie in Pemonian waters and that Pemonian kingdoms have legitimate claim to them dating back to the founding of said kingdoms?"

"They lie in close waters, yes," the Almerian ambassador said through a translator. "But we have owned those islands since before a single Pemonian kingdom existed. We've served as guardians of—"

"Oppressor!" shouted the Rugen ambassador, a pale-faced woman with sharp eyes.

Maillard jumped in again to stave off further tension. "Thank you, and can the Almerians agree that their occupation of said islands is a source of strain between the peoples of the two continents? A disagreement that should be resolved peacefully?"

"Our confederation holds the islands as safe harbors for trade and bases for hunting the pirates that threaten all our merchant vessels," the translator said. "And multiple Pemonian kingdoms claim them. Thus, by holding them for all, we help to prevent war."

"Convenient excuse!" blurted the Calbrian ambassador. "Faukshal and Hildegad, Delnollen and Mollering . . . All of these islands belong to Calbria!"

"Delnollen and Mollering are within twenty and forty marqs of Donovan," Meltres protested. "They have been and should be part of our kingdom!"

"My lords," Maillard said, "can the confederation at least acknowledge Donovan's historical claim to these islands, in the hopes of negotiating a settlement?"

"In return for what?"

"Continued support for the Empire Alliance, from which we all benefit," Maillard said.

"Benefit?" The Rugen ambassador stood from her chair. "There is no benefit to this alliance. It is a relic from the days when our kingdoms were weak and the Almerians were strong. We cling needlessly to a treaty that is naught but dusty rubbish!"

"Ovelia has never been weak in the face of Almerians," the Ovelian ambassador said through a translator. "In the Arukan tradition, we stood alone until joining this endeavor, merely to attempt peace with Calbria. A peace repeatedly broken by the Calbrians with invasion and intrigue. Ovelia will support the Almerian Confederation if it agrees to help dismantle the evil Calbrians and exclude them from trade within the Alliance."

The great hall erupted with shouting. Members of several delegations moved to cross the floor with fists raised, their swords having been surrendered outside, before being forced back by Rachard guards.

It was not the council of diplomacy Arthan had imagined. It seemed that every king and emperor had chosen hot-tempered men and women to represent their interests. In that moment Arthan realized how unique his father was.

"My lords, please!" Maillard shouted above the din. He was standing now, almost begging the delegations. He spoke again when they had settled enough to hear. "For me it's clear. The old treaty governing the Empire Alliance is now untenable, and I hope the Almerian Confederation can agree to amendments. The modern Pemonian kingdoms are not the original New World societies that signed the first treaty. There were nine original signatories, today consolidated into six kingdoms and empires. To say nothing of the free city-states that dot this continent. To ignore this present reality is supreme folly."

"We can accept some amendments, if our demands are met in turn," the Almerian ambassador said.

"Very good." Maillard nodded. "Perhaps we'll turn away from the question of the islands for now and discuss the sea. We can all appreciate that the Almerians, with their larger navy, have been the primary reason that piracy is more limited in every major waterway from Almeria in the north, through Middlesea, to Pemonia in the south. The sea is kept open for—"

"But the Almerians control the routes and tonnages all the same," said the Rugen ambassador. "And they restrict the size of our fleets and control ports like Durgensdil that are rightfully ours."

"Ambassador Vesamune, Durgensdil will never be Rugen," Meltres interrupted. "It is in Alpenon Ministry and will always be part of Donovan."

Vesamune steamed. "We'll no longer be part of any treaty that denies Durgensdil's rightful place in the Rugen Empire!"

"My lords and ladies, we must remain focused, for the sake of peace," Maillard said. "This council has been called to address the alliance, not the claims between Calbria and Ovelia, or between Rugenhav and Donovan, or between anyone. Now, could the Almerian Confederation agree to open the sea routes and relinquish control over certain ports in Pemonia? In return, the kingdoms could grant you free access to said ports, along with shouldering more of the burden of chasing pirates."

"Why should our empire ask theirs for space upon the wide sea?" the Calbrians asked.

The Almerian ambassador stood. "Because our navy is superior to any crew you might muster from your soggy, disjointed lands, cobbled together as they were from realms you dare to call an empire." The Calbrian ambassador jumped to his feet, quivering to think up a response. But the Almerian continued. "And piracy? They'd infest every sea and route and harbor in Pemonia if we relented. Half your ports would be havens within the year."

"Release the city-states!" the Donovards cried.

"Abolish the payments made to faraway crowns," the Austveedes said.

"The islands!"

"Durgensdil!"

Maillard attempted to quell the room but it was the Almerians that got the delegations' attention.

"If the treaty dissolves, our confederation will shut down the trade of your entire continent. We'll release all pirates into your waters and not a single Pemonian ship will visit a Middlesea port without confiscation ever again. And not only will our confederation keep the islands, city-states, and ports, but we'll expand our holdings!"

The hall erupted.

"Just as I said," Medoff shouted as he waved for more guards. "Now it's too much." The general jumped from his seat and went to help contain the chaos himself.

"Do not abandon an imperfect treaty of long peace for hasty war!" Maillard shouted from the dais.

But it was no use. Arthan and Bardil watched Maillard join Medoff in the throng, trying to talk down the delegations face to face. After much effort, he convinced all of them to retire for the day.

❦

"Utterly intractable," Maillard said, exasperated. Arthan had never seen his father complain like this. His counselors nodded in agreement as the fire burned low in the hearth. "Their bickering is childish, incessant, as if they—"

"Want to see it fail," Medoff said.

"I'm afraid the general is right," Alfrem said. "I had hoped there would be common ground to build on. But now that I've heard these ambassadors, well, I fear the kingdoms smell opportunity in forcing the Almerians to withdraw from Pemonia. And they're not wrong. Control of the free city-states alone will swell the coffers of any king."

"But for how long?" Maillard said. "The Empire Alliance should not end this way. War will be certain. No kingdom, no province will escape it."

"Perhaps we'll emerge stronger, Father," Arthan said.

"But at what price, Arthan?"

Everyone was quiet for a moment, then Alfrem spoke up. "My lord, if you were king of Donovan, peace would be possible. But as long as Erech or his brothers are on the throne, peace will only be an unlikely accident."

"I agree," Medoff said. "Pemonia would be different if the House of Valient still ruled the realm."

"Those days are long over," Maillard said, waving his hand dismissively. "Whatever we may think of Erech, he is still the king and we owe him our allegiance."

"Less and less, I think," Alfrem said quietly. "Brugarn, Chaultion, Asteroth, and Erath. All of them usurp the king by day and rule the night."

"Where is Serdot?" Maillard asked. "I've spent all evening speaking in private with each ambassador. I want to know what they are saying when I'm not with them. Tomorrow may be our last chance at this."

"Here, my lord." Serdot stepped into the room with a stack of reports. Arthan was glad to see him, but none of Maillard's counselors bothered to greet him. "These are what I've gathered from talking with our servant-scouts. Mostly petty nonsense. They can only overhear so much without looking suspicious."

Maillard gave the reports a cursory glance. "Then what else do you have for me?"

"Two things. First, the Rugens and Calbrians have every intention of wrecking the alliance. Ambassador Vesamune has explicit orders from Emperor Theudamer himself."

"That much is obvious . . ."

"Second, the Calbrians are considering abandoning tomorrow's council before it begins, while the Rugens are considering killing the Almerian ambassador by dawn."

"My God . . ." Alfrem muttered.

"Medoff, post extra guards at the Almerians' quarters," Maillard said. "And Alfrem, arrange for the Calbrian ambassador to break his night fast with me, so that I can convince him to stay a bit longer. Do you have any good news, Serdot?"

Serdot handed him a folded parchment and glanced at Arthan. "Another letter from Golbane, my lord. He's a bit verbose, but the short of it is that things have not improved."

Maillard read the note before passing it to Arthan.

Lord Minister Valient,

Please accept my apologies, Uncle, for the increasingly complicated situation in Mordmerg. What follows is the most complete report I have had the chance to write, and I request aid and reinforcements as they are available. Yourself, if possible.

I first received word of trouble in Mordmerg while at my residence in Brambard. It was an urgent letter from the free city's alderman, Sir Hurmant, asking for our assistance. I left with a company of my knights and soldiers and found a dozen small fires burning across the city. The damage was not significant and there were no deaths. Our patrols did not uncover the culprits.

Keeping in mind your standing orders to be lenient in the city-state and defer to the local Almerian guards, I went to their garrison, since I had seen no guards on the streets. We found the door locked and no one answered our knocking. We became increasingly suspicious and finally broke down the door, whereupon we found the guards slaughtered, to a man. The garrison did not appear to be looted. Sir Hurmant later claimed to know nothing about it.

The following day the city was beset by riots, though it remains unclear why. If they had been rioting against the greedy Almerians, their deaths had not adequately sated the crowd. It was clearly something else. My knights had acted honorably since entering the gates, and there was no sign of anger against us, until suddenly the rioters turned like the wind. We sheltered at Hurmant's tower keep.

And here we remain trapped. Of course, my men and I could escape but with it would require much bloodshed, so I appeal to you for guidance given the delicate situation. Some of the Donovard guards are still loyal to the alderman and agreed to carry this letter, but I would not trust them as escorts. Given your respected position, I believe only you can put these people at ease.

Your humble servant,
Count Golbane Valient
Mordmerg

"What is happening, Serdot?" Maillard asked.

"Hard to say without seeing it myself. Could be the Almerians giving us a taste of the rebellions they could foment if we try to take the islands or ports or city-states from them. But that wouldn't explain the murder of their garrison. Alternatively, it could be the Rugens instigating rebellion. They've long prided themselves on their lack of free cities, having stamped them out years ago, and may seek to cause problems for us.

"Whatever the cause, I don't think this disturbance is mere criminals. Nor is it coincidence with the timing of the Empire Alliance Council here in Rachard. Nor is it coincidence that the disturbance is in Mordmerg and not other city-states in Donovan."

Arthan recalled Medoff's initial belief that the events in Mordmerg were mere coincidence. The general now wore a frown but did not challenge Serdot's speculation.

"What you say makes sense," Maillard told Serdot. "And it's very soon after Raymond's death."

"Yes, my lord. And interesting that Raymond's family and the Valients are the only lord minister families that are not relatives of the king."

"Bardil said the same thing," Arthan said, wishing his little brother was present to hear his idea validated.

"Something else bothers me," continued Serdot. "In his letter, Golbane requests that you go to Mordmerg to aid him. I don't recall Golbane as someone who lacks the will to trample folk like rioters if he's trapped with the alderman."

"The count is quite right to ask for my guidance," Maillard said. "He knows the free cities are a sensitive issue, especially now."

"But to ask for you personally, my lord, when you have capable generals and commanders at your disposal?"

"A minor detail to me," Maillard said. "More important is what to do about it."

Medoff finally stirred. "It sounds to me like someone has stoked the people of Mordmerg into thinking they're about to lose their free city. That simple. Nothing an additional troop of knights can't extract Golbane from."

"With respect, there is nothing simple about Mordmerg," Serdot said. "It's a place with a long, troubled history."

"As you said, Serdot, you can't know what is going on without being there yourself," Maillard said. "Arthan will lead a company of soldiers to take care of this, and you'll guide him. Arthan, take the Eighth Company, commanded by Sir Livonier. You'll recall he has experience in the area."

"Yes, Father."

"Extract Golbane and return as quickly as possible," Maillard said. "If the rioters want to kill their Almerian partners and Alderman Hurmant, so be it, it's their city-state. It is not part of our realm, so do not stay longer than absolutely necessary."

"My lord, is he ready for this task?" Medoff asked.

Maillard looked at Arthan with pride. "He's twenty now, Medoff. He fought bravely at the southern border when that Austveede baron got aggressive last year. He fought well when the Calbrians tested the Narendrabruk River the year prior. And he'll have Serdot and Livonier."

"I'm honored, Father."

"And if we cannot extract Golbane, for whatever reason?" Serdot asked.

"Return with my son and my nephew, Serdot," Maillard said. "As for you, Medoff, I want more Rachard guards in the great hall in the morning before one foreigner steps foot inside. Enough men to prevent the delegations from leaving their tables. If it all ends badly, protect each ambassador and escort them out."

"Yes, my lord."

13

RODEL

The cold rain glimmered as the clouds choked out the final rays of sunset. A black carriage with barred windows pushed through the rutty, puddle-pocked road. Four glum prisoners sat uncomfortably on their benches and watched the fading light outside. Hands bound in iron, they struggled to stay seated as the carriage bounced and jerked under them.

Rodel watched the rain seep between the slats. If only to be like water now, to infiltrate or escape through any possible space. It reminded him of his training back in Rugenhav, the whole reason for his presence in Donovan.

The horses became unsettled as thunder clapped nearby and wind pushed through the barred windows. The driver attempted to calm them as they came around a bend in the road. Rodel was not surprised that the Donovards plowed through the weather without stopping for shelter, given the sort of men who occupied the carriage with him. He wondered if the Donovards knew for sure who they had caught.

Rodel heard the rush and splash of a river. The wheels clacked over a stone bridge as the flash and crackle of lightning struck too close. He heard the splitting of a tree. Another bolt and the horses lurched. Rodel and the others were thrown from their benches as the horses tried to turn around on the bridge. The carriage slammed into the stone bridge wall, splintering a rear wheel. The carriage reeled again and all the captives struggled to stay upright. A wrenching snap and dragging signaled that the rear axle had broken, yet still the panicked horses pulled. The jailors' shouting faded amid the roar of the swollen river. There was a final bump, then the carriage twisted. White water sprayed inside as the carriage crashed into the river.

Rodel and the others were tossed about as water surged through the bars. The carriage broke in half like an egg and Rodel was the first out, his jet-black hair plastered over his face and neck. He felt another prisoner latch on to his leg but he kicked him off as he struggled to swim loose of the wreck with bound hands.

Rodel popped up to the surface. The carriage planks twisted and crunched as the horses struggled to free themselves. Everything was pulled under the churn. He gasped for breath and kicked as hard as he could toward the riverbank.

Finally wedged between two rocks, he wiggled and elbowed his way up from the water. When he was safe on the embankment he watched what was left of the carriage break apart and sink below the rapids. There was no sign of the others until he noticed movement on the far bank. In the darkness he could not see if it was one of the jailors or one of his own. They sat panting, looking at each other.

"Heingartmer!" yelled the survivor above the noise of the river.

Rodel recognized the voice as Wredegar's. But he hesitated, glancing toward the damaged bridge in the distance. He had had enough. This was his chance for true freedom. He waited for the roll of thunder to pass before yelling back. "Eglamour!"

Wredegar nodded, then disappeared into the woods. Rodel picked himself up and walked toward the bridge. He examined his chains, the iron having rubbed his wrists raw to bleeding. He stumbled up the road, itself a brown river, and soon crossed the bridge. The axle was still there, the last remnant of the fate of the others.

I can still run, Rodel told himself. He didn't have to wait for Wredegar in Eglamour. He could run and be done with everyone. But he knew the Wosmoks would find him. He was almost jealous of the ones who had drowned. Their hunting days were over, and no one would be hunting them anymore either.

Rodel was so distracted with himself that he did not notice another carriage that had stopped on the road before him. Instinctively he darted for the woods.

"Stop!" cried a man who jumped out of the carriage.

Rodel kept going. Then he crouched inside the wood line. He watched as a peculiar man with a bushy red beard and rich robes walked toward the woods, uncaring of the mud soaking into his fine garments. It was evident from his movements that the man was missing his right arm.

"Come," said the man, a Donovard. "I wish you no harm."

After a moment the man repeated his call in Austveede, Rugen, and Calbrian. But there was no need, as Rodel had learned Donovar as a child.

"I saw what happened and I offer you my carriage," continued the man. "Anyone who survives that is marked by destiny. I'll rid you of your shackles and take you where you need to go."

Rodel smiled to himself. If this ignorant nobleman had an inkling of who he was, he would not so freely make the offer. Then again, most noblemen would not have bothered to stop—unless they hoped for something to gain. Rodel considered it his duty to go to Eglamour and wait for Wredegar. The Wosmoks would get suspicious if he did not show up.

"Well?" asked the man, patiently standing in the rain.

Rodel stepped out of the bushes. He did not have to decide now. He could use the carriage to travel to Eglamour or go his own way once and for all. Either way, he was sure he could handle this one-armed nobleman if he was trouble.

"Good," said the man. "You have nothing to fear. I am Count Arasemis Reimvick."

Rodel stopped walking when he heard the surname, reconsidering everything.

Arasemis fished under his cloak and brought out a glass vial that glimmered in the rain. "This will remove your bonds," he said, holding up the vial. "It's best used out of the rain. I assure you, you'll get no awkward questions from me. Won't you come? I have food, wine . . ."

Rodel told himself it was impossible for this man to know who he was. To meet one of the Reimvicks on the road after surviving the river could be nothing but coincidence. For once he suppressed his training and followed Arasemis into the carriage.

"May I?" Arasemis asked, uncorking the vial. Rodel extended his shackled wrists and watched as a few drops sizzled into the iron. They crumbled away from his wrists, leaving his skin unharmed.

"Remarkable, thank you," Rodel said in Donovar.

Arasemis grinned. "I detect a well-hidden Rugen accent."

It was not a question. Arasemis pulled bread and dried sausage from a drawer under his cushioned seat, then filled a silver goblet with wine for Rodel.

"What are you count of?" Rodel asked.

"Nothing, really. Not for a long time. My brothers inherited our father's lands and titles. I spend my days engrossed in ancient books."

"Your brothers must be Raymond and Edmond Reimvick," Rodel said, knowing full well the answer.

"Correct."

"My condolences for Raymond . . ."

"Come now, young Rugen. As a former captive you care not for Donovard noblemen. But I won't ask you questions, as I promised. Just say where you wish to go."

Now that he had a chance at freedom, Rodel could think of no place in particular. Arasemis stared at him kindly, clearly aware of Rodel's uncertainty.

"Surely a man in your position has a destination, other than the office of the chief magistrate of Eglamour," Arasemis said.

"Tell me about your ancient books," Rodel said, eager to delay his decision on a destination.

Arasemis happily sat back in his seat. Rodel felt as if he had been led into this discussion.

"My books are unlike any others. Rarest of the rare. Single extant copies. Dead languages. The ancients of Pemonia and their forgotten secrets. At least, forgotten by most people."

"What secrets?"

"Forgive me, but that is something for me and my students alone."

"You teach?"

Arasemis nodded. "The ancient ways of the original peoples of Pemonia. Their tales, migrations, alliances, weaponry, alchemy, and metallurgy. Probably not what a thief like yourself would be interested in."

"I'm not a thief," Rodel said. He stopped himself before saying more.

"I believe you." Arasemis nodded. "Whatever you were wanted for is no concern of mine. If you have a destination in mind I shall inform my driver."

"Are your students the sons of Donovard nobles?"

"Most definitely not. They are all bold youths, like yourself, who come from all kingdoms and backgrounds. Young men and women who are interested in a . . . special . . . purpose for their lives. A purpose that recognizes no borders, titles, or divine rights of kings. No wealth or poverty, only collective honor and shared fates. And a return to the original ways."

"Who is your benefactor for such an experiment?"

Arasemis chuckled softly. "It is no experiment and the only benefactor is the man before you." Arasemis cocked his head and squinted. "You are interested in my little organization." Again, it was not a question.

"Perhaps . . ."

"The youths of the Order were at a crossroads in their lives when I found them, as you appear to be. They were searching for a different path in life, a new calling. I could be mistaken, of course, but I sense that in you."

Rodel nodded silently, trying to see through Arasemis's plain speaking. But he found no ill intent in this strange man.

"I always keep my eyes open for others who are drawn to the things the Order is drawn to," Arasemis continued, "wherever they come from. You would be most welcome."

"And if I change my mind?"

"My driver will still take you wherever you wish to go, on one condition. You would swear an oath of silence for the things you see and hear."

Rodel considered all Arasemis had said. Something inside him felt an intense curiosity about the Order of which Arasemis spoke. But his training interjected, urging him to be suspicious of this man and to remember his duty in Eglamour. He went back and forth with himself but knew how it should end.

"I must go to Eglamour."

"Then my driver will take you," Arasemis said, seemingly neutral with his decision. "First he will take me home, to Thorendor Castle, just west of Bredahade, the capital of Wallevet. Then he will take you into Toulon. If you change your mind you'll know where to find me. If not, then I expect you to keep our conversation private as thanks for my hospitality."

Rodel nodded. He looked out the window at the slowing rain and peeping moon. When they arrived at Thorendor he almost changed his mind but remained on his seat. As Arasemis's attendant moved to close the carriage door he spoke up, though he was unsure why.

"My name is Rodel. Thank you, Count Arasemis."

"My pleasure." Arasemis smiled. "Remember, if you change your mind, you know where to find me. If not, my best to you."

14

MILISEND

Eglamour, Toulon Ministry
Midspring, 3034

"Go on," Regaume whispered. "You can do this, Thimblegloves . . ."

Milisend briefly glared at him before refocusing on the door. "What if we're caught?"

"Then you'll sprint away and leave me to be arrested by Tronchet's men." Regaume winked. "Go on, or I'll claim the necklace for myself."

"First tell me what it is," she said, peering through the keyhole of the storeroom that served as their hiding place. "We've gotten this far. And if I must abandon you I want to at least get the goods."

Regaume stifled a snicker. "I've trained you well. All right, then. Across the room do you see a gilded door?"

"Yes."

"Behind it is the Benrollen Company's treasury. Benrollen is Donovan's oldest chartered merchant company and the kingdom's best competition against the Almerian trading fleets. Benrollen is also considered the most secure holder of the nobles' jewels and other valuables."

Milisend turned from the keyhole to Regaume. "But not our royal pieces."

"Of course not. Now, your target is a necklace made with Middlesea coral and Terving diamonds. If you can steal that, your training will be complete."

"Who owns the necklace?" she whispered, turning back to the keyhole.

"The wife of one of the company's owners just sold it to one of Duke Brugarn's vassals."

"Good. But the guards won't leave. One of them stays at the door."

Regaume nodded. "Use the candle, as we discussed. It's our only option now."

Milisend turned away from the keyhole. "It doesn't feel right."

"You're jesting. How many jewels have you stolen over the past few years?"

"Not that—the alchemy. It seems . . . dishonorable."

Regaume smiled. "You're the only thief I know who cares for honor."

"I'm also the only royal thief you know. Listen, before Father ended sword training for his daughters, we were taught that alchemy was an old, mystical craft that was beneath the honor of knights and ladies and lords."

Regaume clutched his hands over his mouth to suppress another chuckle. She glared at him longer this time. "I'm sorry," he whispered, "why are you only telling me this now, when we're inside the company?"

"It just occurred to me." She looked away from him and examined the storeroom shelves with feigned interest.

"Look, alchemy is as alive today as it ever was. I'm no bard, but the tales make it plain that, while it's fallen out of fashion with the nobles, it has always played a role in, well, everything. What can be dishonorable about that?"

"We were never taught anything about it . . ."

"Of course not. The high folk are suspicious of alchemy because they fear what a commoner could do with it. But I think it will become widespread again, and soon."

"Why?"

"I've been a thief all my life. I see more and more thieves using candle alchemy, smoke screens, and the like. And high folk, too. It used to be I'd never find an alchemy workshop in a nobleman's home. Now, many of them secretly have one or employ an alchemist. Maybe it's because good steel is now so common, unlike in the old days. A blade treatment can give them an advantage."

"Fine. So the candle, then."

Regaume reached into a pouch and brought out an ordinary-looking candle. "It will take care of the guards you've been watching. The candle alchemist I bought it from in the Borel District of Eglamour said the first few moments of burn will be ordinary. Then its colorless, tasteless vapors will leak out briefly, putting the guards to sleep for about an hour. Then it will burn normally again and we'll be able to get the necklace."

"It doesn't look like a special candle. Are you sure this is going to work?"

"If it fails, we'll use this one to escape." Regaume pulled another candle from his pouch. "This one should smell like the building is on fire, causing panic."

"How do we start?"

"Creep down the dark side of the room," Regaume whispered as he took a turn at the keyhole. "Then light the candle and put it with the candles already on the table. Then come back to the storeroom and we'll wait for them to sleep. You look beautiful in your new leathers, by the way . . ."

She looked down at her black-dyed ensemble.

"The mask and slippers are still being made," he continued, "but you look the part enough. Get ready, Thimblegloves . . ."

He carefully opened the door and she slipped by. She crept along the darker side of the long room, keeping an eye on the guards chatting by the door. She neared the table easily enough, but she hoped the alchemist's candle would not release its vapors too soon.

Milisend tilted the candle into the flame of one already on the table, then set it in an empty spot in the brass candelabra. She turned and headed back to the storeroom, but stopped again when she noticed a faint blue glow growing in the room. She glanced over her shoulder. Her candle had changed color and was belching up thick, black smoke.

Milisend rushed over and blew it out. It flickered back to life. She blew it out again and again it returned, defiant. She blew and blew but it continued to spew the smoke. Then the guards came running. Regaume appeared and grabbed her, ushering her down the corridor. They left the smoke-filled room and the clamor of the guards behind them. They exited out the first-floor window through which they had come and disappeared in the nearby garden.

"What was that, Regaume?" Milisend demanded when they were a safe distance into the surrounding company estate.

"I'm sorry, Mili. This is the first time I've bought materials from the Borel slums. That candle alchemist must have sold me the wrong—"

Milisend snatched the bundle of candles from his pouch, hurled them into the pond, and marched off in the direction of the castle, not bothering to say good night.

15

MAILLARD

Rachard Castle, Delavon Ministry
Midspring, 3034

Maillard watched the delegations carefully as he took his seat on the dais. Their faces were gloomy but quiet. Maillard was fatigued, having spent much of the night attempting last-minute private negotiations and ensuring the Rugens stayed away from the Almerian ambassador. But he found himself surprisingly hopeful. Some delegations seemed amenable to limited concessions, which he hoped would be enough to keep everyone talking.

Maillard sat for a moment in silence as everyone watched expectantly. It was a quiet balance, a peace that he knew could be upturned in a blink. He looked toward Medoff and Bardil and Arthan's empty chair. Pushing Mordmerg out of his mind, he addressed the council.

"My lords and ladies, I'm most grateful that each delegation has returned this morning. After spending many hours of the night with you I'm confident an agreement can be reached that will benefit all of us."

A few grumbles throughout the hall did not deter him.

"Firstly, as noted yesterday, the Almerian Confederation has agreed to some concessions, including the loosening of shipping routes, the conditional return of selected ports, and the joint administration of selected free cities in Donovan and Austveeden.

"Secondly, regarding the disputed islands, the Almerians have agreed to—"

"Bugger off by sundown!" the Calbrian ambassador shouted, followed by more rumblings from the crowd.

Maillard held up his hand and spoke louder. "The Almerians have agreed to open discussion with kingdoms having legitimate claims to allow settlements to be—"

"I won't hear it!" Now it was the Donovard ambassador, Meltres. "They'll sabotage them by planting the seeds of revolt, as they're doing now in the free cities. Nearby Mordmerg is all the proof we need."

"My lords, order, please!"

The Almerian delegation stood from their table and prepared to leave. Maillard called out to them but felt a tug on his arm. It was Medoff.

"My lord, you stand before a dam that is breaking."

"If I won't try, who will?"

Before Maillard could address the crowd a scream rang out. He turned to see the delegates swarming into the middle of the room. Medoff charged in to lead the guards in breaking them apart, but it was too late. Pitchers of water, books, and other items were being hurled as weapons. Maillard stood from his chair in disbelief.

The ambassador from Austveeden perched himself atop his table and shouted over the din. "The Empire Alliance is no more!"

More guards flooded in as delegates attempted to flee. Bardil and Alfrem came to Maillard's side and the lord minister's personal guards stood fast between them and the chaos.

"You're to blame for this, you pigs!" Vesamune, the Rugen ambassador, shouted at him. "It's on your heads!"

A guard shuffled her away from the dais as Bardil spoke.

"You did what you could, Father."

"It matters not, my son. There will be war."

Maillard regretted the letter he would now have to write to the king, even if Erech expected or welcomed the news. Maillard was not proud of having presided over such a violent end to the alliance, nor to have his great city be remembered as its last place of assembly.

"Thus ends the Empire Alliance," Alfrem affirmed, and they solemnly watched the chaos unfolding.

16

ARTHAN

On the Road to Mordmerg, Delavon Ministry
Midspring, 3034

"It is my business to study the minds of kings and princes," Serdot said. "Because of their wealth and power, they often occupy themselves with leisurely pursuits. Hunting, women, court gossip, and games. For widsemers like myself, and those that came before me in the employ of your father, we are occupied with keys, secret correspondence, night rides, and vials of sleep serum. Or more delicate matters."

"A spy who practices alchemy?" Arthan asked.

"A little. Enough to fulfill my duties."

"Perhaps your alchemy can fulfill my belly's desire for a beer," Livonier jested.

The green meadows in the valley before them were dotted with bright flowers, and the streams still swelled with winter thaw. With Livonier riding on his right and Serdot his left, Arthan felt confident in his task.

"No time for alchemical beer if we wish to reach Mordmerg by next morning," Serdot said.

"What do you know of Mordmerg, Serdot?" Arthan asked. "Why is it called a free city?"

"It lies wholly outside your father's control, despite the inhabitants being Donovards by race," Serdot answered. "Even the king cannot take the free cities in Donovan without provoking a war with the Almerians. Mordmerg and the rest are relics of the days before the Empire Alliance, when the early kingdoms of Pemonia broke away from the Brintilian Empire. But the Brintilians kept control of key trading hubs like Mordmerg. In time, the kingdoms of Pemonia agreed not to take the city-states, but the Almerians still garrison soldiers there to guarantee the cities' independence. Thus, the Almerians retain influence inside our kingdoms."

"But the Brintilian Empire is long dead," Arthan said. "What stops us from taking the free cities, once and for all?"

"The Almerian Confederation is just a new incarnation of the Brintilian Empire, and the Almerian Empire before that," Serdot said. "The names change over the centuries, but Old World politics stay the same. If we leave the free cities alone, we benefit from the trade they bring. If we storm them by force, it means war with the confederation."

"The Rugens did just that," Livonier said. "But it was a costly war for them."

"For a long time, Donovard rulers were comfortable with the arrangement," Serdot continued, "because the Almerians mostly stopped raiding their new kingdoms."

"And if the Empire Alliance falls?"

"King Erech will almost certainly order the seizure of every Almerian possession in Donovan," Serdot said. "Whether he has the swords and gold to do it is another matter. Some lord ministers, like your father, would probably take steps to secure the cities from unrest—such as appointing new leaders in each city-state—while granting them some autonomy."

"Perhaps we could prepare Mordmerg while we are there," Arthan said.

"I recommend we follow your father's orders, my lord," Livonier said. "Extract Golbane and return to Rachard. With only a company of knights with us, we should be careful not to provoke the Mordmerg folk."

"I agree," Serdot said.

Arthan turned in his saddle to look at the one hundred knights, soldiers, and mounted archers waiting on the road behind him. Then he turned back to Livonier. "Can you make sure everything is well with the men? I want a private word with Serdot."

"Of course, my lord." Livonier turned his horse down the line to inspect the men.

"You've been to Mordmerg?" Arthan asked.

"Several times. Your father likes to keep an eye on the place."

"Back in Rachard, you mentioned Mordmerg's troubled history. Father never talks about mother's death. What do you know?"

"Only what I've gleaned from Medoff, really. You and Rowen were only children, Bardil just an infant. Men from the free city had raided nearby towns and farmsteads before retreating behind Mordmerg's walls. The Almerians and the alderman would not answer Maillard's calls for justice.

"Months later, while on the road to Austveeden, your father's convoy was attacked, your mother killed, and Bardil nearly so. The attackers were seen returning to Mordmerg but the Almerian guards insisted it wasn't anyone from the city. Maillard marched on Mordmerg anyway. He killed all the guards who resisted and hung fourteen men found to be responsible for the raid.

"Then he left Mordmerg to itself again. The Almerians eventually accepted his actions, having larger disturbances to deal with on the islands. That's the extent of what I know."

"Free cities . . ." Arthan mused.

"Thankfully, Mordmerg is the only one in Delavon. May I speak freely, my lord?"

"Always, Serdot."

"I think Medoff underestimates you. Your courage is proven despite your youth. Your skill with a blade confirms the crusader blood that runs in the veins of the Valients. As Maillard's heir, you will rule well when your time comes."

"Thank you, Serdot. Father is the wisest man in the kingdom, certainly wiser than any in Eglamour. I still have much to learn from him. When the—"

Shouting arose from the column of men behind them. Arrows flew from the nearby woods into his men. Livonier sounded the alarm.

Arthan lowered his visor and drew his sword as Livonier led a contingent of knights toward the woods, shields up.

Other knights from the column rallied around Arthan with their shields.

"Someone doesn't want us going to Mordmerg," Serdot said.

Arthan had no time to answer. Enemy footmen rushed out of the woods screaming war cries. Arthan raised his sword and called the charge. His cavalry followed behind him as the archers softened the enemy.

They met the enemy in the meadow below the road, the full force of their downhill charge easily crashing through the footmen. Another hail of arrows from archers in the woods brought down several Racharders. Arthan's horse took one in the neck and threw him from his saddle.

Stunned from the fall, he looked skyward through blurred eyes. A footman raised an ax above him. Then Serdot appeared, a small crossbow in hand. Blood spurted from the man's neck, then Serdot shoved a dagger in him. Arthan was pulled to his feet and his sword returned to him by another knight. The Rachard cavalry rallied to him as he rejoined the fight.

The enemy was a mix of well-trained armored men alongside ragged poor folk with swords of iron and gode steel. All of them fought fiercely and appeared to outnumber the Racharders. Fear stabbed Arthan's mind when three of his knights fell before him. *Not here.*

"Cursed son of Valients!" a man cried from the wood line.

A knight stepped into the meadow, his black hood obscuring his face. He raised his sword in challenge. Arthan squared his shoulders and waited. The enemy came to him, bringing his blade up high and slashing down at his head. He deflected each blow, then moved to strike, but the hooded knight was quick to parry.

The enemy pressed close, forcing Arthan's backstep. Arthan feigned losing his balance on the lumpy ground, letting his guard down. The hooded knight surged forward recklessly and Arthan dodged him, swiping at the knight's neck, which proved unprotected under the hood. The enemy fell, motionless.

Within a short time the leaderless attackers fled back into the woods. Livonier led the chase as Arthan stayed on the road with the wounded.

"They knew we were coming," Serdot said, nursing a gash on his cheek. "I didn't recognize their lead knight, but the black hood is ominous."

"Brave of them to attack us this far out from Mordmerg though," Arthan said. He was still sore from his fall but unwounded.

"I'd say foolish. I count at least seventy of them dead."

"And thirty of our own knights . . ."

Livonier soon rode up. "We got most of the stragglers, my lord. A few likely escaped, but . . ."

"Do we have enough men to continue?"

Livonier squinted up and down the line, surveying the men as they rested or tended to the wounded. "Thirty-two lost, and as many wounded. To approach Mordmerg with only a troop would be unwise."

"Perhaps it's enough to quickly ride in and out," Arthan said. "Golbane is depending on us. He has men, and we know they are sheltering at Alderman Hurmant's keep. Serdot?"

"Very risky, my lord. But there is another way. I could sneak to the central keep. If Golbane is there I'll set a signal on the tower, or perhaps extract him myself."

Livonier shook his head. "If this skirmish was any indication of what awaits us at Mordmerg, we best turn back to inform the lord minister, drop the wounded, and get reinforcements."

"Let's do both," Arthan said. "If the enemy has come this far from Mordmerg, they may have their eyes on Rachard. Livonier, you hold this road in case they are planning something. Send the wounded back to Rachard with a message for reinforcements, and wait for them here. And send scouts ahead to watch for our signal. Serdot and I will infiltrate the city and either bring Golbane out or signal for your reinforcements from the roof of the keep. Be sure to have scouts watching for us, but keep your men at a distance."

"My lord"—Serdot hesitated—"widsemers are used to working alone. It will be dangerous."

Arthan saw protest in Livonier's eyes, too.

"Nonsense, Serdot. I've made my decision. Golbane is my cousin and I intend to bring him out as Father ordered. Livonier, hold the road."

Arthan and Serdot mounted and pushed on southward.

17

FETZER

Sea of Pemonia
Midspring, 3034

There is only one thing I can do, since I'm stuck on this ship and Captain Renaud will either soon discover my theft or have me killed. If the mysterious passengers' secrets are so valuable, then I need to know them so I might be in a position to barter for my life . . .

Fetzer made his way into the bowels of the *Meurden* as the sun set. He guessed the mystery passengers would be most active at night to better hide from the crew. He came to the cavernous cargo hold where the ship's stolen goods were held, waiting for resale in Lyonseln.

Fetzer could not see or hear anyone, but he spied three empty bedrolls behind a stack of crates. He hid himself in an overturned barrel on the other side of the crates, and there he watched and listened. The growing darkness and sway of the ship soon lulled him to sleep.

It was a while before the creak of the floor slats by the door woke him. He kept still as a lantern was lit. He quietly sat up and peered through the space between the crates.

There was the bulky Almerian named Bertwil he had seen with Renaud, and the slender man and woman Fetzer had seen run with Bertwil to the ship. All three were dressed as commoners and without sailor garb. They appeared to have objects under their tunics but Fetzer could not make out their shapes. All of them wore grass-stuffed moccasins that muffled their footsteps.

Their voices were low and difficult to hear at first. When the trio settled down with their food and drink they talked more openly.

". . . remains in place," Bertwil was saying. "Therefore, Morroy, you will link up with the islander and meet Juhl and me at the place."

"Easy enough," Morroy said. Fetzer pegged him as a Calbrian.

"Why assault the castle if we can catch him in his carriage?" the woman asked. Her accent was strange.

"I think Master Arasemis wants to make a point, Juhl, that we can get them anywhere at any time," Bertwil said.

"Seems like a needless risk," Juhl said.

"With three of us, we can handle any of Duke Gottfried's soldiers," Morroy said.

"It's not enough to kill the pig," Bertwil said. "We are to set fire to the castle before leaving."

"Easily done," Morroy said, pulling a vial from inside his tunic.

"Put that away," Juhl said. "Are you trying to sink us all?"

"Relax," Bertwil said. "You're trained for this. All will go well."

"May the pig taste the fate of Raymond!" Morroy said a bit too loudly.

"Hush, now," Bertwil said. "There'll be time to celebrate after."

Bertwil was a cool, clever man, certainly not the brute Fetzer had pegged him to be. Morroy was a typical northern Calbrian: confident and careless. But Fetzer was still unable to place Juhl's accent or unusual name.

"This is the best part about being part of the Order of the Candlestone," Morroy said. "The training is difficult by far, and the alchemy can be tedious, if not deadly. But the tasks we're sent off on, well, killing these lordly types is what I . . ."

A realization struck Fetzer. They'd spoken of Raymond's death and now were plotting against the king's cousin, Gottfried Avaleau. Both were lord ministers. Fetzer had never heard of Candlestone but he liked what he was hearing. A sudden hope welled up within him that his own lord minister, Sigbert of Barres Ministry, would be their next victim. He turned back to listen to them.

". . . colder heart than yours," Morroy was saying.

Juhl smiled. "We Lambics can endure any cold. We carry it in our heart and blood."

Of course, Fetzer thought. Her accent, pale face, sharp features, and squinty eyes. She was from Lambochardy, one of the coldest and southernmost places of Pemonia. Why were an Almerian, a Calbrian, and a Lambic members of an order tasked with assassinating Donovard lord ministers? Part of him wanted to walk out at once to discuss it.

"You never told us how Arasemis recruited you," Bertwil said to Juhl.

"That's right," Morroy said. "The master never mentioned traveling to Lambochardy."

Fetzer watched Juhl take a bite of stew, taking her time before answering. "Not sure I can tell you."

"Come on, Juhl!" Morroy said. "This is our third task together. I already know Bertwil was kicked off his Almerian merchant vessel at Rilhammor. And you know that I, of course, have the pedigree of a right honorable vagabond. What's your story?"

"I was . . . How do you say? Like a princess. Is that the word? But not so high."

Morroy stopped chewing his stew and Bertwil's smile vanished.

"Princess?" the big Almerian asked.

"Not so high," Juhl repeated. She took another spoonful of stew. "Have you been to Lambochardy?" Both men shook their heads. "It is a difficult land. Very difficult but sacred to us. Rugen tales say the first Lambic was made of stone encased in ice, brought to life by sea spray and lightning. Our kings have always been iron fisted. The queens too. There are no councils as in Donovan or your kingdoms. It's still so primitive."

"How did you meet Arasemis?"

Fetzer felt a hand on his shoulder and jumped, tipping his barrel into the crates. He instinctively jerked the captain's golden knife from his belt, pointing it toward his assailant. It was Greffid, who screamed out. Fetzer exhaled and lowered the knife. By then Bertwil and the others were upon them.

They snatched the unarmed Greffid and met Fetzer's knife with their blades. He noted a peculiar yellow shimmer in Bertwil's blade.

"Get up," Morroy told him.

Juhl blocked any possible escape to the doorway. Fetzer did as he was told, following Bertwil and Morroy, who held fast to Greffid. Fetzer and Greffid were made to sit on the floor by the lamp while the three surrounded them. Greffid's eyes were big as onions.

"What are you doing down here, clerk?" Bertwil asked.

Fetzer, knife still in hand, looked at each of them in turn. They did not seem especially threatened and he saw no reason to lie. "I saw you board the ship in secret, so I was curious. And yes, I overheard you with the captain." From his tunic Fetzer slowly pulled the stolen letter from Bertwil to Renaud, then tossed it toward the Almerian.

"You weren't sent here to stop us?" Morroy asked.

"No." Fetzer lowered his knife as a gesture. "There was no need to order my death."

"Me n-neither," Greffid stammered. "I know nothing about nothing."

"Quiet." Bertwil identified the letter before crumpling it. "Clerks aren't so foolish as you. Who are you?"

"My name is Fetzer and I'm no one of importance. Just trying to run as far from home as possible. What you talked about appeals to me. That's it." Fetzer tossed the knife to the deck, hoping to convince them.

"Search them, Morroy."

Morroy found nothing on Greffid. Fetzer let the Calbrian fish through his pockets, finding nothing of interest until he touched Fetzer's journal in his breast pocket.

"Leave it," Fetzer said. "It is personal to me and of no threat to you."

Morroy plucked out the little book and turned to the pages with the freshest ink. "This fellow has been thinking about us, Bertwil."

"I said it was personal!"

"Quiet," Bertwil said, grabbing the book.

"Your eyes are cold," Juhl said, studying Fetzer's face. "But you are not Lambic."

Fetzer glanced at her pale, beautiful face, then back to Bertwil. The big man's brow furrowed with consideration.

"Please, release me," Greffid said. "I just needed some apples for the—"

"Keep quiet!" Bertwil said, leafing through the journal.

"Last chance," Morroy said, placing his sword point on Fetzer's chest. "Tell us who you really are."

"This is *your* last chance to give my book back," Fetzer said. He felt his anger rising.

Morroy threw back his head in laughter. Fetzer knocked his blade aside and punched him, sending him backward and jerking the sword from his hand. Juhl stepped forward but Fetzer parried and spun past her, shoving her into Bertwil.

Bertwil raised his yellow-glinting sword to avoid harming her. Fetzer kicked Morroy as he recovered himself, then tripped him. Fetzer then scooped up a bedroll blanket. When Bertwil and Juhl came at him he whipped at their blades with the blanket and lunged with Morroy's sword.

Bertwil backed off to give Juhl more room. She flicked a latch on the hilt of her sword, splitting it into two separate blades. With a sword in each hand she spun toward Fetzer and reduced his blanket shield to a rag, forcing him back. He kicked the lantern, spilling the candle's flame into an open bedroll.

Fetzer next kicked over a stand of kegs, causing Juhl to break off her attack as she regained her balance. She dropped one of her swords and Fetzer recovered it, easily deflecting her next attack. Morroy crawled to pat out the flames on the bedroll, but Fetzer kicked him a third time.

Fetzer crossed swords with Juhl, forcing her back. Bertwil finally charged him but Fetzer dove and rolled away. Juhl was on him again but he stabbed with her sword, pinning her cloak to a crate. Bertwil came for him again.

Fetzer saw a sparkle of light from the corner of his eye. He spun and caught the sparkle with his blade, deflecting toward Bertwil the little glass vial that Morroy had thrown. It broke upon his barrel chest and sent him down to the deck, vomiting and sputtering.

Juhl aimed a second vial at Fetzer. He deflected it also, into a barrel. Then Fetzer went to her and put his blade to her throat. He watched Morroy put out the fire with a water flask while Bertwil continued heaving on his hands and knees. Greffid sat frozen on the floor.

"You're good," Juhl whispered softly to Fetzer. Her gray eyes were cold but captivating.

"Get up," Fetzer told Morroy. "Slowly, or I'll spill her blood."

Morroy did so and Bertwil recovered himself. The big man's eyes were puffy and his nose and mouth was caked with mucous.

"Damn it, Juhl!" he said between gasps.

"He's good," she said again with a smile. "Now you must tell us who you are."

Fetzer calmed his breathing. "A nobody who has turned his back on everything he knew."

"Not everything," she said, glancing at his sapphire ring. "And the book?"

"My journal is my only companion. Return it to me—slowly."

Morroy picked up the book and extended it toward Fetzer. Fetzer could see that he'd broken the Calbrian's nose.

Bertwil's eyes began to weep away the puffiness but his breathing was still labored. "If you harm her, you'll not leave this hold alive, I swear it."

Fetzer smiled as he took the journal. "I don't plan to leave. I want to be part of what you're doing. I've heard everything and I like it."

Morroy chuckled as blood dripped from his nose. "You've heard almost nothing . . ."

"You don't know what you're asking for," Bertwil added.

"You'll need more than the three of you to assault Gottfried's castle," Fetzer said. "Let me join your cause, whatever it is. As you've seen in my pages, I'm like you."

"You're not like us," Bertwil said.

Fetzer sensed that Bertwil was considering his suggestion. He took the risk of slowly removing the blade from Juhl's throat. She looked at Fetzer and pulled herself loose of the crate, then stood calmly between Fetzer and the others.

"The master does want more recruits," she said. "If he had meant us harm, he would have done it."

"He broke my nose," Morroy said.

"You took my journal," Fetzer answered, throwing his sword toward the Calbrian. "I killed the last man who did that."

"Why should we trust you?" Bertwil asked.

"You've probably never heard of Perilune Academy. Overseen by Count Atilon of Perilune, vassal of Lord Minister Sigbert."

"I know it," Morroy said.

"I left it in tatters, spilling the blood of its best cadets. I was a petty nobleman's son. But no more. There is nothing for me there except execution, and nothing I want more than revenge. I've never heard of Candlestone, but if it's responsible for killing high lords, then I want to be part of it. I'll take any oath and complete any 'task,' as you call it. You'll find me loyal to this new calling."

"Prove it," Bertwil said, shoving Greffid with his foot. The cook cried out as he landed at Fetzer's feet. Bertwil tossed the gold-bladed knife to Fetzer and he caught it.

"He's not a high lord," Fetzer said. "He's just a cook."

"He'll talk," Bertwil said. "Show me your new loyalty."

Greffid scrambled away from Fetzer but Morroy jerked him up and held him fast. Fetzer swallowed, staring at the panicked, struggling cook. He was no match for Morroy's sinewy strength. Fetzer brought the knife closer as Juhl looked on. Fetzer took hold of Greffid's jaw and with a quick twist of the blade cut out his tongue.

"Release him!" Fetzer shouted and they dropped him to the deck. Greffid, shrieking through his hands, hid himself in the crates.

"That did not demonstrate loyalty," Bertwil said.

"Greffid is illiterate and now he can't talk. We can keep him hidden down here until we're off the ship. He's no threat to us."

"Us?"

"If he wants to join, let him come with us to kill Lord Gottfried," Juhl said. "Master Arasemis will determine his loyalty."

"If this is trickery, you'll not be as fortunate as the cook," Bertwil said. "And stay out of the way."

"You also burned my bed," Morroy said. The Calbrian smiled through crooked teeth. Fetzer smiled back.

"You are most brave," Juhl said to Fetzer, smiling. "And foolish."

"I have nothing to lose," Fetzer said, "but I have the world to gain."

18

ARTHAN

Mordmerg Free City, Delavon Ministry
Midspring, 3034

If one looked past the rising columns of smoke, Mordmerg could be charming. It was wedged between great forests at the bottom of the Bram Valley. From their approach, Arthan and Serdot could easily see the alderman's keep. It was the tallest tower capping one of the five hills inside the city walls. For Arthan, the town looked as foreign as a distant country.

"The streets are paved with red and gray river stones," Serdot said. "The buildings were built with pride and the inhabitants are usually content. Most speak Donovar and one of the Almerian languages. And though Donovards travel there only with special permissions, the city folk have free passage throughout your father's lands."

"Yet something, someone has disturbed all that," Arthan said. "How do we get in?"

"There is a secret door one tower down from the western gatehouse, behind the bushes. It's usually locked but I pilfered a key during my last trip. The trouble is not knowing how many guards will be on the other side. We should wait here until nightfall."

When the sun finally set, the pair scurried through the dark, crossing the ring road between patrols. Serdot led them straight to the door and unlocked it. The wall chamber was dark and abandoned.

"A passage meant for emergencies and otherwise forgotten," Serdot whispered. "Truth be told, luck is often a key part of a widsemer's work. Last time I came to Mordmerg I had to use my dagger."

Serdot led them through several corridors of rough-hewn rock until they reached the gatehouse. He watched through the keyhole for a while.

"Well?" Arthan whispered anxiously.

"Just one guard is posted. He's pacing up and down the stairs and circling through the rooms." Serdot pulled a small steel wedge from his pocket. "Stay here."

When the guard was gone again Serdot slipped through the unlocked door. Arthan watched him creep to the gate cranks. Serdot silently positioned the wedge into the gears of the contraption, then returned to Arthan and closed the door.

"Aren't we going through the gatehouse?" Arthan asked.

Serdot shook his head. "When they open the gate in the morning, they'll not be able to close it until they discover the stopper. But Livonier should be here by then."

"And if they open the gate during the night?"

"They won't. By law the free cities seal their gates at night. Come, this way."

Serdot led them down another corridor and stairs that emptied onto the street from inside the walls. They donned their hoods as it began to rain. At one point a patrolman stopped them. Arthan was surprised by the accent that Serdot quickly employed to talk their way past.

The streets were littered with debris. Some houses and shops were burned out, and horse carcasses and upturned carts blocked some streets. But the city was quiet. When they neared the alderman's keep they saw abandoned barricades across every street.

They pushed their way through broken furniture, barrels, upturned wagons, and heaps of firewood, splashing through puddles and trying to keep their cloaks from catching on the barricades. But Arthan bumped a pewter plate from its perch, sending chicken bones crashing to the cobblestones. They froze and he cringed.

"Hurry," Serdot whispered.

They turned a bend and Arthan could see a hill and the barred gate into the alderman's courtyard ahead. The walls were high and scarred.

"You there, halt!" came a voice from a nearby alley. Two pikemen rushed out. "Halt!"

The pair ran up the hill toward the gate. "Open!" Serdot shouted as men came to the bars, swords drawn. "In the name of the lord minister!"

A lantern was brought up as they approached. The defenders had their own pikes, ready to shove through the bars.

"I am Arthan Valient, son of Maillard! Where is my cousin Golbane?"

"Open the gate!" Serdot shouted again.

"Show a sign!" shouted a knight through the bars.

Arthan's heart pounded under his tunic and mail. First it felt like a skipping, then a squeezing. He doubled over as the pikemen behind them ran up the hill toward them. Serdot took hold of him.

"Arthan! Are you wounded?"

Arthan leaned on Serdot as he tried to calm his breathing. "It's nothing . . ." Arthan leaned toward the lantern and removed his hood to show the knight his face, then showed his wist ring with the Valient seal.

The gate jerked open and the knights pulled them through as the enemy's pikes thrust close. The gate slammed and the knights thrust out their pikes in turn, fending the enemy off.

"I'm sorry, Arthan," said the chief gate guard. "We've had them fake the arrival of your father, so we have to take every precaution."

"Aldon? My cousin has an old man guarding his front door?"

The gray-haired knight laughed. "Well, my lord, we didn't count on being trapped here. But I've a few years left in me."

"Where is Golbane?"

"Follow me."

They walked toward the tower keep as the enemy shouted curses through the gate before retreating back down the hill. Meanwhile, the rain fell harder.

❧

"You need a shave, Cousin."

Golbane looked up from an improvised map of stones and bits of wood, then smiled. "Who let you in here?"

"Your old wet nurse," Arthan said. He extended his hand but Golbane gathered him up in a bear hug.

"It's been too long since I've seen you, Cousin," Golbane said. "But I'd know that pampered face anywhere. Who've you brought with you?"

"This is Serdot."

"Count Golbane." Serdot bowed. "We've met once. Some time ago."

"Yes," Golbane muttered. "That matter with the Temari woman who showed up in Brambard."

Arthan looked at Serdot, puzzled.

"It was . . . a delicate matter," Serdot said.

"Well then, what happened, Cousin? You came to Mordmerg to put out a few fires and you let them trap you here, waiting for me to rescue you? Where is the alderman?"

"Hurmant? Hell if I know," Golbane said. "Probably plotting with his rabble how best to charge through my gate. He's peeved that I took over his keep."

"But your letter said Hurmant asked for your assistance," Arthan said.

"Yes, that's true. But I didn't say—"

"And that the Almerian garrison had been slaughtered."

"Yes, you'll find their bodies outside in the courtyard, at the rear of the keep."

"But Hurmant is not assisting you?"

"Of course not," Golbane said. "I wish I could have written to your father since my arrival, but both messengers I attempted to send out were caught and killed within view of our gate. I don't know why the brutes haven't overrun us by now. They have the numbers and equipment to force the gates and take the keep. Strange, but my father always said poor leadership makes a bad—"

"But we received your letter," Serdot said. "You asked for Maillard to come with reinforcements."

"I sent no such letter."

The three looked at each other for a moment.

"This was a trap," Arthan said.

"And Golbane was the bait," Serdot said.

"Who would do this?" Arthan asked.

"Almerians. Free city folk. Doesn't matter now," Golbane said. "Perhaps now the big assault will come."

"Maybe not, if the letter's request for Maillard means he was the target," Serdot said.

"They'll not mistake two cloaked figures as the lord minister's arrival," Aldon said. "And they must have heard your name at the gate."

"Perhaps I was bait for Maillard but they'll be satisfied with their catch anyhow," Golbane said. "Maybe you're the new bait, Cousin."

"Well, let's figure out our end," Arthan said. "What is our situation?"

"Of my original company, I have seventeen men well enough to fight," Golbane said. "Twenty-three wounded, several of them still guarding the walls."

"Only seventeen, Cousin?"

"The rebels surrounded us when we entered the city under Hurmant's false promises of protection. I didn't think we'd last near this long."

"Rebels?" Serdot asked.

"That's what I'm calling them. They killed their Almerian overlords and Hurmant is part of it. And now we know about their little scheme to lure the Valients here. I don't think all the people of Mordmerg are involved because most of them stay shuttered up in their homes. But I can't say what started it all, or why they set the fires."

"No demands?" Arthan asked.

"None."

"Fine," Arthan began. "We have your seventeen or so, plus Serdot and me, and a few wounded who can still hold a sword. We should be—"

"Cousin," Golbane laughed uneasily, "there are thousands of rebels. Did you not bring a force of men with you?"

"I brought a company, same as you. But we were ambushed on the road from Rachard. I ordered Livonier to hold the road and send word to Father."

"If they'll be satisfied with you, Maillard won't get here in time," Golbane said, sitting down at the map table. "We'll have to get out on our own, or we're lost . . ."

"What else?" Arthan said, looking over the map.

"We are here," Golbane said, pointing to a black stone in the middle. "Here is the council house nearby, where the city-state decides on their little laws with Almerian guidance. Here is the northern garrison and the north gate. The east gate is farther away, here . . ."

"The west gate is best for an escape," Serdot said. "It is closer and rigged to be locked open for a time after they open it, either for our escape or for Livonier's entry."

"And we can signal to Livonier from here," Arthan said. "His scouts will be watching."

"Good, we'll make for it then," Golbane said. "We have nothing to lose in trying. Have yourselves a hot meal, courtesy of Hurmant's kitchen, then get a few hours sleep if you can. We'll load the wounded into the wagons and saddle up the horses. We'll be doubled up and slow, so we'll shed the heavy plate armor. Keep your mail on."

Food was brought to Arthan and Serdot and they found chairs in the corner of the hall to keep out of the way.

"Do you think we'll make it?" Arthan asked.

"The odds are against us, my lord."

"Should I have acted differently with our company?"

"No, I think it was wise to send word back to Rachard and have Livonier protect the road, in case they're planning something more. And there was no way for us to know Golbane's letter was a forgery."

"You suspected something wasn't right, didn't you?"

"It was suspicious that they requested your father come to Mordmerg and I should have been more insistent about that. If I've learned anything living in the shadows, it's to trust my gut. There are no coincidences. Luck, yes. But if something doesn't feel right, by definition it isn't."

"I'll remember that," Arthan said. "Now, let's get some rest while we can."

19

WREDEGAR

Eglamour, Toulon Ministry
Midspring, 3034

"Where is Sir Garentorf?"

Wredegar knew that tone. For an ambassador, Vesamune never attempted to hide her true feelings when barking at him. "The commander is dead," he said.

"And the others?"

"All dead, except for me and Rodel. I saw him survive the river. I expect him in Eglamour any day. Will you look for him while I go to our emperor in Heingartmer?"

"You're not going anywhere," Vesamune snapped. "I just sent a letter to Emperor Theudamer congratulating him on your successful assassination of Raymond. Now I must send another courier to tell him that the Wosmoks cannot claim that victory. You failed, Wredegar."

"We didn't fail. Someone simply reached Raymond before we could."

"I must send a correction regardless. I'm sure the emperor and Meliamour will want you to stay here and not waste time traveling to Heingartmer. They'll undoubtedly have more work for your Wosmoks."

"As ambassador to Donovan, you're not in my chain of command," Wredegar said.

"But I know the emperor's desires, and I know how Meliamour works. And so do you. You will stay in Eglamour and, when Rodel arrives, both of you will stay hidden within the confines of this residence until we hear from the emperor."

Wredegar had always disliked Vesamune. She had no idea what it was like to be a widsemer, to live on the road, always running here and there and evading discovery by the Donovards. She lived in palaces and dined with kings, even pig-kings like Erech. But Wredegar knew the influence she had in the emperor's court, especially with Lady Meliamour, the master of the Wosmoks and her sister.

"I'll stay," he said, "just so Rodel doesn't have to stay here by himself. But if you pin some failure on the Wosmoks, I'll make sure Meliamour knows of your bedding down with General Chaultion."

Vesamune laughed. "You think that is a vice? Meliamour receives information from me about the general's plans. He is quite the pillow talker. The Wosmoks are not the only eyes and ears of Meliamour."

Wredegar disliked her even more in that moment. "I'll be awaiting Meliamour's orders." Then he dismissed himself and went down to the cellar of the ambassador's residence. He knew where the good wine was, and he was going to need it. He only hoped Rodel would arrive soon.

20

MAILLARD

Rachard Castle, Delavon Ministry
Midspring, 3034

"The Empire Alliance was doomed to fail from the start, my lord."

"We had to try, Medoff." Maillard stood from his writing table as the general folded the parchment and readied the wax. Maillard walked to the tall window and silently took in the view.

"I will have a messenger take your letter to Eglamour straightaway," Medoff said. "The wax is ready for your seal when you are ready."

Maillard returned to the table and made a fist with his ring finger pushed out. He pressed his wist ring into the wax, imprinting the Valient coat of arms. "The most difficult letter I've sent in a long time . . ."

"I'm sure the king and his brothers and all their cronies will be delighted."

"Is there no end to your cynicism, Medoff?"

"Not while King Erech has his indolent ass on the throne, my lord."

"Lord minister!" A messenger burst into the room. "Another letter from Count Golbane."

"Still no word from my son?"

"No, sir."

"Arthan is probably still on the road," Medoff said as Maillard unfolded the letter.

> Lord Minister Valient,
> Our situation is dire. We are trapped and lack provisions for much longer. I beg you to come with reinforcements soon. Only you can calm these people.
>
> Your humble servant,
> Count Golbane Valient
> Mordmerg

"Again he asks for me . . ." Maillard said.

"And gives little detail," Medoff said.

"Perhaps Serdot was right: something is amiss. I shouldn't have doubted him."

"You were focused on the alliance negotiations. And it's probably not as bad as Golbane says. He's young and probably took too few men with him, and now the Almerians are having fun with him. When Arthan finds him they will—"

"Golbane says his situation is dire, Medoff . . ." Maillard felt a sudden sense of urgency. "Anytime I ignored the advice of Serdot's father it was to my own detriment. Serdot has his father's gifts, not only as a widsemer but as an adviser. Assemble a regiment at once."

"A whole regiment? For Mordmerg?"

"If nothing else, we'll demonstrate our authority to the city-state in the wake of the alliance collapse. It's not a power I intended to wield, but now that the kingdoms have made their choice I will use it. Make it a brigade, Medoff. No less than three thousand men."

"That will slow our arrival."

"We'll ride in an advance party. Go."

21

ROWAN

"You can't do this!"

Lord Asteroth backhanded the Almerian representative to Ambardil. "Never tell your new master what he can or cannot do."

Rowan wanted to run. He wanted no part of this. But Asteroth turned to him, his giant bulk, deep voice, and hard eyes commanding Rowan to remain still.

"I can see what you're thinking, boy, and you're wrong. The other lord ministers will be doing the same thing. Even your father, if he's as clever as people think." Asteroth turned back to the quivering alderman. "I don't usually give second chances, but today you're lucky. If you don't produce the key right now, however, I'll have my men pick the lock with your breastbone."

Despite his fear, Rowan could see that the trembling Almerian was not going to comply. He stayed on his knees, resigned to his fate.

"Break him," Asteroth told his men.

"Lord Asteroth," Rowan blurted, "surely we don't need it. The city is already yours and its charter void by the collapse of the alliance."

"The people need to see its end, boy, not merely hear about what happened in Rachard. They need to see their charter burn, along with scum like him. As my ward, you should be learning something here. About fear and its power.

And don't forget how many Donovards have died because of the conspiracies hatched in this city."

Rowan watched as the Almerian was brutally beaten and stripped of his clothes by Asteroth's men, every pocket and fold searched. They took their time finding it.

"Here is the key, my lord."

Asteroth snatched it and turned the lock on the bronze chest. He flicked open the lid and reached his big gauntleted hand inside, searching through the parchments and scrolls. Finally he found a scroll wrapped with the faded purple silk of the former Brintilian Empire. Rowan knew the charters of the free city-states dated back to the colonial days but he'd never seen one before.

"Bring him out with me. Bring your torch, Sir Hamon."

Rowan and Asteroth's men followed Asteroth to the balcony of the alderman's tower, with the naked Almerian in tow. Rowan looked down at the people who had gathered in the square below. They gasped when they saw the Almerian representative, who had long controlled the Almerian garrison and jointly ruled the city with the alderman. The latter's body was already splattered below.

Asteroth held up the purple scroll so all could see. He did not bother to unfurl it. He effortlessly ripped it in half, swapping one half for Hamon's torch. He held the torch to the half, then let it go. It flared as it floated down, sprinkling ashes on the weeping, shouting crowd below.

Asteroth then recovered the other half from Hamon, crumpled it, and shoved it into the mouth of the Almerian. As he choked, Asteroth grabbed him by the nape of his neck and tossed him from the balcony to the sound of shrieks below. Rowan turned from the scene as Asteroth waited a moment before addressing them.

"The days of the Almerians meddling in our kingdom through the city-states are over. Join your Donovard brethren and forsake the foreign conspirators! And forsake the rebels in the west!"

The crowd boiled. Rowan watched as they attacked Asteroth's men posted in the square. It was not what Asteroth had expected.

"This is how you repay my liberation of Ambardil?" he shouted. "My mercy and forgiveness?"

The people rushed the entrance to the tower but Asteroth's knights held their ground.

"My lord . . ." Hamon began.

"Let's go down, then. Let them see their new ruler with fresh eyes!"

Asteroth charged down the spiral stairs. As his ward, Rowan was oath-bound to follow him with the others. When they reached the ground, the swelling crowd had become emboldened. Asteroth wasted no time. He drew his sword and hacked at them, armed men and unarmed women alike. His men did as he did.

Rowan kept his distance as much as he could and only defended himself. But the people did not let up. Their poorly made swords shattered as they struck Asteroth's cindersteel armor. All the lord ministers and their senior knights could afford cindersteel, including Maillard. But Asteroth's was ominously spiked. He reminded Rowan of the tales of armored animals called rhinoceroses that lived in Ovelia.

Then something changed. Rowan noticed that among the common folk there began to appear better armored men and women with green sashes. The rebels of the west.

"You see, Rowan?" Asteroth shouted over the din. "These conspirators welcome the Rugen-loving rebels. A thorough cleansing of this city is long overdue."

"My lord," Hamon said, "they are too many . . ."

"Nonsense!" Asteroth shrieked as he killed two rebels with one blow of his giant sword. But Rowan could tell that Asteroth knew they were in trouble. The lord minister was fighting toward where his armored carriages had been left waiting.

When they reached the carriages, the guards left to protect them were dwindling, fighting for their lives. The sight of Asteroth's bulky, bloodstained form charging toward them was enough to scare many of the commoners and rebels. But of the four companies of soldiers Asteroth had brought with him to Ambardil, Rowan was sure less than half would make it out with them.

When they were safely in the carriage and on the road Asteroth laughed wildly. Rowan glared at him. Sir Hamon, Asteroth's right hand, did not laugh either. He was too busy bandaging his shattered hand.

"If you can't smile at that, boy, you have less humor than a leper."

"My lord, what is there to smile about? The leaders of the city are dead and now the people are in league with the Durgensdil rebels."

Asteroth's face fell grim. "Don't ever call it Durgensdil again. Another slip and I'll send you back to your father in a pine box. This realm is Alpenon Ministry. My realm." He sat back in his seat and removed his gauntlets. "And you should smile, because now they've given me the best reason I could ask for to destroy their city."

"Did we need a reason?"

"No. But now I must punish them. You see, it was one thing to rid them of Almerian influence. Killing the alderman and the representative was easy and over time the people would have accepted my rule. But now that they've clearly invited the Rugen-loving rebels from the west to come here to the east of Alpenon, my task is made easier. What do you think, Hamon?"

"Yes, my lord," Hamon said, wincing as he tightened the wrapping around his hand.

"What about the Rugens?" Rowan said. "Aren't you concerned that they could be supporting the rebels' movements in such large numbers?"

Asteroth shrugged. "It's happened before. They send their rats even into my Cantrileme. But we always hunt them out. The difference now is that, with the fall of the Empire Alliance, I can do as I wish under the rubric of settling Ambardil and the free port of Orringholm. Are you learning yet, my little ward? Great rulers must seize opportunity in calamity. And people once ruled by your enemy must be made to submit to the new power. As for the rebels, their days are numbered, too."

Rowan was certain his and Asteroth's days would be numbered if the lord minister kept underestimating his many enemies. Asteroth was laughing now, but his ignominious departure from the city would later grate on the lord minister. Rowan knew Asteroth's temperament would not allow him to forget it.

22

ARTHAN

Mordmerg Free City, Delavon Ministry
Midspring, 3034

The jolt shook bits of mortar from the walls. Arthan sat up in his bedroll, noting the sky outside the window was still dark.

"What was that?"

"Time to go," Serdot said as he scrambled to gather their things.

Arthan rubbed the sleep from his eyes to see Golbane's knights hurriedly doing the same. One of them came over to them.

"We have horses for you, my lord. They are ready."

"Did we signal?" Arthan asked.

"Count Golbane sent a man up there now to wave a torch. Come, we mustn't wait for the rebels to figure it out."

They followed the knight out onto the torchlit steps of the keep where Golbane was standing to survey the men. The courtyard was cluttered with horses, wagons of the wounded, and men darting about.

"Perhaps they've heard of our plan to escape," Aldon said. "There's movement on the street below."

"What was that noise?" Arthan asked.

"We mustn't linger," Golbane said. "Mount up. Prepare to open the gate!"

Arthan and Serdot did so and fell into line. Then the second crash came. A large stone projectile smashed into the face of the keep, showering everyone in the courtyard with rubble, injuring several. Golbane sheltered in the arch of the doorway.

"Catapult!" Aldon yelled from his post at the opening gate. Golbane's men hesitated, bunching up at the gate.

"We must leave!" Serdot shouted. "Arthan!"

He turned to Golbane. "Hurry, Cousin!"

But Golbane was caring for the injured around him. Arthan looked again toward the outer gate. The next boulder rose into the sky like a distant phantom in the moonlight. He watched it fly overhead and crash into the keep's door where Golbane had been standing.

Arthan jumped from his horse, leaving Serdot's shouts behind him. He rushed up the debris-strewn steps and past the heavy oaken doors that had burst from their hinges into the interior. Several bodies were silent or squirming in the rubble. Arthan bent down beside Golbane. His cousin's armor was crushed and oozed bone fragments amid deep crimson. He lifted Golbane's visor and found his neck bent at an awkward angle.

Serdot put his hand on Arthan's shoulder. "You must lead our escape."

Arthan pulled the gauntlet from Golbane's right hand and removed his wist ring. He stood shakily, pocketed the ring, and breathed deeply. He wiped his eye as they walked through the gaping hole where the doors had been. Arthan set his jaw.

"They're reloading!" Aldon cried from the gate, now closed again.

"Prepare yourselves!" Arthan mounted his horse. "We'll not die here under thrown stones. We fight to escape Mordmerg, or we die trying and take them to hell with us!" He lifted his sword and Golbane's men cheered.

Aldon opened the gate, then took his mount. A troop of cavalry sped out first and down the hill toward the long street before them. The catapult waited at the far end. Arthan and Serdot came after, followed by the wagons of wounded and knights in the rear. Another catapult boulder passed overhead from a different direction, narrowly overshooting the keep.

They swept down the hill and channeled like a river of iron into the street, cutting down the enemy as they flooded out of the shadows and alleys with swords and pikes. The cavalry ahead jumped the barricades ahead of Arthan and rode hard for the first catapult, its crew now panicked at the sight of their charge.

Arthan rode up and joined them in dispatching the crew and their black-hooded leader with their swords. They cut the torsion ropes and hacked at the wooden spokes of the wheels, permanently disabling the machine.

"Push on to the western gate!" Arthan shouted.

The cavalry turned and the others followed. As they raced down the street Arthan noticed that the small bands of rebels had grown into organized units fighting as fierce as any Racharder soldier.

"The wagons slow us down, my lord," Serdot said when he caught up.

"We won't make the city gate in time," Aldon added.

Arthan looked the soldiers crowded around him. They were in one of the narrow valleys of the city, between the tall hill of the alderman's keep and the hill of the council house. "We must try," he said. "We've no choice. Forward!"

The cavalry rallied for a second push as the wagons caught up. But they soon found their path blocked by higher barricades, causing the horses and wagons to back up on each other. Rebels descended on them from all directions.

They turned on a side street, finding it broad and clear. They charged down it with little fighting. But once they neared the bend they met rebel cavalry led by three black-hooded knights. Arthan turned to see a similar number had followed them from behind. He readied himself for what was certain to be their final charge.

As they neared the enemy another cavalry unit burst out from an alley. They carried the azure and violet lion banner of the House of Valient. He recognized Livonier's call and spurred his horse harder. All the cavalries crashed together on the broad street, breaking lances, splintering shields, and casting knights from their mounts. Wagons crushed the fallen into the cobblestone and overturned themselves as more rebels poured out from an alley.

"Little Lord Valient!" shouted one of the black-hooded knights. "Die now, in the city that bleeds your kin!"

Arthan turned to him, the fire in his blood rushing into his arms. He spurred his horse and came alongside the hooded knight. Their swords met but each stayed upright. With a second pass Arthan unseated him and Livonier hacked down into his helmet when he got up.

"Has Father come?"

"An hour away at most," Livonier said. "I saw the torch atop the keep and the western gate open, so I didn't wait for Maillard. But the gate is closed again."

"We won't last an hour in this maze of streets," Serdot said. "Most will be lost."

"What happened here?" Livonier asked.

"A trap was set for us," Arthan said. "No time to explain. Aldon, can you lead us to the council house?"

"Probably well fortified," the old knight said. "We suspect the rebel leaders are there."

"Then we have more reason to go there," Arthan said. "And they probably don't expect an attack. We'll fight for that shelter or otherwise make Father's task of rooting them out a bit easier."

The group turned toward the hill where the glass-domed building shimmered with the faint glow of first light in the sky. The men standing guard there seemed ill prepared for an assault. A black-hooded knight attempted to rally them but when he fell to Livonier's sword the guards fled, leaving the courtyard gate wide open.

"Bar it when everyone is inside," Arthan ordered Aldon. He knew the fewer wagons and many riderless horses meant many of Golbane's men had not made it. But Livonier's men were still fresh.

"Aldon, you command the wall," Arthan continued. "Livonier, post half your company to the walls to give Golbane's men a rest. Then bring the other half. We'll go inside to hunt these rebel leaders and make for the roof to signal. Serdot . . . where is he? Did he come in, Aldon?"

"I presume, my lord. He survived the broad street . . ."

Arthan spun on his heels, looking for Serdot in vain. The fighting had not been difficult up this hill, but he couldn't remember Serdot being there when the guards folded. He wondered . . .

"Shall I send someone out?" Aldon asked.

"No, keep the gate secure. Come, Livonier."

23

SERDOT

Mordmerg Free City, Delavon Ministry
Midspring, 3034

Creeping through the streets and burned-out houses was slow work but Serdot knew he was racing against the coming dawn and the speed of Maillard's army. He cursed himself for not doing more at the western gatehouse when they had come through the first time. He had been overly confident the guards would not find the little steel wedge in the gate wench gears. What's more, they'd be looking for the saboteur.

When he finally came within view of the gatehouse, Serdot peeked around the alley wall to see that all the guards were distracted with something beyond the wall. They were also shoring up inside the main gate. Unless Maillard had taken the time to assemble an army capable of laying siege to Mordmerg, which Serdot thought unlikely, he would arrive without a speedy means to ram open the gate.

Serdot slipped out of the alley and hopped in and out of the closed doorways of the houses on the street. The shouts grew louder as he approached. Serdot thought he heard Medoff's voice. The guards reacted to the voice by posting archers on the wall and promptly shooting their arrows.

"Hey, what are you doing?"

Serdot wheeled around. A man dressed in a Mordmerg guard tunic already had him by the cloak. Serdot reached for his dagger but the bigger man smacked it from his hand, then struck him across the jaw. Serdot fell to the ground and rolled, pulling a vial from his pouch. He threw it at the guard's face, obscuring his vision with a burst of burning powder.

Serdot retrieved his dagger and brought it down into the man's neck as he bent to cough. Then he hefted the dying man into the house from which he'd come. Serdot unbuckled the guard's Mordmerg tunic and slipped it over himself. Turning toward the door, he saw a black hood hanging from a peg. He pulled it on and ran toward the gatehouse.

"The lord minister has arrived, sir," said one of the guards when he reached the gatehouse steps.

"How many?" Serdot asked in his best Mordmerg accent, peering out one of the arrow loops in the wall.

"A brigade or more, up on that ridge. We scared off their advance contingent. The fool thought he could just order the gate open."

"Big man, black mustache, haughty?" Serdot asked.

The guard captain nodded. "General Medoff for certain. Fool of fools."

Serdot pulled away from the loop. "And the gate?"

"Reinforced with timber, sir."

"Good. Get all the archers to the roof of the tower so they have the best range. And fan all the soldiers along the wall."

"But the gatehouse, sir . . ."

"It's well fortified. If we spread the men out, our numbers will appear stronger to Maillard."

"But, sir . . . Navarron's standing orders are to—"

"Don't argue with me," Serdot said. "I have command of the gatehouse. Now move it!"

When the guard departed, Serdot turned his attention to the gate mechanism. His steel wedge was cast aside across the room. The mechanism was in proper working order, the counterweights left carelessly unlocked. He rushed to the door and barred it. The same guard, realizing he'd been duped, returned and began pounding on it.

Serdot rushed to bar the second door across the room. Then he grabbed the hammer and knocked the weights from their platform. The chains jerked tight and wrenched the gate open. A few of the reinforcing timbers were cast off but the remainder held, stopping the gate halfway.

But it was enough. When he ran to the arrow loop again, Serdot could see Maillard's brigade descending from the ridge. He jerked off the black hood and, with heavy hammer in hand, did the same thing he had done for the weights for the heavy iron portcullis that hung in front of the half-opened gate. By the time Maillard's cavalry reached it, their path was clear and Serdot was fighting his way down the outside stairs. Most of the guards had fled their posts.

"You're welcome, General!" he called down.

Medoff and Maillard turned to see him as the rest of the cavalry flooded down the major streets.

"Master widsemer," the lord minister said with a smile. He motioned for a horse to be brought to Serdot.

"Not a master yet," Serdot said as he mounted. "Arthan is at the council house. A trap had been set for us, my lord."

"I realize that now, but we bring a new game for them. Come, lead us, Serdot."

When they arrived at the council house hill, they found another catapult aimed up at the courtyard walls. A boulder had already smashed the gate and rebels were fighting with the Racharders who were making their last stand in the rubble.

The cavalry wasted no time attacking the catapult crew and sweeping up the hillside. The sight of the lord minister and his men sent many rebels running.

"Thank God in heaven!" Aldon said as they rode up.

"Where is my son?" Maillard asked.

"He went in, my lord, then someone barricaded the door from the inside. When we attempted to ram it down, the rebels breached our gate and kept us too busy."

Maillard turned to Medoff. "Bring it down this instant."

After a few minutes of withstanding hammering and prying, the council house door finally relented to the charge of a heavy knight named Cuern and his massive horse. Medoff was the first in, followed by Serdot and Maillard. The foyer was a wreck and several bodies lay among strewn papers, books, and weapons.

"Arthan!" Maillard's shout echoed without response.

They went from room to room and down each corridor but no living soul was found.

"Up the stairs," Medoff ordered the Racharders.

They mounted the foyer staircase. When they reached the second-floor corridor, smoke was creeping along the walls.

"We must hurry," Serdot said.

They stepped across the bodies of Rachard soldiers who had been with Arthan, as well as Mordmerg rebels and a few black-hooded ones. Dull light flashed at the hazy end of the corridor. Muffled voices echoed beyond.

They came to a side chamber that was belching out smoke. A large fireplace had its burning wood strewn out onto the rug in the room. Flames chewed on the wall, floor beams, and rebel bodies littered nearby. A mocking voice farther down the hall grew louder.

Then the attack came. Serdot and the others ran out of the smoke-filled room and into the fray in the hall. Three Blackhoods wielded large axes, felling two Rachard knights in front of Serdot.

"Confounded haze!" Medoff shouted as he took down one of the Blackhoods.

More rebels poured from the doorways farther down the hall. Serdot reloaded his small crossbow and realized his steel-tipped bolts were nearly gone. He stowed it, drew his dagger, and picked up one of the fallen knights' swords. The smoke thickened as the fight slowed to a confused brawl.

"We must push forward!" Maillard shouted.

The big knight Cuern and another Racharder raised their shields and charged down the corridor shoulder to shoulder. Medoff and the others followed. Finally they reached the far end, crashing through a door into the domed council chamber where the air was clearer. Several councilmembers were slumped over in chairs or lying on the floor. All dead, except one.

"M . . . m'lord . . ."

"Where is my son?"

"This was n-not . . . our plan . . ."

"What plan? Where is my son?"

"H-hurry . . ."

His head dropped and they rushed across the chamber into another smoke-filled hallway and stairwell to the third floor. Men shouted, then Blackhoods swarmed out.

24

ARTHAN

Mordmerg Free City, Delavon Ministry
Midspring, 3034

Meriam's fingers touched Arthan's face. Her chestnut hair framed her delicate features. Her lips moved, but he could not hear her words. Concern crept across her eyes. He tried to open his mouth but could not. Tears welled in her eyes as she faded from view.

Arthan was startled awake by angry voices and the smell of smoke. He was lying on his side, hands bound in front of him, facing a stone wall. Shadows played across the wall. There was also something near his head. He slowly raised his eyes to see Livonier's head next to his. The knight's eyes were closed and bruised, but he was breathing. Arthan kept still as the voices grew more violent.

"I didn't sign up for this mess! You've opened a—"

"You heard my master. Whatever was 'necessary.' Everything has gone according to his plan, better, actually. New bait, and two Valients for the price of one."

"This was not the plan!"

A table overturned and a sword was drawn.

"Put it away, Navarron," said the man with a master.

"Didn't you see the size of the Racharder force outside?" Navarron asked. "It's over, Marlan."

"It's only the beginning," Marlan answered.

"They will burn our city to the ground for this," Navarron said.

"You think we care what happens to Mordmerg?"

"I want no more of this. We're not interested in his games."

"My master allotted you a small part to play and you've done it well enough," Marlan said. "If you won't finish it, then I will. But don't expect full payment."

"Let him finish it, Navarron," said a third man. "This was not part of the plan. Full payment or not, we shouldn't be here."

"Shut up, Lunfrid," Navarron said. "You'll save your skin soon enough."

Shutters were opened and a light breeze swirled through the room.

"Go then," Marlan said. "The rest will be no problem for me."

"What about the alderman?" Navarron asked. "He knows all about this now."

"Mercy . . . please . . ."

Arthan guessed the weak, trembling voice to be that of Alderman Hurmant. Another sword unsheathed. The alderman convulsed, then the weight of his body fell to the floor beside Arthan.

"What about the others?" Lunfrid asked.

"They are part of the show," Marlan said. "Get out."

"And our payment?" asked a woman.

"My master's word is golden. You'll get it."

Muffled shouting interrupted them. A great struggle arose outside the room. Arthan thought he heard a familiar voice.

"Blackhoods to me!" Navarron shouted.

Arthan heard many more boots than he had guessed were in the room. Then the shutters clacked on the stone as the group departed. The room was quiet, with only the struggle outside.

An ax smashed into the door. Arthan saw a shadow flick across the wall and he felt Livonier's head bump his. Livonier was awake and tried to whisper, but Arthan could not understand him. Livonier struggled against his bonds but it was no use. Desperation seized Livonier and he lurched his body up.

"Trap, my lord!" he shouted as loud as he could toward the door. "It's a—"

Marlan kicked Livonier in the head until again the knight fell unconscious. Arthan feigned unconsciousness, sure he would be discovered. But the door burst in and Marlan stepped away. Arthan turned to see that Marlan wore a cape of forest green and moccasins stuffed with grass. He was holding a long sword in one hand and a small crossbow in the other. Racharder knights and smoke poured into the room. Then Arthan noticed the cord strung behind the doorway.

"Arthan!" Maillard shouted behind them.

"It's a trap, Father!"

The Racharders tripped the cord. A sound like a hundred eggs breaking was followed by clouds of orange and purple dust that mixed with the smoke from the corridor. The green-caped Marlan turned to look at Arthan. On his face was a mask of wood, with only narrow eye slits breaking the smooth surface. Then Marlan spun into the colored smoke, his sword slashing through the Racharders' armor.

Arthan struggled in vain with the rope on his wrists. He pulled a small knife from Livonier's belt and gripped it in his teeth, cutting himself loose. Then he stood, looking for an opening to throw the knife at Marlan. He caught a glimpse of the green cape but Marlan was too quick and the Racharders too many.

Arthan's eyes widened as Marlan sprang from the smoke and ran up the wall as easily as if he were on flat ground, then opened a high window. Arthan bent to vomit as the noxious cloud swept toward him. He pulled a handkerchief from his pocket until the breeze swept out the foul air.

There were bodies everywhere. The live ones were still vomiting and rubbing their eyes. Arthan found Serdot first.

"Almost got him," he said through a scarf he had tied around his face. Serdot held up Marlan's wooden mask.

"Father!" Arthan shouted as he looked around amid the thinning smoke.

"My lord . . ." It was Medoff. The general waved him over, his face bleeding and his eyes all but swollen shut. He was crouching beside a body. Arthan came and took Maillard's hand. There was still breath in him.

"Son . . ."

"Don't speak, Father. We must get you out."

Cuern and the other big knight, both wounded, hefted Maillard up from the floor, leaving a pool of crimson. Arthan returned to Livonier as Serdot cut his bonds. They lifted Livonier to his feet and exited after Maillard.

The hallways were thick with smoke, the fire now spread throughout the building. They stumbled down the corridors and stairs. When they laid Maillard down on the cobblestone outside, he was already dead.

Arthan fell to his knees. Maillard's hair was singed and his face smeared with soot. Arthan stared at the gaping wound in Maillard's chest, the fine cindersteel armor cleaved open, until his eyes welled blurry. Arthan felt a sudden cold grip him despite the blaze behind.

His constitution began to shred and sorrow crept in. He buried his face in his hands, his youth consumed in the flames. The Racharders wept with him.

"May God rest him," Medoff said. Then he raised his hand for the Racharders to join him.

"All hail the new Lord Valient of Delavon!"

25

THEUDAMER

Heingartmer, Ward of Havelbern
Midspring, 3034

"I don't care if I'm hunting in the mountains at the end of the earth, you send someone to me! The collapse of the Empire Alliance is not mere news, but a chance to reshape the continent!"

"A thousand apologies, Your Majesty," Meliamour said. "We did not want to—"

"How long has it been? Never mind, give me the letter."

"We have two letters, Your Majesty. Both from Vesamune in Eglamour."

Theudamer shook his head. "Lady Meliamour, don't bore me with Vesamune's excessive details. Just tell me what has happened," he said as he sat on his onyx throne.

"Ambassador Vesamune attended the Empire Alliance Council hosted by Lord Minister Maillard Valient in Rachard," Meliamour said. "The alliance collapsed because the Almerians would not soften their demands. Maillard was subsequently killed while fighting rebels in Mordmerg Free City. Lord Minister Raymond Reimvick of Wallevet was also murdered prior to the council."

"Didn't we agree to postpone your plan to assassinate King Erech's lord ministers?" Theudamer asked. "You were merely supposed to use the Wosmoks to undermine them politically until we had a candidate to replace Erech."

"I did not order the Wosmoks to kill Maillard and Raymond, Your Majesty. The Wosmoks were not involved."

Theudamer noted the defiance in Meliamour's sharp eyes. It's what he liked most about his spymaster. Meliamour, along with her sister Vesamune, was one of his most competent and daring servants. As their uncle, Theudamer repaid their loyalty with powerful positions.

"Your Majesty," began Graf, "if it wasn't Meliamour's Wosmoks, I would urge you to hire whoever killed them."

"Excellent idea, Graf. What say you, Herzol?" Theudamer looked expectantly at his favorite counselor.

"Your Majesty, you already know my mind on such matters."

"Nevertheless, as Wardenlord of Rugenhav, I want to hear your official opinion."

"Well," began Herzol, stroking his pointy white beard, "if someone is ousting the lord ministers of Donovan, we shouldn't get involved. Whoever they are, they know what they're doing. It would be difficult for us to influence them at this point, even with her Wosmoks."

"The Donovards are certain to blame us for their deaths regardless," Graf said. "We have nothing to lose by helping them kill all the lord ministers."

"Some are already blaming us," Meliamour said. "Not only for the deaths of Maillard and Raymond, but for the collapse of the Empire Alliance. They also say we're plotting to overthrow Erech."

"We should be," Graf said, his tone sharpening. "Better yet, if we invade Donovan it will put us in a stronger position. If we at least take back Durgensdil once and for all, the Donovards will be too frightened to cause us any trouble."

"I disagree," Herzol said. "Attacking Alpenon Ministry— or Durgensdil, if you still insist on calling it that—will only invite a larger war. We should be focused on increasing our influence peacefully at this time. Perhaps strengthening our alliances and—"

"The sword is the only true influence," Graf said.

"Your opinions are noted, Graf," Theudamer said, raising his hand. "We share your lifelong desire to bring Durgensdil back into Rugenhav, but the time to invade has not yet come. Herzol, I heeded your earlier advice not to begin our plan to eliminate Erech's high nobles. But now I must consider how to make the most of the current situation, as well as identify who is behind their deaths."

"Your Majesty, in her letters Vesamune also reported on the status of the Wosmoks," Meliamour said. "Their recent mission failed. Most were killed and the rest captured but subsequently drowned when their prison carriage overturned in a river in Wallevet Ministry."

"Most?" Herzol asked with concern.

"Your son, Wredegar, survived," Meliamour told Herzol. "Along with one other. The rest perished, including Commander Garentorf."

"I warned this council . . ." Herzol said, shaking his head. "Too dangerous, too provocative."

"It seems the Donovards did not know who our Wosmoks actually were," Meliamour said. "I often have them dress as thieves and beggars, and their Donovar speech must be impeccable."

"Promote Wredegar," Theudamer said. "Give him command of the Wosmoks deployed to Donovan, and pull those Wosmoks who can speak Donovar out of Austveeden and send them to Eglamour to serve under Wredegar."

"I'll send the courier at once," Meliamour said.

"Tell Wredegar to find out who is killing the lord ministers, but to stand down on further missions for now. He should stay in Eglamour until his new Wosmoks arrive. And tell Vesamune I want to know how Erech is responding to everything. If he continues to weaken we may be forced to take our opportunities while they are still there for the taking."

"Must Wredegar continue as a Wosmok?" Herzol asked. "My son is eager to take off the cloak of a widsemer and don knight's armor again. It is time he ruled over his ancestral lands."

"Wredegar is one of my most capable ghosts," Meliamour said.

"Herzol, as long as your brother rules the Ward of Auftengardin, your family's ancestral lands are well taken care of," Theudamer said. "Wredegar's current calling is in my service as a Wosmok. If he commands his unit well, he will be rewarded when he returns to Rugenhav."

26

FETZER

Near Lyonseln Port
Midspring, 3034

They won't tell me much, but Juhl has shared that the Order of the Candlestone is ancient, its roots planted before the first kingdom of this continent became independent from the Old World. The aims of the Order, and its current leader, are still hidden from me.

Bertwil remains suspicious of me but has relaxed a bit. Morroy the Calbrian considers him and me to be on equal terms: my damaged journal and his broken nose. Juhl's icy eyes notice everything. If all the Lambic women are as beautiful as she is, then perhaps Lambochardy's many wars start with the jealousy of their men.

Candlestone has been a revelation to me, perhaps from a god of a darker nature than most people believe. What little I've learned about the Order suggests their endeavor to overthrow lords and kings is a most serious and dedicated effort. I look forward to meeting this Arasemis, wherever he dwells . . .

Fetzer looked up to see Bertwil's grass-stuffed moccasins stepping toward him.

"Time to put your little schoolbook away," he said. "And don't make me regret giving this to you."

Bertwil held out the hilt of a sword. Fetzer stood, carefully pocketed his journal, then took the blade.

"No 'thank you'?" the big man asked.

"You need my help," Fetzer said.

Bertwil glared at him but Juhl stepped in. "Let's keep our focus."

"Captain Renaud says we've sighted the port of Lyonseln," Morroy said as he descended the ladder. "Won't be long now, and the sun is going down."

"Get in your barrels," Bertwil said. "Fetzer, you take the one beside Morroy. No one comes out until the islander has us safely in his wagon. Understood?"

Everyone took their places and waited. Fetzer's barrel reeked of mackerel and glidiwots but he kept quiet. When they finally came into port, the crewmen hoisted the barrels out of the ship's hold and onto the dock. Fetzer was a bit unnerved by being stuck in the barrel as it dangled from the dock crane.

Soon he was tipped over and rolled up a ramp into a wagon. Sick from the motion, cramped, and craving fresh air, he hoped it would not be much longer. The horses jerked forward and Fetzer heard a barrel open. Bertwil began whispering, so Fetzer pushed his lid up and peered out.

"Not yet," Bertwil whispered. Morroy and Juhl were peeping out as well.

"The islander will get us to Duke Gottfried's castle," Juhl whispered to Fetzer. "But he doesn't know who we are or what we're about."

Fetzer nodded. Bertwil climbed out of his barrel and poked his head out of the covered wagon's front to speak with the driver. Fetzer assumed this was "the islander." Fetzer glanced around the wagon. There were sacks of spices, a scale, and a stack of merchant ledgers.

"Change of plans," Bertwil said to them. "The islander says if we want to 'meet' the duke we should wait until morning. Apparently the duke is planning to travel."

"Morning is mere hours away," Morroy said.

"Exactly. So I told the islander to take us to the castle anyway and to leave us in the courtyard. He agreed but he's nervous."

"How did you hire this man?" Fetzer asked.

"Not your concern," Bertwil said.

"Our master contacted him," Juhl said. "Just a merchant willing to make a lot of coin to take us inside."

"That's enough," Bertwil hissed. "We'll be inspected, so you'll need this. Keep your head down and don't come out until we do."

Bertwil picked up loose sacks from within the wagon and dumped their contents over each of them, then closed the lids. Fetzer received large dried leaves of some herb he'd never seen before. They smelled like spoiled cream and, along with the lingering fishy smell, made breathing difficult. But he did not complain.

The sway and bump of the wagon and the heavy scents made Fetzer doze. He awoke later to the sound of soldiers' voices.

". . . a look first. Go round there . . ."

The wagon came to a stop and the leather flaps of the wagon cover jerked aside. A soldier or two rummaged around, then Fetzer heard a barrel lid being pulled off, then another. The soldiers did not bother to check them all. Fools, he thought. After a few shouts to the gatehouse, the portcullis drew up. The wagon lurched forward and soon he was being rolled off. Then silence.

The hours passed slowly. Fetzer drifted in and out of sleep amid the occasional whinny of nearby horses or the footsteps of guard patrols. When a rooster crowed the coming dawn, he knew their time would come soon. Fetzer did his best to move his head, hands, and feet to avoid getting stiff.

What he presumed to be the courtyard was soon alive with voices, horses, and laughter. Someone said "My lord." That was all that was needed. A barrel lid shifted nearby.

"We're covered," Bertwil whispered. "Everyone out. Slow."

Fetzer pushed up through the herbs and lifted the lid. The barrels had been placed under a lean-to next to the castle wall. They had a protected view of the courtyard and the main door of Gottfried's castle. Fetzer's eyes fixed on a rotund, richly dressed man speaking with a few knights. Several carriages were being loaded with luggage.

"Everyone ready?" Bertwil asked.

Fetzer turned to see that Bertwil, Morroy, and Juhl were wearing wooden masks with tiny eye slits, and their weapons were ready.

"No mask for you . . .yet," Juhl said. "Just stay away from my alchemical clouds."

"Fetzer, you wait here until the fight has begun," Bertwil said. "Your boots will be too loud."

Fetzer looked down at his boots. Before he could protest, Bertwil rushed out, followed by the others in single file. He could not hear them running, their grass-stuffed moccasins merely a breeze across the ground. He drew his sword and watched impatiently.

Bertwil was faster than his girth suggested. He was halfway across the courtyard before anyone sounded the alarm. The duke's knights turned to see the Order members fan out behind Bertwil. The big man was upon them as they drew their swords. Their surprise was almost total. Bertwil killed one of the knights with his yellow-shimmering sword as Fetzer rushed out to join them.

The duke's head swiveled from side to side as he called his guards, then he drew his sword and ran for one of the carriages. He jumped inside and closed its wooden shutters. Morroy slashed at the door but was attacked by two guards. Many more poured into the courtyard.

Juhl threw something at the carriage that burst gray powdery clouds at the door and shuttered windows. Then she split her sword into two and crashed into the guards. Fetzer came alongside her and they took down several of the guards together. But the courtyard was soon filling with soldiers.

Juhl gave Fetzer one of her swords, then took a crossbow-like device from inside her cloak. She shot little smoking pellets into the approaching guards. Fetzer moved to block a knight approaching her from behind, but not before Juhl noticed. She ran up the side of the castle wall. Fetzer stared as she ran along the rampart, shooting more pellets. They created a foul-smelling smoke screen around the carriage that kept the guards away.

From her perch on the rampart Juhl shot again at the carriage, this time with orange-smoking pellets. The carriage burst into flames amid screams from inside. The duke pushed open the door and stumbled out, a richly dressed woman close behind him. Without hesitating, Bertwil and Morroy slew them both.

By now, different colored smoke was drifting throughout the courtyard, obscuring everyone's view. Fetzer's eyes watered and he could not control bouts of coughing. Bertwil and Morroy continued to move in and out of the smokes with ease, dispatching any knights and guards who came too close. Fetzer, finding it increasingly difficult to breathe, started to fall back.

Then bolts shot through the air. Fetzer caught a glimpse of crossbowmen lined up on top of the outer wall. He lost sight of Juhl and when he turned to Bertwil and Morroy they were running up the outer wall to escape.

Fetzer looked toward the gatehouse but the guards had lowered the portcullis. There was no escape for him. He looked to the wall again. Only Juhl remained, and she had lowered a thin green twine. He ran over and took hold of it, certain it would snap. But it did not, so he pulled himself up.

When he reached the top Juhl jumped over the edge into a tree. Guards were running along the wall toward him. Fetzer took a breath and jumped too. He fell through the tree, hitting limbs and landing in a bush. He felt the trickle of blood on his arm.

"We can't leave him!" Juhl cried.

Fetzer rolled and pushed out of the bush. There in a hidden clearing in the woods was Morroy, blood pumping from his chest and mouth. Two crossbow bolts protruded from his ribs. Fetzer caught his breath and watched.

"He'll not make it," Bertwil said, lifting Morroy's tunic for a better look at his chest. A vial rolled out of one of Morroy's pockets. "We were supposed to burn the castle, too," Bertwil said, nodding at the vial. "But it's too late for that, and for him . . ."

Without a word, Fetzer grabbed the vial and ran back toward the castle wall. Bertwil yelled behind him but he did not stop. Fetzer remembered Juhl's comment to Morroy back on the *Meurden*, about being careful with the vial so as not to sink the ship. Guessing it worked best on wood, Fetzer aimed for the lowest window of a guard tower. He threw it and heard the faint breaking of glass and soldiers shouting. Black smoke appeared at once from the window.

He returned to the others. Bertwil had picked Morroy up. They all ran through the woods, with Fetzer limping from his fall through the tree. They had not gone far when Fetzer noticed Morroy's pale face flapping over Bertwil's shoulder, his eyes staring into the next world.

Bertwil found another place to stop and they hid Morroy's body in the brush. Juhl wept quietly. They looked back to watch a column of black smoke rising before pushing onward.

27

MILISEND

Eglamour Palace, Toulon Ministry
Midspring, 3034

"How can this be happening!"

Her father's outburst startled Milisend out of her thoughts of Regaume. The king's court was quiet otherwise, an eerie silence amid more troubling news.

"Someone in this great hall knows," Brugarn said to the watching courtiers. "One among you, perhaps more, knows who is killing the lord ministers. Someone is trying to overthrow our king and ruin our realm. Someone among us here . . ."

The courtiers squirmed. Milisend wanted to go up and slap her uncle. If there was anyone who usurped her father's authority, it was his youngest brother, Duke Brugarn, the Lord Minister of Toulon.

"Who will rid us of this evil?" Brugarn continued. "Who will uproot it wherever it will be found?" He paced by the courtiers clustered around the throne, peering into the eyes of each. "Who is worthy . . . Who is suspect . . . ?"

Milisend's eyes met Tronchet's a moment before Brugarn came to him. She wondered how long Tronchet had been watching her.

"You!" Brugarn jabbed a finger in his face. "You are the king's Chief Magistrate of Eglamour. What can you say about Lord Maillard's death, or Raymond's before his? They were each on a mission from the king to save the Empire Alliance when they were struck down."

Tronchet regarded him with a puzzled look. "They were both killed in their home ministries, my lord, not in my jurisdiction of the capital."

"The details do not matter to me." Brugarn waved dismissively. "The point is that shadowy men murdered another lord minister. As chief magistrate, you should know more."

"I am not the chief magistrate of Rachard or Bredahade," Tronchet said. "The lawkeepers of those lands answer only to their lord ministers."

Brugarn sneered at him but had already found his next prey.

"What about you, Sir Hamelin? As captain of the king's guard, what can you say? Will this hidden scourge come to Eglamour?"

Milisend knew Hamelin, if anyone, would throttle Brugarn if ever given the chance. But he stood silently next to the king. She urged Erech with her eyes to take back the floor from Brugarn. But her father was entranced with his theatrics.

"Well, Sir Hamelin?" Brugarn asked. Hamelin answered with a hard stare. The duke paced forward, peering. "Perhaps none are worthy . . . all are suspect . . ."

"I wonder . . ." Erech finally spoke. "We are surrounded by enemies now. The Rugens to the south, the Calbrians in the east, the Almerians all around . . . Perhaps the blame is best laid at the feet of a foreign throne."

"Perhaps, great king, perhaps . . ." Brugarn stopped his pacing. "Since none here can say, we can only wait for a sign. All of you, leave at once."

The courtiers exchanged confused looks. Erech's lack of control deeply embarrassed Milisend, but she knew better than to speak out in front of the whole court.

"Go . . ." Erech said.

To Milisend he sounded reluctant. Or indifferent. She approached her father as the courtiers filed out the doors, but Tronchet intercepted her and walked her toward the door.

"Princess Milisend, lovely to see you."

"Magistrate . . ."

"I wonder if I could have a quick word."

"Well, I—"

"You see, there is still the matter of the diamond brooch belonging to the countess, and that ring stolen from Baron Balvene. I would like to—"

"Tronchet, I'm quite sure I know nothing of their unfortunate losses, as I've said before."

"With all due respect, Princess, I'm quite sure that you do. And now there is the mysterious appearance of an alchemical smoking candle set right in front of the Benrollen Company's treasury door. May I ask where you were that evening?"

"Was anything stolen, Tronchet?"

"No, the guards claimed to have foiled a pair of shadows."

"I'm confused, Tronchet." Milisend smiled innocently. "For a moment I thought you were suggesting I had special knowledge of those unfortunate events. But since nothing was taken from the Benrollens I see that you believe me to be a good source of such gossip."

"No, actually—"

"That's all right, Tronchet. I take no offense." Milisend spun on her heel, then sidestepped his attempt to cut her off again. She skirted back toward the throne. "If I hear of anything I'll be sure to speak with you," she said over her shoulder.

"Anything at all!" he called back in frustration.

Milisend set her eyes on Brugarn. The duke saw her coming and positioned himself between her and the king, but she spoke through him.

"Father, I'm troubled by what happened to Lord Maillard. I know he was one of your favorites . . ." Milisend noticed an absent stare on Erech's face. "Excuse me, Uncle," she said, gently pushing Brugarn aside. "Father, are you unwell?"

"Dear Princess," Brugarn said, clutching her arm. "Do not burden the king's mind with womanly worries."

Milisend tried to jerk away from him but he tightened his grip. She turned and slapped him. "Release me, foul-speaker!"

Brugarn recoiled a little; she knew he felt the sting. His eyes flared as he took a step backward. She looked at Erech and his eyes brightened. "What has happened to you, Father?

His absent gaze returned. Milisend took his hand, confused about how he could so quickly shift from bouts of rage to quiet surrender to emptiness.

"You mustn't allow these troubled times to depress you so," she continued, squeezing his limp hand. She glanced over her shoulder as she sensed some movement. Brugarn was drawing close again. "Tell him to leave, Father." She turned to her uncle. "Leave!"

"Leave . . ." Erech repeated softly.

She watched as Brugarn retreated to the dim sides of the great hall. He paced and watched.

"Father," she said, kneeling with his hand in hers. "You must climb out of the ditch he has dug for you. Were it up to me, he would be in a cell, along with Chaultion and the others who crave your crown. Don't you see how they are using you? Do not listen to their poisonous talk and dire ways. Our people need the strength you still possess. Your people, Father."

Erech looked at her and spoke as if explaining a simple game to a child. "Mili, there is nothing that can be done for Donovan. The bright days of the House of Avaleau are waning. Our enemies are too numerous, too strong . . . Who can hold back the tide?"

"Any sail can be turned to catch the changing winds, Father. Do not lose hope. The Avaleaus built this kingdom. You can strengthen it."

"My child, you know nothing of politics and war. There is no end to the greed and hate of men. No end to the lengths men will go to . . . I've grown weary of the burden of keeping the balance . . ."

"If the king will not protect his kingdom, who will, Father? It must fall to you."

"Go, Mili. Keep a free heart while you may . . ."

"Yes. Go, Mili," Brugarn said.

She had not noticed his return. Her uncle's eyes were devious. She looked back at Erech but dark clouds had already fogged his mind again. Brugarn latched on to her arm, tugging her away. She stood and slapped him again, harder.

"Don't touch me," she said.

Brugarn recovered himself with stubborn dignity. Then he escorted her toward the door and whispered, "There will come a time, Princess, when I hope you will appreciate my service to your father. As Lord Minister of Toulon, I have many things to occupy my time and talents. Yet I'm so often here, in his castle, helping the king however I may."

"I appreciate exactly what you're doing. May there come a day, sooner than later, when my father wakes up to who you really are."

"I am but the king's loyal brother," Brugarn said, his voice darkening. "And you'd do well to remember that, since you have no brothers or sons to inherit his crown. One day that most unfortunate time will arrive."

She stopped to regard him and set her jaw. "May Donovan fall before you have any chance of ruling it."

"May you enjoy your days robbing others of their petty possessions, Princess. For those days may be shorter than you've ever thought possible."

She slapped him again but was too distraught to speak. Brugarn laughed as she exited the great hall. She walked at first, then ran to escape the echo of his laughter. She thought of going to her mother, but knew the queen would already be in a stupor from drinking popaver. Milisend considered Hamelin, but what could the captain of the Crownblades do to the king's own brother? And Regaume was traveling. There was no one.

Milisend wept in her chambers. Helpless, she pushed up from her bed and stepped to the window. The warmth of summer was coming, the golden sun its crown. She often wondered how the sun and moon and all the heavens plied their ancient paths without concern for all the turmoil below them. Perhaps it was the normal working of things.

She looked toward the west and thought of Regaume and his desire for her to escape with him. What adventures had he found today? What carefree life was she forgoing? What was keeping her here, if her father had already given up?

28

ARTHAN

Rachard Castle, Delavon Ministry
Flowertide, 3034

Six days of mourning had passed since the bodies of Maillard and Golbane had been brought to Rachard and buried in the cathedral. Then Arthan wasted no time in gathering his closest advisers at his father's table. Count Dardanon and Countess Iserenne came from the ministry's far reaches, joining Bardil, Serdot, Livonier, General Medoff, and Alderman Alfrem.

When everyone was seated, Arthan nodded to Serdot. "Show them."

Serdot held up the mask he had snatched from Marlan. "Maillard's killer wore this in Mordmerg. It's a significant clue for who is behind all this."

"We already know it was those damn Blackhood rebels of Mordmerg," Medoff said.

"Yes," Alfrem said, "weren't they displeased with the fall of the Empire Alliance, and feared we'd seize the free cities?"

"We should have," Bardil said.

"We still can," Count Dardanon said. "Or burn it to the ground. Worthy punishment for the death of Maillard."

Arthan watched Serdot lay the mask on the table as they bantered. It was tempting to punish Mordmerg.

"Burning Mordmerg won't bring Maillard back," Alfrem said. "And if you do punish them, my lord, all the city-states—who already fear being seized—will see it as confirmation of their worst fears. They'll appeal to the

Almerian Confederation for protection, provoking war. As an alternative, you can show yourself to be merciful, especially since the Blackhoods are already defeated."

"I'm not concerned about the Almerians," Medoff said. "Their power has faded. And don't presume the Blackhoods are defeated. They just scampered back into their holes for a while."

"It's the Rugens we should worry about," Countess Iserenne said. "They are the ones who were probably behind the Mordmerg rebels. The Rugens would have seen the free cities' fear as a weapon against us. Maillard's death is proof of that."

"The Blackhoods are certainly still our enemy, and my ears are open to the opinions of my advisers," Arthan said. "But I see nothing to suggest the Rugens encouraged or supported them. The man who wore this mask spoke Donovar. He gave orders to the Blackhoods on behalf of his unnamed master."

"His master could still be a Rugen," Iserenne said. "This is how their agents work, through others."

Arthan shook his head. "It could have been someone else. Serdot, tell them about Marlan's mask."

"It's an ancient design worn by the Naren-Dra natives who lived in the highest reaches of the Narendra Mountains straddling Delavon and Calbria. The complete covering of the face, except for the narrow eye slits, protects from the frigid winds of that place. And it's made of aglanrit wood. Those twisted, stunted trees only grow on those mountains. Finally, it was lined with gray gill ferns, which produce fresh air for the wearer, and the eye slits are windowed with shulmel crystal panes. Those ferns and crystals are known to grow in the Narendra cave systems. It's definitely made by the Naren-Dra tribe."

"So this Marlan collects ancient masks?" Medoff asked. "That's hardly relevant for—"

"He used alchemy against us, too," Arthan said.

"Poison clouds, stun powder, irritants," Serdot said. "He used advanced alchemical mixtures and knew sophisticated deployment techniques."

"How would you know what is advanced in such a dishonorable art?" Dardanon asked.

"A good widsemer knows a thing or two about mixtures," Serdot said with a smile.

"Eggshells?" Alfrem asked.

"I heard the eggshells break when the Racharders burst into the room, tripping the trap Marlan had set," Arthan said. He nodded at Serdot to continue.

"Marlan's use of hollow eggs to dispense the powders is an expert technique called shroud alchemy, developed by the Naren-Dra," Serdot said. "What's more, he wielded a blade that was able to cut through Maillard's cindersteel armor, which should have resisted any steels available in Mordmerg, or most anywhere else."

"And I heard about wall running?" asked Alfrem.

"Yes," Medoff said. "With queer shoes . . ."

"Grass-stuffed moccasins," Arthan clarified. "They completely muffled his steps."

"They were long used by the Gallerlander tribes," Serdot said. "They're the ones who developed wall running and other acrobatics."

"How do you know so much about ancient heathens' fighting habits?" Dardanon asked.

"The Widsemer School of Rangerhood teaches about the wars between the colonists and the natives," Serdot said. "And I've since developed a personal interest in the details."

"Raymond's killer claimed to be 'an ancient flame' when the survivor asked his name," Medoff said. "How do you explain that?"

"I cannot," Serdot said, glancing briefly at Alfrem. "Not yet."

"The point is that Marlan is a sophisticated killer," Arthan said. "Lord Raymond of Wallevet was also killed with alchemy and a small crossbow bolt, which Marlan also had. Someone planned these attacks very well."

"The timing of Raymond's death with the fall of the Empire Alliance," Serdot said. "The forged letters sent to us from Mordmerg with Golbane's name on them that lured Maillard. And using Blackhoods muscle and the discontent of the free city people . . ."

Medoff leaned back in his chair. "Marlan could still be an agent of the Rugens. They've had agents among our people before, as we have theirs."

"I still think the Rugens killed Raymond and the rebels killed Maillard," Iserenne said.

"Did you listen to anything my brother and the widsemer said?" Bardil asked. "This master of Marlan, whoever he is, has killed two lord ministers in the span of a month. I may be the youngest of the Valients, but it's clear to me someone is aiming to break the kingdom."

Iserenne glared at him but held her tongue.

"Medoff, Dardanon, and Iserenne, tell all our guards and garrisons to be on the lookout for a mask like this," Arthan said.

"Assuming he's got another one," Bellumet said.

"And his distinct green cape," Serdot said.

"Any sighting, any rumor, I want to hear about it," Arthan said. "That goes for the Blackhoods' leader, Navarron, and his lieutenants as well. I'm determined to find Marlan before he kills again."

"They've probably already left Delavon if they intend to kill another lord minister," Livonier said.

"Arthan," Alfrem began, "I advise you not to wait here to find Marlan. And I don't think you should wait for King Erech to summon you to Eglamour. Our messenger has probably not arrived there with news of your father's death, and it could be another two weeks for the king's summons to arrive here."

"I agree," Dardanon said. "The sooner you go to Eglamour and have your lord ministership confirmed, the better."

"But there is much for me to do in Rachard," Arthan said. "Must I leave at this critical time for a mere formality?"

"It's not just a formality," Alfrem said. "It's a longstanding custom that should be respected by you, as it was by your father. And with Duke Brugarn increasingly speaking for the king, you should seek your confirmation before his influence becomes an obstacle for you."

"Very well. I will leave in the morning. Medoff, I want Sir Cuern and his brother Erboln to be assigned to my personal guard. They performed admirably in the council house at Mordmerg."

"As you wish."

"And I hereby promote Sir Livonier as your deputy and commander of my personal guard," Arthan said. "Livonier and Serdot will join me in Eglamour while you and Alfrem oversee things here."

The advisers nodded their agreement. Livonier stood from the table and bowed his head.

"Thank you, my lord."

"May I also recommend Bardil stay in Rachard as well and cancel his planned wardship under the king of Austveeden," Dardanon said. "The Austveedes may see that move as rude and ungrateful, but given the circumstances . . ."

Medoff nodded. "We may be at peace with Austveedes now, but who can say with certainty what will happen? If war does come, the Austveedes are likely to provide mercenaries to anyone and everyone, given their history. Not a place for Bardil to be."

"I can stay in Rachard, Brother," Bardil said. "I didn't want to go there anyway."

Arthan nodded. "Alfrem, send the Austveedes our regrets for cancelling the wardship. But Bardil will be coming with me to Eglamour."

"It would give the people of Delavon some confidence if one of you remains in Rachard," Dardanon said.

"I understand. But I want my brother there when I give the king my oath, to solidify our position. And it will be important for both of us to experience Eglamour, to see its problems with our own eyes. Now, about Rowan. Should I recall our brother from his wardship under Lord Asteroth of Alpenon? If war comes, he's in the thick of it on the border with Rugenhav."

"We sent word to him about your father," Alfrem said. "But Alpenon is far. We'll not receive word from him for some time."

"If Rowan is not in Rethsrond he's probably riding with the lord minister out patrolling the borderlands," Medoff said. "Asteroth fears the Alpenon rebels receiving arms from the Rugens."

"If Rowan stays in or near Rethsrond, he's at least an eight days' march north of the border," Serdot said. "That's plenty of time to evacuate if the Rugens cross over. Until then, Rowan could send us useful information about the borderlands."

"Are we now reducing a son of Maillard to be a mere scout?" Alfrem asked.

"It's an uncertain time," Serdot said. "We can't expect Eglamour to keep us informed, and Asteroth answers to no one."

"It would be useful to know what they're doing at the border," Iserenne said.

"Then I will write to Rowan," Arthan said. "He can stay in Alpenon Ministry for now, but I want him to be aware of everything we know. Also, he'll be upset he couldn't be here for Father's burial."

"We can have his messengers routed to you in Eglamour," Alfrem said.

"Fine. Now, regarding my travel to the capital, how much tribute shall I bring to the king?"

Alfrem shifted through a stack of parchments. "Before we discuss tribute, let me read your father's will because it describes the possessions you've inherited. Then you'll understand what I will advise regarding the tribute."

"Go on," Arthan said.

"Firstly, as the eldest living son, you are his heir. He leaves everything to you, pending the king's consent, and makes a large gift to the Messengian Church. He places the welfare of your two brothers in your hands.

"Secondly, I am to read this list of possessions bequeathed to you, so that you are aware of your holdings. You inherit a treasury wealthier than any of the lord ministers, as your father did. You control the main trade routes between Donovan and the kingdoms of Calbria and Austveeden, from which you extract taxes on behalf of the king, keeping half for yourself.

"You have the mines of the western Narendra Mountains, rich in iron, cinder, electrum, wist, and silver. You have lesser mines rich in gold, corbalt, and copper. Your rivers are well bridged and stocked with good fish. The Garnault riverbed is most plentiful of tuning stones, for which you have skilled divers to harvest. Your fields are full of wheat, rye, and all manner of vegetables, orchards, and vineyards.

"You have several seaports, notably Count Dardanon's seat of Oradrond, from which you access the Calbrian Sea. Your naval fleet numbers thirty ships. Small, but their crews are well trained and trade with nearly every kingdom on the continent.

"Upon the land you have under your command the Army of Delavon, numbering ten thousand knights, soldiers, archers, and others, all garrisoned in castles and fortified towns across the ministry. Your lands are divided into four regions: Bram in the north, overseen by you from Rachard. Imvorlon, ruled by Count Dardanon, in the east. Sobel, ruled by Countess Iserenne, in the west. And Caval in the south, ruled by your late cousin Count Golbane . . ."

Arthan tapped his fingers on the table. He already knew much of what Alfrem was reading, but he kept silent as the alderman continued the custom. Maillard would have expected as much.

"You have a population that is primarily Messengian in faith, with Congregants making up the bulk of Sobel County. Your people are, on the whole, contented, and of course proud to be ruled and protected by the famed House of Valient. The former Royal House of Valient still lives in the memory of your subjects despite the time that has passed, and they have great expectations that you will follow in your father's footsteps as a wise, benevolent, and influential lord minister.

"That concludes the will and inheritance. I'm instructed to keep possession of the signet of Maillard's wist ring until the king confirms your lord ministership. Thereupon you may dismiss me from my duties as Alderman of Rachard, should you wish to do so."

"Thank you, Alfrem," Arthan said. "You will continue as keeper of my capital, and Medoff as head of the army. As for the vacant Count of Caval, I will keep that title for myself for now."

"Regarding your question of tribute," Alfrem said, "I advise you to cement your loyalty in the eyes of the king by giving him a handsome gift. The Valients have never wasted nor been stingy with their fortune."

"Erech is weak and firmly in the hands of others," Medoff said. "Giving him more gold will not help him, nor the kingdom, and any tribute you give will probably end up in Brugarn's pockets—maybe even provoke Brugarn and the other brothers to ask for more."

"Then Arthan should give it," Alfrem said, surprising Arthan and everyone else. "History is full of kings who seized the wealth of their vassals because they considered rich heirs to be potential competitors. As long as Erech is on the throne, he should view Arthan as an indispensable and trustworthy ally, not a threat. Maillard and his forefathers did the same, as the Valients and Avaleaus have long been allies. Furthermore, the Valients' status as former royalty demands the spigot stays open to keep the favor of the people."

"If war comes, the king will demand every coin," Medoff said.

"And we'll adjust our position at that time," Alfrem said.

"Will three chests of gold suffice for a tribute, wise alderman?" Arthan asked.

"Quite."

"Very well. Now, I see you still have a stack of parchments."

"A few letters, my lord, from your lesser vassals who could not attend your father's burial. Regrets and well wishes and professions of loyalty. A few seek your favor or forgiveness for petty things, which is common after the death of a lord. Others propose various political alliances or request support for others. There are also letters from various Austveede border barons. Your counts and the countess can handle most of these. But this letter is from the heir-apparent lord minister of Wallevet. Edmond Reimvick, Raymond's younger brother."

Alfrem handed the letter to Arthan and he read.

> Lord Arthan Valient,
> My deepest condolences to you and your brothers
> for the unexpected loss of your father. My
> brothers and I lost our father to similar violence

when we were your age. Know that whether I am confirmed as your neighboring lord minister or not, you may always count me among your loyal friends. Like Raymond, I knew your father well and cherished his wisdom and friendship. May he rest in peace.

I will be traveling to Eglamour for the royal confirmation, as I presume you will be. I propose we travel together to get to better know each other. As you know, your shortest road to Eglamour is via my capital, Bredahade. I would be honored for you to accompany me and exchange news about the royal court and the effects of the Empire Alliance's fall.

I hope you will accept my invitation, and I look forward to serving the Crown beside you in these uncertain times.

Most Respectfully,
Lord Edmond Reimvick
Bredahade

Arthan passed the letter around for the others to read. "Well?"

"I say accept his invitation," Alfrem said. "Like his late brother, Reimvick is a well-respected and knowledgeable, if gossipy, man. He is not shy with his probing questions and loves a tasty new rumor, but he should be among your allies in the king's court. You can learn a lot from him."

"I cannot stand the man and his prying demeanor," Medoff said, cringing. "He should be called the Queen's Royal Neb."

"Fortunately, you don't have to stomach him," Alfrem said. "That is Arthan's task."

"Very well," Arthan said with a smile. "Please arrange for a messenger to go ahead of us to accept his invitation."

As Arthan's advisers departed he motioned for Serdot to stay behind. Serdot closed the door.

"Why, when they asked if you could explain Marlan's calling himself 'an ancient flame,' did you glance at Alfrem and say 'not yet'?"

Serdot smiled. "I was hoping you'd catch that. I was trying to pressure the alderman into talking, but you were too polite to call him out in front of everyone."

"Talk about what?"

"Alfrem is sworn to silence about something until the right time."

"When? And by whom?"

"I cannot speak about it, my lord."

"If I am your lord, you must speak of it. And how did you learn of it if he is sworn?"

"I know more than he knows, simply because I was in the service of your father. But it is Alfrem's place to tell you."

"Tell me what, Serdot?"

Serdot wiped the smile off his face. "I'm sorry, my lord. This is the only secret I will ever keep from you, because it is not my place to tell. When the time comes, you will understand. This is the way your father wanted it."

"My father . . ."

"Please excuse me. I must prepare for our travel to the capital."

Arthan stepped out of the way and the widsemer departed. Arthan could not imagine why Maillard would keep a secret from him, a secret Alfrem was tasked with keeping. Serdot was supposed to be the dealer of secrets. He wondered if it had anything to do with his inheritance, which Alfrem alone was entrusted with handling.

He shook the curiosity from his mind as best he could. He knew Maillard had chosen trustworthy men to surround him. Arthan needed to focus on his visit to the royal court. He stepped toward the door and saw Meriam approaching. She clasped her hands anxiously.

"I don't have time for this," he said.

"I heard you would probably be leaving. I wanted to wish you safe travel."

"Thank you, Meriam. I'm . . ." Arthan wanted to say he was sorry, but he was not sure why. He'd seen her only briefly since Mordmerg and knew she'd like to see him more.

He wanted that too, but he could not find the right time. "Meriam, I . . ."

"Just be careful," she said. "I'll be here, waiting for your return."

PART II

ARCANAE

29

RODEL

Eglamour, Toulon Ministry
Flowertide, 3034

"You've returned just in time, Rodel."

"For what?"

"New orders from Heingartmer," Wredegar said, holding up a letter. "Emperor Theudamer wants us to determine who killed the Donovard lord ministers. He wants to know whether the assassins are someone we can harness for our own ends."

"Since when have the Wosmoks become magistrates in a foreign land?"

"I don't like it any more than you do," Wredegar said. "You know I'd rather be at the head of an honorable army marching across Donovan than skulking around this cursed kingdom in rags and without honor."

That stung Rodel. Wredegar was right, of course, and it had long bothered him.

"You know what I mean," Wredegar said. "I'm not a natural widsemer like you and the other Wosmoks. This work is not befitting my House of Auftengardin. We're meant to be the right hands of emperors, not shadow-cloaked thieves and assassins. Alas, Theudamer gave me command, since Garentorf is dead."

Wredegar did not seem to lament Garentorf's death as Rodel did. All Wosmok deaths affected him. Wasted lives, yet Rodel wanted nothing to do with them. Not anymore.

"What now, then?" Rodel asked, sitting in a chair that was completely in tatters. He hated Vesamune's cellar. She lived in opulence above while the Wosmoks were always hidden far below.

"We're to wait here until some Wosmoks from Austveeden, led by Etzel, arrive to assist us. I'd like to go at once to Wallevet Ministry, since Raymond's death was the first, but we're ordered to stay in Eglamour for now."

Rodel fiddled with a string unstitching from the chair arm. Wallevet. That was where he'd met that eccentric one-armed man, Arasemis. He still thought it peculiar that Arasemis did not seem distraught over the death of his brother, Raymond. Rodel considered telling Wredegar about Arasemis but kept his mouth shut as Wredegar continued his rant against the emperor's orders.

"Are you listening to me?" Wredegar asked. "What's distracting you?"

"I'm listening."

"We'll request to start in Wallevet instead of staying here in Eglamour. How else do they expect us to—"

"I'd rather not see that river again," Rodel said.

Wredegar nodded with a smirk. "As Wosmoks, we've seen worse . . ."

"You'll return to your lands and titles after all this," Rodel said after a moment. "Most Wosmoks die in foreign lands, like at the river . . ."

"But it's an honor to serve as a Wosmok, doing the things the knights and ambassadors can't. That's why we're named after the ancient Raffen word for *ghost*. Wosmoks stay hidden, silent. It's honorable to—"

"No it's not. You said as much."

"What's gotten into you, Rodel? We've served together for years."

Rodel turned away. From the corner of his eye he saw Wredegar straighten up before speaking formally.

"As your commander, I order you to shake off whatever is souring your mind. We nearly drowned, yes, and there's nothing we can do about Garentorf and the rest. We have our orders, magistrate work though it seems. But you know it will be different soon. Donovan is on the cusp of falling apart. Can't you feel it?"

Rodel nodded absently, fiddling with the chair's frayed stitching again.

"Good," Wredegar said. "Then cast off that dark mood that's grabbed you."

❧

Rodel could not sleep. He could not cast it off. And he could not stay any longer. He quietly got out of bed, taking his dagger and hooded cloak. Wredegar breathed steadily as he took the stairs.

Sneaking up into Vesamune's residence and out a window was routine. Her guards were either lazy or too used to the fact that shadowy figures often came and went from her home. Rodel took no provisions; he knew how to live off the land.

Outside, the spring night was fresh and clear. He considered the possibility that leaving could be a mistake but he tried not to care. He knew the Wosmoks and how they operated. He would notice if they came to hunt him down. They might not bother, given the pace of change in the kingdom. And Wredegar would not readily soil his reputation by reporting a deserter under his new command.

Rodel looked forward to the countryside again. And to seeing Arasemis's Thorendor Castle perched high in the hills of Wallevet.

30

MARLAN

Thorendor Castle, Wallevet Ministry
Flowertide, 3034

Marlan stared down into the barrel, his eyes fixed on the soaking blade. It had darkened considerably in the past few days. The sachets of stones fixed at the barrel's lip were now empty, having completely dissolved in the solution.

"The blade is nearly black now," he said when he found Arasemis. The master was reading a letter at his great writing table and did not look up. Marlan waited a few moments before trying again. "I think my sword is almost ready."

Arasemis finally looked up. "There is one more step in the treatment process."

Marlan could see he was distracted. "News?"

"No, a letter from a friend." Arasemis handed the letter to him. Marlan took it carefully, as the master rarely let his students read his correspondence.

> A,
>
> I wish to inform you that Lord Minister Valient, the new one, will likely be visiting Bredahade soon. He must go to Eglamour to receive the king's confirmation and Bredahade is his shortest route.
>
> You will no doubt see this as an opportunity. I strongly urge you not to attack him on the road. If you do, you'll bring too much attention to your

location. It's best if you stay at Thorendor while Valient travels, and stay quiet.

Separately, I received your letter about your current task. I wish you had informed me about your plans to kill Raymond earlier. I think I deserved—and had a right—to know, though I do appreciate the rewards his death has brought. I also would have liked to have known about Maillard. Nevertheless, I would caution you to take your time and not be hasty. If you change things too quickly we'll not have the chance to seize the advantage.

Finally, I wish that you would spend less time on aerina and chemina, and more time on unlocking the mythic machines. That is the future; you've only to look eastward to Calbria to see that. Teaching your pupils to run up trees and boil gourd warts will only get us so far. But airships, now that is something in the old tales that would be worth all this effort.

E

Marlan returned the letter. "Who is E?"

"Someone I trust."

"I thought no one else knew about our work."

Arasemis regarded him carefully. "As your master, you must trust my judgment. I shared this letter with you because I trust yours."

"I'm sorry, Master Arasemis. I suppose I'm restless here by myself without a task to look forward to." Marlan knew there would be new tasks, of course. He simply wanted to know what or where they would be.

"Bertwil, Morroy, and Juhl will return soon enough," Arasemis said. "Then, the next phase of your training will begin. As for this letter, you cannot know who E is at this point. Suffice it to say that he is a supporter of the Order who would have us focus on reviving and improving on the ancient machines of the Rahlampian folk rather than the acrobatics or mixture making. But he's the hasty one. We must make full use of all three ancient arts before we can hope to use the great machines of old. Only then can we strike down whole armies."

"Will we build landships, like the Rahlampian tribes did?"

"Of course, Marlan. But not for some time still."

"What about airships, as this man suggested?"

"I'm not certain they ever existed. The tales began long ago with Hilsingor's self-serving speculation and continue to this day. But no one has seen even the remnants of a ship that could sail in the clouds. There are still some places we could search for them, but . . ."

"Imagine what the Order could be with airships," Marlan marveled aloud.

"We must keep our focus where it is. There will be a time to investigate the machina arcana. But right now, there are too many crowned heads yet to fall."

"Must we heed this man's advice? I could kill the new Lord Valient on the road much quicker and easier than I killed his father. I could stalk him until he crosses into Toulon so no one has cause to suspect Wallevet locations."

"I considered that. It's especially tempting since the Valients are descendants of Marshal Hilsingor himself. And you know what the marshal did to Rildning. But we'll let the young Valient live for now, to preserve the safety of Thorendor. There will be other opportunities."

"Soon?"

"Yes, soon."

31

ARTHAN

On the Road to Bredahade, Wallevet Ministry
Flowertide, 3034

"Well, I'm unaccustomed to traveling in a carriage," Arthan said, looking up at the velvet ceiling and shoving the bench cushions aside. "I prefer my horse and the sky above me."

"Me too," Bardil said.

"Alderman Alfrem was right, my lord," Serdot said. "Taking your father's carriage is a symbol of your new status. Additionally, I arranged a few modifications."

Serdot peeled back a corner of cloth on the wall, exposing iron plating.

"An armored carriage?" Arthan said, impressed.

"That's why there's a larger team of horses," Bardil said.

"It's not as good as what they're building in the Calbrian foundries these days, but it will afford some protection."

"Thank you, Serdot."

"That's not all . . ." Serdot leaned over and pulled a drawer out from under his bench. Three wine bottles clinked.

"Well done!" Bardil said.

Serdot continued to pull on the drawer, exposing a back section that held a small crossbow.

"Like the one you carry," Arthan said.

"You never know when it will come in handy," Serdot said, restoring the hidden weapon.

"More foreign than sitting in this carriage was sitting in Rachard's great hall . . ." Arthan mused.

159

"My lord?"

"During the feast to break the mourning."

"Well, you can't argue with tradition," Serdot said. "But yes, celebrating the life of the deceased with roast pigs, jugglers, and music is also meant to turn our eyes to the future."

"Yet that same hall hosted the foreign delegations that came to rip down the Empire Alliance that Father was attempting to shoulder. How the hall was transformed . . ."

"The halls of power are built for such things," Serdot said. "Feasts and funerals. Mercy and judgment. War and peace. But it's men like your father, and yourself, who are destined to rule men well from such halls. I believe the destiny of the Valients is to be kings once again."

"Destiny . . ." Arthan mused as he glanced at Bardil before looking out the window. "And what governs destiny, Serdot?"

"Some say God, others say the stars. But I'm a simple shadow, my lord. My counsel will always be that your destiny lies in your own hands."

Arthan turned from the window. "You leave no role for the actions of other powerful people?"

"Nor God," Bardil added.

"That's how I prefer it," Serdot said with a smile.

"Is there anything else I should know about Lord Reimvick before we arrive in Bredahade?" Arthan asked. "If I travel with him to Eglamour, what will that say about me in the royal court, that I am a gossiper? You did not speak of Reimvick when we held council."

"Because I had nothing to add. I agree with Alfrem that you can learn a lot from Reimvick. But I also agree with General Medoff that Reimvick's incessant gossip is a distraction. Otherwise, I see no danger in him."

"What are your methods for discerning the minds of such high nobles?"

Serdot laughed. "I know no methods you are not already familiar with, my lord. Ask me for the contents of their secret letters or the names of their mistresses, and I can deliver with ease."

"I'm sure. It's a dark side of the world most never see, isn't it?"

"Everyone sees shadows. Not everyone pays attention to them."

Arthan nodded. "I suppose I must employ the skills of widsemers like you selectively, or otherwise upset the balance and provoke them to spy on me."

"There is no balance," Serdot said. "They'll spy on you whether you are careful or not, I assure you. Even now, for although your enemies are fewer as a young lord, you have inherited the enemies of your father."

Arthan knew Serdot was right. He felt it in his gut and in his father's absence. "So you are my hidden shield, then, Serdot?"

"For as long as you wish it."

"What about me and my other counselors? Have you turned your discerning eyes and ears upon us?"

"There's been much change of late," Serdot said. "For example, Medoff hides this from you well, but the guilt of your father's death will consume him if he is not kept busy. He is a formidable and worthy general, much as I spar with him at times."

"And Alfrem?"

"The alderman is one of the wisest administrators I've ever met. Sometimes I wonder if he knows Rachard better than me. But his flaw is that he too often sees good where there is none. If Medoff is too quick to condemn, Alfrem is too quick to excuse. But a good balance between them, I would say."

"Count Dardanon and Countess Iserenne?"

"Dardanon loves the pleasures of life too much. Even homely women of Port Oradrond receive his gaze. His eyes equally scrutinize the bottom of any bottle of wine or spirit, especially those imported from across the sea. And he loves a game of chance, especially if it risks a coin. Despite his vices, your father judged him to be a loyal and competent keeper of eastern Delavon, and I still agree.

"As for the Countess of Sobel, there could be no better opposite of Dardanon. Prudish, serious, and afflicted with constant worry. But Iserenne is utterly reliable and commands the respect of her knights. And she is a follower of the Congregant religious sect, making her a useful bastion against any disquiet from that minority."

"I'm impressed."

"What about me?" Bardil asked.

"May we stop there, my lords?" Serdot asked. "I take my observations of people seriously and don't wish to insult anyone, particularly you sirs."

"Sounds like you have a touch of countess," Arthan said.

"Undeniable. My critical observation of people includes myself, and I'm prudent enough to know when to keep my mouth shut."

"I don't care," Bardil protested. "I'd like to know if—"

Arthan waved Bardil off. "Serdot, do keep me appraised of Medoff. No one laments Father's death more than Bardil and me, but if Medoff does not cope as we are . . ."

"Of course, my lord."

༒

On the third day, Arthan's convoy arrived in Bredahade. Lord Reimvick's castle was near the center of the old city. In the foothills beyond, toward the semicircular ridge of the beautiful Vaudreuil Mountains, Arthan could make out a second, peculiar castle looking out over the forest.

"What is that?"

Serdot followed his gaze. "Thorendor Castle. An ancient place inhabited by the youngest of the three Reimvick brothers. Well, two, now that Raymond has been killed . . ."

"What is his name?"

"I don't know. He's just a hermit, lost his professorship at Bredahade Academy years ago."

"For what offense?" Arthan asked.

Serdot shrugged as if it was a meaningless detail.

"How can you claim to know everything of importance about everyone if you don't even know his name?"

"I will look into it when we return to Delavon, my lord."

As they approached Reimvick's castle in the city they found the lord minister ready, standing by his own carriage. Their carriage pulled up alongside, and Arthan stepped out.

"Welcome to Bredahade, Lord Valient!" Reimvick smiled broadly. He was a tallish man yet potbellied, with locks of graying brown hair. His mustache was too long at the ends and fading to gray under his nose. But he was cheerful. "I'm honored that you accepted my invitation to travel together."

"The honor is mine, Lord Reimvick," Arthan said. "Please, ride with me for a time."

"I'm very sorry for Maillard," Reimvick said as he stepped into Arthan's carriage. "It pains me to know that his wise counsel will no longer fall upon the king's ear, perhaps when he needs it most. Your father was the most honorable knight, loyal friend, and able servant of the Crown."

"Thank you, and thank you for your letter. It's still difficult for me to think of him lying in a cold tomb."

"The feeling of loss will never pass, but it will get easier," Reimvick said.

"My condolences for Raymond as well. I know Father held him in high regard."

"Thank you. I can't help but think that Maillard might be alive today if he hadn't taken on Raymond's burden to keep the Empire Alliance afloat. Though I initially supported my brother's efforts, I soured on them once I realized how little King Erech cared. It certainly wasn't worth the lives of Raymond and Maillard."

"Or my cousin Count Golbane. And our knights."

Reimvick's tone changed and his eyes grew wide. "Oh yes. I must confess: never in my years at the royal court have I been so concerned for the future of our kingdom. And now I fear for our personal safety. Three lord ministers dead."

"Three?"

"Have you not heard? Duke Gottfried, the king's cousin, was killed at his castle in Lyonseln. The assassins attacked him with poisonous gas and swords, similar to what happened with Raymond."

"And Father . . ." Arthan glanced at the silent Serdot seated beside Reimvick. The look on his face told Arthan that Serdot was not surprised at the news.

"I cannot help but wonder if you and I are being lured to Eglamour so that we may fall victim to these plots as well," Reimvick said.

"That thought crossed my mind as well," Arthan said. "Yet, we have our duty."

"Of course. Have you heard any good rumors about who is behind it all? If you have cause to suspect the Rugens, then I would agree. But I can't help but wonder, given all the change that is afoot."

"No theories as of yet," Arthan said. "But my gut tells me the Rugens, or perhaps the Almerians, must be involved." Arthan glanced at Serdot as he spoke. Serdot gave a quick wink to approve Arthan's discretion with the information about Marlan's use of ancient tribal methods.

"Yes, that seems certain. I hear the Rugen ambassador, that sharp-eyed Vesamune, still remains in the capital despite all that has happened. Maybe she is pulling the strings on all this?"

"Perhaps we'll know more once we're in Eglamour," Arthan said.

"May I ask, have you ever been to the royal court?"

"Not for a while. Perhaps Father wished to shelter me from the storm."

"Much has changed," Reimvick said. "But some things have not. Surely you've heard about the king's growing weakness?"

"I've heard a bit . . ."

"As you know, Erech trusted Maillard early in his reign, before the king's mind rotted and his confidence withered. It's a holy shame that Maillard's final duty to the king was to preside over the doomed Alliance, but I digress.

"Erech's mind is now easily swayed, controlled even. He surrounds himself with aggressive vassals who usurp his power daily. Everyone from Nore to Hanovel sees it, except for the king himself. In a nutshell, that is the situation in which we will pay homage and gain our confirmation, before God and all the corrupted court.

"Now," Reimvick continued, barely taking a breath, "you should know a thing or two about these usurpers you'll encounter. First is Duke Brugarn, the king's youngest brother and lord minister of Toulon. He oversees the largest ministry but spends all his time behind the throne, whispering in Erech's ear. Since Toulon is not enough for him, I can only guess that Brugarn covets the crown for himself. At the same time, he does his best to seem like Erech's most loyal servant."

Arthan caught a slight nod from Serdot. He was not sure if it was confirming what Reimvick had said, or confirming Reimvick's long-windedness.

"Second is Chaultion," Reimvick continued. "He is general of all the armies of Donovan, potentially including yours and mine. He has the authority, in consultation with the Council of Lord Ministers, to march your brigades where he needs them to protect the Crown, at your expense. Much like Brugarn, Chaultion is a vain, greedy, self-centered man with too much anger and not enough brains. He's a ruthless plunderer, eager to make war for his own profit. And though he is an ally of Brugarn, Chaultion may also have his own designs on the crown.

"Lastly, beware of Meltres, the man who represented Erech at the Empire Alliance Council in Rachard. You undoubtedly saw his love for prodding the Rugens to anger. I'm convinced Erech, or rather Brugarn and Chaultion, chose Meltres because they were sure he would properly sink that ship."

"Why does the king tolerate such men?" Arthan asked.

Reimvick smiled. "You'll learn how weak he is. These usurpers have him firmly in their grasp. And they will test and isolate you, too, if you let them." Arthan nodded solemnly. "I've already talked enough, as I'm apt to do, young Arthan. But suffice it to say that Erech's court is a snake pit. Then there are Erech's middle brothers, the twins Asteroth and Erath, lord ministers of Alpenon and Gadolin, respectively. They're also heavy-handed brutes, but too far away right now to cause you many problems."

"I cannot thank you enough, Lord Reimvick. I hope I can depend on your insight in the weeks ahead."

"It would be my pleasure. Speaking of the royal court, have you heard about the chambermaid who was found in the—"

Arthan was surprised at how quickly Reimvick bounced from grave matters to gossip. He feigned interest in

Reimvick's latest hearsay for a while before announcing his need to rest.

For the remainder of the journey to the capital, the two lords often rode together until Arthan needed a break from Reimvick's talking. But, just as his father would have advised, he intended to maintain the friendship.

32

FETZER

On the Road to Thorendor, Lundwynland Ministry
Flowertide, 3034

Fetzer opened his journal carefully. The binding was beginning to tear at the edges, but it was still reliable, trustworthy, and always willing to listen.

Our journey back has been slow and stained with the death of Morroy. Juhl says they have not lost anyone before but Bertwil noted that the Order has a long history of sacrifice. Both of them are uncertain as to how Master Arasemis will react to the loss of Morroy.

We escaped the island ministry of Leauvenna easily enough, this time on an Ovelian merchant ship named the *Taranoga*. Like the *Meurden*, her crew was oblivious to our presence and the captain well paid for her trouble.

We made port in Quayrond on the northern coast of Lundwynland. There we purchased horses and rode steadily south, camping away from the roads. Bertwil says we'll reach Thorendor within four or five days.

I've met Juhl's gaze more than once now. She is beautiful, but her eyes are dangerous. Bertwil has finally acknowledged my contribution and offered what passed for an apology for nearly leaving me stranded inside the duke's walls. If not for Juhl, I'd be dead. But I don't feel like one of them yet, despite our success with Gottfried.

I live still and my wounds are minor and healing. My mind is on Thorendor and what I might find there . . .

33

MILISEND

Eglamour Palace, Toulon Ministry
Flowertide, 3034

"They are beautiful. Thank you, Regaume."

"Try them on."

Milisend dipped her toe into the black slippers. They fit perfectly and would match the slim outfit Regaume had bought her earlier.

"Walk and jump," he said. "See how they feel."

Milisend made a show of her thief acrobatics, slinking along the wall of her bedchamber, sprinting to the door, then leaping like a cat onto a table. She finished with a smile. "Silent shoes," she said approvingly.

"And the shape of the toe points will get you around narrow ledges for the more difficult windows," Regaume said.

"You bought these from that special tanner in Goyngard?"

Regaume nodded. "No one makes better clothing and equipment for professional thieves, widsemers, and quillshades. And I just got this, too."

Milisend's eyes widened when he pulled a matching hood and mask from his bag. She smiled as she put them on. The hood was tight on her hair, like a second skin. The mask covered her face with similar black cloth, with narrow cutouts for her eyes.

"Is this what the thieves of your band wear?" she asked. "I still wonder when I will meet them."

"Maybe now you can, since they'll have no chance of recognizing you. They wear similar clothing, but this is the best. Look at this." Regaume showed her a jointed seam in her outfit. "Thin plates of steel are sewn into the leather in the entire suit. It won't stop a crossbow and most sword blows, but you'll escape knives and glancing slashes."

Milisend cocked her hooded head. "What thievery do you plan for us next, Regaume? I told you I don't want to be involved in anything violent. Stealing jewels is fine, not anything like—"

"I know, Mili . . ." His voice turned grim. "But given how things are going with the lord ministers and the riots, I want you to be safe if the assassins come to Eglamour."

She smiled. "What have you done with Regaume the Readyfingers? He is fearless and—"

"I'm serious, Mili. Many cities are having riots now. Bandits less discerning than my little band are prowling every major road. Normally I'd see opportunity in that, but with you, I . . ."

There was a knock at Milisend's door. She jerked off the mask and hood as Regaume straightened up in his stolen soldier's uniform. "Yes, who is it?"

A rotund, red-cloaked woman just entered as Milisend hid the hood and mask behind her. "Princess Milisend, I . . . who is this?"

"Greetings, Marielle," Milisend said, relieved that it was only her mother's lady-in-waiting. "This is a castle guard, of course." It always made her nervous when Regaume showed up like this—but she did like the look of him in a uniform. "He was delivering . . . this . . . bag for me."

"Filthy homespun?" Marielle scoffed at the bag in Regaume's hands. "Who would send you such an item? Get out of here and don't bother the princess with empty errands. If something needs to be delivered, it should be given to Rosellen or one of the others."

"Yes, my lady," Regaume said with a curt bow. He made for the door, winking behind Marielle's back as he exited.

Marielle turned to close the door behind him. Milisend quickly stuffed the hood and mask into a nearby drawer.

"Princess, your mother sent me to fetch you. She wishes to discuss the question of marriage."

"Not again . . ."

"Avalane is already wed to Duke Henrey. You are twenty-one, well past ready. And Brielle will not be allowed to wed until you are."

"She's only sixteen."

"But not too young for initial suitors. Regardless, the queen wants to discuss it with you."

Milisend sighed, knowing there was no way around it. "I will visit her later this evening."

"The queen gave me strict orders to bring you at once."

Milisend considered simply running, as she had done before. Regaume was probably waiting for her somewhere close by. He'd have her run away permanently. But something had been growing inside her, a determination to confront her mother's designs once and for all. She would not have this question hanging over her head any longer.

"Then I will go."

"Princess, what are you wearing on your feet?"

She looked down at her black leather slippers with the peculiar ledge-walking toes and searched for an answer. "I, well, I found them. They fit, so . . . Never mind, they're hideous." She kicked them off and stepped into her silver-threaded slippers.

"Hideous, indeed," Marielle muttered.

❧

When Milisend arrived in the queen's solar, she found her mother sitting, exhausted. The queen's physician was mixing her afternoon drink of popaver and licorice. It always made Milisend sad to see her addicted in this way.

"Come, Mili . . . sit," said the queen, patting the cushion next to her.

Milisend sat quietly, watching the sips. Her mother had once been a beautiful queen. Milisend remembered being a child and looking into her mother's amber eyes and her warm smile. Her long shining chestnut hair. Like Father, Mother never smiled anymore. She kept her hair hidden in a twist of silk. And, like Father, the life had dimmed from her eyes.

"I do not wish to wed yet, Mother. There is no suitable—"

"Silence, child. Our times are darkening but you won't hear me dwell on it. Your father does enough brooding for all of us. I know your heart, Mili, and I will not ask you to wed Lord Reimvick. He is too old for you. And Gottfried had no clear heir for you to wed, so you will be spared a life isolated on his island."

"Thank you, Mother . . ."

"But Lord Arthan Valient would be most suitable. He is from a good house, formerly of royal blood. It would solidify the Valients as our allies at a time when our enemies encircle us. And he is gallant, charming, and wealthy."

"I met Arthan only once, Mother. He was arrogant and talked only of himself. And he's younger than I."

"By a year or so. Heaven's sakes, you're both young. But he has matured beyond his years. You would have a long, productive life together for the benefit of the kingdom."

"I do not love him, Mother."

"We are duty bound to marry for politics, not love, Mili. But, like me and your grandmother before, you can grow to love him, and he you. It is your lot in life and one you must never shun." The queen took a long sip from her popaver.

"I will not marry Arthan."

"Consider this, then. Who is next in line if your father dies, either in battle or from his depression?"

"One of the twins, Uncle Erath or Uncle Asteroth."

"They will either kill each other for the crown, tearing Donovan apart, or let Brugarn claim it if they get their war with Rugenhav and win the lands they think they'll win."

"But there's also Avalane and Henrey."

"Your sister's husband has the blood sickness. He wouldn't rule long, if at all. Who would have the crown, then, since a queen would break Donovard tradition by ruling alone?"

"I suppose Uncle Brugarn . . ."

"Correct. Also consider that Brugarn would attempt to take you as his wife in order to strengthen his claim regardless of his route to the throne. You know that no one wants your father's crown more than Brugarn, and no one wants to be free of the crown more than your father. Brugarn is dangerously close to having whatever he wants, even with Erech on the throne."

"How would marrying Arthan stop any of this, Mother?"

"At the least, you wouldn't belong to Brugarn. At best, the Valients' past royalty would be rekindled with the marriage, strengthening the House of Avaleau while helping to block your father's brothers."

"But won't they still have superior claims?"

"The kings of Donovan still need the support of the lord ministers, lower nobles, and the Messengian Church to rule. Most will never be coerced into supporting Brugarn. One of the twins could be more palatable initially as king, but they would eventually commit the kingdom to perpetual war. However, if you wed Arthan, the elites would be more likely to support your joint claim over theirs."

Milisend looked down at her hands as the queen took longer sips. This was what she hated about royal life: every privilege, every luxury, but no freedom to take her own path. She thought of Regaume and knew what he would say. But the notion that she had a higher duty to the kingdom gnawed at her. And the notion of wedding Brugarn was worse. It made her understand why her mother drank popaver with such regularity.

"How much have you arranged, Mother?"

"Your father is ambivalent. Brugarn knows nothing of my ideas, of course. Arthan will arrive in Eglamour soon to give the king his oath. I will look for ways to press your father to speak to Arthan about this arrangement."

"May I have more time to consid— to get used to the idea?"

"Time runs short, Mili. Prepare your heart for this necessity, for all of our sakes."

જ્

Milisend walked alone back to her chambers. She was not surprised when a castle guard approached her.

"Princess, do you require an escort?"

"You're going to have to stop entering the palace like this," she whispered. "One day they will see through your disguise. You don't walk like a soldier."

"I see through your disguise of happy royalty," Regaume said with a smile.

She turned to him when they were out of view. "I *am* royalty. Duty and responsibility are my burdens." She didn't mean to be so stern, but the conversation with her mother had shaken her.

"I meant I know your heart, Mili . . . Where is this coming from? Did Marielle tell Andrilenne about your new black slippers?"

"You must call her the queen . . ." Milisend could not bring herself to tell him about her mother's plans. He would be heartbroken. But surely he knew this would eventually happen. It was her lot, after all. "I'm sorry, I just . . . I need to be alone tonight."

"All right . . ."

She fought the tears welling in her eyes. "I'm sorry . . ."

Regaume reached his hand out to her, but she turned and hurried to her chambers.

34

ARTHAN

Eglamour, Toulon Ministry
Flowertide, 3034

"There it is," Reimvick said as they crested a hill. "Eglamour!"

Arthan could see the sprawling city of white marble down in the valley before them, straddling the Toulon River. Everyone knew the tales of its founding as the greatest city of Pemonia, back when the famed Frontier Corps pushed the colonial borders deep into the unexplored forests of the New World. But that did not stop Reimvick from talking about it.

"There, see the king's palace? And over there, the outer districts that creep up the slopes of the foothills? The rows of violet and crimson flags of the Avaleaus. Magnificent."

"Yes, it is . . ." Arthan said. After a long journey listening to Reimvick's incessant gossip and storytelling, Arthan was looking forward to the city for other reasons.

"But don't let the sight fool you, young Arthan," Reimvick continued. "The white city has an underlying rot centered in the palace itself. Leadership is lacking, the treasury is a place of cobwebs, and usurpers lurk in every hall and corridor like adders. You can almost smell the rot from here."

Prior to descending into the valley, Reimvick dispatched a messenger to announce their approach. Word soon came back that the royal court was assembled and expecting them. Upon entering the city gates they made straight for the palace, passing by the Valient estate at Clonmel where his servants were waiting for him in front of the great oaken doors. He waved, looking forward to the respite he knew would be waiting for him there.

The grand gates of the palace grounds were already open. The trumpets of a dozen heralds sounded their coming. Reimvick and Arthan dismounted, and their retinues gathered behind them as everyone prepared to parade into the great hall.

"I dislike all this ceremony," Arthan whispered to Serdot.

"It won't be too cheerful. I've just learned that the king only learned of Gottfried's death this morning."

"How could you possibly know that? We've only just arrived."

"I spoke to one of my contacts while everyone was lining up. Things are not good here in the capital, my lord."

Arthan sighed as they waited. A moment later a blue-robed man approached with several of the king's Crownblades behind him. His face was familiar but Arthan could not remember his name.

"Welcome, Lord Valient and Lord Reimvick," said the man. "I am Waldemar, the steward of the palace and deputy alderman of Eglamour. Our king's hospitality awaits you. Please, follow me."

The trumpets sounded again as everyone followed Waldemar toward the great doors. The palace's white marble facade and columns were carved with scenes from the settling of the New World and the subsequent founding of Donovan as an independent kingdom. Many of the scenes were decorated with bright-shining electrum. The great doors were also inset with electrum and precious stones.

Arthan recognized the cavernous interior when they stepped inside. All manner of animals, birds, fish, and plants were carved from marble or cast from polished electrum and set upon the massive columns. The violet and crimson carpet led down the cathedral-like grand hall, and fountains studded the side wings. If the treasury was truly broken, he thought, selling the decorations of the palace alone would surely pay off a portion of the royal debt.

Arthan could see the throne ahead was crowded with courtiers despite the large space. He tried to keep his eyes straight ahead, chin high. The courtiers bowed respectfully as the two lords passed by. He felt unworthy of lord ministership in the presence of all these people unknown to him. He tried to think of Maillard and the respect he had always garnered wherever he went. He knew it had been hard earned. Would they ever respect him in the same way?

He tried to calm his mind as they approached the dais. The king looked haggard and sleepless. Erech's golden beard had faded, and his mustache was drawn in a frown. He was hunched well before his time, not sitting proudly as he once had. To his left was Queen Andrilenne, her eyes distant and glassy. Brugarn, Chaultion, Meltres, and others Arthan did not recognize were clustered on the king's right.

Waldemar stopped and bowed. "Your Majesty, may I present Lord Arthan Valient of Delavon and Count of Bram, heir to his father Lord Maillard Valient. And his brother Bardil Valient." They bowed their heads. "And may I present Lord Edmond Reimvick of Wallevet, heir to his brother Lord Raymond Reimvick." Reimvick bowed in turn.

"Come forth, young Valient," muttered the king.

Arthan stepped forward while Bardil and Livonier guided his servants carrying the chests of gold. They opened the chests to show his tribute as Arthan knelt before the king. He drew his sword and lay the blade across his palm, ceremoniously offering it to Erech. He noticed Erech's sword at his side. It was the famous Rhunegeld, the ancient symbol of Donovan's first king.

"I know this young face," Erech said. "Eldest son of the most honorable and loyal Maillard . . . I have grieved for the loss of your father. Few burdens surpass what he willingly shouldered time and again, unto death. Do you freely wish to inherit such duties as may be placed upon you?"

Arthan had not expected Erech to speak so coherently. He did notice a small light in the king's eyes. "Yes, Your Majesty. It would be my life's honor."

"Your oath, then," Brugarn said.

Arthan inhaled deeply, recalling the sacred words of his family. "I, heir of the House of Valient, which was born in the Crusade of Pemonia, do swear fealty to Erech, King of Donovan, pledging my sword, my vassals, and my resources in loyalty to you, my king. In my life, or by my death, I shall serve, as God wills. *Honora thering Valienta Crusadis.*"

"Then rise," Erech said, "lord minister of Delavon."

Brugarn reluctantly addressed the crowd. "In the tradition of our fathers, you may hereby recognize the new member of the Lord Ministers Council, a first noble of the king."

The court applauded to recognize Arthan, then he waited as the same ceremony was repeated with Reimvick. When this was done, Waldemar turned to the courtiers.

"Let us feast in celebration!"

It was the grandest meal Arthan had ever attended, but it was more for the enjoyment of Brugarn and his ilk than for anyone else. Arthan guessed that his chests of gold had been anticipated but wondered for how long the lavish spending could continue. He also noticed that Erech simply watched and ate little. The light in his eyes faded, as if he was being swept in and out of a foggy dream.

"My lord," Serdot whispered in Arthan's ear. "The steward wishes to have a word with you." Serdot pointed him to where Waldemar had been sitting near the king. "He waits for you in the side hall, near the ivy fountain."

"What does he want?"

"Talk. These high officers of the royal court like to talk. Shall I accompany you?"

"No, thank you, Serdot. I will meet him alone first."

Arthan excused himself as the courtiers refilled their wine cups. Arthan noticed Reimvick's cautious glance as he stood from the table, certain that Reimvick hoped to glean good gossip from Arthan later.

Arthan found Waldemar pacing around one of the fountains by the light of a torch sconce. They were well out of earshot of the feast.

"I am glad to have lived to see the day when you take your father's place as the king's vassal," Waldemar said, "despite the unfortunate circumstances, of course. Maillard was the elder lord minister, you know. Not by age, but by wisdom."

"Thank you, lord steward. I remember Father speaking highly of you as well."

"Maillard leaves a great hole that I and others hope you will grow to fill. That is why I wanted to speak with you privately from the beginning, before any of the others. I hope you will count me among your friends . . ."

"Of course . . ." Arthan said. He searched Waldemar's eyes for malice, but the old man seemed genuine, though anxious.

"Let me tell you that many others here will pander to your power, but they pander only for themselves. Unlike the old days, when kings were kings and nobles were nothing, the lord ministers are the power behind the throne. Or at least they should be. One lord minister, Duke Brugarn, the king's youngest brother, rules out of balance with the rest, as you've undoubtedly heard."

"I have," Arthan said, understanding that Waldemar was trying to gauge where he stood.

"You must know, Lord Valient, that your father had been a unifier among the ministers. Brugarn had slowly chipped away at Maillard's influence within the Lord Ministers Council. Now that Maillard is gone, Brugarn's influence is unbounded. The wolves are circling the vulnerable sheep, my lord."

"What are you asking of me, Waldemar?"

"None of the other ministers admit as much, but some wonder if you're willing and capable of doing as Maillard would have done. Before Brugarn ascends."

Waldemar looked down and shook his head before continuing. "Court politics is always about the power and favors one can gain for oneself. But these are especially trying times. I wanted you to know about the respected position your father held in the minister council, which I mediate as steward. And I wanted you to know the hope of some of us that you'll aspire to fill his shoes, for the good of Donovan. Alas, you've officially been lord minister for less than a day, but in time I think you'll appreciate what's been said."

"I do, and I thank you," Arthan said. "But don't you fear the wrath of Brugarn if he discovers you're against him?"

"Of course we do. But we tell ourselves there must be plenty of Maillard's bold diplomacy and influence in you.

Undoubtedly a burden during these times, as the king said, and your enemies will be many. But you're not alone."

Arthan could not help but be wary. He did not expect to find allies in the king's court, ruled as it was by Brugarn. And although Waldemar seemed genuine, he looked forward to Serdot's assessment. Arthan wished Maillard had brought him to Eglamour more often, to teach Arthan how to weigh the words and deeds of powerful people. He realized in that moment that he feared being deceived.

Waldemar stepped closer and dropped to the lowest whisper. "The king has lost himself to shadow, usurped by those closest to him. Everyone can see it. Some say he's utterly unfit to be king. This is treachery, of course. But our kingdom faces new perils all around. When the quake comes, can such a man continue to stand?"

Reimvick's words echoed in Arthan's mind. *They will test and isolate you if you let them.* He could not help but feel as if he was being baited. Waldemar was simply being too open with him. Dangerously open for the chief royal servant. Waldemar was either desperate for an ally to fill the void left by Maillard, or Waldemar was sent by Brugarn to test Arthan.

When Arthan's answer did not come, Waldemar took a step back. "I'm sure I've said too much. Before you return to Delavon you must attend the Lord Ministers Council. It will be Brugarn's first opportunity to test you. Remember, your enemies may be many, but you're not without allies."

"Thank you," Arthan said. Waldemar did not return to the feast but walked into the dark.

"What did he want?" Reimvick asked when Arthan returned to his seat.

Arthan glanced at Serdot, who twitched his head as if to say *don't tell him.*

"Just news from Delavon and condolences for Father," Arthan said.

"Waldemar is a collector of gossip," Reimvick said, "like me. But I don't trust him. As the king's man, he's effectively Brugarn's man."

"I suppose that is beyond me," Arthan said before taking a long drink of wine.

Reimvick stopped chewing. "No it isn't. You'll need to learn who is who in this court, beyond the primary usurpers I named on the road. This place is a snake pit, perhaps more so than when Maillard was last here. You'll need to learn where the traps are, perhaps better than your father did."

Arthan nodded but kept eating.

As the courtiers' bellies filled and the wine fogged each head, the king retired early to his bedchamber. Eager to go to Clonmel, Arthan said his farewells.

Riding through the white-paved streets, Arthan's head was heavy with proffered advice and foolishness. It was difficult to tell everything apart. He pondered Reimvick's words about his destiny and Serdot's similar words from before. Then there was Waldemar's anxious and pushy talk.

"How can I tell friend from foe, Serdot?" he asked as he readied for bed. "The chaos of a battlefield is easier to navigate than the royal court."

"I do not trust Waldemar," Serdot answered. "Brugarn would have every reason to corrupt the steward. However, as master of the palace, Waldemar is someone you must keep close at hand. Don't let him think you distrust him."

"What about Reimvick? His advice seems sound, but I half wish we hadn't traveled together. His gossipy concerns are endless, yet he spoke to me of destiny as if he had looked into a witch's well."

"Your father had much respect for both men. But they did not gain power merely by being respected."

"Father also respected our neighbor to the north, Lord Sigbert of Barres Ministry."

"Sigbert is headstrong. His temper is a liability."

"Then who can be trusted, Serdot? How is life at court possible without trusting someone at some time?"

"None of them can be fully trusted, my lord. You must be cautious and discerning, aware that their loyalties and whims will constantly shift. And Reimvick was right: you'll have to learn the court well, better than Maillard. I will help you."

"At least Reimvick and I were confirmed together. Which reminds me, I did not see anyone from Leauvenna at court. Has the king not decided on a new lord minister?"

"Gottfried and his wife had no children, so his heir for lord ministership remains uncertain. The queen's mind has been shaded with popaver since our arrival, and the king is said to go in and out of bitter depression. Frankly, my lord, I was surprised that Erech conducted the confirmation ceremony as well as he did, and that Brugarn largely let it be."

"When is the Lord Ministers' Council meeting?"

"A few days still. Not all the ministers who will attend have arrived. The fall of the Empire Alliance, the poor state of the treasury, the assassinations, the riots across several ministries, the potential for war with Rugenhav and Calbria and the Almerians. Much will be discussed. But tomorrow you should attend court. I hear something important will be announced."

"An announcement before the council meets? What is the king—or Brugarn—planning?"

"I don't know yet, my lord."

"Engage whomever you need. I want to be the best-informed nobleman in the city. Pay anyone you need to."

"And I'll keep a close eye on your known and potential enemies," Serdot said with a nod. "Listening to what everyone else was saying was one reason your father was such an effective mediator. He wanted to know as much as he could about everyone. That's how court games are played, and perhaps why Reimvick loves gossip."

"Get some rest, my friend. We'll need it."

"No rest for me yet, my lord. Too many people I need to reacquaint myself with in this city. And most are best reached at this time of night."

35

RODEL

Rodel's long ride back to Wallevet on a stolen horse gave him time to reconsider his initial confidence that the Wosmoks would not hunt him down. He wished he'd not gone back to Eglamour at all. Wredegar saw him survive the river but if he had accepted Arasemis's original invitation, Wredegar would have assumed Rodel had been captured or killed on his way to Eglamour. But it was too late now.

His fears evaporated when he saw Thorendor. It was unlike any castle he'd seen in Donovan or any other kingdom. Modestly sized, yellowish-brown stone, and like a temple. It was ringed with a standard curtain wall and moat fed by the mountain springs shimmering through the woods behind it. But its central keep was pyramidal at the top, with towers studding the four corners. The towers widened toward a common foundation, so the whole construction was like a shrunken mountain.

Rodel finally reached the fork in the road. Straight ahead was the bridge where he'd been dumped into the river. To the right was the road to Thorendor. He steered his horse right, hoping Arasemis would be as welcoming as he had been.

As he approached the outer guard house he was surprised to find it empty. He peeked inside a door left ajar. It looked like it hadn't been occupied for many years. Only cobwebs, birds' nests, and animal prints in the dirt-strewn floor. The bridge across the moat was completely unguarded, and the gate of the curtain wall wide open.

Rodel paced his horse slowly across, struck by the quiet of the place. If not for the faint curl of smoke coming from a chimney, he would have been sure the castle was abandoned. When he reached the far side of the bridge he passed through the open gate and into a large courtyard. The main door was closed, as were two side doors through the interior walls that divided the courtyard.

"Anyone there?" When no one answered he dismounted and slowly stepped toward the main door. "It is I, Rodel, from the river." He approached the door and knocked. "Count Arasemis?"

Still nothing. Rodel wondered if the one-armed man had died alone within. He turned and remounted his horse, intending to exit the way he had come. He turned the horse just as the portcullis of the gate crashed down. The horse reared back. Rodel instinctively reached for his long dagger.

"Arasemis! I am Rodel. I come at your invitation and mean you no harm!"

He turned back toward the main door, but it was unchanged. He turned to his right and left, considering whether to try the side doors. A flash of color on the right interior wall caught his eye. It was a green-caped man, running silently along the top of the wall. And he wore a mask.

"You there!" Rodel called out. But the man kept running. He was thinner than Arasemis and had both arms. He jumped from the interior courtyard wall up onto the curtain wall, ran along the top of the gatehouse, then down to the left interior wall, nearly circling Rodel. In midjump he pulled out a crossbow and shot Rodel's horse in the chest. Rodel struggled for control, but the steed tossed him off. He scrambled away as the man, completing his running circle on the wall, shot the horse again, in the head.

"I'm not here to fight!" Rodel shouted.

The man jumped from the wall and rolled when he hit the ground, all silently. He drew a sword out from his cape when he came to his feet.

"No," Rodel said as he backed away. "I didn't come to fight . . ."

The masked man rushed him. Rodel pulled his dagger to defend himself. He dodged the man's first swipe by rolling to the side and parried the second. The green cape flashed in his face. Rodel stabbed at empty air with his dagger as the man ran up the courtyard wall. He watched in awe as the man ran along the top again, then back down the wall on the far side.

Rodel defended himself again, clashing his long dagger with the man's sword. The man was quick, a blur of metal and green, and utterly silent behind the mask. Eventually Rodel found an opening to strike. He missed, but his jab caused the man to break off his attack and back away.

The man seemed bored, turning his back on Rodel. He prepared to throw his dagger, lifting it up to his shoulder. The man turned his head, one eye slit watching over his shoulder.

Rodel lowered the dagger. "I did not come to fight. I came to see Arasemis, by his invitation."

"Then you did come to fight," said the man in Donovar-accented Rugen.

Rodel shook his head. The man spun around and rushed him again. Rodel stabbed toward the mask but missed. The man landed a punch across Rodel's jaw, disarmed him, and flung him to the ground. He then placed his sword at his neck.

"I want no more of this!" Rodel cried. "I've come to the wrong place."

"You've come to the right place," said the man. He held the sword aloft, but Rodel rolled away.

Rodel grasped a handful of dirt as he came to his feet. When the man rushed him again he tossed the dirt. It bounced off the mask and the man laughed. Rodel evaded the attack, rolled to his dagger on the ground, and tripped the man. Rodel pounced on him, striking the sword from his hand, and readied his dagger.

"Do you yield?"

"We never yield."

"You must, or—"

The man head-butted Rodel's dagger hand. Rodel shifted to regain control, and the man wrenched his arm loose, throwing Rodel off him. Rodel quickly regained his feet but turned to see the man run up the wall, then run back down. A black object flew from his hands on the way down. In a blink Rodel was choking on a cloud of brown powder.

The powder made him feel drunk. He gasped as it coated his eyes, nostrils, and throat with sublime warmth. He staggered and found himself lying on his back gazing at the sky. The mask appeared above him, and he closed his eyes. The man spoke as his own heartbeat slowed down . . .

When Rodel awoke he found himself sitting upright in a chair. The room was completely dark except for one candle on a small table before him. He moved to stand but his arms and legs ignored him. He looked down at his leaden arms, resting on the cushioned armrests of the chair, but they still would not move.

The candle's flame was green and elongated, as if the fire had been stretched one hand length. He heard movement and looked into the dim beyond.

"I must apologize," said a voice. "Marlan used a bit too much flashoak tincture." A familiar bushy red beard leaned toward the green light.

"Count Arasemis?"

"But you're lucky because he used to confuse flashoak with earth nut oil, in which case you would have awoken blind instead of dizzy. If you've never seen flashoaks, we have a grove of them on my land. Acorn to full grown to rotting log in two years. Quite a fascinating species."

"Why . . ." Rodel closed his eyes, but the fog wouldn't clear. "I did not . . ."

"It's all right," Arasemis said, moving his chair closer to the light. "This rising candle will wear away the haze in your head soon. Since you are new, Marlan thought it best to test your skills. You did well, considering."

"Your . . . invitation . . ."

"It still stands. But it's not too late to leave either. I haven't told you anything yet, and you've not seen much."

"No, I . . ." Rodel shook his head vigorously.

"So now's your last chance to turn back," Arasemis continued. "Thereafter you will be bound to us by an oath that cannot be broken, for our lives depend on it."

Rodel blinked hard. Then he noticed the candle's flame shorten considerably, and the light changed from green to common yellow. Arasemis looked at it too and smiled.

"There. How do you feel now?"

Rodel looked up, surprised to feel refreshed. "Much better."

"The rising candle could taste the flashoak on your breath, you see? Just as the flashoak dies within two years, its essence escapes from your lungs within two hours. Remarkably potent stuff, but easily countered by time and the vapors of the right rising candle."

"When I first met you, after the river, you spoke of an Order," Rodel said. "And teachings."

"So you've come to another of life's crossroads and chose the path to Thorendor?" Arasemis asked, and Rodel nodded. "Then you are most welcome, as promised."

Arasemis stood and walked around behind Rodel's chair. Rodel felt the feeling in his arms and legs return. He stood and followed Arasemis. Light flooded in as Arasemis opened the door.

"These will be your quarters," Arasemis said, opening another door across the hallway. "Not much larger, but it has a bed, blankets, and a washbasin. Shelves for the many books you'll study. And that bag of candles will provide your first alchemy lessons. But you are never confined to this cell. All of Thorendor Castle will be yours to explore. Follow me."

They walked down the corridor. There were many more hermit-like cells, their doors left open. Only one was closed.

"How many students do you have?" Rodel asked.

"That number is not important right now. Unfortunately, I just lost one, but now I've gained you and one other." Arasemis gestured to the closed door. "I will meet with him now, as I did with you. I'll meet you in the great hall after.

Take this corridor and go down the stairs to the left. The others are waiting for you there."

Rodel did as he was told, walking slowly and taking the opportunity to observe his surroundings. The stone walls were carved with whimsical designs, sprinkled with animals, plants, and peoples. The floor was covered with a fine rug with a repeating design that looked like a jagged arch with a flame.

The grand hall was unmistakable. The large doors of reddish wood were propped open. Rodel heard friendly banter and smelled good food. He stood at the threshold, watching two men and a woman talking at a table.

"Come, join us, Rodel the Rugen," bellowed a large man in Donovar. All of them turned to look.

Rodel was not surprised to hear his name, since he had given it to Arasemis the night he crawled out of the river. But he was surprised that they knew he spoke Donovar. He walked toward the table as the second man held a mug of beer out for him.

"No hard feelings about our dance in the courtyard," the man said. "I'm Marlan."

Rodel took the beer. "Perhaps we'll have a fairer fight next time. You have my dagger?"

Marlan handed it to Rodel with a smile.

"Don't worry, Rodel," the young woman said. "You'll learn what he's learned soon enough."

"If he's able," the big man said. "I'm Bertwil. She's Juhl."

"My condolences to you all," Rodel said. "Arasemis told me a student was recently lost." He raised his mug. "To the lost."

Bertwil paused before joining the others in a drink. "His name was Morroy. A finicky, prim Calbrian, but a good swordsman."

"You're our first Rugen," Juhl said.

"You're a Lambic," Rodel said with a nod. "And a Donovard and an Almerian," he said, looking at Marlan and Bertwil in turn. They nodded.

"The other new student is also a Donovard," Marlan said, "as is Master Arasemis and a few others. So we have you outnumbered when the War of All Kingdoms comes."

"He jests," Bertwil said.

"He knows," Juhl said, turning to Rodel. "Where do you come from?"

"Rugenhav."

"Yes, but what did you do before?"

Rodel took a long drink. "I was in the shadows . . . But I've left them."

"You've stepped into new ones," Marlan said.

The sound of footsteps at the door drew their attention. Arasemis entered alongside a young blond man with sharp eyes. "Rodel, this is Fetzer, from Perilune in Barres Ministry. He's almost as new as you are."

Rodel detected unease in Fetzer's handshake and mannerisms. He wondered if it was because he disliked Rugens.

"Everyone please sit," Arasemis said. "Let us eat."

"Their oaths?" Bertwil asked.

"After we dine together," Arasemis said. "I'm confident of their commitment."

"In the beginning, Garion and I had to give the oath before setting foot in Thorendor," Marlan said.

"I can read youngsters' confidence better now," Arasemis said with a smile.

"There are more of us?" Rodel asked.

"Garion is on a special task in Eglamour at the moment," Arasemis said. "I'm hopeful he will return here soon with good news."

"Garion was the master's second pupil, after Marlan," Juhl explained.

"Then me, and then Morroy," Bertwil said. "Juhl came after."

"And now the two of you," Arasemis said to the newcomers. Then he turned toward a side door. "Yorand!"

Rodel watched a man wearing a cook's uniform shuffle out, followed by a woman.

"Yorand, some meat and bread," Arasemis said. "And something good to finish." When he departed back into the kitchen, Arasemis turned to Rodel. "Yorand is mute, and Adalane is deaf. I brought them over from the academy, where I once taught. They're a little slow, but we treat them better than anyone did at the academy."

"They are part of our little family," Juhl said.

"But they don't know what we're all about," Bertwil added.

"I'm not sure I know what we're about," Rodel said.

"You've not been on a task yet," Fetzer said. "It's about blood. Lots of blood, in the most wonderful way."

"Now, Fetzer . . ." Arasemis wagged his finger. "Leave the lessons to me. The Order of the Candlestone is not merely about blood. It is a name that few ears have heard for a long time, buried by kings who survived the Order's halcyon days. But with all of you, Candlestone is rising again."

"You mentioned the ancient peoples of Pemonia when I was with you in the carriage," Rodel said. "Is that where Marlan learned wall running?"

"Of course," Arasemis said. "Everyone at the table has learned the various techniques. Tomorrow you and Fetzer will begin your training, too. But for now, a story."

Yorand and Adalane reappeared with plates of roasted chicken, vegetables, and brown bread, and they refilled their mugs. Arasemis continued after they had departed.

"Long ago, the lands now known as Wallevet Ministry were completely forested. Before the Brintilian colonists settled here, there were giant trees that were inhabited by natives called the Gallerlanders. Their realm was larger than any of the other tribes of early Pemonia, stretching from the Bomlofoss Mountains on the western shore to the Narendra Mountains in the east. And from Leauvenna in the north to the Orringholm River Valley in the south. A massive network of forests ruled by their high king. He was elected from among the lower kings, who were also elected from among the clan and family chieftains.

"When the settlers came, the Gallerlanders—despite their overwhelming numbers and knowledge of their lands—could do little against mounted knights and armored soldiers. For religious reasons, the natives shunned horses and metal weaponry. And so their forests burned and there was a great exodus southward where they joined with a few other tribes to resist the expansion of the Brintilian Empire, the Second Crusade. But with time they fell to the empire and were absorbed into it.

"Now, there was one among the Gallerlanders who organized the initial resistance. He was a colonial knight named Rildning who helped lead an expedition into the frontier but eventually joined the natives and wed one of their princesses. Although the natives eventually lost, they would have succumbed to the empire much sooner had it not been for Rildning and his followers. And much of what we know about the various natives would have been lost forever."

"Why did Rildning turn against his own people?" Rodel asked.

"Like many, he had become disenchanted with the empire and the cyclical violence of the Old World, which, as you may have noticed, still plagues the Almerian Confederation to this day. But Rildning saw an opportunity to unite the tribes of the New World. He hoped to strengthen them against the empire and protect them from the rot of the endless warring dynasties of the Old World."

"Clearly he wasn't successful," Fetzer said.

"Obviously the native kingdoms eventually fell, otherwise we'd be speaking Gali right now," Arasemis said. "But the natives prophesied Rildning's coming, and he laid the foundation of an order of warriors that would live on in secret within the Brintilian Empire. Candlestone, originally formed by seven members of various tribes and another colonial, worked to subvert the empire from the inside. Marlan, continue this part of the tale while I taste this chicken."

"Official histories do not acknowledge most Candlestone victories," Marlan said, "such as the assassination of Marshal Hilsingor, the leader of the Frontier Corps who destroyed many tribes of western and central Pemonia.

"But Candlestone was responsible for such tasks, as we call them, which slowed the empire's march, contributed to its eventual breakup, and helped preserve pockets of the original peoples of Pemonia that still exist today. You've heard of them as the wildermen of the Merbredel Mountains and the Black Forest Wildermen.

"The Order thrived for centuries and killed many kings and other powerful people, until it was aggressively hunted down. The Order nearly died out, but the flame was kept alive in secret for revival. We call it the War of All Kingdoms, the overthrow of all tyrants and continent kings, and the return to elected chieftains. That revival has begun."

"How can so few overthrow so many?" Fetzer asked.

"Rodel may be able to explain it . . ." Arasemis said.

Rodel turned his eyes to his plate and quickly filled his mouth. He wished to keep his history with the Wosmoks to himself. Yet Arasemis appeared to know it.

"Perhaps it's best if I explain," Arasemis continued. "It may seem far-fetched, young Fetzer, but our methods are well developed, precise, and effective. You will start learning the methods of Candlestone tomorrow. But you must understand and accept the Order's reason for being before you can be part of the revival."

"Candlestone killed the lord ministers of Wallevet, Delavon, and Leauvenna?" Rodel asked.

Arasemis nodded. "They are only the beginning."

"Why must we waste time on the nobles?" Fetzer asked. "Why not focus on the king?"

"Patience," Arasemis said. "Everything is as I've planned it. Marlan?"

"King Erech is the weakest of the Avaleau men. If we killed him first, then one of his three violence-prone brothers would fill his place. So we benefit by keeping Erech on the throne. Aside from his brothers, several of the nobles would also have claim to the crown, such as the House of Valient. So by starting in the middle and working our way up, there will be no one left to legitimately claim the throne of Donovan."

"The chaos created by the lower nobles squabbling among themselves will give Candlestone opportunity to grow," Arasemis said. "By the time foreign rulers try to step in to take a part of Donovan for themselves, we'll already have Candlestone branches in their kingdoms, ready to strike when they are distracted with the ruins of Donovan."

"Magnificent . . ." Fetzer said.

Rodel was also impressed. "Where did all of this come from? Rildning's history, the deeds of the Order, these plans, all of it?"

"The heart of Thorendor Castle is my beloved library," Arasemis said. "You will spend many hours reading and learning for yourself. But these plans have been shaped by generations of Order members. We have Rildning's journal and books written by his companions and his son. Texts written by the natives. And many other things. Then, when you're ready, perhaps one day you'll take the light of Candlestone into Rugenhav."

Rodel contemplated the gravity of what he'd been told. To be a Wosmok, turned against the Rugen emperor. He did not lament this path, but the notion of a continental war was unsettling.

Bertwil slapped the table. "This chicken is delicious."

Arasemis chuckled, turning to Rodel. "Bertwil is the son of an Almerian merchant and has probably seen more conflict in the Old World than any of you. Juhl is an erstwhile princess of the iceberg-hearted Lambics. Fetzer you've met. Marlan and Garion were among my students at Bredahade Academy. You were not able to meet Morroy, but he was a brave Calbrian who would have willingly taken the torch of Candlestone into Tiberon. So you see, Rodel? You are in familiar company."

Rodel changed the subject quickly. "What happened at the academy?"

"I once taught ancient history and native martial arts. When the academy had no further use for—or perhaps patience with—my skills, they forced me out. I retired to my family's estate here at Thorendor to focus on my studies. Marlan and Garion soon followed, abandoning the academy."

Fetzer cocked his head. "How did you come to possess the histories of Candlestone?"

"You could say I inherited them," Arasemis said. "But that is a story for another day. I believe you've heard enough. It is time to take the oath. Rise, both of you."

Rodel and Fetzer pushed up from the bench. Arasemis stood with them.

"Repeat after me. Like the long memories of the trees, we will never forget the prophecy and sacrifice. Like the electrum of the earth, we will be unseen until our time has come. Like the flame, we will keep the ancient truths alive.

And like the stone, we will find strength in ourselves and each other. We will carry the truths and defend the original lands . . . Until the End of Days."

❧

Juhl caught up with Rodel as he was on his way back to his quarters that night.

"It's good to see a Rugen here," she said in his language. "I don't care what past you're hiding, but the others will pester you until you tell them."

"What led you here, Juhl? Are you really a princess?"

"I was at a crossroads, as Arasemis likes to say. Betrothed to a young prince that I loathed. Forced by a father who saw me as a political pawn, not a daughter. And faded from the memory of a mother driven mad by the sickness of the southern winds."

Rodel did not expect this softer side of her. She had a severe look and cold eyes. Every pale-skinned Lambic he had ever met was the same way.

"I'm sorry, Juhl . . . Do you believe Candlestone can remake the world?"

"Yes. You see this symbol?" She pointed to the repeating jagged ridge and flame design in the corridor rugs that Rodel had noticed earlier. "That stone and flame is the symbol of Candlestone," she said. "You'll see it everywhere in Thorendor. It is a reminder that we are already walking a path toward a remade world. Do you not believe it can be remade?"

"I've never cared enough about the world to consider how to change it," Rodel said. "My life has always been about death . . ."

"You were a Wosmok, weren't you?"

Rodel stopped walking and turned to her. "How could you know that?"

"Master Arasemis told us about your fall into the river from the prison carriage, and he said you'd be back. Didn't sound like a common thief to me. Listen, everyone here has a difficult past. And none of the Donovard members of the

Order are going to judge you for what the Wosmoks have done in Donovan. None of us hold allegiance to any king."

"I'm not ashamed for what the Wosmoks have done," Rodel said. "I just can't do it anymore."

"I'll keep it to myself." Juhl eyed him curiously. "Why did you join us?"

"I wanted to leave the Wosmoks. All of it . . . We were just pawns . . ."

"Of a foul emperor," Juhl finished. Rodel nodded. "There are no pawns in Candlestone," Juhl continued. "We will rid the world of families like the Theudamers and Avaleaus. We are the king breakers. Pursuers of rebellion. Agents of death."

"Like the Wosmoks . . ." Rodel muttered.

"No, like nothing else. We seek to change this whole continent for the better. To the way it used to be."

"And a handful of misfits will accomplish all that?"

"Tomorrow, you'll see . . ." Juhl stepped closer to him, her gray eyes brightening like crystal in the torchlight. "I look forward to learning more about you, Rodel Once a Wosmok."

"What about your Lambic title?" he asked, feeling his back press against the wall.

"Juhl Empty Hearted Stone."

"Not sure I believe it . . ."

"No?" She winked before striding to her quarters. She paused in the doorway. "If you're awakened in the night, don't fear the rolling noises from the chamber above. The master sleeps little and often toys with a contraption at the top of Thorendor."

Rodel nodded and watched her close her door before entering his own cell. For the first time in a long time he slept soundly.

36

ROWAN

Near the Rugenhav Border, Alpenon Ministry
Flowertide, 3034

"What's happened? Give me that letter, boy."

Lord Asteroth snatched the messge from Rowan's hands, snapping Rowan out of his daze. Why did Arthan not send for him to attend Father's funeral? He would have gladly left Asteroth's side and made the journey back to Rachard.

Asteroth returned the parchment. "I'm sorry to hear this, Rowan. Maillard was a . . . good man." He cleared his throat and straightened up in his saddle. "When men lose their fathers it is a time to stand tall and take up the burden."

"My brother will be lord minister of Delavon," Rowan said. "What is left for me?"

"Don't give me that nonsense," Asteroth said. "My older brother is the king and my younger brother is his right hand. It's fallen to me and Erath to protect his kingdom for him. We protect the southern border because we're the strong ones. Your burden is to help your brother when the time comes. But as my ward, you still have much to learn."

Rowan looked up at the massive Asteroth, clad in fine-gilded cindersteel armor. The sword belted to his back was as wide as a man. Only the largest war chargers could carry Asteroth's weight. There was little sympathy in his hard face. It was not the first time Rowan regretted Maillard's decision to ward him under Asteroth.

"My lord," said a nearby knight captain, "more Rugen scouts have been spotted near Merl."

"That far in? God, they are getting bold. Turn around, we'll squash them."

Rowan sighed to himself. Asteroth cherished patrolling the border towns himself. He was not a lord who sat idle in his castle at Cantrileme. As his ward, Rowan went everywhere with him. He had become intimately familiar with the Rugen and Austveede border regions and had seen much of Alpenon Ministry. But Asteroth never let Rowan cross into Rugenhav.

Within a few hours they arrived on the outskirts of Merl. Rowan knew the town's watchmen would cringe at the sight of Asteroth's brigade approaching, heavy-handed as he was about rooting out the frequent scouts that Rugenhav was sending into Donovan these days. But this time the soldier had already captured the scouts, three of them, and waited in a field within view of the town.

Asteroth and Rowan dismounted and walked to the soldiers and their prisoners, who sat in the grass with hands bound. One was a woman.

"Lord Minister Asteroth," began one of the soldiers, "we caught them coming up the road from the southeast. Only this one claims to speak Donovar." He gestured to the woman. "She was also carrying this." The soldier dumped the contents of small coin pouch into his hand. "Austveede bloone. Twenty or so coins."

"Stand them up," Asteroth said. "Let's have a look at them."

The soldiers jerked them to their feet. Their garments and possessions clearly marked them as Rugen scouts. But Rowan thought it odd that they would be coming from Austveeden. He wondered if Asteroth would let them sit in the Merl magistrate's jail for a few days, or take them back to the capital for questioning.

"Why are you here?" Asteroth said to them. They answered with silent stares. "Your names then?" he asked. Nothing.

For a large man, Asteroth moved quickly. He pulled his massive sword off his back and crashed it down on one of the scouts. When the woman lashed out, he backhanded her into the grass, then prepared to strike the third scout.

"Wait!" she shrieked from the grass.

"You wish to speak now?" Asteroth said, halting his blade over the man's head.

"My name is Etzel," she said. "We are merely travelers, returning to Rugenhav."

"If that were true, you would have exited Austveeden directly into Toninbern, not through my lands," Asteroth said, still holding his sword above the scout. "Surely you don't deny coming from Austveeden. Who else carries square bloone?"

Etzel glanced at her companion, the shadow of Asteroth's wide sword darkening his face. She nodded weakly.

"Why?" Asteroth shouted.

Etzel looked at her companion again, and the fear melted from his face. Her companion pulled a hidden dagger from his tunic and stabbed toward Asteroth's unprotected neck. Asteroth dodged the stab and brought his sword down, severing the scout's arm. Then his head.

Etzel got up to run.

"Let her go!" Asteroth shouted. He sheathed his great sword and mounted, following after her through the long grass. Rowan and a few others came after them. Rowan knew Asteroth enjoyed a good chase. The lord minister quickly caught up with Etzel, fast as she was, and planted his big boot between her shoulder blades. Rowan halted his horse above her still body, facedown in the grass.

Asteroth came alongside him. "A mere scout, young Rowan?"

"No, my lord. Something more . . ."

"The scouts who probe our border always come direct from Rugenhav, never through Erath's lands from Austveeden."

"What should we do with her?"

"Crush her skull, like the others," Asteroth said with a smile. "After she tells us what they were up to." Asteroth turned to Sir Hamon, his top commander. "They would have come through Fanedor. Send a troop of knights to that city to ask about them. As for this one, bring her with us back to Cantrileme in the morning. We'll overnight in Merl."

That night Rowan thought about his father and his struggles. It was strange to hear of the important and tragic events happening across the other ministries. The assassinations of the lord ministers, the riots led by soldiers discharged by a broken treasury, and the growing number of hungry in Toulon. Then there was the disquiet here in Alpenon, Asteroth's brutal seizure of Ambardil Free City and several Almerian ships and properties on the coast.

Rowan simply wanted to go home and touch his father's tomb. He would never forgive Arthan for keeping him in Alpenon with this tyrant. Asteroth's advice about supporting older brothers echoed in his mind, but he did not need the tyrant's wisdom. He had his father's.

So be it, he thought. He would serve his brother, if unhappily, and provide the information about the borderlands that Arthan requested. But Rowan would expect something from his brother in return. He was not sure what.

37

ARTHAN

Eglamour Palace, Toulon Ministry
Flowertide, 3034

"None of you have any answers." Duke Brugarn scowled at the courtiers. "None of you care that you might be the next to feel an assassin's dagger in your throat." His glare settled on Arthan.

Arthan was not worried. It was Brugarn's second rant today about the deaths of the lord ministers. Arthan disliked being in the duke's presence but reminded himself that he was no longer simply a lord minister's son. He looked at the other lord ministers now present at court, including the newly arrived Sigbert of Barres, Halevane of Merbredel, and Voufon of Laume.

"Shall we move on to the matter of the treasury, given the lack of information on the killings?" Waldemar said. "I'm sure that with time we'll learn—"

"Silence, steward," Brugarn said. "The treasury is none of your concern. But we'll let the matter of the killings rest for now. Now, give me the scroll." The duke snatched it from Waldemar. "I'll read it myself," Brugarn said as he faced the court. A cruel grin spread across his ugly face as General Chaultion stepped up beside Brugarn.

"The king hereby issues a new proclamation," Brugarn said. "It will be effective at once . . ."

"Interesting that he rushed to do this before your Lord Ministers' Council meeting," Bardil whispered to Arthan.

200

Serdot nodded. "Official proclamations are traditionally put through the council first, when possible."

Arthan shushed them as Brugarn finished his prefatory remarks.

"And now," the duke continued, "the first ruling of this Proclamation of Expediency is the revival of the treasury. All monies collected as taxes by the vassal lords will be doubled, with the vassal's portion reduced to one-tenth."

"How are we to keep the peace and feed ourselves?" Sigbert asked. Others complained similarly.

Brugarn ignored them and continued. "Additionally, all noble prisoners and hostages, Donovard and foreigner, will be sold their freedom. First among them will be Geras Vilarwef, who shall be sold to Austveeden for three hundred guldirs. Lord Asteroth has already agreed to this, given the criminal killed an Austveede prince. Ambassador Vesamune, if your emperor wants Geras he'll have to pay a double ransom."

Arthan turned to see Vesamune's reaction, but she was already walking swiftly toward the door.

"The Rugens will probably pay it," Serdot whispered to him. "Geras is the leader of the Alpenon rebellion. The Rugens have given him much more money and support over the years."

"Treasury monies will also be saved by reducing the wages of all soldiers of the Army of Donovan, the city guards of Eglamour, and the king's Crownblades," Brugarn continued. "Every garrison will be reduced in number. Surplus soldiers will be sent to the Rugen border in Alpenon and Gadolin. And finally, Donovan will demand that monies paid into the defunct Empire Alliance for the maintenance of Austveeden's erstwhile neutrality be paid back by the Austveedes before Midsummer has passed."

"Does he want a kingdom-wide riot?" Reimvick whispered to Arthan. The other courtiers also grumbled.

"The second ruling of the proclamation addresses the hostility from our enemies on every front," Brugarn said. "We demand the Almerian Confederation vacate the occupied islands or suffer our attack. Similarly, Calbria must recognize our right to certain islands, especially in the Calbrian Sea, or face our attack.

"As for Rugenhav, which for untold generations has plotted against us, has supported the Alpenon rebels, has daily harassed our southern border, and may have had a hand in the recent assassinations . . . Rugenhav will be made to cower. If Emperor Theudamer does not give up his games, Donovan will march on Heingartmer!"

Arthan noticed that the one member of Vesamune's retinue who had remained behind suddenly departed. The rest of the courtiers complained loudly now, with big Sigbert protesting the loudest. But Brugarn showed no cracks in his resolve.

"Brugarn probably wrote it himself," Serdot said to Arthan. "Heavy-handed like Asteroth and Erath, yet the king says nothing . . ."

Arthan looked at Erech. He was slumped on the throne, staring down the length of the great hall and oblivious to the commotion around him. Queen Andrilenne, surprisingly present, watched Brugarn with apparent curiosity. She seemed surprised by the proclamation and yet impressed with Brugarn's nerve.

"And finally," Brugarn continued, "the third ruling of the Proclamation of Expediency is the creation of a new servant of the king. The Marshal of Inquiry will investigate the recent assassinations, superseding the authority of chief magistrates of all ministries and territories. The king will confirm the holder of this title in due course."

"Which means him," Serdot whispered.

Brugarn permitted himself a vile smirk. Clearly satisfied with himself, Brugarn turned to the king. "Your Majesty?"

Erech snapped out of his thoughts and stood. As he stepped from the throne to address the court, he stumbled and dropped the ancient sword of Rhunegeld. The courtiers cringed to see the blade clatter down the steps of the dais onto the stone floor, to hear the dissonant sound.

There was a collective gasp as the finest symbol of Donovan's storied past crashed to the floor. Erech's eyes widened, for he knew the great dishonor he had inflicted on himself and all present. He froze in his pitiful position, unable to speak or recover the relic. Even Brugarn and Chaultion were appalled. But none moved to pick it up.

Arthan felt Serdot nudge him. Without thinking, he stepped forward slowly, carefully. As reverently as he could, Arthan picked up the sword, holding the blade and hilt, and gracefully offered it back to Erech with palms up.

A small light appeared in the king's eyes, which Arthan had not seen since his arrival. Erech gave a slight nod of appreciation. Regaining a dram of dignity, he sheathed Rhunegeld with a quick snap. Then, without a word, the king retreated to his chambers alone.

38

FETZER

Thorendor Castle, Wallevet Ministry
Flowertide, 3034

Fetzer was finishing breaking his night fast with the other students in the great hall when a bell clanged three times.

"To the training hall," Marlan said.

The veteran pupils broke into a jog down the corridors, with Fetzer and Rodel following behind. Up they went past their quarters to the third floor of the castle. Bertwil led them through a large square room filled with many exotic weapons and armor. Wooden tables and racks were laden with swords and axes. Weaponry such as Fetzer had never seen before hung on the walls flanked by shields painted with foreign markings.

Bertwil continued through the armory into the large training hall. The ceiling was a dome with many windows and beneath them, a balcony ringed the whole chamber. Countless years of practice battles scarred the gray stone walls. The floor was waxed tiles of hardwood bolted down in the corners.

"Welcome," Arasemis said. He stood in the center of the hardwood tiles, his one arm holding a long quarterstaff behind his back. Fetzer glanced around; no one else was armed.

"Shall I fetch equipment, Master?" Marlan asked.

Arasemis twirled the quarterstaff and pointed it toward a pile by the wall. "Leathers only," he said.

The students donned padded shirts, open-faced padded helmets, and kneepads. But no weapons. When they were ready, Arasemis, who wore his usual robes, glanced down at his right side. Fetzer noticed a small red pouch dangling from his belt.

"Your objective is this purse," Arasemis said. "Rodel, you first."

Fetzer reluctantly stepped aside to let Rodel past. Again the Rugen got the attention that should have been reserved for him, he thought. He watched impatiently as Rodel walked cautiously onto the hardwood tiles. Arasemis did not move until Rodel was within reach of his quarterstaff. Then the master swept it out, forcing Rodel to duck and roll. Arasemis easily sidestepped Rodel's grab for the purse, then whacked him in the back of the head.

"Too slow," Arasemis pronounced. "Who's next?"

Fetzer rushed in, dodging Arasemis's quarterstaff jab. Another step, and he found the quarterstaff at his legs. Arasemis tripped him, and he landed on his back.

"Too reckless," Arasemis said.

Fetzer rolled away as Bertwil came forward, blocking a strike with his broad forearm. Arasemis twirled the quarterstaff, landing blows to Bertwil's head, belly, and knee. He went down, and Arasemis pinned him by his neck with the staff.

"Work together!" the master shouted.

Juhl and Marlan bolted in. They were both exceptionally fast. Marlan feigned a rush for the purse, then ran toward the wall. Juhl got close to Arasemis but he twisted away, the red purse lifting from his belt as he spun like a top. He tripped her with the staff as Marlan ran up the wall to the balcony.

Rodel rolled in and came at Arasemis opposite Juhl, then Fetzer joined them. The three students struggled to keep their heads from getting whacked. The quarterstaff caught Fetzer's legs, and he was soon on his back again. Marlan flipped off the high balcony.

Arasemis whacked Rodel, tripped Juhl, then guided Marlan's fall with the staff so that he landed on Bertwil. All the students slowly came to their feet, panting. Arasemis breathed calmly, as if he were simply out for a stroll.

"Again!" he shouted.

Fetzer grew determined. He joined the others in rushing Arasemis from all sides. Using his one arm, Arasemis pole-vaulted from the floor and bounded off Bertwil's chest before crashing into Marlan. Then he jabbed the quarterstaff at Fetzer's padded forehead and hooked Juhl's foot, sending them both down. Rodel lunged for the purse when the master's back was turned but received a forehead jab without Arasemis bothering to turn around.

"Better . . ." Arasemis said. He walked to the wall and opened a wooden panel set in the stone. It was like a little cabinet, with several iron rings tied to ropes coming out of the wall. Arasemis pulled one of the rings. Fetzer crouched when flapping and creaking sounds emerged from beneath the floor. Arasemis grew taller. Fetzer watched as a section of the hardwood floor rose up on a stone column. Then another section rose, forming an X-shaped wall with the first. It stopped waist-high, with Arasemis standing in the center. "Again!" he shouted.

The students hoisted themselves onto the short wall and ran toward Arasemis. He easily plucked them from the wall, disrupting their balance by jabbing at their feet, heads, and hands. None got close until Juhl somersaulted along the wall, just touching the purse. Arasemis struck her legs hard, sending her to the floor.

Bertwil rushed in and managed to clutch the quarterstaff in one big hand. Fetzer saw his opening and lunged for the purse. Arasemis rotated his wrist, twisting a hidden joint in the staff. It separated into two halves. He beat Fetzer in the ribs until he fell from the wall.

Bertwil charged with his half of the staff as Juhl and Marlan ran along the walls toward the master. Arasemis turned to parry Bertwil but the big Almerian tossed the half staff to Marlan, letting Arasemis beat him from the wall. Marlan caught the half staff, rolled under Arasemis's preemptive strike, then knocked the purse off his belt and into the air.

Arasemis cast Marlan from the wall as Juhl leaned out to catch the purse. She did not see his half staff come from behind. Arasemis next batted the purse back into the air and hooked the string on the end of the staff. He calmly walked to the wall panel and pulled another iron ring in the cabinet.

Fetzer stepped away as the short walls sank back into the floor, then deeper, forming an X-shaped waist-deep ditch. Arasemis walked to the center and straddled the gap, the purse held aloft on the tip of his half staff.

The students regrouped with Rodel holding the half staff now. Everyone except Rodel rushed along the wedges of floor toward the master. Arasemis danced above the gap while batting the purse up and down between striking them. Rodel crouched down in the ditch and edged toward Arasemis. Marlan fell into the ditch opposite him, then Rodel stabbed up at Arasemis's legs. He could not touch the master and was soon disarmed.

Arasemis flipped Rodel's half staff up and twisted the two halves back together, restoring its full length but letting the purse fall into the center of the ditch under him. Every time Rodel or Marlan reached for it Arasemis blocked their hands with the quarterstaff, all while simultaneously fending off Bertwil and Juhl. Fetzer dove into the ditch for a chance at the purse.

With the three pairs of reaching hands and the distraction from Bertwil and Juhl, Arasemis was unable to prevent Fetzer from snatching the purse. Fetzer was elated for the briefest of moments before finding that Rodel had also snatched the string of the purse. He jerked it out of Rodel's grasp, then rolled backward through the ditch. Fetzer stood up victoriously, but again it was brief. Arasemis caught the purse with the staff, lobbed it up into the air, then swatted it back down into Fetzer's face.

An acrid yellow smoke burst out of the purse, sending Fetzer back into the ditch, coughing and sputtering to his knees. He wiped frantically at his eyes as his vision darkened. His eyes numbed so much that he could not tell if his eyelids were open or closed.

"Help me!" he shrieked. "I cannot see!"

"Calm yourself," Arasemis said. "It is only temporary . . ."

Fetzer, still crouched in the ditch, struggled to control himself. There was flapping and creaking underfoot as the floor leveled out again. Then he noticed a peculiar sensation of knowing, somehow, exactly where each iron gear, rope, and pulley was under the floor. It was a massive contraption.

As he brought his head up, he could hear everyone's breath and movements, and smell every drip of sweat. In his mind's eye, he could see exactly where everyone was standing. Fetzer felt his body grow colder. Even with the padded leathers and wooden plates that had softened the blows, his body had grown sore. But now the soreness drifted away. He stood upright, facing the one he somehow knew was Arasemis.

"How do you feel?"

"Peculiar . . . but well enough . . ."

"Do not fear the mixture," Arasemis said. "Defend yourself before it wears off."

"Can he not see us?" Rodel asked.

"To us his eyes appear to see, but they are blind," Arasemis said. "And yet, he can see much more than you can. Observe."

Arasemis tossed the quarterstaff to Fetzer. The latter instinctively ducked but outstretched his hand and caught the weapon, surprising himself. Fetzer heard Arasemis return to the wall cabinet and then there was more shifting underfoot. He could envision the movements, each vibration. He knew the pattern in the floor was repeating, with the tiles varying between heights and depths of one finger length up to two hand lengths. A trip hazard, like a rock field. The students adjusted their stances as the whole floor changed. Bertwil's breathing suggested great stress.

"Proceed," Arasemis said.

Fetzer could not help but smile. He could see his opponents' approach in his mind's eye. Juhl was close, her steps the lightest. He lashed out at her and heard Marlan charge, followed by the rest. Fetzer felt his thinking recede to the back of his mind as a natural instinct came to the forefront. He whirled the quarterstaff like an extension of his body. Though he did not know acrobatics like wall running, his swordcraft blended easily with whatever ability was flowing through him. He heard the others struggle over the irregular floor, but his balance was effortless.

It took some time before anyone could land a blow. Fetzer felt himself grow tired. It came on quickly. Arasemis, who Fetzer knew had stayed by the wall cabinet, finally spoke.

"Enough, leave him be."

The floor evened out again and Fetzer sat down, rolling his eyes around to find light. He heard Arasemis and the others approach.

"How was that possible?" Rodel asked.

"Much more is possible with alchemy," Marlan said.

"Not only that," Arasemis said, "the melding of aerina arcana and chemina arcana. A more advanced arcanae always augments a lesser one. How do you feel, Fetzer?"

"Exhausted. But I want to breathe more of that stuff."

"A little can give you an advantage," Arasemis said. "A lot can kill you."

Fetzer stopped smiling.

"What is arcanae?" Rodel asked.

"Aerina and chemina are two of the three schools of the ancient arts. Remove your leathers. It is time to take you to the library."

39

MILISEND

Eglamour Palace, Toulon Ministry
Flowertide, 3034

"You'd like me to believe you've been idle, Princess. But I know you are plotting your next theft."

Milisend tried to hide her surprise as Magistrate Tronchet came around the corner.

"I must say, I'm disappointed that you've taken to dabbling in alchemical ruses. As if thievery were not enough to dishonor your house, you must stoop to embracing ancient crackpottery."

"Enough, rat catcher!" Her echo rattled down the empty corridor. The smug self-assurance on Tronchet's face melted into genuine hurt. She wondered how the soft-skinned man had ever become the most senior lawkeeper in the capital.

"I apologize for shouting," she went on. "I did not steal those things, and I do not dabble in alchemy. I'm the king's daughter . . ." She did not enjoy lying to Tronchet, even if he did not believe her.

"You must stop thieving," he said. "It is not becoming of a princess. And it's not proper for a lord minister's wife, nor a queen."

Milisend's eyes narrowed. "What have you heard about marriage?"

"I—I presumed . . . Well, like Princess Avalane, that you would—"

"Don't presume anything about me!" she snapped. And yet she was unsure why it made her angry.

210

"I was merely saying that theft is below a royal princess."

"Even if your accusations were true, is it not a trifle? Of all the problems plaguing Eglamour . . . the rioting, the intrigue, the enemies on our borderlands. You of all people should be more concerned about that and less concerned about me."

"I take my duties as chief magistrate very seriously, Princess, from the most sinister crime to the pettiest offenses." Tronchet paused and blinked. "Did you just confess to the thievery?" he asked slowly, his silver mustache twitching expectantly.

Milisend looked away from his wide eyes. "No."

Tronchet seemed oddly relieved. "Then I will continue my duty and will not rest until I've caught you in the act." He turned and, almost triumphantly, left Milisend alone and confused.

"Is everything all right?"

The voice came from the end of the corridor.

"Lord Valient?"

"I'm sorry, I don't mean to intrude," he said. "It's just, I was leaving the palace and heard—"

"Nothing of importance, Lord Minister," she said, uncertain of what he'd overheard. "He keeps bothering me about a trivial complaint."

"Who was that—Tronchet?"

"Never mind. Are you departing for Delavon Ministry?" She walked beside him, thinking of her mother's designs on them as a pair. He was handsome—but distant.

"No, though I do miss Rachard," Arthan said. "I have an estate here in the city, Clonmel. I'm retiring there for the evening."

"It must be wonderful to escape the madness of this palace."

Arthan cleared his throat. "It is a nice respite."

Milisend stopped and faced him. "Have you known love, Lord Minister?"

He looked confused but quickly recovered. "I . . . have known love, yes."

"Has it ever been forced upon you?"

"Well, no. I suppose not." He gave a little nod. "But as a princess, I assume you must—"

"Don't assume anything about me."

Arthan nodded again. His eyes traced his path to the door. Before she could apologize, a man with shorn hair and a dark cloak walked in and went straight to Arthan, barely acknowledging her.

"My lord, a letter has arrived from your brother in Alpenon."

"I was on my way to Clonmel," Arthan said, eagerly taking the parchment from the man. He glanced at Milisend, trying to extricate himself from a situation she knew she'd made awkward.

"Who is this?" she asked, extending the discomfort.

"My political counselor," Arthan said. "Now, if you'll excuse me."

"A good night to you," Milisend said as she turned to leave.

"Good night."

They left the building as she walked toward her chambers. She wished she had been more polite. She wished she had not been so frustrated with Tronchet. Most of all, she wished to fly away and be wrapped in Regaume's arms.

40

ARTHAN

Clonmel Estate in Eglamour, Toulon Ministry
Flowertide, 3034

"A letter from your brother in the south borderlands, my lord." The messenger handed the letter to Arthan.

Dear Brother,
Thank you for your letter about Father, though I wish I could thank you for calling me back to Rachard. Since you were never given as a ward to a man like Asteroth, I'll tell you there is nothing worse than being far from home when Father died and being absent when he was entombed.

But I know you represented our house well, and now in the king's capital. Moreover, if you had perished in Mordmerg, I would have nothing to do with my rage. I think you can understand why I'm upset with you, Brother.

My own life was in danger of being cut short in Ambardil Free City when Asteroth tried to take the place by force. You've probably heard what he did to the Almerian garrison and the alderman by now, before the people ran us out of the city. It's a matter of time before he sets his eyes on it again with a large force.

Regarding your request for information from the borderlands, I will of course comply. Father would have expected as much. But don't leave me down here too long, Brother. I often think Asteroth wants the Rugens to invade so he can sate his hunger for their blood. His every action seems designed to provoke them. I hope you can help defray the tension, as both sides ready themselves for war.

The Rugens regularly send scouts across the border to observe us. No doubt they suspect us of prodding their border as well. Asteroth imprisons or kills any Rugens that wander into our lands, sometimes ransoming the wealthy ones back to their Rugen lords, other times executing them within view of the nearest Rugen town. He is a dangerous man.

Most recently we caught a few Rugen scouts near Merl, south of the lord minister's seat at Cantrileme. Oddly, the scouts had come from Austveeden. Though they initially claimed to be traveling to Rugenhav, the last surviving one admitted they were going to Eglamour. Her name is Etzel. She holds up well under the cruel tools of Asteroth's jailors, so far refusing to provide details. Her fortitude suggests she is more than a mere scout.

That is all the news for now, Brother. Pass my greetings to Bardil and do not forget about me, ward to one of the most violent men among the Avaleaus.

Rowan Valient
Rethsrond

"Typical Rowan bitterness," Arthan said, handing the letter to Serdot and Bardil. He gave them a moment to read.

"His comments about Lord Asteroth match what I've heard from my sources," Serdot said. "He provokes the Rugens as much as they provoke us."

"And I'm guessing there won't be an opportunity to talk with Asteroth at the Lord Ministers Council," Bardil said.

Serdot shook his head. "Asteroth and Erath won't be coming for the council. Guarding the southern border is their priority. They've always left courtly matters to Erech, so long as they get their monies and soldiers. Another reason to keep Rowan down there as long as he can stand it."

"Yes, for now," Arthan said. "But our brother is not one of your agents, Serdot. I'm glad to keep him with Asteroth until the risk to him outweighs the value of the information he sends. Not a day longer."

"Of course, my lord."

"Thank you for Rowan's letter. Was there anything else?"

Serdot nodded. "I don't have all the details yet, but there is something amiss about one of Brugarn's guards, a man by the name of Garion. He's one of the king's Crownblades under Sir Hamelin. Garion joined the guard only about a year ago. I saw him sneaking outside Brugarn's quarters. When I confronted him he simply walked away."

"Unusual for a guard who would have good reason to be there."

"Exactly."

"Did you ask Hamlin about Garion?" Bardil asked.

"I prefer to do my own investigating, until I have something worth saying."

"Get it quickly, Serdot," Arthan said. "No one knows much about the recent assassinations other than that alchemy and ancient heathen masks were used. If Brugarn is next, we need to know."

41

RODEL

Thorendor Castle, Wallevet Ministry
Flowertide, 3034

The library at the heart of Thorendor was the largest Rodel had ever seen. Three long, open floors with balconies and shelves crammed with books, folded parchments, scrolls, and massive atlases spread out across tables. Every free patch of wall was covered in maps and old tapestries, bronze busts of wild-looking men looked out from the ends of the shelves, and rolling ladders were scattered around the room. Arasemis's table was at the head of the hall and had pillars of books blockading all but one path to it.

Arasemis guided the students to the table nearest his and gestured for them to sit. "Rodel, you asked about the arcanae. You just experienced one of them when you observed the others' fighting techniques and wall running. Fetzer, you experienced another firsthand when you were blinded but still able to fight, and fight well. But everyone experienced all three types of ancient arts without realizing it. Marlan, tell them about the first."

"Aerina arcana is the knowledge of oneself in the where and when," Marlan said. "It comprises general movements, such as running or swimming, as well as special methods of fighting and evasion."

"All of aerina is rooted in the acrobatics of the ancient natives of Pemonia, particularly the Gallerlanders," Arasemis rejoined. "The Brintilian colonists were surprised to find natives who could run up into the trees. Their unique skills contributed to the convenient and preposterous belief that the natives were children of Memelos, according to old colonial records and the Candlestone histories.

"For us, aerina is a family of disciplines that weaponizes your body, especially when you have no other means to defend yourself or complete your task. Even the best trained, most experienced knights are ignorant of what their bodies can do, how far they can push themselves."

"Why didn't the colonists adopt these natives' tactics?" Rodel asked.

"Two reasons: they thought the natives were inferior, and they didn't need to," Arasemis said. "The Frontier Corps had horses and steel, both of which the natives lacked. Most importantly, the colonists were united, whereas the Gallerlanders were fractured from the start. So no amount of acrobatics could adequately defend their realm."

"Just like training this morning," Marlan said. "When we took our own approach to the red purse, we failed. When we cooperated, we succeeded."

Rodel listened intently, but this concept was nothing new to him. The Wosmoks executed their missions as a cooperative unit skilled in fighting with no weapons if necessary. And it was essential for any squad of soldiers, whether on the battlefield or in the shadows. But he kept his thoughts to himself.

"Then why was Marlan sent alone to execute Lord Raymond?" Fetzer asked. "And Garion, whatever he is doing in Eglamour?"

"Some tasks do not require a cooperative unit," Arasemis answered. "A single assassin is usually harder to detect. As for Marlan and Garion, both have mastered not only aerina arcana but nearly chemina arcana as well. Juhl and Bertwil have made great strides in chemina, too. But aerina must be mastered before chemina can be mastered."

"What about the fighting styles of the Ovelians in the east?" Rodel asked. "They must have mastered this aerina."

Arasemis nodded. "Yes. But, unfortunately for them, they ignore anything having to do with chemina, beyond burning incense."

"Too many wives," Bertwil said with a smile.

"Perhaps," Arasemis said. "Now consider the western kingdoms of Pemonia: Donovan, Rugenhav, and Austveeden, and the Old World Almerians as well. All are deeply traditional in their fighting styles. Cavalry still rules the battlefield, and spies still sneak into cities. None of them has taken any real steps to master aerina, although the various schools of swordcraft—including Crusaders, Broadblades, and Temple Knights—certainly fall under the aerina family of disciplines. But they stop there, ignorant of how chemina and machina can be applied to their swordcraft."

"Tell us about machina arcana," Fetzer said.

"Patience," Arasemis said. "First, let us speak of chemina, the second of the arcanae." Arasemis walked to the nearest hearth and took a glass flask from the mantel. He set it on the students' table, then retrieved a few bottles from his table. "Marlan, narrate as I work."

"Master Arasemis is pouring a tincture of miasma into the flask. Now he is adding bear fat and vole gems."

"Vole gems?" Fetzer scoffed.

"Just a nickname," Marlan said. "Also known as children's jewels. They are tiny crystals that grow under milkweed. Salt and sap are woven together among its root tendrils."

Arasemis picked up the flask, swirled it around, and tipped it carefully. A few drops fell to the table. Smoke arose as little holes burned in the wood.

"This solution is simply called wood acid," Marlan continued. "It eats through most woods, but the vapors are harmless and—"

"Stop there," Arasemis said. "Your hand, please, Fetzer." Fetzer refused to give it, so Arasemis turned to Rodel. "What about your hand?"

Rodel remembered the liquid Arasemis had used to burn through his shackles after he survived the river. He extended his hand slowly. Arasemis poured the contents of the flask into his hand. It fell through his fingers and splashed to the table, searing into the wood while leaving his hand unharmed. Rodel smiled as Fetzer pouted.

"And the solution will not harm the skin," Marlan said. "It is activated only by wood. Should you place your hand below the table to catch the drops, you'll be burned."

Arasemis nodded. "Very good, Marlan and Rodel. Fetzer, you are right to be cautious, and there is no shame in it. Chemina arcanae is often unforgiving of mistakes, and sometimes lethal. Had I substituted the tincture of miasma for wireworm juice, the solution would have eventually vaporized from the flask. Without a stopper in it we'd all asphyxiate.

"Rodel here gave his hand because he has seen the power of a similar solution called rust vex that defeated his chains without harming him. This works because the rust vex goes after even the tiniest specks of rust on and inside iron-bearing metals. We call such things tool alchemy, pioneered by the ancient Raffen natives. As you'll learn, there are many branches of chemina."

"So the natives of Pemonia were the only users of chemina?" Rodel asked.

"No, and don't confuse chemina with alchemy. Chemina is one of the three overarching arcanae. Alchemy is one of two divisions of chemina, the other being metallurgy. Each of the arcanae has two divisions like that. To answer your question, the ancient Almerics developed many branches of alchemy and metallurgy completely independent of the original Pemonians. For example, medicinal alchemy, candle alchemy, alloys, and beast lore. The Arukans were the most skilled at chemina among the Old World peoples."

"What branch of alchemy did I sample during the training?" Fetzer asked.

Arasemis looked at Marlan. "Explain it."

"A watered-down version of an ancient furywine recipe from the Hral natives," Marlan said. "According to the earliest Candlestone records, the original version was made with the blood of adders from the Black Forest, among other things. Hral warriors used furywine to achieve a battle frenzy that sometimes killed them. Half of the ingredients are still a mystery, so we supplement with risper nut oil in the laboratory beneath the great hall."

Arasemis nodded. "Good. Now that you've all seen some examples of chemina, you're ready to learn what it's really about. Consider the growth of plants. Does everything in a tree first exist in its original seed? Fetzer?"

"Of course not."

"Go on."

"It needs water . . ."

"Right. The seed draws what it needs from the soil, sunlight, and water. We cannot see the transfer of this material, only its result: the growth of a tree. And Rodel, what happens when the tree falls and dies?"

"It decays."

"And returns to the soil," Arasemis said, "its material dispersed and repurposed for the next tree or plant, and so on. It is the same for all living things—and the nonliving as well. Mountains reduce to sand, sand recalcifies and is pushed back up toward the sky by the quakes of the earth. We see these transformations, the breaking down and building up, as natural conversions.

"Similarly, the crafting of a powder that burns when touched by water, as the ancient Raffen did, seems unnatural—even wicked—to most. But that view reflects an ignorance that led alchemy to eventually be shunned. These things only seem unnatural to those who don't understand all of chemina as naturally as they do the mighty tree from the humble seed.

"Experimentation by generations of alchemists and metallurgists, sometimes including fatal trial and error, has revealed these hidden conversions that surround us in nature. Discoveries are always waiting to be made because the choice of ingredients and combinations of mixtures are limitless, bounded only by our curiosity and willingness to take risks. All of it can be harnessed for those with an open mind."

"You mentioned metallurgists," Rodel said. "Why are alloys considered chemina? Blacksmithing is an ancient art but hardly a secret."

Arasemis nodded. "Metallurgists mix metals to form alloys, just as an alchemist would mix powders or liquids. Again, metallurgy and alchemy comprise the two branches of chemina. As for blacksmithing, it is not considered pure chemina but rather a blend of chemina and aerina. You're right: anyone with a strong back and an eye for detail can learn blacksmithing. But when the original members of the

Order of the Candlestone defined and organized the schools of arcanae, they grouped and enhanced existing skills. Remember that the Order was formed by a diverse set of people from across the world. They found great utility in merging their diverse skills to combat the colonists."

"Wait a moment," Fetzer said. "The Order created the arcanae? I thought the skills were older . . ."

"It was almost eight hundred years ago . . ." Marlan said.

"So the founders of the Order merely trained each other and gave it a name like arcanae?" Fetzer asked. "It didn't help them prevent the colonization of Pemonia."

"Watch your tone, newcomer," Bertwil said.

Arasemis held up his hand to calm Bertwil, then visibly summoned his patience. "Fetzer, you've done well proving yourself at Gottfried's castle and in our training hall, but you are still a novice. The arcanae is both a system of learning and a body of knowledge unlike anything on earth. Although the founders of Candlestone did oppose the colonization of Pemonia, I don't think they believed they would stop it. A joining of the Old and New Worlds was prophesied before a restoration and ultimate peace could be attained. I don't think you're ready to understand all of that yet, but that is—"

"I'm not interested in prophesies and peace," Fetzer said. "I thought we were here to overthrow kings."

"We are," Arasemis sighed, "but killing kings is a means to an end. You know nothing about the prophecy, and you've merely scratched the surface of arcanae. Those skills are the bedrock of how Candlestone can succeed in not only overthrowing tyrants, but in restoring balance on earth."

Rodel could see that Fetzer was becoming more agitated. He put himself between him and Arasemis. "I can understand Fetzer's frustration. This is a lot of new information for us as newcomers." Rodel turned to Fetzer. "We'll do our best to grasp the master's teachings, recalling our oath to the Order."

Fetzer glared at him, but Arasemis was appreciative.

"You were explaining that blacksmithing was a blend of chemina and aerina," Rodel said.

Arasemis nodded. "Yes, the Almerians were masters at making alloys such as steel, but they did not fully exploit the wide range of materials and plants to give their metal weaponry unique properties. So they never mastered chemina. They were also masters of the swordcraft division of aerina, but they did not absorb native skills like running up trees and walls. So they never mastered aerina either.

"Thus, the bloodlines of the Almerics never advanced far into machina arcana. They learned the simple mechanics behind things like pendulums, rudders, and sails. And they built devices like windmills, cranes, crossbows, and ships. But they never touched the theoretical branches of machina."

"Like the moving floor in the training hall?" Fetzer asked.

"That floor is a mere toy compared to what should be possible within machina arcana," Arasemis corrected. "If any kingdom or people were able to master aerina and chemina, they could potentially go far into machina. Notice I did not say individuals, because the great workings of machina require much cooperation to be mastered. I believe this has been done before, to varying degrees, by the ancient Rahlampian natives and their Agnesci forebears. To the point, and all history aside, the Agnesci may have discovered the secrets of building ships of the air."

"Impossible," Rodel said.

"Not if you master all three arcanae. Chemina can create the lifting airs you'd need. And one of the best examples of machina was the Rahlampians' landships, capable of sailing across almost anything besides mountains. They invented them long before the Calbrians.

"I believe airships are possible, but hard evidence that they were ever built is lacking. Even Rildning, the knight who led the natives against the colonists, did not believe airships existed. But he lived in times of momentous change. Despite his role as the seed of Candlestone, he could not have known all the natives' secrets."

"Kings would bow to us if we built airships," Fetzer said.

"It is a distant goal, young Fetzer. I mastered aerina and chemina long ago but still have much to learn about machina despite many years of study and experimentation."

"What about the Calbrians?" Rodel asked. "Might they be close to lifting their wheeled landships into the sky?"

"The Calbrians have a knack for building things. Most have some Rahlampian blood in them. But their work is misguided and unbalanced because they've not mastered aerina and chemina first. So their ships will not fly. I aim to teach you the arcane in the proper order with the ultimate goal of combining them. Perhaps airships are one embodiment of this, but I suspect we'll discover many ways we can use the ancient, blended knowledge to affect the downfall of kings and restore the balance of creation."

All the students nodded solemnly, even Fetzer. Rodel caught Juhl's gaze. He gave her a small smile, but it was all still a bit opaque to him.

"You mentioned mixing alloys with plants," Fetzer said. "It that why Bertwil's sword flashed yellow when we attacked Gottfried?"

"Bertwil, tell him about your sword," Arasemis said.

"It's an alchemical process that treats the blade, as tempering toughens the steel. The yellow tint comes from chalice vine flower, which leaves an unseen, poisonous residue in wounds. A scratch can rot a limb, and a good cut is certain to kill."

"There are two other methods of imbuing weapons with such effects," Arasemis said. "Marlan, lead everyone to your sword. It's time we go to the laboratory anyway."

The group followed Marlan down to the chamber below the great hall. The laboratory reminded Rodel of the Master of Poisons building in Heingartmer, where the Wosmoks procured their poisons. He knew basic methods of dipping an arrow or knife into some foul mix, but he had never imagined a blade could permanently hold poisons.

Marlan brought them to the barrel in the corner of the room, wherein the sword was submerged in a solution. Fetzer reached out to touch the liquid.

"Careful! It's not water," Marlan said. "This acid of fysic and royal water will burn. It eats away the trace impurities in the steel and replaces them with components drawn from a sachet of stones that have are now dissolved in the barrel."

"What stones?" Rodel asked.

"Brassember, corbalt, sulfur, ardnamur, and napthar seed paste."

"What will happen to it?" Fetzer asked.

"The blade will flame when it strikes steel," Marlan said with pride.

Rodel nodded. "A clever treatment."

"It isn't a treatment like Bertwil's," Arasemis said. "What you see here is a combination of the other two metallurgical methods: alterlocum and glading. Glading is a method of folding in special materials when the alloy is first made. Alterlocum is what Marlan described with the removal of impurities and the dissolved stones. Glading and alterlocum are more painstaking than simple treatment, but rewarding when done right. Not as exquisite as a glyphblade, but still very good."

"What is a glyphblade?" Rodel asked.

"Never mind that now," Arasemis said. "We'll discuss that when—"

"I want a flaming sword," Fetzer interrupted.

Arasemis chuckled. "You have much to learn still."

Fetzer's eyes sharpened as Rodel quickly thought of another question. "What about your current sword, Marlan, the one you killed Maillard Valient with?"

"It is not an alchemical sword, but it is made of anchiclade. The purified ore permits a very thin, very long blade when paired with bog iron. It's an ancient method developed by the Rahlampians."

"Their swords could cut through colonial Brintilian steel, gode steel, even trees," Arasemis said. "They called them windrazors, though Marlan's is a shorter variant."

"How long will it take to master aerina arcana?" Fetzer asked.

"Depends on you, Fetzer," Arasemis said. "Thorendor will feed, clothe, and shelter you. Your mind and body will be free to read and train. Alongside the three arcanae, you'll also be required to study languages, navigation, politics, persuasion, and other things you'll need to infiltrate, blend in, subvert, and destroy. With the more advanced students beside you, perhaps you'll learn faster than you might otherwise."

"Then let's get on with it," Fetzer said.

"First, back to the library," Arasemis said. "Later, the training hall."

42

THEUDAMER

Heingartmer, Ward of Havelbern
Flowertide, 3034

"King Erech is in a precarious position," Meliamour said as she handed a letter to Theudamer. "You should read this yourself, Your Majesty."

Your Majesty,
My apologies for not writing sooner. Eglamour is a city transformed by King Erech's decrees known as the Proclamation of Expediency. His actions have spurred riots, killings, and various calamities the Donovards are ill-equipped to manage.

However, as your ambassador to these people, it is my pleasure to inform you of two developments of note. First, Lord Minister Gottfried of Leauvenna has become the third high lord to be assassinated. He and his wife were killed at their castle, which was torched by a fire said to be unquenchable.

Second, the defenses of Eglamour are significantly weakened. Despite calls for war by Duke Brugarn and General Chaultion, Erech's proclamation has effectively disbanded several army units, sending these former soldiers into the streets as beggars and thieves. They join common folk who lack enough to eat despite the season.

Should you ever order the march on Eglamour, laying siege to the city should not take long.

Separately, I regret to report that Wredegar and his Wosmoks have made no progress in determining who is behind the lord ministers' killings. Wredegar requests your permission to leave the capital to discern fact from rumor. Regarding the Wosmoks, the unit led by Etzel from Austveeden is overdue to arrive here. What's more, the only known survivor of Wredegar's unit, Rodel, is now missing. Thus, the Wosmoks of Donovan are effectively one man, Wredegar.

Regarding court politics, I plan to meet with the newly confirmed Lord Minister Valient of Delavon, son of the slain Maillard. He is young but ambitious and well respected. I intend to open communication with him to gauge his willingness as a potential partner. Perhaps his inexperience and position will make him ideal for your plans to replace Erech with someone more agreeable to our needs when that decision is made.

Lastly, the Donovards will sell Geras Vilarwef to the Austveedes unless we ransom him for double, meaning six hundred guldirs. Given the Austveedes will likely kill the man who has been our best rebel leader for some time, I advise we pay the ransom. The Donovards won't have long to enjoy the money in any case.

Your humble servant,
Ambassador Vesamune Theudamer
Eglamour

The emperor set down the letter and looked at his council. "I'm glad to hear about Erech's situation." He turned to Meliamour. "Though I cannot thank the Wosmoks for making it happen."

"My apologies," Meliamour said. "This is the first time that I'm aware we've lost two Wosmok units at once. I must offer my resignation and my seat at this council." She stood and bowed, then waited for him to dismiss her.

Theudamer let her wait a few moments before he spoke. "The Wosmoks have accomplished nothing of late, but neither have they created problems for me. Sit down, Meliamour. If I had wanted someone's head, it would have been Garentorf's, and he's already fish food in a river."

He watched as she retook her seat with dignity. He favored Meliamour and her sister Vesamune for their loyalty, competency, and dedication to the tasks he gave them. He stroked his graying beard. "What happened to Etzel's unit?"

"I fear they all must be dead, Your Majesty," Meliamour said. "Those in Austveeden confirmed their departure some time ago. And I sent a courier to our supporter in Fanedor, but the courier found the supporter dead. The area in Alpenon that Etzel would have traveled through is difficult. Lord Asteroth Avaleau is always prowling the borderlands. As for Wredegar's subordinate Rodel, I can offer no explanation of his missing status if Wredegar cannot."

"Write to Vesamune," Theudamer said. "Tell her to keep Wredegar in Eglamour. We'll assume Etzel was intercepted, so take your pick of men and women from the Army of Havelbern to build a new unit to send to Wredegar."

"But, Your Majesty," Graf interrupted," I'll need my best knights for the invasion of Donovan."

"You'll have plenty of knights. And while I appreciate all your preparations, we will not attack Donovan yet. Something is eating away at Erech's court from the inside and I want to let it continue for our benefit."

Herzol cleared his throat. "Perhaps this is a good time to deem my son's service in the Wosmoks fulfilled. Wredegar would welcome returning to his knighthood and you can appoint a fresh commander in Eglamour."

"Again, I must deny your request, old friend," Theudamer said. "Wredegar is still one of our best, and I need a commander who knows Donovan well. He will have plenty of time with the regular army later."

"Meliamour," the emperor continued, "I want Wosmoks ready in Donovan when I need them. Regardless of what is happening in Erech's court, his brothers on the borderlands are brutal and reckless, and I'll not stomach them much longer."

"Yes, Your Majesty."

Theudamer turned back to his favorite pacifist. "Herzol, what is your opinion of Lord Arthan Valient? Vesamune thinks he may be malleable."

"If Valient becomes as influential in Erech's court as his father was, negotiating with him could help avoid a war. If we can control him."

"I don't want to avoid a war!" Graf shouted. "I want to hasten it. We have every cause to attack them. We can't trust any Donovard lords no matter how much we may think they are our puppet."

"If war comes, our ambassador will no longer be welcome in Eglamour," Meliamour said. "Having one of their lords in our pocket would help us know what is happening, and maybe facilitate Vesamune's evacuation."

"You'll know what's happening there when I march my army into the city," Graf said.

"Meliamour, tell Vesamune to proceed with her talks with Valient," Theudamer said. "As long as Asteroth and Erath don't do anything foolish, she should have time to judge if he is someone we can deal with."

"Vesamune will be bedding the young Valient now, will she?" Graf said. "Perhaps old Chaultion has become too boring for her."

"No one asked your opinion," Meliamour said.

"I require your counsel on military matters only, Graf," Theudamer said, "not on the means the ambassador uses to gather information. The truth is I don't care about her liaisons. If Valient is a high lord we can control, then we'll use him however we can. If not, we'll look elsewhere."

"Why the intrigue, Your Majesty?" Graf asked. "If Donovan is to be ours, then let us take it by force and straightforwardly."

"Donovan is not some small territory," Theudamer said. "Even if without a competent king, the local lords will band together to fight us. If we want all of Donovan, we must prepare the way for your knights by offing some leaders and driving wedges between the rest."

"What do you want to do about Geras Vilarwef?" Meliamour asked. "I agree with Vesamune: we should pay his ransom."

Theudamer shook his head. "I grow weary of dealing with the House of Vilarwef . . . All we have done for them over the years, for generations!"

"They are still an excellent thorn in the side of Lord Asteroth," Graf said. "There is no better rebel leader than Geras. The Donovards were fools not to have executed him when they got their hands on him. They fear him, and what the rebels would do if he were killed."

"Or maybe their offer to ransom him shows how desperate they are for gold," Herzol said. "Erech's treasury has long been dry."

"Desperate, yes, but not foolish," Meliamour said. "The Donovards know that if they kill Geras, the rebellion that simmers now will erupt in their faces. It's clever of them to sell Geras to the Austveedes, to let them kill him. I say buy him back."

"I agree," Herzol said. "If we must have a war, it would be best to have him lead Durgensdil. No one can lead them better, except Gothal, of course."

"So you're all united against me on this," Theudamer said. "The Vilarwefs are as much a thorn in my side as the Donovards. Unlike all of you, I think the rebels' claim to join our empire is an illusion meant to secure our assistance against the Donovards."

"It's a difficult problem," Meliamour said. "The mostly mountain folk of the Durgens have been independent minded since its founding as a Brintilian colony. But they are ethnic Rugens, so it's natural for them to look to us for protection. It's only a matter of time before Asteroth attacks them again."

"So be it," Theudamer said. "But I want their Port of Orringholm and half their tin mines. And a portion of their yew forests to increase our stocks of bows. And I want them to give up their pitiful Congregantism. All of that, as payment for ransoming Geras and renewing our protection of them."

"They will never give up their religion, Your Majesty," Herzol said, "nor should they be made to, in my opinion."

"As head of the House of Vilarwef, Gothal and his brother Geras are powerful symbols of resistance to the people of Durgensdil," Meliamour said. "If we buy Geras and keep him in Rugenhav with Gothal for a while, we can send him back into Donovan later when the time is right. But if we place too many demands on him, he'll sit back and watch us fight the war for him."

"If you think Geras is worth six hundred guldirs, then I want more from the Vilarwefs in return," Theudamer said.

"It's payment for all of Durgensdil in the end," Graf said.

"They might be persuaded to open their mines and yew forests for a war effort," Meliamour said, "if we time it right. And I do think Geras is worth the investment. Gothal is frail, and he has been a king in exile for too long. When Geras becomes king of the Durgens, his people will follow him."

"As long as he follows us," Theudamer said. "Graf, as warden of Havelbern, you shall personally take the ransom money and meet the dirty Donovards at the border to take custody of Geras. Then bring him here to me."

"Of course, Your Majesty."

43

ARTHAN

Eglamour Palace, Toulon Ministry
Flowertide, 3034

"Serdot, this better not be a jest. The Lord Ministers' Council is mere hours away."

"You know I never jest about such matters, my lord. I'm certain Garion is an assassin. You'll need no further proof than this small letter, clumsily left by him in a closet in his quarters down in the Crownblades' barracks." Serdot handed Arthan the paper.

> Garion,
> You have done well. Your next task, which I relay
> from your master, is Brugarn on the last day of
> Flowertide.
>
> E

"Could anyone have planted this note?" Arthan asked, handing the note to Bardil to read.

"I also found this among Garion's personal effects." Serdot revealed a wooden mask. "As you can see, it is identical to the one I took from Marlan in Mordmerg."

"My God . . ." Bardil mumbled.

"What day is it?" Arthan asked.

"There are five days remaining in Flowertide. If you wish, we can expose Garion and save Brugarn. But you shouldn't expect much in return from Brugarn. It may even give him cause to suspect you, more than he may already. Alternatively, you can let Brugarn die."

"Let him die then," Bardil said.

"No, we must expose this assassin," Arthan said. "Brugarn is still a member of the royal family who—"

"—wouldn't save your life if given the same choice," Serdot said.

"I'm of the House of Valient, not a wicked slug like Brugarn. We'll expose Garion at the council."

Serdot nodded. "Best to do it in front of the king and his whole court, ensuring your enhanced reputation among the most people. I will make sure Sir Hamelin brings Garion to court."

"Who is behind all of this, Serdot? Who is this E person, and who is their common master?"

"We will press Garion to tell us."

"What will this do to Hamelin? Garion is one of his men, after all."

"He may lose command of the Crownblades. Also, Hamelin could be part of this."

"I didn't consider that . . ."

"Even if Hamelin isn't part of the plot, Brugarn could make this very ugly."

"Find out all you can, Serdot, while I'm at the council. It is imperative."

⌘

Arthan walked into the assembly chamber used by the lord ministers for councils. His head was a bit light, and his heart raced. Aside from it being his first Lord Ministers Council, he had never been in possession of information that determined the life and death of a royal. He was unused to this world of shadows and secrets. But the knowledge that Brugarn's life was in his hands gave him a calm confidence.

"You look as if you've stumbled into the wrong place," Reimvick said as Arthan took his seat beside him. "Is everything all right?"

"Yes, I just . . . I'm learning much about the court."

"Oh, do share," Reimvick whispered, his eyes widening at the prospect of juicy rumor.

"I'm afraid not at this time," Arthan said. "But soon, my friend."

"Most mysterious . . . Am I in any danger, Arthan?"

"You'd be the first to know if that were the case."

"If it's Brugarn who wishes to see me killed next, then your news is old indeed." Reimvick smiled. "If he had his way, this council would not exist."

"I cannot say more," Arthan said. "The council has many important matters to discuss."

"Yes, but whatever is troubling you seems more important."

Arthan turned to watch the others take their seats at the meeting table. The knowledge that an assassin was waiting in the palace was difficult to sequester in his mind. Reimvick's gentle prodding did not make it any easier. Arthan wondered if any of the other lords knew what he knew, or were part of the conspiracy.

He looked around. Sigbert had arrived from Barres Ministry. Duke Henrey of Elmbrel, who had married Erech's eldest daughter, Avalane, was also present. Duchess Voufon, the queen's sister, was lord ministeress of Laume and also ruled the Donovard side of Nore Island. Another woman, Eperude, was lord ministeress of Lundwynland. Dukes Asteroth and Erath were absent as Serdot had predicted, as was Ferin of Hanovel. Couriers relayed his preoccupation with Donovan's claims to the Almerian-occupied islands. The chair for the Lord Minister of Leauvenna was still vacant, Gottfried's successor still undetermined.

Then there was Duke Brugarn. The Lord Minister of Toulon arrived last, entering the chamber as if he were already king. Arthan could not help but picture a bloody corpse as he watched Brugarn make his opening statement to the council.

"And since it is the first meeting since the assassinations, I want everyone to endorse my plan to replace you if you're killed. Given the speed with which these killers strike, we need to have lord ministers ready to succeed you when . . ."

Arthan realized his knowledge of Brugarn's potential fate gave him more patience to listen to his bluster. Still, the more Brugarn talked the more Arthan was tempted to keep the warning about Garion to himself. But he remembered Maillard and knew what he would have done with the information.

"Preposterous!" Sigbert shouted at the duke. "You've no right to upend centuries of tradition. My heirs take my lands and title, subject to the confirmation of the king. Not the Lord of Toulon!"

"Desperate times, Sigbert . . ." Brugarn said with a sly grin. "And the king is less able to manage all the affairs of the kingdom. We must preserve Erech's strength for the important . . ."

Arthan noticed that the longer Brugarn talked, the more the other lord ministers turned to watch his own reaction. It was a few moments before Arthan recalled Waldemar's words, that Maillard had been the elder minister. Arthan realized the others were accustomed to having Maillard open and adjudicate the council, as he had for the Empire Alliance.

Arthan took a deep breath and stood from his chair. Brugarn stopped talking, shocked to be interrupted in such a way.

"My lords, it is my honor to sit among you as a recently confirmed heir to a lord ministership. My father was taken far too soon from us, but I'm proud to fill his chair. Maillard's broad shoulders carried more burdens than I can know, but I will do my best to serve as he did, for the good of all Donovan." He retook his seat.

"Welcome, son of Maillard," Duchess Voufon said with a small clap.

Reimvick patted his back and the others nodded their approval. All except Brugarn.

"Time will tell whether you have your father's fool wits or half wits," Brugarn said.

Arthan ignored the comment, tactfully acting as though he was adjusting his chair and had not heard him.

"Perhaps we should discuss the Empire Alliance," Henrey said. "I believe we are well positioned to benefit from trade no longer dominated by Almerian shipping."

"Good riddance to it," Brugarn said. "The attempt to preserve the alliance was a fool's errand," he added, glancing at Arthan, "and its demise, a heavenly blessing."

"The absence of Lord Ferin speaks to the complexities of the aftermath," Sigbert said. "The Calbrians are threatening to invade the islands in the Strait of Delnollen. If they take them from the Almerians, the Calbrians will control all trade in the Calbrian Sea."

Arthan knew this problem directly affected his own ports, but he kept his silence. It was a much bigger problem for lords with coastlines far longer than Delavon's.

"I think we can all agree to recommend to the king that a naval force should be sent to help Lord Ferin," Reimvick said. "He faces the prospect of simultaneously fighting the Almerians and the Calbrians for islands that are rightfully part of Donovan, with fewer ships and sailors than is required for the task."

"Any opposed?" Henrey asked. "If not, I will broach it with the king."

"No you won't," Brugarn said. "I will discuss it with him. Now, the threats on our land borders. My brothers in the south say the Rugens regularly probe our defenses. What's more, the rebels in Alpenon are becoming more aggressive. Aside from Calbria's island grabbing, the Rugens appear to be the greater threat. Any opposed to the armies of Donovan marching to Heingartmer to put an end to all of this?"

"You're mad," Voufon said.

"Start a war with the Rugens?" Eperude asked.

Everyone voiced their concerns at once, and few spared harsh words for Brugarn. Reimvick leaned over to whisper to Arthan.

"This idea must have been planted by that warmongering Chaultion."

Arthan opened his mouth to respond, but Brugarn erupted, pounding on the table.

"How many of you are agents of the Rugen emperor, then? How can the king's own council attempt to deny him his holy right to defend our kingdom from these aggressors?"

"The king is my father-in-law," Henrey said. "I'm certain he does not want war. Nor should we."

"We wouldn't gain anything from attacking them," Eperude said.

"The Rugens are trying to provoke us, that much is true," Voufon said. "But that is their way. It has always been their way. They are driven by fear. Even in our condition, the Rugens know they would attack us at great cost."

"What condition is that?" Brugarn asked.

"You know exactly what I mean," Voufon said, wagging a finger like a grandmother. "You attempt to steal this council's influence at every turn, as you do the king's. You deny him—and us—the ability to solve the many problems plaguing Donovan. To say nothing of your abuse of the treasury and the—"

"Hold your asp tongue!" Brugarn shouted. "Is it a crime for a king to depend on his own blood kin for advice? But sowing divisions in the king's court, now that is a treasonous—"

"Am I not also the king's kin?" Henrey asked.

"And I the queen's?" Voufon asked.

"*Blood* kin," Brugarn said. "And the sister of a drug-drunk queen is no sound counsel. Silence, all of you! I will discuss this Rugen matter further with the king and his generals."

"And who keeps up the queen's steady supply of popaver, Brugarn?" Henrey asked.

Lord Sigbert slowly rose from his chair. The big man paused until he had Brugarn's attention, then smashed his goblet onto the table, spattering wine across it like blood.

"Storm clouds circle above and wolves below," he said. "The king's mind rots, his counselors bicker, and riots sweep our cities and countryside. Will you not put aside your greed this one time? I stand for our common good."

Arthan shot up from his chair. "I stand with you, Lord Sigbert. We must unify in the face of many challenges."

Reimvick stood beside him, then Eperude. As Brugarn glared at Henrey and Voufon, Arthan realized that most of these rivals were the king's relatives. The rest were houses of longstanding vassals who had survived successive Avaleau rulers.

Sigbert walked toward the door. "Then, like my neighbor Ferin in the north, I have better things to attend to. When this council is ready to act, then perhaps I'll return to Eglamour."

"He's making a mistake," Reimvick whispered to Arthan. "He's as hot tempered as Brugarn. Leaving is easy, even gratifying. But staying to make a difference, hard as it may be, should be our path."

Arthan knew he was right. Maillard would never have abandoned a lords' council. But Sigbert was gone. The lords looked at each other.

"Shall we discuss the proclamation?" Arthan asked.

"What is there to discuss?" Brugarn said, clearly happy with Sigbert's departure.

"Though I'm the most junior vassal among you, I'm aware that kings traditionally consult with this council prior to issuing proclamations."

"The king consulted with me," Brugarn said.

"You are not the council," Voufon said.

"You broke with tradition," Henrey said.

"None of you were here, and the need was urgent," Brugarn said. "Must I wait until assassins have killed a few more of you, or me, before taking action?"

"The proposed taxes are excessive," Voufon said. "The cuts to the soldiery are unnecessary. And the ransoming of top Durgensdil rebels to replace money you wasted is beyond unwise. Your skull is empty."

"Careful, Voufon, you and your soldiers are with Toulon on the Rugen front," Brugarn said. "And someone will need to absorb the initial blows. Anyway, they are not proposals. They are now the law of the land. Ignore the king at your own peril."

"You're ignoring the riots across Toulon at your peril," Eperude said. "Your proclamation also seems timed to give you new powers. This Marshal of Inquiry title will be yours, no?"

"And the proclamation also provoked Rugenhav," Henrey said. "You can't simply order our enemies off the islands and away from the borderlands. They'll see it as a threat."

"It is a threat, you mumbling fool," Brugarn said. "We must protect what is ours. As for the new marshal, the king has yet to choose a worthy servant for what will undoubtedly be a burdensome and difficult role, but if asked, I would gladly serve."

"This is not the way of wise kings," Reimvick said.

"Then we should be glad the royal blood of the Reimvicks died out ages ago," Brugarn said. "In fact, perhaps it's not in the best interests of the Crown to have has-beens so close to the throne." Arthan caught Brugarn's glance, but he did not take the bait.

"There is no shame in my house," Reimvick said. "My forefathers ruled the Kingdom of Gidemond well during its short existence. In fact, it was our peaceful diplomacy that made the unification of Donovan possible. But I wouldn't expect you to know such history."

Brugarn's face burned red, but Reimvick continued.

"Now, unless your objective is to see additional lord ministers leave this council, which is permitted by tradition, I suggest you stop hoarding the king's decisions. As they are your war plans, I think you have the wits to reconsider. Toulon is large and wealthy, at least it used to be. But remember that you'll need help from our ministries to defend Toulon after you and Chaultion wreck the peace."

Arthan looked at Reimvick, impressed. Everyone clapped while Brugarn stared a hole through Reimvick. Again Arthan found himself reconsidering warning Brugarn. He was having difficulty seeing the harm it would bring. The duke was divisive and dangerous.

"Let us adjourn this council and consider what has been discussed," Voufon said.

"I second that," Henrey said.

"As do I," Reimvick said, turning away from Brugarn's silent stare.

"My lords, I request your presence tonight at court," Arthan said as everyone rose. "I have an important announcement that will be of interest to all of you."

"Who do you think you are?" Brugarn said. "You should be back in Rachard riding ponies and learning a wooden sword."

Arthan set his jaw but remained calm. "I am the Lord Minister of Delavon, Count of Bram, and head of the House of Valient. I will respect your position and expect the same from you. When I speak tonight, you'll welcome the news more than anyone."

Arthan realized his mistake as soon as the words left his mouth. He quickly turned toward the door, but Brugarn lurched for his arm.

"The only thing I care to hear is when a whelp like you decides to return home. You do not know with whom you're dealing."

"I look forward to your apology," Arthan said.

Brugarn laughed in his face. Reimvick firmly removed Arthan's arm from Brugarn's grasp, then took Arthan by the shoulder and led him to the corridor.

"You shouldn't have provoked him," Reimvick said when they were alone.

"That was not my intention."

"Whatever you intend to announce tonight is unlikely to impress Brugarn."

"Yes, of course . . ." Arthan silently cursed himself for his indiscretion. He wanted all the lord ministers to be present at court, but he regretted singling Brugarn out.

Reimvick drew Arthan closer. "You know me as an addicted collector of rumor and news, young Arthan. I can smell a juicy secret. You can share it with your father's old friend."

"I'm afraid you'll have to wait until court."

"Very well, I respect that. If it's something that will make Brugarn squirm, it's worth waiting for."

44

FETZER

Thorendor Castle, Wallevet Ministry
Flowertide, 3034

Fetzer dipped the quill again, pausing to look at the flicker of the candle. It made him think of burning his uncle's house down. He wondered how long his uncle suffered before dying, and hoped it wasn't too short.

. . . while our training continues at a rapid pace. I think I've convinced the old master that I'm best suited for this work. More than his other apprentices.

Wall running is not as difficult as I first thought. It boils down to momentum, balance, and careful footing. And we were given grass-stuffed moccasins that mute our footfalls and make gripping the wall easier. Marlan also helped teach us how to throw tiny knives while running up a wall and how to grasp ledges to rest.

After a week or so of constant training and laborious reading, Arasemis finally let us try some alchemy. We learned how to prepare some basic powders and feed them into drained eggs, just as the Naren-Dra did long ago. We also made Gallerlander stone knives treated with a solution that causes the onset of sleep. But still nothing about making my own flaming sword.

I've hid the fact that I speak fluent Rugen thanks to all those lessons from the Sember family tutor when I was a child. Arasemis let us choose a language to study. Choosing Rugen means I finish my studies early, giving me more time in the training hall with Arasemis and Marlan, both of whom speak multiple languages.

I'm sure I'm not fooling Rodel. He's tried to coax more Rugen out of me, but I pretend not to understand him. It irks me that Arasemis brought him here just before my own arrival. The more students he brings in, the less time the old master will have to focus on teaching me.

It's my hope that we'll be given another task soon. If Arasemis will not send me to Eglamour, then perhaps to the castle of a different lord minister. I very much want to put my new techniques to the test.

I also hope it's not too long before we kill a king—any king. I'm beginning to wonder if Arasemis enjoys all the lore and history of Candlestone more than keeping the flame alive with the blood of tyrants, as it has been kept alive through the centuries.

I'm also suspicious of the master's desire to replace kings with elected chieftains. What did elected chiefs do for the ancient tribes? They didn't stop the Brintilians from conquering and colonizing Pemonia. They didn't do anything.

Nobles and kings should be overthrown, and nothing allowed to replace them. Their divine right, as they call it, is a sham, a clever ordering of men devised by an unjust god to divide people for his own amusement . . .

45

MILISEND

Eglamour Palace, Toulon Ministry
Flowertide, 3034

"What about Lord Valient?" Regaume asked. "He's one of the wealthiest. I heard he gave ten chests of gold to the king as tribute."

"He gave three chests," Milisend said. "But, no, I don't want to steal from him. Especially not while he's here at the palace."

"Why not?"

"He lost his father, Regaume."

"Well, it should be one of the lord ministers while they're all here. It's simply too good of an opportunity to waste."

"I'm glad you're back," Milisend said, "but you need to recognize how difficult the situation is for everyone here. Things have gone badly for Father and the kingdom as a whole."

"Kings and houses come and go, Mili. It's not my concern, and it shouldn't be yours."

"I'm a princess, Regaume."

"Not in your heart. You could be a master thief much earlier than most, if you'd only follow that path. Bagging the lord ministers' valuables while they're clustered in the capital will get you there."

"Half of them are my relatives. You know I don't want to steal from them."

"What about Lord Reimvick? He's wealthy and childless. His money will be used to build a cathedral or some other useless thing when he dies. Stealing from him is a gift to others, really."

"Why must my next target be a lord minister?"

"I told you. They are the wealthiest and most powerful nobles of the kingdom. I'm the only thief among my circles to have stolen from a lord minister. This would be an accomplishment for you that would win respect among the thief bands."

"I've stolen from people in the palace before," she said, "but things are difficult now. If I was caught, with everything that is happening, it would embarrass Father at the worst time for him."

"You won't be caught, Thimblegloves. You're one of the best thieves I know. So, what is your decision?"

Milisend sighed. "Lord Reimvick it is . . ." She hugged Regaume close and noticed a slight distraction. "What's wrong?"

"I must travel again."

"What? You just came back. Then you task me to rob a lord minister and leave again?"

"One of my men was caught on the road to Ralmogard with loot from his heist. He's in a prison there awaiting execution."

"Your band of men can't go without you for once?" She tightened her arms around him.

"I'm the head thief, Mili. Freeing him should not be difficult, but I'm the only one who will risk it."

"What about us? Me and you?"

"Of course, Mili. But you're not facing death. He needs my help."

"So I'm to sack Reimvick's chambers alone?"

Regaume nodded. "You'll do perfectly well. Thimblegloves is ready for this. And I promise, when I return, that I'll let you run away with me, once and for all."

Milisend smiled and tapped her finger on his cleft chin. "Oh, did I ask for that?"

"Your heart desires it, even if your lips will not voice it."

"My heart is yours all the same," she said. "Go to Ralmogard, but don't be long."

46

ARTHAN

Eglamour Palace, Toulon Ministry
Flowertide, 3034

"My king, there is another subject I wish to discuss," Tronchet said. "The Benrollen Company was recently the target of an attempted burglary. I believe she may have been—"

"You are bringing this insignificant matter to the king again?" Brugarn said.

"She's unable to control herself, my lord. If His Majesty would simply—"

"That will be all, Tronchet," Erech said with a wave of his hand.

Arthan watched impatiently as Tronchet stumbled through his excuses. "What is this the chief magistrate is always pestering the king about?" Arthan whispered to Serdot.

"From what I gather, Tronchet believes the king's middle daughter, Milisend, is repeatedly involved in jewel thefts."

"The princess is a thief?" Bardil asked.

"Quiet," Arthan whispered.

"Get out!" Brugarn shouted, raising his hand to strike Tronchet.

The magistrate kept his composure and rejoined the crowd of courtiers. Arthan watched impatiently as the king looked toward Waldemar the steward for the next petitioner.

244

"Your Majesty, next is the Lord Minister of Delavon," Waldemar announced. "He wishes to address you and the court on an important matter of security."

Erech's expression was dull, but he nodded his acceptance.

"Security?" Brugarn's face wrinkled. "Whose security?"

"Yours," Arthan said, taking the floor. He turned, looking at all the courtiers to catch any reaction among them. Then he settled his gaze on the king. "Your Majesty, I have reason to believe an assassin hides among us."

The court collectively gasped and murmured. Erech squinted, his interest finally piqued. Brugarn also listened intently, as did Sir Hamelin. Arthan noticed that the Crownblades commander stood close to one of his guardsmen, presumably the one Serdot had arranged to be present. Arthan was careful not to meet this guard's eyes, for fear of spooking Garion too quickly, if it was him.

"Speak what you know," Erech said.

"Your Majesty, as one who has suffered firsthand the pain inflicted by the recent assassinations, I've been most attentive to any information that might hint at the identities of the assassins—including within this court. It is my honor and duty to reveal this . . ."

Arthan pulled Garion's mask from his cloak and held it up high to more gasps and whispering. "This, lords and ladies, was found here in the palace. This wicked tool of concealment is identical to one taken from the face of my father's killer before he escaped.

"And this," he continued, holding up the small parchment, "is a letter ordering a named Crownblade knight to assassinate Duke Brugarn before the turn of Flowertide." Arthan paused for effect, glancing at Hamelin, who was in shock. Then Arthan focused on the guard at Hamelin's side. The man's eyes were wide as eggs, shifting left and right, his mouth agape.

"This letter and the mask were found in the Crownblades' barracks among the belongings of a guard named Garion . . ." Arthan stepped toward the guard, who had now fixed on him burning eyes. "This letter was addressed to him, the assassin among us. Tasked by his mysterious master to kill the king's brother. Arrest him!"

Sir Hamelin snatched Garion's arm. "Crownblades, to me!" he said. "Protect the king!"

The court erupted as Garion punched Hamelin and wrenched away. Brugarn repeated the order to arrest Garion. But Hamelin needed no orders. The Crownblade captain drew his sword and rushed after him.

"No! He must tell what he knows!" Arthan yelled. He stayed near the throne, clutching the mask and letter.

As Hamelin and the others closed in on Garion, he pulled something from his tunic and glared at Arthan. The sound of breaking glass preceded a sparkling gray cloud that billowed around the struggling knot of Crownblades. Nearby courtiers screamed as the cloud swelled and they pushed at each other to escape the alchemical smoke.

Garion rose above the fray by running up the wall, then paused with one hand grasping a ledge. With the other he threw a tiny glinting object at Arthan. Arthan turned away and crouched to the floor. Pain seared up the side of his face. He felt blood pulse between his fingers as he held his jaw but stood to draw his sword even so.

Garion was running to the high windows. Arthan was astonished at the feat despite having seen Marlan do the same in the Mordmerg Council House. Other courtiers were frozen or clamored to escape the hall. The king and Brugarn, now protected by Crownblades and lord ministers, also watched Garion skitter like an insect.

Arthan was certain he was going to escape. But Hamelin's crossbowmen worked quicker than Garion's attempt to break through the leadlight window. He lost his balance when crossbow bolts shot into his leg and grazed his neck. He fell onto the guards below him, and they dragged him shouting and kicking before the king and his brother.

"Who sent you?" Brugarn said.

"The ancient flame," Garion said, proud defiance bright in his eyes. The Crownblades twisted his arms.

"Your death can be quick or slow," Brugarn said, drawing his sword.

"I would have made yours slow," Garion said, "but you wouldn't have lasted."

Brugarn stepped forward and raised his sword high.

"Stop!" Erech shouted. He stood from the throne and peered down at Garion, waving Brugarn aside. "You were a Crownblade, Garion. Why have you done this?"

Hamelin cringed at the king's words. Garion licked his bloodied lips and glared through winces. "Because the reign of tyrants is over."

"We'll get everything out of him," Hamelin told the king. "I assure you. I'll personally—"

"No you won't," Brugarn said. "You have more to answer for. Garion will answer to me alone."

Hamelin blinked through his shame and silent rage, his whole body quivering. Erech stepped in. "Neither of you will question him." The king turned to Arthan. "You will."

"Your Majesty?" Arthan felt the blood seep between his fingers as he spoke.

"You discovered him," the king said. "As my new Marshal of Inquiry, you'll get the rest of it out of him."

Brugarn steamed. "Erech, you cannot name him marshal."

"Silence, Brugarn!"

The duke hushed up, stunned, like everyone else, at the king's sudden return to command. Erech's eyes were bright again, as when Arthan had returned the sword Rhunegeld to him the day prior.

"As my new chief lawkeeper, you are responsible for unraveling this conspiracy," Erech said. "No more lord ministers shall be lost, and no more corrupted Crownblades. Find them out, Lord Valient. By my order, every person and resource of my kingdom is at your disposal."

Arthan bowed low. "Humbly, Your Majesty. I will find them."

∾

"Not too deep, despite the blood . . ." Arthan held still as the king's physician finished the stiches in his cheek. "There, all done. You'll want to talk a bit less over the next few days, I'll wager."

"I have my duties, Doctor," Arthan replied with a wince.

"And you'll have a handsome scar when it's done," Serdot said. He walked into the physician's chamber and handed Arthan a small object.

"A stone . . . tooth?" Arthan asked, inspecting the object in his palm.

"Look at the edge. A tiny throwing blade made of flint. I found it on the court floor. If you hadn't turned, Garion would have buried it in your throat."

"How did he throw such a tiny thing with such force from the wall?"

"And how did he run up it, like Marlan in Mordmerg?" Serdot asked.

"Quite impossible," the physician said. "You've all had too much wine at court."

Arthan looked at Serdot as the physician affixed a bandage over his stitches. Then Arthan thanked him and joined Serdot in walking down the corridor.

"I've taken the liberty of arranging for Garion to be chained up in the cellar at Clonmel, my lord."

"Why at my residence?" Arthan asked, wincing as he touched the bandage.

"To keep Brugarn from meddling and to keep Garion secure, in case he's not alone here. Additionally, Waldemar told me the king has assigned twenty soldiers to Clonmel, and more are available for the Office of the Marshal of Inquiry, should you need them. Clonmel is no longer merely your residence."

"This is all happening so quickly, Serdot. I'm a new lord minister and far from knowing how to be the king's chief lawkeeper."

"Tronchet will still handle most things as chief magistrate of the capital," Serdot said. "And as a lord minister you are already the top lawkeeper in Delavon. Now your lawkeeping powers are expanded over the whole kingdom in terms of hunting down the assassins."

"I'll have to consider that responsibility in detail . . ."

"That's why you have me, my lord. And we have Garion."

"Has Brugarn finally accepted this?"

"He's still steaming, trying to change Erech's mind at every opportunity. But Waldemar assured me it's final. The steward said the king has not appeared so resolute in years."

"That is a change," Arthan said. He pulled out the Naren-Dra mask again and turned it in his hands. "Who are these people, Serdot? What 'ancient flame' drives them?"

"Let us ask Garion."

47

RODEL

Thorendor Castle, Wallevet Ministry
Flowertide, 3034

Rodel peered through the narrow slits in his Naren-Dra mask, watching the other students ready themselves. He tried to breathe normally, remembering what Arasemis had taught them about the small fronds of gill ferns that lined the inside of the mask to convert the "fixed air" that he exhaled into fresh "common air." It was also difficult to see with the mask on at first, but Arasemis's techniques of anticipating an opponent and outmatching his speed and economy of motion made seeing everything less important.

Arasemis and Marlan stood at the far end of the training hall, the floor of which was raised. From there, the floor gradually stepped downward so that the whole room was a stepped slope. The master and veteran occupied the top, while Rodel and Juhl were paired up at the bottom. Fetzer and Bertwil formed a second team beside them.

"The first student to reach the top of the slope wins," Arasemis said. "Use any means to prevent the opposing team from reaching the top. And if Marlan's shroud eggs hit you twice you are done. Do not fear the eggs, however, as they are merely filled with powdered dyes, no alchemical ingredients."

Rodel gripped his quarterstaff and adjusted his leather padding. They had not been told about the eggs until now, which made him nervous. Like Fetzer and his temporary blindness, all the pupils had been made to sample many

250

different mixtures and solutions over the past few days so they could better understand the effects. Despite Arasemis's assurance that Marlan's eggs were inert, Rodel did not completely trust him. He did not look forward to more vomiting, brief blindness, or temporary paralysis.

"Begin!" Arasemis shouted.

Bertwil charged up the stepped slope with Fetzer close behind him. Rodel and Juhl sprinted up together. Bertwil reached out with his long arm and whacked the back of Rodel's legs with his quarterstaff, sending Rodel down. Juhl came to his defense, parrying Bertwil's next blow as Rodel regained his feet. Fetzer sprinted ahead of everyone.

"Run, Juhl!" Rodel cried.

She gave Bertwil a last jab and followed Fetzer up. Rodel saw a puff of yellow burst on his own chest. He instinctively pressed his eyes shut and held his breath until he remembered the mask that protected him. He cursed himself for being too concerned about Fetzer's run up the slope and not watching Marlan.

Juhl paused to pull Rodel by the arm, dodging an egg as she jerked him forward. Rodel made good progress again until he felt a blow to his back. Bertwil had thrown his quarterstaff. When Rodel recovered and focused again, Fetzer was far ahead. He picked up Bertwil's quarterstaff.

"The wall!" Rodel shouted to Juhl through the mask. Together they bounded between the slope and the wall. Juhl gained speed quickly.

A green cloud burst on Juhl just ahead of him. She moved faster, and he tried to do the same. When he stole a glance toward the top he saw a red cloud burst on Fetzer as he was looking back at them. Fetzer lost his balance and fell backward. Rodel aimed Bertwil's quarterstaff at him when he stood, sending him rolling down the slope a second time.

By now Juhl had reached Fetzer and engaged him until Rodel caught up. The three fought and bounded up the slope while watching for Marlan's black eggs. Then Marlan changed tactics, bursting the eggs on the slope ahead of them to obscure their paths.

Bertwil shouted behind them. The big man was forced out of the race when the back half of the slope fell away and flattened on the main floor. Rodel narrowly dodged an egg. He rushed to catch up with Juhl and Fetzer, who were still fighting and making slow progress.

Rodel engaged Fetzer and shoved Juhl forward. Fetzer grabbed Rodel's arm and slung him toward the wall. Rodel kicked his feet up and backflipped, knocking Fetzer off balance. In the same instant an egg burst on Juhl, her second, and a row of tiles fell away from the back end of the slope. The raised floor was now rhythmically falling away behind them.

Disoriented from the smoke and surprised by Fetzer's fresh attack, Juhl teetered at the edge of the slope. Rodel threw his quarterstaff at Fetzer with little effect, and then ran to Juhl. He caught her by the hand as the tiles she stood on dropped away from her feet.

Bertwil positioned himself below to catch her. She would probably be fine, Rodel told himself, but they were a team. He pulled frantically, knowing his tiles would soon fall away, too. As he hefted her up an egg burst on the back of his head, enveloping him in a purple cloud. They rode the column down to the floor, where Bertwil waited.

Rodel stood with Juhl as Fetzer cheered from above. The entire remaining slope lowered with him and Arasemis and Marlan riding it down. The master approached the vanquished students.

"Don't remove your masks yet," he said. He walked to the wall cabinet and pulled on a steel ring, opening the windows in the dome high above. The dustiness of the eggs that hung in the air started to clear. Arasemis ushered them into the adjacent armory, where they took off their equipment.

"Once again," Fetzer said with a smirk, "victory for me. Master, you need more students to give me more of a challenge."

Everyone ignored him, having become accustomed to his constant boasting.

"What did you do wrong, Rodel?" Arasemis asked.

Rodel frowned. "I wasn't quick enough?"

"You are quick enough. But you were distracted by Juhl's problems."

"She would have fallen."

"It is better to complete the task than to save others at the expense of the task," Arasemis said.

"But if I hadn't helped her, our team wouldn't have made it to the top."

"I said the first student to make the top of the slope would win, not the first team. You were a team for defensive purposes only. But only one of you had to complete the task. This is the way it works for real tasks."

Rodel considered the lesson. It contradicted what he had learned as a Wosmok and what he had read in the library. "But the books about Rildning . . . he had been rescued, even while his friends were besieged and on the verge of falling to the enemy. If they hadn't saved Rildning, there would be no Candlestone."

"Rildning was extraordinary," Arasemis said. "The rest of us must be willing to sacrifice anything to complete our task. Certainly our lives, if necessary, but also the lives of others—including allies and innocents."

Rodel nodded obediently, but he disagreed. No Wosmok was ever left behind, dead or alive, if at all possible.

Arasemis turned to the other students. "It's a lesson for all of you. The task is everything. That is all the training for today. Return to your studies."

"Thank you," Juhl said when the master departed.

Rodel simply nodded again.

"I would have caught her," Bertwil said.

"Makes no difference," Fetzer said. "I would have won even if Rodel had let her drop."

"So sure of yourself," Juhl said.

"You should be sure of me, too," Fetzer said. "This Rugen belongs in a prison somewhere, not here with you and me and the rest."

"You were a nobleman's son, weren't you?" Rodel asked. "Your arrogance gives away your ignorance."

"My blood will not prevent me from spilling more of the same when we are assigned tasks again," Fetzer said. "And I won't need anyone to save me."

Marlan stepped forward. "None of us doubt your skill, Fetzer. But all of us are in this together. Born for it. Rodel is as much a part of Candlestone as any of us. Helping each other is important and only put aside if completion of a task is in jeopardy. Otherwise we are united to the end."

"Maybe you're right," Fetzer said as he strolled to the door. "United in purpose, even if unbalanced in ability . . . But I got it right in Leauvenna without this training. It was me who took the fire-starting vial from Morroy's pocket while you waited for him to die in the woods. I'll be in the library."

"I remember . . ." Juhl said as Fetzer disappeared.

"He wasn't like this when we were in Leauvenna," Bertwil said.

"Perhaps he is sour stomached when not on a task," Marlan said. "Garion is the same way."

"Yes, but Fetzer hasn't proven himself," Juhl said.

"The master considers Leauvenna sufficient proof," Marlan said. "But enough of this. To our studies."

48

BRUGARN

Eglamour Palace, Toulon Ministry
Flowertide, 3034

"Insolent bastard," Brugarn mumbled. "Curses on his house . . ."

"We could have Arthan and his army sent to buttress Alpenon," General Chaultion said. "Asteroth could put him at the front, ensuring Arthan is one of the first to die when the Rugens invade."

Brugarn stopped his pacing. "I like that idea, but Erech will never agree to it now that he's made Arthan his new marshal."

"Perhaps death at the enemy's hands is too honorable anyway," Chaultion said, twisting his white mustache.

Brugarn always wondered how the general, a man younger than himself, could be so prematurely white headed. Perhaps it was the price for a mind that never ceased strategizing. That was why Brugarn prized the general, along with his control of the army.

"The Valients are weakhearted fools," Brugarn said. "Yet the king already favors Arthan as much as he did Maillard."

"Then look at it this way: the king's dependence on the young Arthan is a blessing," Chaultion said. "The king once more leans on weak men, which should only hasten his fall. Arthan is inexperienced. We will outmaneuver him like everyone else."

Brugarn eyed the general. "This is why I'm the brains, Chaultion. You know nothing of court politics. Did you see how Erech visibly changed when Arthan restored the sword of Rhunegeld to his hands? And the way the courtiers approved of that. Arthan is popular already. His appointment as Marshal of Inquiry only strengthens his hand. And I created that damn post for myself!"

"Accuse him," Chaultion said. "Plant the seeds that he was Garion's mysterious master, sacrificing his own operative to cover himself. Spread rumors that Arthan was behind it all to benefit himself. Sow the seeds of doubt."

"I will, Chaultion. But it won't be enough. Only war can shake Eglamour enough . . ."

"You have riots in every major city of the kingdom. The treasury is broken. And the Rugens are probing our southern underbelly. I'll be the last to delay a good war, but it seems you've got plenty to undermine your brother's claim to the throne."

"I want the war too," Brugarn said. "A broad, all-consuming war. Asteroth and Erath will be compelled to fight it in the south. Erech will fail to lead, and I will supplant him. Then we'll crush Rugenhav, and I'll be hailed as Donovan's savior."

The general twisted his mustache again. "How do you want it done?"

"You're the general. Has the Rugen ambassador provided any clues about their weaknesses?"

"Vesamune's pillow talk is worthless. It's entertaining to feed her false information, but overall we don't need her. The Rugens will eventually make the mistake of probing too far into Alpenon. Perhaps they'll renew their claim on those lands, maybe by force."

"Provoke them, make them want to invade. Then you and the twins can invade Rugenhav and lay waste to every city, farm, and hovel between Gardwerp and Heingartmer."

"That is what I love to do."

"You were born to break Rugenhav, general. I will fight the politics of the court. You give me a war to win."

49

ARTHAN

Clonmel Estate in Eglamour, Toulon Ministry
Flowertide, 3034

"I don't like having all these palace guards here, my lord. I just don't trust them."

Arthan nodded. "It's all right, Livonier. They are now assigned to us as inquiry office soldiers. Have them fan out over the estate and guard the cellar, which we'll convert to a jail. Your Racharders will still have the interior of the house."

"How do we know one of them is not another assassin, Brother?" Bardil asked. "Or one of Brugarn's lackeys?"

"We don't," Serdot said. "I'm still evaluating them. Their commander is Waldemar's son."

"This is the best arrangement we have for now," Arthan said. "The king favors us and wants to know who is behind the killings. We must accept any assistance he gives along with the risks. Where is the prisoner?"

"Garion is waiting in your study with a few soldiers," Livonier said.

"We'll talk with him privately," Arthan said. "Everyone come with me."

When they entered his large study, they found Garion, hands chained behind him, hunched in a chair in the middle of the room before Arthan's writing table.

"Thank you," Arthan said to the guards, "you may leave him with us."

"But, my lord, shouldn't we stay to protect you?"

"Are you the lead knight, the son of Waldemar? What is your name?"

"Debanor, sir. The king and steward instructed me to serve you however I can."

"Very well, Sir Debanor. I hope your father is proud that you now serve the Marshal of Inquiry. But you must understand that these most sensitive matters are best left to me and my circle. As knight captain of my inquiry soldiers, you can organize the men into patrols throughout the estate. No one comes in or out of Clonmel without my knowledge. And heed any orders that Livonier, Serdot, or Bardil provide you."

"Yes, my lord," Debanor said. He nodded to his men and they filed out of the room. Debanor turned before leaving. "Almost forgot. We found this on him, my lord."

Arthan accepted a key from him. "Thank you."

Serdot and Livonier took their places on either side of the glaring Garion, while Bardil positioned a chair behind the prisoner. Arthan paced in front of the assassin.

"You know those pitiful soldiers won't stop us once my master learns you are here," Garion said.

Arthan kept silent, watching Garion sweat. He wanted him to feel the weight of silence, the uncertainty of his fate, before beginning. "Tell me more about your master."

Garion grinned, exercising his own silence.

"Answer the lord minister," Livonier said.

"Who instructed you to kill Duke Brugarn?" Arthan asked.

"You have my letter," Garion said.

"But who is represented by the initial 'E'?"

"A servant of my master. We are many."

"Tell me more."

"Even a few members of our Order will overwhelm your soldiers, as Maillard was overwhelmed."

"Do not speak his name!" Bardil shouted. He had shot up from his chair. Arthan cut his eyes at his brother until he reseated himself.

Garion grinned again. "Oh yes, you'll know soon enough."

"Did your master teach you to run walls?"

"Of course."

"And make cloaking powders? Poisonous powders?"

"He taught me much."

"What is his purpose?"

"The ancient flame is relit. And it grows stronger."

Serdot brought out Garion's mask. "The Naren-Dra were masters of a forgotten alchemy that your ilk has revived. Why?"

"We embrace the ancient ways that are forsaken by modern men."

"It was forsaken for good reason," Arthan said. "No knight would dishonor himself with such trickery." He noticed a sideways glance Serdot gave him, as if he wanted to say something but held back.

"Kings fear it for good reason," Garion said. "They have only to see Maillard's swollen throat, smell the vomit in his lungs, and see the wound inflicted to his chest that no armor could have prevented."

Bardil lunged up again, but Livonier reached Garion first, cracking the prisoner across his jaw.

"Who is your master?" Arthan repeated.

Garion spit blood at Arthan, earning another punch from Livonier. He shook the pain from his head. "You . . . you will know his name . . . in time. All shall tremble at the sound . . ."

"If you do not tell me, I won't protect you from Brugarn's plans for your slow death," Arthan said. "There is no crueler hand in this kingdom. You've seen him in court."

"Squabbling, reaching men of greed . . ." Garion muttered.

"What about Marlan, where is he now?"

"All of you will suffer the same fate when Candlestone comes . . ." Garion said.

"Is Candlestone the Rugens?" Arthan asked.

Garion laughed heartily, shaking with the pain throbbing in his wounds.

"The ancient flame?" Serdot asked.

"You can ask Maillard, when you see him in hell," Garion answered.

Bardil rushed up and struck him in the back of the head, tossing him out of the chair. Arthan came to his brother as Livonier moved to pick up Garion.

"Bardil, if you cannot control yourself, then leave," Arthan whispered. "I want revenge for Father, too, but we must stay—"

"My lord," Serdot whispered over his shoulder. "Garion is opening up. We must keep on him."

Livonier's shout turned them around. Garion had struck the knight in his face with his shackles and was limping toward the window. They rushed to Garion but he threw himself at the glass. They reached him just as his body tumbled through. Breathless they watched him plummet to the courtyard, where he fell broken and lifeless.

"Only a true believer does such things," Serdot said, breaking Arthan's shock.

Arthan reached into his pocket and pulled out the key found by Debanor. "Search everywhere, Serdot. Find where this key fits. It's all we have now . . ."

"I will. My lord, we need to discuss Candlestone."

"What is it?"

"There is a professor here in Eglamour who specializes in ancient heathen histories. I think he will be of help."

"How could some scribe possibly help? We're dealing with assassins, probably hired by the Rugens. Or maybe the Calbrians. You heard how he laughed when I asked about the Rugens."

"With respect, my lord, I think this is different. I've never known agents of Rugenhav or Calbria to run up walls and wear Naren-Dra masks."

"Fine, we'll talk with him sometime. But for now, focus on that key. Garion is dead, but Marlan and E may be close by."

"I'm sorry, Brother," Bardil said. "I was a distraction . . ."

"No, I let him get through me," Livonier said, nursing a bleeding nose.

"We must be vigilant."

50

MARLAN

Thorendor Castle, Wallevet Ministry
Flowertide, 3034

"Master, the others are becoming more irritated with Fetzer's arrogance."

"Well, he is arrogant," Arasemis said. "But you're not as bothered by it, are you?"

Marlan paused. He had been thinking quite a bit about this. "Remember when Enildir's book quoted Rildning as saying he wouldn't be the last to unite the defenders of the tribal lands?"

"It was a new prophecy that foretold the coming of another leader like Rildning."

"And you've never thought you might be this leader?" Marlan asked.

"Not at all. I'm the reviver, not the uniter."

"Since Fetzer's arrival, I can't help but wonder if he is the uniter who was prophesied. Fetzer's personal story is compelling, and he took a risk by volunteering to help with the Leauvenna task. I agree that he is arrogant and sometimes reckless, but he has vigor unlike anyone else. And his skill with a sword is unmatched."

"I appreciate your observations, Marlan. But if the other students dislike him, then by definition Fetzer is divisive, not a uniter."

"Sometimes leaders are abrasive until they master their own abilities and others get used to their talents. You taught me that. Rildning certainly had his problems unifying the tribes, as did Eniri, Enildir, and the later leaders of Candlestone. Perhaps it takes an aggressive warrior like Fetzer to fulfill Candlestone's destiny."

"You may be right, Marlan, but it's too soon to tell. Fetzer took part in Gottfried's killing, but there are still many tests ahead of him, ahead of all of us. Be careful with your theory that Fetzer is Rildning's prophesied leader."

Marlan nodded.

"Now," continued Arasemis, "there is something else I wanted to see you about. Come and sit." Arasemis cleared a stool near his table. Marlan walked around the book stacks and took his seat. "You once told me you are synthic. What forms of this condition do you have?"

"Words, letters, and numbers have a specific color in my mind's eye," Marlan said. "Sounds and music also have color and shape and movement. And the days and months are mapped on a loop."

"I think my grandfather Erwold was also a synthic. I've come to the end of his journal that you retrieved for me from the academy's archives. His writings confirmed my suspicion that he was involved in Candlestone despite my father's efforts to hide it from me and my brothers when we were children. But there must be more written somewhere."

"I looked everywhere you told me to at the academy," Marlan said. "This journal was it."

"Not at the academy. I think Erwold hid something here at Thorendor that will tell me more about him and Candlestone. Look at this last page of his journal."

> THORENDOR IS YYWRGRVWR,
> YWPRG WO OWWP.
> RYGRG BWTB BRGGRR,
> GRV YGGY TGGRR.
> YYY RYWRG RWWP.

"I've run through various treatises on coded language, but this passage does not fit any methods. I'm wondering if it is synthic lettering—since synthics 'see' black-inked letters in colors, as you do, this must be a hidden message."

Marlan nodded. "Color graphemes. But I can't read it, because no two synthics see the colors the same way. So Erwold's writing is like a code within a code."

"I must know what he was protecting, Marlan. Walk me through what you mean."

"No one knows why, but synthics associate every letter and number with a specific color that never changes in their mind's eye, regardless of the color of the actual ink. And multiple letters can share the same color, so there are many combinations. Looking at Erwold's page, it's clear to me that the letters signify the colors that he associated with each encrypted letter. For example, 'Y' just means yellow."

"I'm following you, Marlan, but why is he saying Thorendor is yellow yellow white red and so on? It's just gibberish."

"The colors are just a clue to the actual letters." Marlan pointed to the bottom of the page. "See the first word in the last line, *YYY*? Obviously no word has three of the same letters like that, Erwold simply associated the three actual letters with the color yellow. So, and this is just an example, if the three-letter word is sky then that means Erwold associated 'S,' 'K,' and 'Y' with the color yellow. I just have to figure out how he really saw them, based on the number of colors he saw. This will take some time."

"Then get started."

᳁

Well after nightfall Marlan jumped up from his chair. "I've got it!"

Arasemis and the other students who were hunched over books in the library looked up at him with curiosity. Arasemis explained to them what Marlan had been working on, then turned back to Marlan. "Are you sure?"

"Quite sure, because Erwold provided a partial key in the first line. The 'TH' in the unencrypted word *THORENDOR* is the first 'YY' in *YYWRGRVWR*. If 'Y' signifies yellow letters, then 'T' and 'H' must be yellow. That means the 'O' in *THORENDOR* is white, the 'R' is red, the 'E' is green . . ."

"What is he talking about?" Fetzer asked.

". . . Erwold's 'N' is red," Marlan continued. "Also his 'G,' 'V,' and 'D' are violet. The number seven is yellow, like mine. And his—"

"Spare us all the odd synthic details," Bertwil said. "What does the message say?"

"If I substituted the color graphemes correctly, which the first line key suggests, then it should read . . . 'Thorendor is Thorendor / House of book. / Where cold creeps, / And heat leaps. / Seventh stone nook.' Sounds interesting, whatever it means."

Juhl rolled her eyes. "So now it's a riddle within a riddle."

"A riddle within a synthic code," Arasemis said. "House of book could be a library, or maybe a writing table or shelf."

"But where does hot and cold coexist?" Bertwil mused.

"And made of stone?" Fetzer asked.

Rodel stood and stepped away from his bench. "This is no difficult riddle," he said, stopping in front of the fireplace nearest Arasemis's table. He rested his arm on the mantel.

"My grandfather was a clever man," Arasemis said. "He may have wrapped his clues in several layers."

"Look at Rodel's face," Juhl said. "He has it . . ."

"Tell us, then," Fetzer said.

"Yes, go on," Marlan said.

"An unlit hearth is a creeping place for cold," Rodel said, "and a leaping place for flames otherwise. It need not be simultaneous."

"Why would it be this hearth?" Fetzer said.

"Just a guess," Rodel said. "If this was Erwold's writing table long ago, perhaps he hid something in the fireplace closest to where he worked."

"Brilliant!" Arasemis said.

"And 'seventh stone nook'?" Bertwil asked.

Rodel pointed to the stack of stones above the mantel that formed the chimney, counting seven upward.

"There must be a movable stone," Marlan murmured.

The students crowded around the hearth, counting and tugging every seventh stone above the mantel, around the sides, and from the floor. They found nothing.

"This has to be it," Arasemis said.

Fetzer glared at Rodel. "Not as clever as you thought, Rugen."

Rodel and the others ignored him as they rechecked the seventh stones.

"What about inside the hearth itself?" Juhl asked.

"Anything hidden behind there would be ashes by now," Marlan said.

Rodel hunched inside and counted on all three sides. "The mortar on this one is loose enough. Hand me the poker."

Marlan handed it to him, and Rodel pried at the stone. After a few moments Marlan grabbed the tongs and bent inside to help. He took hold of the stone with the tongs as Rodel rocked it back and forth. The stone edged out and kept sliding.

"Unusual for a hearthstone to be so long," Arasemis said.

Marlan and Rodel ushered the arm-length stone out with both hands, and Bertwil grasped its far end to help. Marlan caught a glimpse of a lid as they set the stone on a bench.

"A compartment," Fetzer said, reaching for it.

"Let me do this," Arasemis said. They watched as he lifted a shale plate cover and gently pulled out a set of tightly rolled papers. Arasemis retreated to his writing table as the students gathered around.

"It's written in ancient Gali," he said of the first scroll, "but the parchment is not from the colonial era. It's a more recent document . . ." He looked up at Marlan. "Well done, synthic. Perhaps you excel at more than chemina arcana. Perhaps I should have you encode my correspondence with our supporters as well."

Marlan smiled. "But who would decode it? We'll have to begin recruiting synthics."

"Not a bad idea . . . And excellent thinking by riddle-master Rodel as well," Arasemis said. "Now, it will take me some time to translate all of this. Everyone is excused."

Marlan corralled the others toward the door.

"Marlan," Arasemis called, "have them clean the laboratory before bed, and practice jumps in the training hall tomorrow. I do not wish to be disturbed."

"Of course, Master."

51

MILISEND

Milisend's feet and calves were quivering with fatigue. She had practiced with her black leather slippers, but now, clutching the ledge outside Lord Reimvick's window with her fingers and toes, her muscles were cramping.

She had not planned on waiting this long. She had crept out of her window at dusk with her mask and outfit, lightly skipping across the rooftops and ledges of the palace. She had been all over the high exterior of the complex many times with Regaume and knew the best path to the apartments reserved for the lord ministers. And she knew which one was Lord Reimvick's after observing him in the palace over several days.

But Reimvick's pattern had changed. His timing was erratic, and his movements were hurried. Milisend had heard about Garion's treachery, so she presumed Reimvick and the others were taking steps to protect themselves. But now Reimvick was leaving his chambers well after nightfall.

It had taken him longer to leave tonight. When he finally departed, Milisend climbed to the window sill and opened one of her belt pouches. She wedged a tiny blade into the gap between the shutter windows, just below the lock. The blade was a handy tool Regaume had given her. A twist of the first knob on the tool's handle unhinged a little arm. A twist of the second turned the arm until it caught the hook on the inside of the window. A final twist pushed the hook off its rest.

She slowly pulled opened the window and crawled inside, closing and locking it behind her. The warm light of a single candle greeted her. She reasoned that Reimvick had either forgotten to snuff it out or that he would be back soon. She hurried around the room, pulling open drawers and opening pouches. She found gold coins in plenty but left them lest their bulk and noise burden her. She wanted jewels. Silky chains of gold and silver. Soundless gem-studded rings and brooches. And silent scarves of gold thread and pearl.

As Milisend neared the candle and opened table drawers, she noticed the candle's flame turn red. She let out a half breath, then froze, and her eyes grew wide as the flame reddened further. "Oh, no . . ." she whispered as its hue deepened. A presence candle.

Regaume had warned her about these before, but she had not expected a lord minister to use alchemical candles. Had the Garion incident caused Reimvick to take such precaution? She considered blowing it out, but that might be just as alerting. She let it burn and controlled her breathing in the hopes that the red would fade away after she left.

Milisend skipped across the room to the side door, finding it unlocked. Inside was Reimvick's wardrobe, travel and ceremonial armors, and other personal effects. She diligently and quickly searched everything, but still found no jewels worth taking. She had to leave with something.

She gave up on the wardrobe and approached a small door that had been left ajar. She guessed it to be the privy, given the washbasin resting by the door. She was surprised to find makeshift shelving throughout the small room. A multitude of glass jars, vials, and flasks filled every shelf, some with strange liquids and powders. Candlewax drippings and various herb fronds littered the floor. A sheathed sword leaned in a corner beside an iron apparatus that seemed designed for holding a fire beneath a stone bowl.

Milisend had never seen an alchemist's laboratory but had imagined that this is what one would look and smell like. As she stepped inside to look around, she heard the turn of the lock of Reimvick's main chamber door. She quickly pulled the little door back ajar, then dove in the gap between one of the wardrobe cabinets and the wall. She held her breath but knew the presence candle flame would still be red.

Hurried footsteps raced from the main chamber through the wardrobe and into the privy. She dared not poke her head out to see whether it was Reimvick or a servant. Whoever it was did not bother to check the candle or anything else. Next she heard the distant breaking of glass, as in a tunnel. Milisend realized the secret laboratory was being destroyed, the bottles and vials thrown down the privy chute.

When this was finished the person closed the privy door and locked it. Then they left the apartment as quickly as they had come. Afraid, Milisend waited.

It was a mistake to come here, she thought. She could not guess why Reimvick had a secret laboratory, and she did not care. She had come for jewels and was frustrated to find that the wealthy lord minister kept few among his things. She was unsure when it would be safe to escape. Should she go now and chance another sudden entry? Should she wait until he was fast asleep in his bed? Or worse, wait until the next day?

Her mind wandered as she considered her options. Given the alchemical tactics Garion had used, she wondered now if Reimvick and Garion were connected. But Reimvick was a respected lord minister who, like other high nobles, scorned ancient mischief like alchemy. His house had long served the Avaleaus honorably.

Milisend thought it best to leave at once so she could warn Hamelin about what she'd seen. She carefully extracted herself from the wardrobe and stepped toward the main chamber. Then footsteps returned and the lock of the door turned again. She retreated back to her hiding place, now angry for hesitating earlier.

It was certainly Reimvick. He locked the door behind him, and the sounds he made suggested he was relaxing and retiring for the night. Then there was a pause in his activity. Milisend envisioned him inspecting the presence candle.

"Must have been me . . ." he muttered.

Footsteps came past the wardrobe and the privy was unlocked. Something was thrown down the chute, possibly the candle, before the door was relocked. Reimvick passed through the wardrobe and locked that door, too, then prepared for sleep.

Reluctantly, Milisend accepted her error. Regaume had taught her to move quickly and often, never to hesitate while on a heist. She vowed to never make this mistake again as she tried to get comfortable.

52

ARTHAN

Eglamour Palace, Toulon Ministry
Flowertide, 3034

"Out the window?"

"Yes, Your Majesty," Arthan said.

"How peculiar. Did he say anything?"

"Garion said little of use. He mentioned something about a candle stone, which Serdot is investigating. Garion also had a key on him. Steward Waldemar confirmed it was made in the style of the palace locks, but we haven't found the correct one yet."

"Candles and keys, death and pain . . ." Erech mumbled, gazing off.

Arthan waited. "My lord . . . ?"

"What? Oh, yes . . . Well, keep at it, marshal."

Out of the corner of his eye Arthan spotted Brugarn moving in the shadows of the great hall columns, despite Arthan's request for a private audience with the king.

"Thank you again, Your Majesty, for the trust you've placed in me," Arthan said. "I will not rest until these assassins and their master are found."

Erech blinked several times, as if clearing a fog in his head. "Very good, young Valient. Your father would be as proud as I am. Since Garion is no more, return to Delavon to get your affairs in order, then hasten back to me. I want your regular counsel in the months ahead as the Rugens do more than threaten our borderlands. They'll undoubtedly be sending more assassins like Garion to Eglamour, and you must smoke them out."

"Counsel from me?"

"I can see you have Maillard's mind. Your thinking will be useful in this regard. And, on a separate matter, please consider wedding my middle daughter, Milisend."

Arthan, taken aback, glanced at Brugarn. The duke was also surprised. "My king, that is a most gracious and humbling offer, but . . ."

"Don't answer now," Erech said. "Just think on it. The queen favors you, Milisend needs direction, and I would see the ties between our houses strengthened for the times ahead. We'll talk more when you return."

"Thank you, Your Majesty."

"The king is overdue for his rest hour, Lord Valient," Brugarn said, stepping into the light.

"I will return as soon as possible," Arthan said with a bow to the king.

"Please do," Brugarn said as he turned to walk Arthan from the hall. He lowered his voice further. "For I cannot bear to think who will protect us while you're gone."

"I know you'll manage," Arthan said.

"You mustn't keep your audiences with the king overly long," Brugarn said as they exited the throne room. "You've seen how his mind can wander."

"Yes." Arthan recalled Erech's mumbling and empty gazes. "Still, sometimes his speech is clear and thoughtful, even decisive."

Brugarn waved his hand dismissively. "His mind grows weary from the toil of a crowned head. And just when I saw renewed brightness in his eyes . . . Perhaps offering the hand of Princess Milisend is merely one of his whimsical passing thoughts."

Brugarn halted and brought his ugly face close to Arthan's. "One day his mind will die, whether or not his body endures. He'll no longer be king, and I'll no longer have use for a marshal of inquiry. Perhaps not even a lord minister of Delavon."

"Until that time, Duke, I shall serve the king and protect you from the menace in the shadows. Garion did not work alone."

Brugarn gave a cruel smile. "Safe journey."

❧

As Arthan and Livonier approached the doors of Clonmel, they were greeted by Sir Debanor.

"My lord, your brother Bardil told me to inform you that he is waiting inside with the Rugen ambassador. She insisted on meeting with you."

"Thank you, Debanor. Is anyone accompanying her?"

"She came alone, my lord."

Arthan and Livonier made for the great room, where they found Bardil and the ambassador seated silently. Bardil was clearly uncomfortable, and Vesamune was confidently quiet. She stood when Arthan entered and introduced herself. Arthan sat down with them. He wished Serdot was present, but he knew the widsemer was busy trying Garion's key in every palace door.

"May we talk privately?" Vesamune asked, glancing at Livonier and Bardil.

"Your kingdom is widely believed to be behind the assassinations," Arthan said. "What you came here to say can be said in front of my brother and Livonier, my protector. I'm sure you'll agree that's prudent in these uncertain times."

"Not yet a diplomat of your father's quality, are you?" she said. Her Donovar speech was impeccable, to the point that Arthan wondered if she were wholly Rugen. "Even so, please accept my apologies for the abrupt meeting, and thank you for granting it."

Arthan shifted in his chair, irritated that she had taken the higher ground. "Certainly. Why are you here?"

"I came to tell you that we, the Rugen Empire, had no part in Garion's plot, nor the death of your father and the others. We are not part of this conspiracy, nor did we have foreknowledge of it."

"And yet, as I said, many believe you are behind it, including me."

"We wouldn't have shed a tear for Brugarn," Vesamune said, allowing herself a small grin. "And I'm certain many of the king's lords would be glad to see the duke gone as well. But we did not have anything to do with any of this."

"Your folk are continuously harassing our southern border, risking a wider war," Arthan said. "You send your widsemer agents across our lands, such as the ones Lord Asteroth recently caught coming from Austveeden. And your emperors have funded the rebellion in the mountains of Durgensdil for generations. How are we to believe—"

"My lord!"

Arthan turned toward Serdot's shout from the corridor. He soon burst through the door.

"Serdot, this is the Rugen ambassador," Arthan said hastily.

Serdot bowed. "My apologies, my lord and ambassador. I've had a breakthrough on the investigation."

"Excuse me for a moment," Arthan said. He slipped out into the corridor with Serdot. "What is it?"

"Why is she here?"

"She wanted to tell us the killings were not their doing. I think she is a convincing liar, but not convincing enough. My guess is she wanted to open communication with the new lord minister of Delavon."

"And the new Marshal of Inquiry," Serdot said. "As always, I advise you to keep your enemies close. Have open dialogue with them if they're offering it, but keep it secret so no one in the king's court can use it against you. If the talking is exposed, you can claim it as part of your official duties as marshal."

"I shall. Now, what was so important?"

"The key," Serdot said as he pulled it from his pocket. "The master smithy of the palace told me Garion's key was part of a new set made for the apartments used by visiting dignitaries. Currently, the lord ministers who do not have residences in the capital, like Clonmel, could be the next target. Alternatively, one of them could be linked to Garion."

"So the key is for lord ministers' chambers . . . which ones are staying in the palace?"

"Eperude of Lundwynland, Reimvick of Wallevet, and Sigbert of Barres. Ferin of Hanovel's room is unoccupied, since he was unexpectedly absent. I wanted you to know before I start sneaking around the quarters of your fellow lord ministers."

"Begin with Ferin's vacant chambers. Then Sigbert's, as he is due to leave the capital today. Then the others."

"Yes, my lord."

"And Serdot, much as I would like your counsel, you should remain here to work while I return to Delavon briefly."

"You could delegate your affairs to Bardil and send him back."

"I considered that, but I want to ensure Delavon is prepared for anything. And I plan to leave Bardil in charge of Rachard."

"And I presume there is a certain young woman you'll want to see . . ."

Arthan was a bit surprised that he knew. "Meriam is my personal business, Serdot." He paused a moment. "I'm sorry. You are privy to all of my affairs, personal or otherwise. Meriam is always in the back of my mind. And she should stay there, given everything that demands my attention."

"I understand."

"Serdot, I'm a bit torn over all this coming and going. You previously told me to focus on Mordmerg, the near threat, rather than the court politics of Eglamour."

"Yes, but that was before we realized Mordmerg was merely a symptom of a broader sickness. Before the collapse of the Empire Alliance unleashed all this trouble."

"So I must focus on Eglamour, at the expense of my own lands?"

"You'll manage both with able help, as Maillard did. Go to Delavon and get things in order. I'll strive to have answers upon your return."

"Thank you, my friend. Search carefully."

Arthan reentered the room to find Vesamune locked in an unpleasant stare with Livonier and Bardil. Despite Serdot's advice to talk with her, Arthan did not sit down. He had a lot on his mind and wanted to be done with her.

"My apologies, Ambassador. As I was saying, how are we to believe the Rugens have nothing to do with the present crisis?"

"I can tell you as much," she said. "We can list equally provocative actions from Donovan, most recently your king's Proclamation of Expediency."

"I'm sure you've had this conversation many times with the king's envoys, but it's not something I'm in a position to discuss. In fact, I have other matters to attend to."

Vesamune bolted up from her chair and rushed toward him, her eyes intense. Arthan noticed Livonier reach for his sword but Arthan raised a hand to stay him.

"We may always be enemies," Vesamune said, "but these killings were not our doing. You must believe me." Her voice was laden with concern.

"Why should I, Ambassador?"

"Because you are Maillard's son. The lords of Donovan respect the House of Valient, and no one else will consider my appeal."

"What does your emperor want?"

"Emperor Theudamer wants a treaty to decisively settle Durgensdil—I beg your pardon—Alpenon Ministry. A treaty that recognizes Rugenhav's historical and cultural claim to the region and allows our trade and travel without undue suspicion."

"You've already taken that much, and more," Arthan said.

"The wealth of those mountains could be shared while remaining part of your kingdom."

"I'm a lord minister of the east and, again, in no position to negotiate lands ruled by the king's own brother."

"Of course. I came to give my condolences for your father and absolve us from all these killings, and I've done that. I will leave you with this final thought. If we wanted to destroy the high nobles of Donovan, as someone else is doing, why would we choose the distant Gottfried, diplomatic Maillard, and the small-landed Raymond? Wouldn't Asteroth, Erath, and Brugarn be our primary targets?"

"Brugarn was targeted."

"True, but the rest do not fit. We did not do this."

"Thank you for your visit, Ambassador."

"Thank you, Lord Minister. I hope the efforts of your inquiry office are fruitful, if only to absolve my people. And I hope we can continue to talk when necessary."

Arthan nodded. "When necessary."

53

FETZER

Fetzer grinned as he wrote this part. He was proud of himself and certain the others could sense his cunning intellect but were powerless to counter him.

Eavesdropping on Marlan and Arasemis is easy and well worth the risk. It was enlightening to hear Marlan report the other students' "irritation" with my "arrogance," and valuable to hear Marlan defend me as a unifying leader prophesied by Rildning. Although Arasemis is unconvinced about my potential, I must continue to cultivate Marlan's friendship.

Marlan does not have a jealous bone in his body. When others have resented my abilities, he has only encouraged and defended me. If Marlan were older and in Arasemis's position as master of the Candlestone recruits, this Order would be better led. And Marlan is the only one whose swordcraft rivals my own. None of the others are a challenge, except the master, of course. But one day I will defeat the one-armed oddity in the training hall.

Marlan's alchemical abilities are also unmatched. Now that Arasemis practically lives in the library, Marlan has taken over most of the teaching. The beautiful Juhl contributes in the laboratory as well, but she is usually too quick to help Rodel and hasn't yet recognized that her time is better spent with me.

While training we've also witnessed Marlan's new sword. Gladed and treated over many months, his sword, which he has named Banebrand, is truly a marvel. We set up an armored frame of wood, complete with steel helmet, breastplate, pauldrons, and mail, for him to slash at a few times. Sparks flew and flames danced along the armor, heating it to a red glow. When he was done fighting it, well past the point when the wearer would already have been cooked, the armor was partially melted and dripped to the floor in little heaps.

If Marlan and Bertwil can have alchemical swords, I should have one. Even Juhl has a sword that is being treated. If I cannot convince Arasemis that I'm ready for one then perhaps Marlan will help me build one in secret. Not that we have a new task on which to use it. Arasemis has kept himself locked away with his dusty books instead of planning our next task. Even Marlan is becoming restless.

54

ARTHAN

Eglamour Palace, Toulon Ministry
Flowertide, 3034

"Will you be leaving Eglamour soon?" Arthan asked. "No, I should stay at court for a while longer," Reimvick answered. "With you, Eperude, and Sigbert leaving, someone should stay and prevent Brugarn and Voufon from killing each other. And the king needs balanced counsel, should he decide to listen to advice."

"Who will care for Wallevet during your extended absence?"

"I have an able cousin as alderman of Bredahade. I cannot count on my reclusive younger brother to manage anything."

"Write to me if something of note happens," Arthan said. "Serdot will be here, but sometimes I wonder if your gossip circles have information that is as good as his networks of shadows."

"I cannot match the skill of a widsemer, but I certainly will keep you informed." Reimvick smiled. "Don't come back with that cheek bandage; show your trophy scar. Safe journey."

⚭

The uneventful ride south from Eglamour gave Arthan time to think about all that had happened. Arthan looked out on the open plains of the Toulon River Valley. His role as the king's Marshal of Inquiry, his diplomatic channel to the

Rugens, his stature at court. His future was as full of promise as the fields before him.

Arthan was reflecting on Reimvick's decision to remain in the capital when Bardil woke from his nap on the other side of the carriage.

"Will you not rest, Brother?" Bardil asked, rubbing the sleep from his eyes. "You're going to need it."

"I suppose I've let the affairs of Eglamour overtake my mind," Arthan answered.

Bardil shook his head and smiled. "Too soon."

"Father was the mortar between all those lords of stone. That's plain to me now. And everyone expects me to be the same way."

"Perhaps that means your destiny is to be either the trowel or the chisel," Bardil said.

Arthan was struck by the truth in his jest. "Add more mortar or pick it apart. What would Father have done in these strange times?"

"He would have done his best, as will you. If you can help keep Donovan unified in the face of our enemies, then you should. And if you can protect our Delavon, come what may in Eglamour, you will."

"Wise words from youth." Arthan smiled.

"I have more for you. Everyone has seen the way you look at Meriam. You should—"

"Bellumet's assistant? She is merely—"

"—the object of your affection, don't deny it. Brother, no woman has touched you as she has."

"Meriam is a commoner," Arthan said. "Beautiful, kind, and tenderhearted. But a commoner."

"Father wed below his rank. You should visit Meriam before you return to Eglamour."

"Of course. I will see Bellumet and Meriam to discuss strengthening Delavon's defenses."

"See *her*. When you are caught up in the maelstrom of politics and intrigue of Eglamour, you will think back on her sweet face and wish to touch it again."

"The king offered me the hand of Princess Milisend," Arthan said.

"That changes things . . ."

"I saw the princess briefly at court. She was shy and awkward, probably aware of the king's offer. I do not know her."

"She is beautiful, Brother. And if you wed her, you'll certainly cement your position at court."

"To wed for love alone is a luxury lord ministers lack. To wed for politics is expected. A duty."

"You have all the difficult decisions," Bardil said with a smile.

"And I have brothers who are little help."

On the third day of travel, Arthan's convoy reached the outskirts of Ralmogard. He knew it to be Toulon Ministry's only free city-state. The columns of smoke rising from behind the city walls reminded him of Mordmerg. Arthan, who had finally shunned his carriage to ride on his horse alongside Livonier, stopped to question a group of peasants near the roadside about what had happened.

"We've been turned out of Ralmogard, my lord," volunteered one man.

"Forced into tents and lean-tos on the farmlands," said another.

"Who turned you out?" Arthan asked.

"Duke Brugarn's men," said a stiff-chinned washerwoman. "Turned us all out for failing to pay a tax."

"And the Almerian garrison?" Arthan asked.

"Butchered," said the first man. "And some of our folk besides."

"Insane," Arthan whispered to Livonier. He turned to the peasants again. "Are the duke's men still in the city?"

The woman nodded. "Otherwise my children would be in their beds tonight."

"We cannot help them," Livonier told Arthan. "Brugarn is lord of Toulon. Like Asteroth and Erath, if he wants to wreck a city loyal to the Almerians, who can stop him?"

"These people of the free cities are still Donovards," Arthan said. "You saw the rioting in Eglamour. Every city will be touched by the disaster that is the Proclamation of

Expediency, not just the city-states. Brugarn is ruining the heart of the kingdom."

"There is nothing we can do here, my lord. There wasn't much we could do for Mordmerg."

Arthan turned to Bardil. "How much do we have?"

"About four hundred guldirs or so in the carriage."

"Livonier, make sure all of it is distributed. Find the alderman of Ralmogard if you can."

"My lord," Livonier muttered, "Brugarn's men will hear of this. They'll take your gold from these people, or even kill them for it."

Arthan knew Livonier was right, but he was compelled to help. "Maybe it will be enough for most of them to find better shelter first. We're rebuilding Mordmerg. We can help them do the same."

✤

A few days later Arthan arrived in Wallevet's capital of Bredahade.

"Lord Reimvick's alderman has taken great care of his city for him," Bardil said as they entered.

Arthan nodded. "No sign of riots here. Unlike the royal treasury, the Reimvicks protect their wealth by protecting their people, as our house does. After Brugarn's proclamation, Lord Reimvick told me he would not increase taxes on the people or cut his soldiers. He said he'd pay Eglamour from his own purse and equip his men without help from the king's coffers."

"I thought the lord ministers were required to do that anyway," Bardil said.

"They were, in the old days," Arthan said. "But Erech's father made many of the lord ministers dependent on his largess. So they'll have no way around the proclamation."

"I'm glad to be a Valient," Bardil said as they rode onward.

55

TRONCHET

"Come now, Waldemar, as steward you must acknowledge how inappropriate it was for the king to appoint young Arthan to be marshal."

"The king may appoint whomever he wishes, Tronchet," Waldemar said. "Do you have Arthan's motivation to find the assassins, given that he lost his father to them?"

Tronchet knew Waldemar was right but did not respond.

"It's a slap in the face," Hamelin said. "Why didn't Arthan come to me about Garion? Why keep it to himself? Because he wanted to make a show of it for his own benefit, I say."

"Then perhaps Arthan is not as inexperienced as you both think. He is a learned, if young, politician," Waldemar said.

"He embarrassed the Crownblades," Hamelin said. "It's a great dishonor to—"

"You embarrassed and dishonored the Crownblades yourself by not detecting Garion in the first place," Waldemar said. "As captain of the king's personal guard, that was—and still is—your responsibility. If it hadn't been for Arthan, Garion would have killed Brugarn and perhaps the king, and you'd be more than disgraced. Yet you've kept your position and nursed your jealousy.

"As for you, Tronchet," the steward continued, "you come to me asking what can be done? You are still Chief Magistrate of Eglamour. If the riots, bandits, and Milisend's heists aren't keeping you busy enough, I suggest you offer

Arthan whatever help you can spare him, instead of complaining. And be thankful that the king named him marshal instead of Brugarn."

❧

Tronchet and Hamelin strolled along in the courtyard after leaving Waldemar's chamber.

"The steward speaks as if everything is well and fine," Hamelin said.

"How did you not suspect Garion?" Tronchet asked. "He was one of your own knights."

"Do you think I need you to tell me that? Garion joined the Crownblades nearly a year ago. He was talented with a sword and seemed loyal. I never would have picked him out as a hidden assassin. What could I have done?"

"He never acted abnormally at all?"

"Never. But I'll freely admit to you, my friend, that my distraction with the king may have contributed. Erech drops in and out of deep melancholy. One moment he's occupied with the smallest matter, the next he's ambivalent about matters that will determine the fate of the kingdom. Brugarn's whisperings are also making the king increasingly paranoid."

"The king is spending more and more time alone," Tronchet said. "Such self-imposed isolation is unhealthy . . . He's slowly withdrawing into himself."

"Will he ever come out of it?"

"That is my prayer," Tronchet said. "In the meantime Waldemar is right. We must accept Arthan's appointment as Marshal of Inquiry. Perhaps Arthan will help us smoke out the assassins."

"If Erech's mind doesn't heal, that will be the larger problem. Any of his brothers would make a more able king, even Brugarn. Their lineage is God-chosen for a reason. But don't misunderstand: my loyalty remains with Erech."

"I've never questioned your loyalty, Hamelin, nor does anyone else. Let us make sure there are no more Garions. Will you assist Arthan as you're able, as I will?"

"I suppose . . ."

56

MARLAN

Thorendor Castle, Wallevet Ministry
Flowertide, 3034

"Master?"

Marlan poked his head into the library. Arasemis's writing table at the far end of the room was obscured by newly stacked books and parchments. Hearing no reply, he walked in. When he got close enough to see over the clutter, he saw Arasemis's shaggy red-haired head lying on the table, unmoving.

"Master Arasemis . . ."

Marlan reached out and touched his armless right shoulder. Arasemis jolted up, his face gaunt, with heavy dark bags under his wide eyes. Marlan was certain he had not eaten for days.

"Master, are you all right?"

"What? Ah, yes. Yes, Marlan." Arasemis cleared his throat. "Thank you, I . . ."

Marlan noticed a tray of untouched food on a nearby table, probably brought in by Yorand or Adalane. "How long has it been since you've had a good sleep and a bite to eat?"

"No time," Arasemis said. "Grandfather Erwold's writings have kept my full attention."

"Drink this," Marlan said, handing him a cup of water from the tray. "Can you share what Erwold wrote?"

"Not yet, Marlan. I'm still piecing it together. The Gali is not difficult. You could easily translate it. It's all of his mention of other books and things. I've had to cross-reference many other texts to understand what he's written."

"Can you let the students help? Everyone is growing restless and there's only so much training and teaching I can give them. They need your direction."

"I have neglected them," Arasemis said. "But this small bundle of parchments from the hearth may be the most significant discovery for Candlestone's revival since I acquired the books of Rildning and Enildir."

"Share it with us, whatever you have thus far. It will help your apprentices understand."

"Not yet, Marlan. But I'll give you a taste. Read this." Arasemis pointed to part of his translation.

> However, the names Ahrazimujz, Arazemus, and Arasemis have been part of every generation of the Order since it was led by Dimanus and Nothild, an Arukan and Bronhildi, respectively. They were probably the seventh generation of Candlestone. It was around this time that the secret seat of Candlestone moved from Aggarwal northward to . . .

"You share your first name with ancient Order members," Marlan said. "Are they family?"

"Appears so. One of them, by the name of Bevil Ahrazmis, was a scribe to a senior general of the Wartemur Army, one of the units that replaced the Frontier Corps in western Pemonia. Bevil would have held an ideal post within the Brintilian Empire to help Candlestone subvert it from the inside."

"Now I see why your parents named you Arasemis."

"Actually, they named me Osmond. My father hated my grandfather's obsession with Candlestone and forbade me and my brothers from studying it. But Erwold encouraged us in secret. He liked to call me Arasemis, so I took that name for myself. I never understood why he liked that name until now. My ancestors have been members of Candlestone for many generations."

Marlan shook his head in disbelief. "Destiny . . . You're reviving an order that they kept alive all these years."

"They did more than that. My grandfather wrote about Wallon Arazmis of Candlestone's fifth generation. Wallon assassinated Seralin, the last Exarch of Pemonia, in 2356. Her death sped the decline of the Brintilian Empire's influence on the continent. Donovan was founded as an independent kingdom during the seventh generation."

"What generation are we?"

"There are gaps in Erwold's lists, and sometimes Candlestone passed from old men to their grandchildren. But if Erwold claimed to be the thirty-sixth, that would make me thirty-seventh, and you, Garion, and the others, thirty-eighth."

"Fascinating to know our roots since the days of Rildning's companions . . ."

"There's much more. Read this."

> And the old Uoricke Book of Aberynbane has a much more accurate history of the Order, although the damage done to the book at the academy hinders my view of this issue. Despite this, I suspect that the Aberynbanes took this burden upon their shoulders and welcomed the Order, permitting Candlestone to build its new seat on Thorendor's forested lands, obscured from the cities and trade routes but having good access to them . . .

"What does that mean?" Marlan asked.

"Thorendor was the name of a petty king of a small realm called Aberynbane. It was later absorbed into the new Kingdom of Donovan. Official histories describe King Thorendor as an ignorant, brutish tyrant who warred often with his neighbors until he was killed, cementing the unification of Donovan. His lands were absorbed into what became Wallevet Ministry."

The information struck Marlan. "King Thorendor must have welcomed the Order when they moved from Aggarwal, then let them build a new capital here."

Arasemis nodded. "And named their castle after him, which suggests he was not what the official histories portrayed him to be."

"How could we not know we lived in such an historic place?" Marlan asked, glancing around the library.

"I always suspected it was different for a reason. The architecture is distinct and its location isolated. Erwold told me it was a special place that must always remain in our family. My father wanted to tear it down but Erwold willed it to me."

"Not your older brothers?"

"Raymond and Edmond were always more concerned with politics than anything else. Raymond especially, since he was the eldest and would inherit father's lord ministership. That's why when Bredahade Academy ran me out, I came here."

"I'm still surprised this castle has belonged to Candlestone all this time . . ."

"Marlan, I'm not finished with my grandfather's writings yet, but he suggests there is more to this place than we currently realize. Secret places underground. But Erwold could never find them. I know the students need guidance in their studies, but I need more time to piece together those secrets."

"I'll do my best," Marlan said.

"I know you will. Take them to see the observatory at the top of Thorendor's pyramid as well. That should be eye-opening for them."

"Wouldn't you prefer to show them the far-seer yourself?"

"You've been reading too much Naren-Dra. You may call it a telescope. Take them up there so they can—"

"Master Arasemis!" It was Juhl, sprinting into the library. "A messenger brought this to the gate. Yorand received it and gave it to me." She handed a letter sealed with green wax to Arasemis.

Arasemis pulled the twine from the letter and glanced at Marlan. "Perhaps Garion's task is complete . . ."

"I'm sure he did well," Marlan said. They read the letter.

O,

The pupil you sent is dead. I'm no teacher, but I warned you he was arrogant and sloppy. Somehow Lord Arthan Valient discovered his mask and his orders. So far they have no reason to suspect me, and I've been able to destroy Garion's little laboratory.

Regarding Arthan, I retract my earlier advice to let him be. He is much too aggressive and will threaten our work. He will be traveling home soon, but his stay in Delavon will be brief. The king asked him to lead the search for the ministers' killers.

Take care not to kill him too near your precious castle or Bredahade. Wait until he has crossed into Delavon. Above all, do not allow him to return to Eglamour.

E

Arasemis crumpled the letter as Juhl cursed under her breath.

"Garion dead . . ." Marlan muttered. "And Morroy . . . Two lost within two months."

"And this young Arthan could make things worse," Arasemis said. "Marlan, you will lead the students, including the new recruits. Get them each a shirt of the gladed elinderum mail, forest cape, and Naren-Dra masks."

"Do you think they're ready?" Marlan asked. "Arthan will be well protected."

"Kill Arthan and anyone else important traveling with him. He'll likely be in a lord minister's carriage with a large contingent of cavalry. Hunt them but don't attack until they've crossed out of Wallevet. Get them on a narrow path or at camp so you can avoid the bulk of his knights. Arthan may already be in Wallevet by now. Make haste!"

57

ARTHAN

On the Road to Beldmerg, Delavon Ministry
Flowertide, 3034

Arthan rubbed his bandaged cheek but felt content as his convoy crossed from Wallevet into Delavon. He looked forward to seeing Rachard again. He hoped Medoff had lifted himself from the doldrums following Father's death. And Arthan was eager to spend time with Meriam. Bardil was right about her, though he still had not figured out how to balance her with his growing duties.

As the evening shadows lengthened, his men found a place to camp. He knew that by midday tomorrow they'd be in Beldmerg. Then only three more days to Rachard, if he kept his men moving.

"This way, my lord," Livonier said, pointing to the right side of the road. His tent was being erected on a flat green between bald hills and a small woods.

"Don't have them bother with the tent," Arthan said. "Sleeping under the sky of my lands will refresh me."

"Rain is coming," Livonier said, nodding toward the west.

"And lord ministers don't sleep outside," Bardil said with a smile.

"Very well . . ."

When the tent was up Arthan and Bardil took their meal inside. They sat comfortably around a brazier eating roasted heath hens while the rain poured outside.

"So how does it feel, Brother, to be a new lord and the right hand of the king?"

"Duke Brugarn remains the king's right hand," Arthan said. "I don't covet his position. My burden as marshal, though an honor, is already enough."

"Brugarn is more to blame for the kingdom's ills than anyone," Bardil said. "After seeing him in court, it's clear he is a master usurper."

"Erech still wears the crown. Not every king is great, but most have able counselors around them. Erech is both weak and surrounded by unworthy men. Bardil, I've been giving some thought to something . . ."

"Don't tell me you're going to accept Erech's offer to wed Princess Milisend. You'd make a better king, Brother, with her hand to cement your claim—but Meriam's face would haunt you."

Arthan shook his head in frustration at the distraction. "Bardil, listen, this is important. I'm not talking about women. Remember the Rugens' offer to keep in touch? I've thought a lot about this and talked several times with Serdot before we left."

"Father talked with all his enemies," Bardil said. "Keeping them close means you'll know what they're up to."

"Right. But Serdot thinks the Rugens are looking for a Donovard lord to supplant Erech. I could let the Rugens think I'm the one to support rather than someone to tear down. But I'll risk looking like a traitor to my own people if the relationship is revealed."

"Why would you consider it, then? You'd be a good king in your own right, Brother. Without their support."

"The king's brothers will rule if Erech is overthrown or killed," Arthan said. "And it would mean war with Rugenhav. But if I were king, I could prevent such a war, since I already have a channel open with the Rugens."

"It sounds tricky. I've never met a Rugen I could trust."

"You're young, Bardil. How many Rugens have you met in Rachard?"

"None should have command over the Valients."

"Father took up the task of keeping the Empire Alliance alive before he died, despite being called a traitor by some. He tried to prevent war by talking with all sides. My talking with them may be our only hope of preventing war. I'm compelled to try because I know that's what Father would have done to preserve Donovan."

"Is Erech's kingdom worth the risk?" Bardil asked. "Even if the worst comes, we can defend Delavon."

"The Rugens have the second-largest standing army in Pemonia, behind the Calbrians. And they can call up twice as many. Their fleets are second to none on the continent. And they have strong claims to Donovard lands where ethnic Rugens are a majority, like in Alpenon. And the Rugens are unified under their strong emperor.

"We, on the other hand, are floundering under a weak king. The royal treasury is empty and indebted. The standing army has been gutted, the discharged soldiers have turned to begging or banditry. Some ministry armies remain intact and paid, like ours, but the high nobles are adrift and being slaughtered one by one."

"But Delavon is strong and far from the border," Bardil said. "We could weather a Rugen attack."

"The border that Rowan is currently at with Asteroth?"

Bardil looked down into the fire, ashamed.

"We would get Rowan home," Arthan continued, "but Delavon cannot shelter all Donovards. Could we so easily stand by, safe in our lands, while the rest of the kingdom is conquered? And later, when it's done and we're surrounded by the new Rugenhav, would we face a negotiated subjugation? Would Delavon simply be another Austveeden, a small kingdom permitted to exist as a buffer between greater powers?"

"You paint a dark future for us."

"It's not written in stone, Bardil. Men like Brugarn, Chaultion, Asteroth, and Erath want nothing more than to have their war with Rugenhav to demonstrate a strength we don't have, all for lands and wealth and honor. But men like Father would find an alternative."

Bardil nodded. "You speak the truth about Father. But he was his own man, and so are you. If after much thought you think getting cozy with the Rugens would be the best path, then take it. I'm young, I know, but I know one man cannot take the world on his shoulders. If everyone else wants war badly enough, how can you stop them merely by making yourself the Rugens' favorite to support your bid for the crown?"

"It must be worth a try, otherwise Brugarn is certain to be king, and it will be war anyway," Arthan said. "Delavon will always be my prime concern. But successful kings must think more broadly than their own house and home."

A ripping sound caused them to look toward the canvas wall. There was a small tear, and another hole appeared on the opposite side.

"Was that an arrow?" Bardil asked as they jumped to their feet.

Another rip was followed by something ricocheting off the brazier. It fell on the rug before them, and Arthan picked it up.

"This barb is exactly like the hand arrows Garion used."

"Our shadows," Bardil gasped. "Quick, cover the brazier!"

Several more darts shot through the tent. The brothers dove to the rug.

"To arms!" Arthan shouted to his men.

Livonier burst into the tent, sword drawn, followed by Arthan's personal guards, the big twins Cuern and Erboln.

"Someone is shooting at us, Livonier! Weaponry like Garion's."

Darts now poured into the tent, including from above.

"Take cover, they're in the trees!" Livonier shouted. He and the guards rushed outside as Arthan and Bardil rolled under the travel bed. Bardil cried out and Arthan saw the blood trail.

"Shoulder," Bardil muttered.

Arthan pushed a meal cloth into Bardil's good hand and brought it up to his shoulder. "Hold tight!" Then he rolled out and lunged for his armor. He quickly pulled on his mail shirt and seated his helmet, then grabbed his sword. The commotion grew outside.

When Arthan exited the tent he saw several soldiers lying dead and injured. The attackers still eluded the rest.

"Livonier?"

"There, my lord," said a wounded knight.

Arthan turned to see a squad of crossbowmen clustered around Livonier just inside the woods. They were shooting up into the trees, looking for the enemy. The mysterious darts had stopped.

"Send scouts up and down the road," Arthan ordered. "Don't let them escape." Arthan walked toward the nearby woods, his eyes searching the dark trees backlit by the stars.

"My lord, it isn't safe here," Livonier said as he approached.

"I'm safer out here in armor than I was inside without it. What have you found?"

"Just a small bag of those hand arrows. Perhaps they've gone . . ."

At that moment men on the other side of the camp shouted. Livonier escorted Arthan back to his tent. "If they can't see you, they can't aim."

Arthan opened his mouth to protest but no words came. A whirlwind of masked figures in green capes burst out from the bushes, cutting down every soldier too slow to react and granting a short but fatal parley to those who did.

It was difficult to number them. They sprinted between the tents and jumped the fires, ran up into the scattered trees and bounded off obstacles like squirrels. Cuern and Erboln stepped in front of Arthan as the darts came again.

Arthan ran between the two big knights, his heart pounding in his ears and skipping in his chest as he raced to confront his father's killers. But it was difficult to focus on one mask as they moved. Arthan would sprint to where they were attacking but they'd be gone when he got there. He became frustrated, as did Livonier, whose orders made no difference.

Arthan rounded a tent and found a masked figure striking down a soldier. Arthan rushed the slim figure as the enemy's sword became two. The woman cartwheeled toward them, wounding Erboln with a slash to his arm, then tripping Cuern with a kick to his knee. Arthan crossed swords with her but she soon disappeared in a glittering cloud that smelled of soot and wet stones.

The action had moved back to the other side of camp. By now Arthan's men were organized into small groups that roved wherever the masked figures reappeared. When Livonier called out, Arthan saw a large masked man lying faceup in the grass. A Racharder pulled his spear from his rib cage.

Arthan knelt and ripped off the mask, exposing unseeing eyes set in a pale face. He was unarmed except for a simple knife.

"Looks foreign," Livonier said.

"There are more of them," Arthan said. "Find them!"

"To your tent, please. So that we can surround it and protect you."

Arthan glanced at a few soldiers struggling to breathe in the grass.

"This enemy is using mysterious powder to choke our men," Livonier said. "You must let me escort you to safety."

Arthan followed his protector back to his tent, noting that the commotion had died down again. A guard rushed out of the tent when they arrived, his face pained. Arthan read his face and felt his stomach turn.

"Bardil!" he shouted.

"They came from there," said another guard inside, gesturing to a gap cut into the rear of the tent. "We didn't see them, but when we came in . . ."

Arthan fell to his knees beside Bardil and cradled his head. "Bardil, I have you . . ." His brother's chest had been opened from his injured shoulder to his lower ribs. Blood oozed along with a sticky yellow liquid.

"A poisoned blade," Livonier whispered.

"I have you . . . You're going to make it . . ."

Arthan wept as Bardil's shallow breathing ceased. He put his hand over Bardil's eyes as they jerked back and forth randomly under the lids.

58

SERDOT

Eglamour Palace, Toulon Ministry
Bloomfade, 3034

Trying the key found on Garion in the doors of the lord ministers' apartments had been tedious. The lords or their servants kept coming and going. Serdot knew he could invoke Arthan's authority as Marshal of Inquiry and simply try the key as they watched. But he preferred to be discreet, trying the locks when he was certain none would see or hear him. If he found a match, Arthan would be the first to know, not one of Garion's collaborators.

Today Serdot would try Lord Reimvick's apartment. He knew Reimvick would be at court. The corridor was clear, so Serdot approached the door. Garion's key turned the lock and Serdot smiled to himself.

He cautiously stepped inside. The room was nothing unusual, spacious and luxurious like the other apartments of the palace. But Lord Reimvick was not a showy man. He traveled light and kept his possessions to a minimum, despite the wealth of his house. But Serdot was certain the materially humble yet socially gregarious man had something to hide.

Serdot took his time picking through the drawers, books, pockets, and pouches. A dish of parchment ashes caught his attention. Serdot knew it was not unusual for high lords to destroy sensitive correspondence, but it was just another hint stored away in Serdot's mind.

He came to the wardroom door and found it locked. Garion's key turned it and Serdot proceeded to search. He froze when he thought he heard a breath. The only sound that followed was a bird at the window. Even so, Serdot's widsemer training urged him out of the room.

He left the wardroom door ajar and returned to the main chamber. He opened the main door and after a moment closed and locked it again, as if he'd left. Then he waited. Sure as the summer sun, he heard movement in the wardroom.

He placed his hand on the dagger in his belt as he watched a black-gloved hand reach out and push the wardroom door open. Then a black-slippered foot stepped through. The dark figure spotted Serdot as he inched along the wall toward the figure. The figure hesitated briefly, then sprinted for the window.

"Stop!" Serdot shouted. "In the name of the Marshal of Inq—"

The dark figure wheeled around and jabbed at his face with a small fist. Serdot blocked the attempt and punched back at the black mask. The sound of a woman surprised him. She recovered quickly and they traded punches, blocks, and kicks.

"Who are you?" Serdot managed to ask as she pulled away toward the window.

The woman surprised him with a backflip from the windowsill. Her feet caught him in the chest and he stumbled back. But he kept his balance and grasped her ankle, twisting her down to the floor. When she grabbed a paring knife from the table, Serdot realized she had been unarmed.

"I'm not going to let you leave," he said, pulling out his long dagger. "Who are you and what are you doing here?"

The woman behind the mask rushed him with the knife but her attempts were halfhearted. His opponent was more intent on escaping than fighting. In his attempt to disarm her, Serdot slashed at her arm. The black leather parted, revealing a shaped plate of thin steel. She stabbed at him but he caught her hand and twisted. Then he landed a fist across her jaw, opening the mask. Fair skin shone out from the black.

Serdot threw her to the floor. "I'll not be bothered with your armor for my next strike," he said. "Who are you!"

"Get off!" she yelled, driving her little fist into his ear.

Disoriented, he loosened his grip on her. He let go of her as she slowly came to her feet. Knife still in hand, she removed the torn mask and pulled back her hood. Serdot swallowed his breath as her brown hair tumbled out of the leather. Her beautiful lips were split and bleeding, her eye already black and blue.

"Princess Milisend . . . ?"

"Lord Valient never gave me the name of his supposed political counselor," she said.

He took a deep breath and lowered his dagger. "My name is Serdot. I'm sorry to have hurt you, but I . . . Forgive me for asking, but why are you dressed like an assassin and hiding in a room accessed by a suspected assassin?"

"Garion is dead, is he not? *He* was the assassin."

"He is . . . was. But we found this key on him. And it fits this door. And here you are."

It was Milisend's turn to take a deep breath. She tossed the paring knife onto the table but Serdot kept his. "You must believe I had nothing to do with Garion," she said. "This was all a mistake."

"I want to believe that, Princess, I do. But . . ."

"What I tell you now you must not repeat to anyone," Milisend said. "Is that clear?"

"My lord learns everything I learn, Princess."

"Then perhaps you'll withhold it this one time, in the interests of the kingdom. I'm to be betrothed to Lord Valient. Against my will, of course."

"I'm listening."

"I'm a jewel thief, Serdot, trained by the best. I desired only the adventure that comes with the game, not the jewels themselves."

"That much is known by many, thanks to Tronchet. I only care about why you're here."

"I came to Lord Reimvick's quarters to search for a worthy heist. Instead I was locked in his wardrobe."

"He caught you?"

"He didn't see me. I hid all night."

Serdot smiled as he sheathed his dagger. "I can see you've been well outfitted, but I wouldn't say you were taught by the best. Aside from becoming trapped, you were not able to pick your way out, you need to scout your targets better, and your thievery is not the best-kept secret. More importantly, Princess, I could have wounded you gravely if not for your armor."

"Will you let me leave now? I'm starving."

"Of course, Princess." Serdot regarded her closely as she made for the window. "Would you like to use the door? In your weakened condition I don't recommend climbing out there."

"But I . . ." Milisend looked down at her black leathers.

"Here," Serdot said, going into the wardrobe and coming out with a fine silk robe. "Much too big for you, but Reimvick is going to be in too much trouble to worry about a missing robe. Everyone is at court, so you should be able to make it to your chambers unseen."

Milisend wrapped herself in the silk. "Yes, it appears he may be in some trouble . . . Why did Garion's key open Reimvick's door?"

"That's what I'm here to find out. It's possible the key was meant to provide Garion access to kill Reimvick, if he was the next target. But something more nefarious seems likely."

"If it's helpful, Reimvick may be an alchemist. I saw a laboratory in his privy and he had a presence candle lit on this table last night when I broke in."

Serdot reentered the wardrobe and unlocked the privy door. "My God . . ." he muttered, staring at the wax and herb remnants on the floor. Bits of broken glass were still strewn about and the shelving smashed.

"I didn't see Reimvick destroy it himself," Milisend said over his shoulder. "But I'm sure it was him. Why would he have a laboratory, then destroy it?"

Serdot crouched to the floor and dipped his finger into spilled powder to smell it. "Because he didn't want Garion to lead us here and see it."

"Could a man like Lord Reimvick have been involved with Garion?"

Serdot looked at her. "You'd better return to your chambers, Princess. It's not safe to be here. Garion and Reimvick may not be the only ones in the palace."

Serdot watched her turn to leave, but then she hesitated.

"Even if there are many rumors about my . . . activity, you'll not tell Lord Valient or Tronchet that I was here?"

Serdot sighed before giving her a small bow. She smiled and retreated from the apartment.

59

WREDEGAR

Eglamour, Toulon Ministry
Bloomfade, 3034

"I can't take this boredom much longer," Wredegar said.

"The emperor has ordered that you will remain here," Vesamune said.

"To waste away in your cellar, Ambassador?"

"Consider it a great compliment that the emperor is keeping you as commander of the Wosmoks in Donovan. And that Meliamour is sending you new recruits. But if you disobey me I will inform her of your insubordination."

"As of now there are no Wosmoks in Donovan for me to command," Wredegar said. "It's easy for you, Vesamune. You spend your days in luxury here and at Erech's palace. I don't mean to complain, but I'd much rather return to my post as a knight in the regular army than skulk in foreign shadows. I will miss out on the war while hiding down in your cellar."

"You are permitted to go anywhere in Eglamour, so long as you take precautions. You still have no clues about Rodel's disappearance?"

"Many nights I've walked the streets of Eglamour searching for any sign of him. I can't help but wonder if he has . . ."

"If he what?"

Wredegar knew Rodel had been unhappy, but he was not about to suggest to Meliamour's sister that one of the

Wosmoks had abandoned the empire. "I wonder how he may have died. I presume he's dead, that is."

Vesamune sat straighter in her chair. "Do you suppose we're being hunted now too?"

Wredegar smiled. "If the assassins have any interest in killing Rugens, you'd be the most visible and senior official in Eglamour."

"Don't," she said, annoyed. "Could Rodel have betrayed us?"

"Wosmoks do not turn against their own. They give their lives for the empire."

"Could Rodel have wanted his life back, as you long for rejoining the regular army?"

"Not possible."

60

MARLAN

Thorendor Castle, Wallevet Ministry
Bloomfade, 3034

"Wrong! You got his brother." Arasemis pounded the table.

"He was in the lord minister's tent," Fetzer said. "Richly dressed son of a high noble. It must have been him!"

Frustrated, Arasemis turned to Marlan and gestured for him to speak.

"We failed, Fetzer. Master Arasemis heard the news before we returned to Thorendor. Everyone is talking about how the Delavon minister's camp was attacked in his own lands. And that his brother was killed."

Arasemis glared at Fetzer. "Perhaps if you'd been less interested in recovering Bertwil's gladed sword you'd have known where Arthan was. You could have completed the task and Bertwil would still be alive."

"Don't blame me," Fetzer said. "You sent us on this mission, and we nearly succeeded."

"Nearly?" Arasemis snorted. "You had a clean chance and wasted it. I blame myself for sending you out on a task so early in your training."

"If you'd given me the proper tools, this wouldn't have happened," Fetzer retorted. "I'm the only one without an alchemical sword or advanced alchemy. If I had a good sword, we would never fail."

Arasemis set stern eyes on Fetzer. "The history of Candlestone is one of many small failures and some big ones. But Candlestone has claimed many great victories because we're persistent. And only when its members are ready for the tasks."

"I am ready!" Fetzer shouted, stepping toward Arasemis. "If you'd get your face out of dusty books and crumbling parchments, I'd have—"

"Hold your tongue!" Arasemis shouted. "Candlestone is not about you. Get out of my sight before I—"

Marlan stepped between them as Juhl and Rodel looked on. "Candlestone can only be undone by us. If we stand together, no king or emperor can stand against us. You taught me that, Master."

Fetzer stepped back, sulking. Arasemis kept his eyes on him.

"He's young," the master said. "I should never have let him or Rodel go on this task. They need more training, though Rodel performed admirably."

"Fetzer did as well," Marlan said. "The new recruits do need more training. But if Arthan had been in his tent he'd be dead. We were unlucky, and so was Bertwil."

Still steaming, Arasemis pointed at Fetzer. "You will relinquish Bertwil's sword at once." Fetzer pretended not to hear him. "At once!"

Fetzer turned to Marlan. "You tell him. Tell the master."

Marlan hesitated but eventually met Arasemis's eyes. "Fetzer tried to save Bertwil. The distraction was going well but there were too many soldiers. It was Bertwil who wouldn't listen to me. Fetzer tried to go to him, but it was too late."

"The sword!" Arasemis shouted at Fetzer.

Fetzer slowly drew the yellow-tinted sword from his belt and walked toward Arasemis. He extended the sword at arm's length, pointing it at Arasemis, then he let it fall to the floor in front of the master.

Arasemis paced around the library and forced himself to breathe calmly as Marlan watched from a bench.

"Serious revolt has happened within Candlestone before," Arasemis said. "The punishment has often been death. The Order cannot afford divisions, distractions, and discovery."

"Fetzer is just eager," Marlan said. "Headstrong and arrogant, but eager to learn and contribute."

"He's reckless and dangerous. You brought him here. But since you're my senior apprentice, I will stomach him a while longer. But get him under control, or I will deal with him."

"Shall we try again against Arthan? It would give Fetzer an opportunity to redeem himself."

"You and Juhl will go to Rachard and try again," Arasemis said. "Fetzer and Rodel will remain here with me to continue their training."

Marlan stood and nodded. He turned to leave the library but hesitated.

"Speak your mind, Marlan."

"I agree with you, Master, that Fetzer is dangerous. But if his mind can be focused, the only danger he'll present is to the enemy."

Arasemis sighed. "You still think he is a prophetic leader of Candlestone?"

"He's no Rildning, but he's bold and talented. I have no doubt that you can shape him into a potent weapon."

Arasemis nodded slowly. "He has potential. But I see *you* as my best weapon, Marlan. If you see something in Fetzer, I will give him some time. But I'll only let him go so far. I'll not have generations of work undone by an undisciplined deviant."

"Tempering and honing, glading and treating, just like our blades."

"We shall see. Now, time to go to Rachard. Do it quietly and quickly."

61

THEUDAMER

Heingartmer, Ward of Havelbern
Bloomfade, 3034

"How are the new Wosmoks progressing, Meliamour?" Emperor Theudamer asked as he received a letter from her.

"Eleven have done well in the training, Your Majesty. They should be ready earlier than expected."

"Good," he said, opening the letter. "Inform Vesamune and Wredegar. Now, what news from your sister?"

> Your Majesty,
>
> Eglamour has become a more hostile place for me as your ambassador. Duke Brugarn continually rejects my request to have an audience with King Erech, and various courtiers regularly insult the Rugen Empire and blame us for their ills. As ever, I'm honored to serve as your representative, but merely wish to inform you of the increasing difficulty of my position.
>
> Regarding the assassinations of the high lords, Wredegar and I are no closer to understanding who is behind it all than the Donovards are. However, one assassin was recently captured. He was among the elite knights known as the Crownblades, who are entrusted with protecting the king and his family. This assassin, Garion by

name, nearly killed Brugarn and Arthan, the young lord I spoke of in previous letters.

Arthan somehow uncovered Garion and interrogated him before Garion killed himself by jumping from a window at Arthan's estate in the capital. Rumors say Arthan pushed Garion to his death, and others say Arthan was behind everything from the start. Regardless, Arthan is viewed by the king as a hero and was appointed by him to a post called the Marshal of Inquiry. He is now responsible for finding and eliminating other assassins.

You'll recall my previous thoughts about approaching Arthan as someone we may be able to work with to serve the interests of the empire. His reputation is climbing despite the dark rumors spread by his enemies.

Importantly, I did gain a private audience with him at his estate and he agreed to keep talking with me. He is under no illusions and appears to love Donovan as a loyal lord should. But he is very pragmatic, self-interested, and potentially corruptible.

Regarding the ransom for Geras Vilarwef, the negotiations have been slow but I managed to persuade the Donovards not to send him to Austveeden. In return, they want the gold now. I'm confident I'll be able to convince them of the exchange as you requested. It will simply take a bit more time to negotiate.

Finally, Wredegar is restless. Any information on the progress of the training of his new Wosmok unit would be appreciated.

Your humble servant,
Vesamune Theudamer
Eglamour

Theudamer looked at Meliamour. "I want Vesamune to continue speaking to Valient. He's the sort we'll want."

"Certainly," Meliamour said.

"What about my war?" Graf asked. "The army is prepared. The border garrisons are double-manned. We're waiting for your order to invade, Your Majesty."

"Don't be so hasty," Herzol said.

"We must wait for the right moment," Theudamer said.

"Whoever these assassins are, they are doing our work for us," Meliamour said. "Infiltrating Erech's personal guard demonstrates their skill, even if Garion's capture is a setback for them."

"But now should be the right time, while Donovan slowly crumbles," Graf said.

"We'll wait to see if these assassins are successful in overthrowing the Avaleaus," Theudamer said. "That would be a better time to invade, once their house is destroyed with the nobles in disarray."

"If we attack now, the high nobles will still rally around Erech," Meliamour said.

"Lord Minister Asteroth took Ambardil Free City," Graf said. "Messengers say he slew many, including every Rugen he found in the city."

"We expected as much," Meliamour said.

"Surely we can at least invade Durgensdil, to protect the ethnic Rugens?" Graf asked. "King Erech has already lost the confidence of his high nobles, and perhaps their loyalty. It's not inconceivable that the Almerians or the Calbrians own these mysterious assassins or will take advantage of Donovan's woes before we do. Perhaps they're preparing their own grab of Donovard lands while we watch idly."

"The Almerians cannot be behind the assassinations with the intent to invade Donovan," Meliamour said. "While the Almerians may wish to punish the Donovards for the collapse of the Empire Alliance, they can barely hold on to their measly islands off Donovan's northern coasts."

"The assassins also first targeted Raymond Reimvick," Herzol said. "Since he was the principal negotiator in support of the alliance, it makes no sense that the Almerians would have killed him."

"The Calbrians also have their own problems, given the patchwork of peoples they've forced together there," Meliamour said.

"If you know their minds so well, why do you bother deploying your spies?" Graf asked her.

"I know them so well because I *do* bother," she said. "I don't expect you to understand such complicated matters."

"Donovan will be ours for the picking soon enough," Theudamer said, "but we must wait until the kingdom is ripe, Graf. Then, you'll have your war, be sure of that."

"And our people in Durgensdil?"

The emperor nodded. "We will send them more support. Food, horses, weapons, soldiers. And, Meliamour, send more of your regular spies to Durgensdil. Don't wait for more Wosmoks. We must stay informed of Lord Asteroth's movements, looking for any hint that he, or Erath in Gadolin, intend to invade us first.

"As for you, Graf, prepare to go to the borderlands to pay the ransom for Geras and escort him here to me."

"Of course, Your Majesty."

❧

"Stay please, Meliamour," the emperor said as his counselors began to depart. He stepped down from his wolf-headed throne and walked with her to the window.

"When war comes, the campaigns will be long and fierce. Even if these mysterious assassins or your Wosmoks are successful in sabotaging Donovan's leadership and defenses, the Donovards will not fold easily."

Meliamour nodded. "It's a large kingdom with many resources at hand."

"Long ago, the ancient Raffen heathens cooperated with the newly independent colonists of this realm. More recently, during Rugenhav's Wars of Unification, many petty kings and princelets were conquered and consolidated, and naval campaigns established our empire. Both of those events strengthened our people. I long for a third revival borne by the collapse and conquest of Donovan."

Meliamour nodded. "Too many Rugen lands are still part of our enemy's kingdom. The time has come."

Theudamer turned from the window and glanced at one of the dark columns lining his great hall. The figure of his great-great-grandfather, Ebronin the Elder, was carved into it. Ebronin stood impossibly tall, sword in hand, confident and strong.

"The statues are a constant reminder of our golden eras, and the third one to come. I feel the power of my ancestors and the Raffen blood in my veins. I intend to redefine what it means to be Rugen emperor, lord of these and vast foreign lands. And now that the empress is finally with child, my legacy will only grow."

"We will return Rugenhav to its rightful place as the dominant power of Pemonia, Your Majesty."

"Yes, our rightful place . . ."

62

MILISEND

Eglamour Palace, Toulon Ministry
Bloomfade, 3034

"I'm sure he'll return soon, Princess."

Milisend shook her head. "I don't know what I'd do if something happened to him, Rosellen. Regaume was supposed to be back from Ralmogard by now. You've had someone check his band's hideaway in the Borel District again?"

"Just this morning."

"Of course you have, thank you. You've always been so helpful in passing our letters back and forth. I'm forever grateful for your protection of this forbidden love."

Rosellen smiled. "I'm always on edge wondering what you and Regaume will bring back from the heists . . . and to hear about his kissing."

"Oh, Rosellen, do not live through my vices. I don't take great pride in the thefts."

"But in Regaume . . ."

"Him I treasure above all the jewels. My heart flutters to think of him, and sinks to think of what might befall him."

"Perhaps he's used an alchemical candle to capture your heart," Rosellen said.

"There is no such thing. And no need, as Regaume won my heart long ago."

"Yes, I remember. The carriage ride to see your sister in Elmbrel Ministry. We had stopped in that little town . . ."

"Oladet. And he stole the heirloom turquoise pendant Mother wanted Avalane to have after she married Henrey. When I saw the bandit's eyes I freely gave it."

"And he promised to see you again."

"Yes, here in Eglamour. And that was that . . ." Milisend looked down at her black leathers in her lap and continued sewing up Serdot's dagger cut.

"Regaume has survived much," Rosellen said. "He will return."

"If I lose him, I lose any chance of escaping all of this. I've always said no to his offers to run away with him, hoping one day I will have the courage to say yes. Otherwise, my heart would die and I'd be forced to wed Lord Valient."

"It won't come to that, Princess. Regaume will return."

Milisend turned to her handmaiden. "All this time thinking, waiting . . . I've made up my mind. When Regaume returns, I will leave with him. You've seen Father at court. Every day is worse. For too long I've forced myself into thinking I could do something to help, but I'm no match for all these clever politicians. I'm just a princess, Rosellen, waiting in the wings. A pawn to be married off like Avalane."

Rosellen smiled. "You're also a master thief, with the outfit to prove it."

"Hardly a master. My last two heists were disasters."

"Bad luck. You have a jewel chest to prove it. I'm happy for your decision about Regaume. He'll whisk you away from the palace the moment you say it."

"You'll be all right?" Milisend asked. "I don't want to abandon you . . ."

"I'll be fine. Your mother will double her popaver when she hears what you've done. Her maidens will need an extra hand."

"Is it better to have them think I was dead?" Milisend wondered aloud. "They wouldn't come looking for me. They would leave me be."

"It would crush your mother," Rosellen said. "And perhaps be the final stroke for the king."

Milisend looked down again. "I am ashamed to think only of myself."

"It is no crime to desire a life of love for oneself," Rosellen said. "With a dash of adventure, of course. When the time comes, you'll know what to do."

63

ARTHAN

Rachard Cathedral, Delavon Ministry
Bloomfade, 3034

The morning was fresh and clear, the sun providing welcome warmth that burned away the fog of the night. But the interior of Rachard Cathedral was still dour. All came to mourn the death of the youngest member of the House of Valient.

Arthan watched glassy eyed as Bishop Nestorath said Bardil's last rites, but he could not bring himself to listen to the words. He could only watch as Bardil's linen-wrapped body was lowered into the granite tomb. Part of Arthan still hoped Bardil would sit up, the poisoned wound healed, before they slid the heavy lid over him.

Arthan was startled when the trumpets sounded to herald the ascension of Bardil's soul. He looked at Maillard's tomb, the newly finished likeness of him carved from the stone. It lay on a stone cushion, eyes aimed skyward and unblinking. In time, the mason would craft a stone face for Bardil.

He knew it was like this for all the Valients, since the times when they were royalty. As a boy he had looked upon these faces and thought about the cracks and worn places. He did not know them and never thought about seeing those he was closest to buried beneath them. Now he saw them and knew they were cold inside their vaults. He pictured himself in one, his stony likeness lying atop.

Arthan felt a heavy hand on his shoulder. It was Medoff. The general looked tired. The ceremony had ended, and those who had come to pay their respects were scattering away.

"Your father's death was my fault," Medoff said. "I was with him, right there beside him, in Mordmerg. But I could not defend him. Bardil was not your fault. You defended him from the enemy."

"It doesn't seem that way . . ." Arthan said. "Perhaps I never should have taken him to Eglamour."

"These masked assassins are everywhere at once. Bredahade, Mordmerg, Lyonseln, Eglamour, and in our countryside. The Army of Delavon awaits your orders, my lord."

Arthan nodded. "A moment, please, Medoff."

The general bowed and left Arthan alone with the tombs. He sat, thinking. Bishop Nestorath had joined the choir in singing the burial dirge. Amid the hymn, other voices flooded into Arthan's mind. He could hear Bardil's laughter and his words urging him to see Meriam. He could hear Bardil's caution against colluding with the Rugens against Brugarn. Then there was Reimvick's voice, telling him the high lords depended on him to lead as Maillard had done. He could see it in Waldemar's eyes when the steward talked of the imbalance of power between the king, Brugarn, and the lord ministers.

Arthan heard Serdot's voice telling him no one could be fully trusted. He saw Brugarn's ugly face and heard his thinly veiled threats. Ambassador Vesamune's negotiations. Desperation in Erech's frightened eyes. Everything faded into a flurry of wooden masks, green capes, screaming, and flames.

Arthan looked up, finding himself kneeling before Maillard's tomb. His eyes welled as he searched for answers and guidance. He lifted his eyes to the rainbow light cast by the cathedral windows and scattered across the carved stone. His eyes settled on the text etched into Maillard's tomb. A single word was alit in red amid the writing: *BOLD*. It was part of the description of Maillard's bygone battles.

Arthan stopped breathing. He turned to see the sunbeams burst through the window. The red light came from the ruby-encrusted crown of Bardhon, first of the House of Valient to be king of Donovan. Arthan looked to the window and saw Rikhard, ancient father of the House of Valient and grandson of Marshal Hilsingor of Ned Gollen.

"I am of the Valients," he said aloud. He felt strength and confidence flow from a hidden fountain within him. "I am lord of Delavon," he said louder. His voice echoed alone, the hymn of the choir having ceased. "I am Arthan Valient, Lord Minister of Delavon, Count of Bram, son of Maillard, and descendant of Hilsingor!" he shouted. He looked at the hard faces shining down on him from the windows and tombs. Then he turned to Maillard's likeness.

"I promise to lead boldly, for realm and kingdom, and continent if need be. Usurpers of the crown, foreign enemies, and masked assassins—none will sway me. These shoulders were built for the burden you've passed to me . . . carried by all of you who have gone before me. Now it falls to me . . ." He stepped to Bardil's tomb and laid his hand on it. "And I will avenge you."

PART III

DARK CORNERS

64

FETZER

Thorendor Castle, Wallevet Ministry
Bloomfade, 3034

Fetzer walked slowly into his cell and closed the door. He collapsed on the bed and looked up at the ceiling, tracing the ancient Candlestone symbols carved in the beams with his eyes. He glanced at the table by the wall. His journal waited for him. He got up and pinched the quill.

> I must admit that since Marlan and the others departed for Rachard, the training under Arasemis has been rigorous. I know he is trying to test me, to punish me, but I'll not give the one-armed hermit the satisfaction of uncovering any weakness. Nor will I give Rodel the chance to get ahead.
>
> Rodel is an annoying, pompous Rugen. I don't care where he came from or what he did. He's not worthy to be part of what I know Candlestone can become. I respect only his persistence. That quality is where our similarities end. He seems to have been bred at the dagger point, but his swordcraft is no match for me.
>
> Rodel has tried to act friendly, but I know he is false. Marlan is a true believer in Candlestone and good with a sword. And Marlan knows talent when he sees it. Juhl is as beautiful as she is dangerous, and quicker than all of us. Although

she is infatuated with Rodel, I know in time she will favor me and our destiny.

Marlan and Juhl will be worthy companions in my eventual leadership of Candlestone. Bertwil was slow, thickheaded, and never acknowledged my dominance. If he had listened to me he'd still be alive, useless as he was.

But this Rodel . . . I suspect his intentions. Could he be an agent of the Rugen emperor, sent to infiltrate and destroy Candlestone from within? He claims to follow our path, but he is less fervent than he should be. After we complete our tasks in Donovan, his loyalty to us will be tested when we turn our attention to Rugenhav and beyond.

I resent not being sent with Marlan and Juhl to finish off the Valients. But I've taken great pleasure in succeeding at whatever Arasemis throws at me. He cannot defeat me. No one can. Perhaps he was formidable when he was young, before he lost his arm. But there is a limit to what he can teach me. I'm fast approaching that point. Then what purpose does he serve? How would he serve Candlestone except to be a book-drunk obstacle to the greatness and speed that we could achieve?

In anticipation of my ascendancy, I've explored every nook and corridor of Thorendor while Arasemis studies and Rodel sleeps. I've seen everything, inside and out, past all but the best-locked doors. It is a magnificent place but still fast asleep under dust and lost memories. One day Thorendor will be great again, when it is no longer shackled by the hermit. When the name of Candlestone is no longer kept secret. And when our deeds spark fear and submission.

65

SERDOT

Eglamour Palace, Toulon Ministry
Bloomfade, 3034

"Not now, Serdot," Reimvick said. "I'm due to meet with Waldemar."

Reimvick tried to sidestep Serdot, but he blocked his path. "I'm afraid it's urgent," Serdot said. "I just received word that Arthan arrived in Rachard, but that more assassins killed his brother, Bardil."

"How dreadful. But Arthan is in one piece?"

Serdot nodded. "For now . . ."

"Please relay my condolences. Arthan has endured more loss to his house than any high noble should in the absence of war."

"I will, Lord Reimvick."

"Now, if you'll excuse me, I must see Waldemar."

"I have another matter to discuss," Serdot said. "I need to speak with you about Garion."

"He's long dead now, isn't he? You and Lord Valient tied the bow on that whole conspiracy very nicely. Shouldn't you be focused on the assassins who attacked them in Delavon?"

"I didn't say they were attacked in Delavon, my lord. Did you already hear a rumor?"

"No, no . . . I just assumed . . ."

"Despite what happened to Lord Valient and Bardil, I have reason to believe a danger still lurks here in the palace. Surely you have time to speak with me for one moment?"

"Fine, fine. What is it then?"

"I wanted to ask you about Garion's alchemy. You recall his use of a cloaking cloud before he was arrested?"

"Yes, go on, go on . . ."

"Items like that take some skill and time to prepare. I've questioned Sir Hamelin about it, but neither he nor any of the other Crownblades ever saw Garion prepare alchemical mixtures. They never once smelled anything peculiar among his personal effects."

"Garion was a weasel, Serdot. He hid from us all this time. I'm not surprised that he would hide his alchemy."

"But he was foolish enough to keep his mask and his orders among his things in the Crownblades' barracks. My lord, I suspect Garion had help. He clearly knew how to use alchemical items, but I think someone must have helped him make them or hide his laboratory."

Serdot noticed Reimvick's brow glisten. The lord minister's breathing also quickened.

"I suppose you're right, Serdot. But who and where? As the king's protectors, the Crownblades have access to the entire palace and everyone within it. Proving your theory correct will take some time."

"I wonder, given your extensive social connections within the royal court, my lord, whether you know of anyone practicing alchemy. Presumably in secret."

Reimvick swallowed. "Alchemy is most dishonorable. If anyone in this palace has such a deplorable pastime, they've done a good job of keeping it to themselves. I could not guess who would—"

Serdot held up a fragment of crystal, the upper half of a vial taken from Reimvick's privy. "I found this in the corridor where the lord ministers' apartments are located. It could have been anyone passing through, of course. Stuck to the bottom of anyone's slipper or boot. But I wanted to show it to you and to you only, in case you'd seen anything like it before."

"No, no I haven't. Is it dangerous?"

Serdot shook his head. "Just a shard of equipment typically used to mix or store solutions."

"Oh, well, thank God for that. Now, Serdot, I must be going. I do hope your search turns up more clues."

"May I continue to ask you about my findings, my lord, with the understanding that they will remain a secret until our investigation is complete?"

"Of course, of course. Your trust in me is well placed." Reimvick wiped his brow with a handkerchief. "Will Lord Valient be returning to the capital soon?"

"As soon as he's able, my lord."

"Yes, of course. Now, excuse me, Serdot. Waldemar is waiting."

Serdot stepped out of his way and watched Reimvick scurry down the corridor. "Thank you for your time, Lord Minister."

Reimvick did not turn around but waved a hand. Serdot gritted his teeth as he watched him go. He had gotten the response he expected from Reimvick but wished he could push harder. He knew he'd have to wait until Arthan returned before accusing a lord minister of ties to the assassins.

Serdot also could not silence a small doubt, given that Reimvick's own brother, Raymond, had been the first high lord to die. Reimvick could have simply coveted Raymond's lord ministership, but that did not explain the attacks on Maillard, Gottfried, and Brugarn. Despite Reimvick's behavior and the certainty that his privy held a secret laboratory, Serdot felt no closer to unraveling the mystery.

66

ARTHAN

Rachard Castle, Delavon Ministry
Bloomfade, 3034

"As I said before, they had the same masks as Marlan and Garion," Arthan said. "All of these killings are related."

General Medoff turned to Livonier. "You were supposed to protect him."

"Our scouts gave us no warning," Livonier said. "And they came from the trees."

Medoff pounded his fist on the table. "There is no excuse!"

"Sir Livonier fought honorably," Arthan said. "Everyone did. But we're not accustomed to fighting an enemy like this. Their methods are not traditional."

"If I may . . ." Alfrem began quietly, handing Arthan a sealed letter. "You father had me keep this alongside his will. Maillard didn't tell me much, but I believe his letter is relevant to these assassins' untraditional methods. I think the time has come for you to read it, aloud, as your father intended."

Arthan complied.

> Arthan, my son,
> If the alderman has given you this letter then the rot in Eglamour has worsened, as I long feared it would. If you are called to war, either on the fields of battle or in the shadows of court intrigue,

know that you have more tools at your disposal beyond what Master Pelinaud could teach you with a sword. Alchemy, Arthan. Don't shudder at the word.

Have you ever wondered why the House of Valient stayed loyal to the Avaleaus despite losing the crown to them? It was a time when alchemy was not shunned as it is today. Your ancestors were good at chemina arcana. The Avaleaus were novices at best.

A secret pact was made whereby the Valients would support the Avaleaus with their alchemical and political skills, and the Avaleaus permitted our house to keep our ancestral lands. The Avaleaus wished to wrap themselves with the legitimacy of Hilsingor's heirs.

This addendum to my will was recent but necessary. When I heard what happened to Lord Raymond I knew where things were going, even if I didn't have the courage to take this path myself. Do not make the modern man's mistake of viewing alchemy as merely an extension of pagan mysticism.

While it's true the original natives of Pemonia had outlandish beliefs, some of their methods were real and not unlike Old World physicians and widsemers. Indeed, the ancient Almerics practiced what is called classical alchemy before the Church labeled it as incompatible with Messengian teachings.

This letter should be accompanied by a sword named Adrithayn. It's very old, forged by the alchemist smiths back when our house ruled Delavon as kings. I never raised it in battle, nor did your grandfather. But if things change as much as I believe they will, you will need Adrithayn.

Do not worry about what others will say. Many have secretly kept these ancient ways alive, lest their enemies rekindle an old advantage. In

time, those who possess these methods may make
all the difference, for better or for worse. Do not
forget that.

Your father, Maillard

When Arthan finished reading the letter, he looked around the room. All eyes were fixed in uncomfortable stares. Alfrem moved first, placing a linen-wrapped parcel on the table and unfolding it to reveal a sword. Arthan recognized the colors of his house in the intricate sapphire and spinel gemstones set in gilded designs. The top of the hilt was fashioned like a lion's mouth, with a white-glinting blade protruding from it.

Alfrem finally spoke. "Adrithayn. The anchiclade blade is old but will still defeat most steels. Unfortunately, that is all I was told about it."

"How long have you known?" Arthan asked.

"Maillard kept the sword hidden from me until Raymond's murder. I was as surprised as you are now."

"Anyone else at this table familiar with chemina arcana?" Arthan asked. Heads shook all around. "Does anyone know what this blade can do? And why it shines white?" Only stares answered him.

"I suggest you consult Master Pelinaud," Alfrem said. "As you know, he is knowledgeable about most any weapon. Perhaps even alchemical."

"If keeping Adrithayn at my side will help me survive these persistent assassins, then I will do so. It's clearly what Father wanted and he seemed to know more than he was willing to write down. I'll ask Pelinaud, but for now, no one outside this council will know about this sword or Father's letter. I'll not have rumors about the Marshal of Inquiry turning to pagan beliefs. Father gave clear warning about dismissing these old ways and hinted that others may hide similar blades, but I need to know more first."

"I think that is wise," Medoff said as the others nodded. "As the newly appointed Marshal of Inquiry, many eyes will be upon you. If you reveal this sword too soon . . ."

Arthan nodded. "I wish I could have spoken to Father about this," he said. "These are difficult times. Rioting in

Eglamour. The weakness of Erech. The influence of Brugarn and his ilk. The skirmishes on the border with Rugenhav . . . I want to end Rowan's wardship under Lord Asteroth, and I want him to return to Rachard as soon as possible. It may only be a matter of time before serious conflict erupts on the border. I sent him a letter prior to leaving Eglamour, but I suppose a messenger has not arrived?"

Alfrem shook his head. "It will be difficult to convince Asteroth. Once warded, Rowan is like an adopted son to Asteroth. He'll want him to experience the strife on the borderlands, to harden him."

"I want him recalled from Alpenon regardless of Asteroth's wishes. Aside from Rowan's safety, if Erech is overthrown by Brugarn, he could hold Rowan as a hostage to force my cooperation."

"I agree," Medoff said. "I can send a troop of men down to Alpenon to retrieve Rowan."

"Just a messenger," Arthan said, shaking his head. "We must not provoke Asteroth by sending a large escort, at least for now."

"Do you need more soldiers to guard you at Clonmel when you return to the capital?" Medoff asked.

"The king has provided me with a new force as marshal, any number I need. I certainly don't trust them as I would my own Racharders, but I'll have Livonier and his men with me again. As for the Delavon Army, ensure we are ready for a war with Rugenhav, should it come."

"Countess Iserenne's troops are already on alert," Medoff said. "Since she shares a border with Gadolin Ministry, her lands would be the first to meet Rugen invaders."

"The Rugens could also come up through Austveeden," Livonier said. "My lord, you've not yet appointed a new Count of Caval to replace your slain cousin, Golbane."

"When Rowan returns he will have the title," Arthan said. "Perhaps it will help him leave Asteroth, if he needs a reason. Rowan's experience on the borderlands will certainly help him manage Caval, if the Rugens take a path through Austveeden."

"Invading Austveeden would bring the Calbrians into the war," Medoff said. "So it's more likely the Rugens would attack Alpenon and Gadolin first, then attempt to take Eglamour. Delavon is far out of their way."

"We mustn't limit Rugen aggression to the south and west alone," Alfrem said. "Given the state of the kingdom, they may be tempted to take more of Donovan than we'd expect."

"Which is why I want to fortify Delavon," Arthan said. "Bellumet, as my chief engineer, what do you advise?"

Arthan could not help but steal a look at Meriam, seated beside Bellumet at the far end of the table. He missed her face but had not had the time to see her much since bringing Bardil's body into Rachard.

The bald, pointy-nosed Bellumet cleared his throat. "Since the collapse of the Empire Alliance, I've been giving some thought to an idea. It's extensive, expensive, but nothing would better defend Delavon if the worst comes."

"Go on," Arthan said with a nod.

Bellumet gestured to Meriam. She unfurled a scroll of loose parchments, scattering a collection of maps and sketches on the table.

"These show the locations of three ancient warcastles: Hullen in the west, Rampilar in the south, and Zulgauet in the southeast."

"Warcastles . . ." Arthan said. "The old Brintilian ruins?"

Bellumet nodded. "They were your ancestor Hilsingor's idea. He designed warcastles to house multiple legions to hold the frontier during the colonial push into the interior of the New World. All of them were built by Frontier Corps soldiers and tribal slaves. Too expensive to keep up, their stones were later cannibalized to build castles and cities when the threat from the tribes subsided."

"They've been ruined for hundreds of years," Alfrem said. "Surely it would be cheaper and easier to build new border castles."

Bellumet shook his head. "No, sir. The foundations are still good. I sent Meriam to study them. These are her drawings. Meriam?"

"You can see in this sketch, my lord, that the Frontier Corps used large rough-hewn blocks to build most foundations and walls," she said. "Even some towers still stand today, though the grounds of all three ruins are now forested, or, in the case of Zulgauet, boggy."

"Wonderful," Arthan said as he stared into her eyes. His advisers looked at him. "What I mean is, were these cities or castles? They look more extensive that I remember hearing." He marveled at the intricate detail her slender, gentle hands had rendered.

"Both, my lord," Meriam said. "They were the largest fortifications ever built in Pemonia, rivalling even Arcodum in Arukia. The heathen hordes repeatedly overwhelmed traditional castles in the original colonies. The formation of the Frontier Corps put the tribes on the defensive, and the warcastles helped the Brintilians take vast swathes of tribal lands. Warcastles were self-sufficient, with fortified farms, granaries, workshops, barracks—everything."

"Hilsingor had the first warcastle built here," Bellumet said. "Rachard Castle was the core of a warcastle by the same name, the rest of it torn down to build and expand the city and pave roads to new cities. Rebuilding on the weathered skeletons of Hullen, Rampilar, and Zulgauet would be a daunting task, but there would be no better defense."

"Many Brintilian high nobles went bankrupt attempting to rebuild or maintain these colossal fortresses," Alfrem said. "I do not advise wasting time and gold on them, my lord."

"None of the warcastles, once completed, were ever taken," Bellumet said. "That includes the warcastles elsewhere in the kingdom and in Austveeden. These three once formed an impenetrable curtain across the underbelly of Donovan, and they could serve this purpose again."

"The utility of the warcastles in olden days, when the Brintilians mined the electrum fountains and other metals here, may have made sense," Alfrem said.

"Does anyone still use warcastles today?" Arthan asked.

"Other than the core of Rachard, there is Riddertin Castle in Gadolin," Bellumet said. "It's right on the Rugen border, just a sliver of the original warcastle."

"I cannot imagine what this scheme would cost," Alfrem said.

"Meriam has calculated it," Bellumet said.

"About seventy thousand guldirs would be required to complete restoration of all three simultaneously within a year," she said.

"Longer, if the money is reduced," Bellumet said. "The cost includes labor, granite, timber, everything."

"Impossible and impractical, to say the least," Alfrem said.

"We'll likely have a war on our hands well before a year's time," Medoff said.

"Asteroth and Erath will slow the Rugens down enough to buy us more time," Lunfrid countered.

"This is folly," Alfrem said. "Seventy thousand guldirs . . ."

"How soon could Hullen be completed, if we focused on just one for now?" Arthan asked.

"About three months," Meriam said. "And only because it's in better condition than the others. Rampilar is foundation only, but close to quarries in the Caval Moors. Zulgauet is the most isolated. If Hullen were reconstructed first, Rampilar and Zulgauet could be completed by this time next year."

"Who would build this?" Alfrem said. "The Army of Delavon?"

"Labor should not be a problem," Bellumet said. "Soldiers put out of service in Eglamour and elsewhere could be hired."

"Other ministers will demand a tax to use them, just as we would," Alfrem said.

"The expense would be negotiable," Bellumet said, "and the northern ministers would have an interest in seeing our fortresses stand up."

"Thereby keeping up the popularity of the Marshal of Inquiry," Meriam said with a smile.

"I don't see it," Alfrem said. "Beyond expending a quarter of our lord minister's treasury, lore says these warcastles took fifty years to construct."

"But that was in an age of few good roads," Bellumet said. "And they had to clear the land and defend against frequent tribal raids and dig the deep foundations and moats. Most of the lengthy work has been done."

"Even if it could be done, these warcastles wouldn't protect our northern or eastern borders," Alfrem said.

"Our northern neighbor Lord Sigbert is of the least concern," Medoff said. "And unless we've insulted the Calbrians in the east, they are probably focused on snatching the channel islands from Hanovel Ministry."

"I agree," Arthan said. "I acknowledge your concerns about the warcastles, Alfrem. But I want them to be rebuilt. Delavon should be its strongest while I'm away in Eglamour. We have the resources and the skill of Bellumet and Meriam. And any labor that is drawn from other ministries will be capable of picking up a sword if the worst comes."

"I can see you've made your decision," Alfrem said. "But let us not neglect Rachard. If the warcastle line is not ready in time, the capital must be defensible. And we shouldn't expect aid from other ministries, including Sigbert."

"The Army of Delavon will be ready," Medoff said.

Arthan nodded. "Rachard will have whatever it needs." He turned to Bellumet and Meriam. "I'd like to see one of the ruins while I'm here, to know of the effort firsthand."

"Rampilar is the closest but merely foundations," Meriam said. "Hullen is not much farther, but there is more to see there."

"I will show him," Bellumet told her. "You stay here and finish the plans."

"I would like Meriam to come along," Arthan said. "She is intimately familiar with the ruins. Alfrem, send word to Countess Iserenne to meet us at Hullen so we can discuss these plans with her."

"Of course, my lord."

67

RODEL

Thorendor Castle, Wallevet Ministry
Bloomfade, 3034

"Well done, Rodel!" Arasemis shouted.

It was the Rugen's turn to play the mouse, and he was enjoying himself. Rodel narrowly evaded Fetzer's quarterstaff, then bounded off the wall and somersaulted over his pursuer. When Fetzer turned, Rodel again ran to the wall and this time up to the balcony that ringed the top of the training hall. Fetzer simply could not spin around quickly enough.

"I didn't know he was allowed to combine techniques," Fetzer complained.

"Why wouldn't he be?" Arasemis asked. "This was an all-out session, so both of you were free to use everything you've learned."

Rodel jumped from the balcony, flipped, and landed perfectly on his moccasined feet. And yet his movements were no louder than a summer breeze. Fetzer scoffed and tossed the quarterstaff. Rodel beamed.

"You've both proven your acrobatic skill in such a short time," Arasemis said. "Even shorter than Marlan and Garion did, I dare say. The competition between the two of you pushes you forward like wind in sails. But beware the squalls and remember that you're both Candlestone. Well done."

"Thank you, Master," Rodel said.

"Have we learned enough aerina arcana to practice more alchemy?" Fetzer asked.

"Actually, yes," Arasemis said with a nod. "Let us return to the laboratory for your next chemina lesson."

As they followed Arasemis down the corridors and stairwells, Rodel turned to Fetzer.

"I know you resent my being here, Fetzer. But we've done well, don't you think?" Fetzer ignored him, so he continued. "It's been good to receive the master's focused attention, hasn't it?"

"I'd rather be on the Valient task," Fetzer said.

"Agreed, but our chance will come."

"I don't wait for chances," Fetzer said, glaring at him. "And I don't like Rugens, especially ones who upstage my destiny."

Rodel was unsure how to respond without provoking him. Fetzer was always dour, serious, and critical. Rodel wondered if Fetzer ever thought about anything beyond what he could do or get for himself.

"I'm sorry to have offended you in any way," Rodel said. "We are brothers in the Order."

"I suppose I should like your people," Fetzer said. "After all, they're responsible for the growing chaos on the continent that will feed the Order's power and speed my destiny."

Rodel kept his mouth shut. In truth, he did not care why Fetzer disliked Rugens, nor did he understand all his talk of destiny. Rodel had learned it was best to keep Fetzer at arm's length when he was in this sort of mood, which was sharper since the other students had departed on their task.

"Gather over here," Arasemis said, pointing to the tall shelves on the laboratory wall. "Rodel, what do you see?"

Fetzer sighed with exasperation as Rodel glanced up and down the shelves. "Jars, containers, bundles," he said. "Alchemical ingredients."

"Wrong," Arasemis said. "You see what the uninitiated folk see. Fetzer?"

"Well, I . . ." Fetzer mumbled. "Materials for mixing . . ."

Rodel did not feel so bad after watching Fetzer be caught off guard.

"Also wrong," Arasemis said with a grin. "You need to see all of these things as small prisons, keeping their essences locked tight within. You'll learn the keys to unlocking and extracting the essences properly. Only then will they be useful for a higher effort that most people never see.

"Chemina arcana is about harvesting and harnessing the innumerable essences of the earth and everything in it. These essences are hidden by nature for a secret purpose—our purpose—and our ancient knowledge is the key to unlocking them. Take this one, for example. Rodel, can you identify it from the textbook?"

Rodel stared at the lump of waxy brown spherules. "A plant resin?"

"Correct. It seeps from the heartwood of the eucalyptus trees of southern Ovelia every winter when the trunks crack open. What is it used for, Fetzer?"

"It's a sleeping agent," Fetzer said.

"Well done. How is it processed alchemically, either of you?" The two students pondered until Arasemis spoke again. "That is your next lesson, to learn the basics of processing, or, more formally, alchemical conversions. In this case the eucalyptus resin must be boiled in clean water with about fifty grains of lead at the bottom for twelve hours. The sticky foam is skimmed from the top and mixed with pigeon bone powder, then heated again until no moisture remains. Finally, brown dye from oak galls is mixed in and dried again. As novice alchemists, you should add dyes to powders and liquids to more easily identify their ingredient family."

"Brown for sleep agents and orange for poisons, for example," Rodel said.

"Correct. Now, Fetzer, can you identify and retrieve caustic sulfur? To give you a hint, you'll need the rolling ladder to reach it."

Fetzer looked at the upper shelves before ascending the ladder.

"Very good," Arasemis said. "I see both of you read the Naren-Dra and Arukan texts I assigned. Both texts were translated by Enthiri, the great-granddaughter of Rildning. Now, Rodel, locate the smoke quartz."

Rodel walked around until he saw a ceramic jar with Naren-Dra glyphs painted on it.

"Very good," Arasemis said. "Take the caustic sulfur and smoke quartz to the worktable. I will bring this jar of garlic balm."

Rodel and Fetzer watched as Arasemis donned his Naren-Dra mask. He ground up the caustic sulfur and smoke quartz with a mortar and pestle, layering the powders into a flask. When he poured the garlic juice into the flask, the reaction was instant. Arasemis let the solution bubble and fizz a moment before corking the flask.

"This solution is called ditch fume," Arasemis said. "Very dangerous if inhaled, but useful for warding off parasites, funguses, and insects. And it demonstrates that not all alchemical conversions require boiling, distilling, or similar methods. Some essences react violently with others because they are so potent even while in their small prisons, so to speak. But most useful mixtures and solutions do require conversion in a laboratory."

"Why do we funnel so many of the alchemical powders into eggs?" Rodel asked.

"There is no better means of delivering a mixture to the enemy at a short distance that is also discreet and silent," Arasemis said. "The Naren-Dra developed the technique. Draining the eggs takes practice and is time-consuming, but not difficult.

"Soot-painted eggs are silent and usually unseen. They break only when needed, if you're careful. You can carry many of them in specially designed pouch belts like this one." Arasemis pointed to Marlan's belt on the worktable. "Depending on the size of the egg—bird, quail, chicken, duck—you can fit up to two dozen eggs in one belt. Marlan usually wears two belts, while Garion wore one because he preferred throwing arrows. The choice comes down to skill, preferences, and the tools required for the task."

"Can we make poisons?" Fetzer asked.

"Novices start with illusory powders," Arasemis said. "They are harmless, such as cloaking and escape smokes, and will help you hone your technique before mixing things that can kill you. Remember this one truth about the arcanae: Mastering aerina is unlikely to kill you, but chemina is dangerous to you and machina is dangerous to many."

"Can we make poison eggs after illusory eggs?" Fetzer asked.

"There is more to alchemy than poison, my eager student. There are many branches you must learn. The subtlety of candle alchemy. The necessity of medicine. The strength of alloys. And the revelatory advantage of telescope crystals, just to name a few. You have many years of study ahead of you at Thorendor, including tasks you'll complete on the outside, before you can hope to master chemina arcana."

"Years?" Fetzer scoffed. "The crowned heads of Pemonia should have shorter spans to live!"

"The work of Candlestone has been a thousand-year struggle," Arasemis said. "These methods have been carefully preserved and handed down through the ages because they are effective and worthy of your time to learn them."

"If machina arcana is more lethal to more people, we shouldn't waste time with anything else," Fetzer said.

Arasemis raised his voice. "You'll recall my lesson about the failure of many peoples to master the advanced methods because they hadn't mastered lesser ones first. You *must* have patience."

Fetzer backhanded the corked flask holding the ditch fume. It crashed to the floor and a searing vapor arose. Arasemis and the students quickly put on their masks. Arasemis shouted something, and Rodel heard the breaking of stone. A white cloud filled the room as Arasemis ushered them out of the laboratory.

They stumbled out into the corridor, and Arasemis closed the door behind them. "Is everyone unharmed?" he asked.

"What was that?" Fetzer asked.

"A neutralizing agent called cloudcarry. If only I had one for your temper!"

"Will the laboratory be damaged?" Rodel asked.

"All will be well after a few hours and a little ventilation," Arasemis said. Then his voice turned sharp. "As for you, Fetzer, you'll be doing extra laps around Thorendor for the next week."

68

MILISEND

Eglamour Palace, Toulon Ministry
Bloomfade, 3034

"But it's been too long now, Rosellen. Something has happened to him."

"Regaume knows how to care for himself, Princess. Don't assume the worst."

Milisend walked among the flowers and herbs, taking in their delicate scents. She lacked the motivation to try another jewel heist since Serdot had caught her in Reimvick's apartment. It was not as much fun without Regaume. She felt empty and longed for him. Then an idea struck her.

"Rosellen, what if I reported him missing to Tronchet?"

"Then the chief magistrate will know you're a thief for sure."

"He already knows, and there's nothing he can do about it anyway. But Tronchet may know something. He may have heard whether something has happened in Ralmogard that might involve Regaume, since that was his destination."

"Yes, but Tronchet will surely use your admitted liaison with Regaume against you with the king or Brugarn."

"It won't come to anything," Milisend said. "Regardless, I cannot bear not knowing what happened to Regaume. Come with me. Tronchet is probably at his prison tower office."

The pair rushed through the palace toward the fortified tower that served as an armory and prison. Milisend bypassed the magistrate's guards and stepped into Tronchet's empty chamber.

"I'm sorry, Princess Milisend," said his assistant. "He left to look for you."

"Me? Why?"

"He had something important to discuss with you. I must let him know that—"

"When will he return? How long has he been gone?"

"He just left. My apologies, Princess."

"I'll wait then."

"The chief magistrate may not—"

"I said I'll wait."

Milisend and Rosellen sat in the nearest chairs, and the assistant tried to return to his work. Satisfied with herself, Milisend glanced around. Tall ledger books filled the dark wood shelves, doubtless full of innumerable investigations, court laws, criminal records, and the like. Out the window was the prison tower's twin, which held the king's private quarters and the treasury. She thought of her father and mother, but quickly pushed them from her mind.

Milisend recited to herself what she would tell Tronchet about Regaume. She would not go into details of their relationship, of course, but she would have to make clear to him that Regaume was precious to her. Should she tell Tronchet she loved Regaume, to help persuade the magistrate? Perhaps it would not be necessary. Tronchet was not a stupid man. Obsessive and sometimes doddering, but not a fool.

If he had useful information, as she hoped, should she swear Tronchet to secrecy? Would he try to dissuade her from seeing Regaume again? The questions continued to swirl in her mind until the magistrate appeared.

"Ah, yes, Sir Tronchet," the assistant said, rising from his chair. "May I present Princess Milisend, who has come to visit you."

Tronchet was surprised. "I was looking for you . . ."

"I wish to speak with you privately," she said.

The magistrate shooed his assistant away, then looked at her cautiously.

"I wish to confess something," Milisend continued. "Not for myself, but to secure your help for someone. And I require your strictest confidence. You must swear to keep your silence."

Tronchet shook his head. "Princess, I think you should listen to me first. I know why you have come. I tried to come to you before . . ."

"Yes, I will confess that I—what?"

"I said I know why you've come. I know about Regaume."

"You do?" Panic crept into her voice.

"You don't need to confess anything to me, Princess. I've known for a long time, and you know I've known."

"Please help me, Tronchet. I fear the worst has happened to Regaume. I miss him dearly and, well, I love him."

"Princess . . ." The magistrate held up his hand and sighed. He had something difficult to say.

"What's happened, Tronchet?"

"Princess, I didn't know about him, I mean him and you. I caught him here in the palace some time back and arrested him for thievery. I kept him here in the tower until I could find the rest of his little band. I learned about the arrest of the thieves in Ralmogard and suspected they were linked to Regaume."

"So he never went to Ralmogard? Where is he then?" she asked.

"He is still here, in the tower."

"Take me to him."

"He only recently confessed to his relationship with you. I would not have kept his arrest from you otherwise. But, well, it's too late . . ."

"What do you mean?"

"Regaume will be sent to Ralmogard tomorrow to be hung for crimes he committed there, alongside the other members of his band."

"You will not send him!"

"I'm a lawkeeper, Princess. I must do as—"

"Take me to him at once!"

Milisend and Rosellen followed Tronchet through corridors and up several spiral stairs. At least Regaume had been kept in the tower and not in the palace dungeon. Milisend's head spun as she considered how to approach her father to secure Regaume's release without informing Brugarn.

Tronchet fumbled with a ring of keys and unlocked a door. They stepped into a dim corridor of barred doors. He led them to one and turned the lock. Milisend stood in the doorway and looked down. Regaume was sitting in the straw, one ankle shackled to the stone wall.

"My love . . ." she said, dropping to her knees to embrace him. He was surprised at first but quickly took her in his arms. He was still strong despite his time in the cell. "Are you hurt?" she asked.

"I'm fine, Mili. Mild beatings early on but they forgot about me for a while."

"I'm sorry," Tronchet said. "My men were trying to determine—"

"Silence," she said before turning back to Regaume. "Have you been here the whole time?"

He nodded. "I'm certain they've killed my friend by now."

"And the others are to be hung as well," she said. "Stand up, Regaume. We're leaving."

"He cannot leave," Tronchet said, his voice firm. Milisend slapped him, but he stayed where he was.

"Release him from this chain!"

Tronchet put the ring of keys in his pocket. "He must pay for his crimes."

"What are his crimes? Stealing from the wealthiest Donovards and spending his gains in the slums?"

"Theft and murder," Tronchet said. "Two witnesses saw him stab the nephew of Baron Frum in Ralmogard."

"Don't believe it, Mili," Regaume said. "I'd wager these witnesses are members of a rival band, is all."

"What proof do you have, Tronchet?"

"Two witnesses are proof enough for the magistrate of Ralmogard," he said. "Regaume must face the charges there, as the other members of his band have."

"Others?" Regaume said. "Who?"

"That is privileged information," Tronchet said. "You'll be told the charges and the rest when you're in the custody of the Ralmogard lawkeepers."

"Lies," Regaume said.

"I came to you," Milisend said to Tronchet, her eyes welling. "I came to you in good faith. I came for help only to find you've locked him away in your wretched tower. Hiding the only love I've known . . ."

"I'm sorry, Princess. Truly."

"Enough!" Milisend said, wiping her eyes. She bent to hug Regaume again. "I will think of something. I will speak with Father if I must."

Regaume nodded and kissed her. She stood, smoothed her dress, and calmed her breathing. She glared at Tronchet as she exited the cell, but the magistrate would not meet her eyes.

❧

"I won't let you bother the king right now," Brugarn said. "He is due to discuss moving another army down into Alpenon in case the Rugens are foolish enough to attack us."

"This is important, Uncle," Milisend said, putting her hand on the door as he tried to close it on her.

Brugarn looked at her hand as if it were a disgusting creature affronting him. "I said we'll not be bothered with petty prisoner requests at this time!" He flicked her hand from the door and tried to close it, but she stabbed her foot in the jamb.

"But I love Regaume," she said. "You must help me!"

A cruel grin crept into the corners of Brugarn's ugly mouth. "In love with a murderous thief? Is he the one who has taught you his craft? What a dishonor you are to this house. Stealing in the night like a wicked rat, giving yourself to such scum, then pleading with me. Death to the filth! May you not dirty yourself with wretched brigands henceforth."

Brugarn kicked her foot away and slammed the door, turning the lock. Milisend pounded her fist on it once, then leaned into it and began to cry. She pushed away and composed herself, walking past the guards, who pretended not to have seen or heard any of it.

❧

That evening Milisend sat at her window, watching the city's night fires come to life. Rosellen had tried to cheer her up but she insisted on being left alone. Milisend was surprised to hear a knock at the door so soon after excusing Rosellen.

"Princess, please forgive me . . ." It was Rosellen, peeking around the door. "The magistrate's assistant has come."

"For what? To tell me Regaume's been sent to Ralmogard early?"

"He's asking to see you."

Milisend sighed and reluctantly slipped her evening robe over her gown. She would not deny she was desperate for news about Regaume, good or bad. She exited her bedchamber and came out into the solar, where the assistant was waiting awkwardly.

"Princess Milisend." He bowed. "Forgive my intrusion. Chief Magistrate Tronchet ordered me to deliver this letter to you."

Milisend unfolded the little parchment, her jaw set.

> Dear Princess,
>
> Please know it was never my intention to hurt you. As a lawkeeper I'm simply doing my duty, as ordered by your father the king. However, I've sent word to the magistrate of Ralmogard to delay Regaume's travel. I've claimed I lack enough guards to escort him.
>
> This tactic will not delay him for long, as they will likely send their own cart and guards. But perhaps it will be long enough for your father to intercede on Regaume's behalf.
>
> Chief Magistrate Tronchet

Milisend wiped a tear from her cheek. "Please tell the magistrate I'm grateful."

"Of course." The assistant quickly departed, and Milisend handed the letter to Rosellen.

"Oh, Mili . . . The lawkeeper has a heart after all," she said.

"I cannot be too glad," Milisend said. "Brugarn takes pleasure in my misery, and he and Chaultion have Father stolen away more and more. I must think of something . . ."

"What about Lord Valient?" Rosellen asked. "As Marshal of Inquiry, surely he is now a lawkeeper himself."

Milisend straightened. "Rosellen, that is brilliant. Though, as Serdot has witnessed, Valient will have much to frown on me about. Still, if I'm to wed Valient, perhaps he would do me this favor."

"Ask him."

"I shall, when he returns to Eglamour."

69

ARTHAN

Hullen Warcastle, Delavon Ministry
Bloomfade, 3034

"And over here you can see this was the central keep of Hullen," Bellumet said to the group. "The walls were thicker than anything else built at the time in Pemonia, which is why they have weathered time so well."

Arthan turned to his vassal of Sobel, Countess Iserenne. "If Meriam's calculations are correct, you will take command of Hullen in about three months' time. Choose your castellan well."

"My lord," Iserenne said, "you should have the honor of naming the first castellan of a modern warcastle."

"Very well, I will send you someone worthy from Rachard."

"If you'll follow me through here . . ." Bellumet said, stepping into a ruined corridor. Livonier, Meriam, and several guards followed him. Ivy lay thick across the roofless stone structures, grasping at and in some places pulling out weathered stones. Iserenne spoke in a hushed tone as she walked beside Arthan toward the rear.

"Troubling news from Gadolin Ministry. Do you think war will be upon us?"

"I wouldn't bother to repair this place if I didn't think so," he answered. "What have you heard?"

"Rumors say Lord Erath regularly catches and tortures Rugen spies sent across the border. And that Rugen soldiers are massing on Gadolin's border."

"My brother Rowan has said the same about Alpenon. If they do invade, the Rugens must pass through Gadolin before reaching Delavon. Erath would slow them down so we'd have plenty of warning. We'll be ready."

"Is Rowan safe, my lord?"

"I've not heard from him in some time. I expect he is roving the borderlands with Asteroth. But I intend for him to come home. He'll be in charge at Rachard while I'm in Eglamour. He will rely on your advice, as well as the advice of Count Dardanon and the others. Trying times are ahead."

"This way!" Bellumet called from up ahead.

Arthan and Iserenne found themselves lagging behind the main group. The ruin of Hullen was a vast maze of weathered stone, crooked trees, and thick brush.

"My lord?" Livonier called from ahead.

Arthan could hear the worry in his voice. He quickened his pace.

"Lord Valient!" Livonier shouted.

Arthan heard swords unsheathe. Bellumet cried out in pain. Arthan and Iserenne looked upward to the sound of someone running along the top of the ruined wall.

Arthan drew his father's alchemical sword. Adrithayn's blade shone with a white gleam brighter than any steel. Arthan sprinted ahead as Meriam screamed, with Iserenne close behind him. The sound of the fighting grew louder as they rounded a corner. A quick-moving masked figure crossed swords with Livonier, Cuern, Erboln, and the other guards. When the assassin saw Arthan, he backflipped and sprinted toward him.

Arthan charged the assassin. Before he could close the distance the assassin threw a tiny knife at Arthan. He chopped it from the air with Adrithayn, feeling the vibration of metal against metal. When they met, Arthan brought his sword down hard against the assassin's blade.

Their engagement was short, Sir Cuern having approached the assassin from behind. Arthan tried to jab the masked figure in the ribs but his opponent was too quick. A puff of orange smoke burst at the feet of the assassin. The assassin disappeared as the cloud grew. Arthan took a last swipe before backing away, expecting the cloud to be poisonous.

At once Adrithayn took on an orange glow, its brilliant white gleam replaced by the hue of the assassin's smoke. All the smoke was soon drawn toward Adrithayn, seemingly absorbed by the blade itself.

But Arthan had no time to puzzle over this. The assassin reappeared behind him, intercepted by Cuern as Arthan turned. The knight caught a moccasined foot in the face as the assassin jumped. His brother Erboln came next. The assassin jumped from Cuern to Erboln, stabbing deep between the knight's neck and shoulder armor. The assassin jumped from Erboln's falling body to the top of the wall and disappeared.

"There were two!" Livonier cried as they looked around and above.

"They came from nowhere," Cuern said, rising to his feet.

"Who were they?" Iserenne asked, sheathing her short sword.

"They are the ones . . ." Arthan mumbled as his guards clustered around him.

They watched the walls as the injured Racharders groaned on the ground. Arthan marveled at the speed and silence of this enemy, and their persistence in following him on his travels. As the threat faded, his eyes fell to Adrithayn, still glowing sickly orange. Meriam peered out from her place in the bushes, her eyes welling at the sight of Bellumet's torn body.

"Come, my lord," Livonier said, glancing at Adrithayn. "We must get you back to your protective carriage."

A hail of hand arrows cut off Arthan's reply. Four of the Racharders fell to the ground and the two assassins jumped down from opposite walls with swords in hand. Both masks were fixed on him. One of them, a woman, split her sword into two halves and reached Arthan first. She maneuvered past Livonier and crossed swords with Arthan.

Adrithayn's orange hue soon faded. The cloud jumped from its blade toward the female assassin's swords with each strike. Arthan could hear the woman cough from behind the mask. He too was forced to back away as the cloud swirled about them. He felt a burning in his eyes and mouth. His opponent had clearly inhaled more of it.

She was shaken and distracted. It was enough for Livonier to strike a blow across her back. The second assassin broke from his engagement with Cuern and the Racharders who were protecting Arthan's flank. Cuern, now enraged by the death of Erboln, did not let him go easily. He struck toward him with his great sword, forcing him to run toward the wall.

The woman turned toward another wall and lifted her mask to breathe, then ran up the wall and disappeared, leaving one of her swords behind. The second assassin followed after her.

Arthan held out his hand for Meriam, and she rushed to him. Livonier and Cuern ushered them and Iserenne back to the carriage. Arthan looked back, realizing most of his guard force had been slain.

"They will not stop until they have you," Livonier said as they trotted. "I cannot protect you without a larger force, my lord."

"They always know where I am . . ." Arthan suddenly bent at the waist. Something throttled low in the middle of his chest. When he caught his breath Meriam was staring at him.

"What was that?" Serdot asked.

"Nothing . . ." Arthan said.

"You've been hiding this long enough," Meriam said before turning to Serdot. "It's his heart. He won't see a physician."

"I have seen physicians," Arthan. "They all prescribe different things that waste my time. It's nothing. Let's get moving."

"The less you're seen publicly, the better," Iserenne said, her eyes still wide from her first encounter.

"The countess is right," Livonier said. "Your location and planned movements should be privileged information. I'm sure Serdot will agree."

"You should go to Eglamour," Meriam said. Arthan glanced at her with surprise and saw fear in her eyes. "I would rather have you alive there than dead here," she said.

"Not before I'm sure you'll be safe," he said. "And not before I talk to Master Pelinaud about this sword."

70

GRAF

Borderlands, Ward of Havelbern
Bloomfade, 3034

"There they are, warden," said a solider.

Graf squinted toward the patchy mist floating up from the river separating Alpenon Ministry from the Ward of Havelbern. He could make out the Donovards' Torgsbad Castle on the hilltop in the distance and the small force of cavalry riding down the road from its gate. They were headed toward the stone bridge that spanned the two kingdoms.

"Looks like Lord Asteroth himself is among them," said one of Graf's commanders.

Graf could plainly see Asteroth's huge form on the most massive warhorse. "Can you see Geras Vilarwef?" he asked.

"There," said a soldier, "a covered wagon is following behind Asteroth."

"Let us meet them on the bridge as agreed," Graf said.

He spurred his horse as the Donovards drew near. The Rugen force followed Graf down from the ridge toward the river. Graf had not seen Geras for some time and looked forward to it. Graf liked the people of the Durgens and the leverage they provided Rugenhav over the Donovards. In time, Emperor Theudamer would better appreciate what the Durgensdil rebels could do for the Rugens.

Graf held up his hand to stop his men as they reached the bridge. Asteroth did the same on the far side. Graf motioned for his two commanders and the soldier with the small coin chests buckled to his saddle to follow him at a slow trot toward the apex of the bridge. Asteroth got there first with only one attendant by his side.

"It is an honor, Lord Asteroth," Graf said in spotty Donovar. "We have the ransom. Where is Geras?"

"In the wagon, you damn Raffenbeak," Asteroth said, using the slur for a person of Raffen ancestry.

Graf bristled. He wanted to cut down the big oaf and bring his head to the emperor, but he reminded himself of the importance of his task. "Bring the wagon over the bridge."

"The gold first," Asteroth said.

"Half now, half after," Graf said.

Asteroth nodded to his attendant, who promptly accepted two small chests from Graf's attendant. Graf was surprised to see Asteroth turn his horse and depart the bridge with his attendant. He was further surprised to see the driver of the wagon jump from his bench and smack the horse on the rump.

The wagon came across the bridge. Graf's commanders halted the horse and jerked the canvas open, exposing Geras's headless, tortured body. Graf's horse struggled to move backward at the smell. He cursed and shouted at Asteroth, who was already on his way back to his border castle. A Donovard soldier tossed Geras's head down the hill and into the river as they rode away.

Graf ventured alone over the bridge onto Donovard soil, shouting as loud as he could and taunting Asteroth. But the big man never turned to look. Graf turned around to look at his cavalry. His force was larger, but he knew he did not have enough men mustered to lay siege to Torgsbad Castle.

It was all he could do to restrain himself. When it was clear Asteroth would not face him, Graf jerked his horse around and rode furiously back into Rugenhav to prepare.

71

MARLAN

Thorendor Castle, Wallevet Ministry
Bloomfade, 3034

"He had a sword that absorbed it."

"Impossible," Arasemis said. "Is this your excuse for yet another failure?"

"I'm telling you his sword absorbed the cloud," Marlan continued. "Juhl became sick when it came back to her."

"Didn't you have your mask on?" Arasemis asked.

"The gill fern fronds needed replacing," Juhl said. "It was my mistake, Master."

"You see?" Arasemis said, his voice heavy with frustration. "This is why I teach *finishing* the task above all else. Because one operative's mistake should not hinder the others from completing the task."

"She would have been killed," Marlan said. "She vomited in her mask twice. Her pupils were already small by the time I escaped with her and pulled her mask off again. Thankfully, I brought an antidote for the poison cloud. With rest she'll be all right."

Arasemis shook his head. "This is your third failure to kill Arthan Valient."

"Only his father was the target at Mordmerg," Marlan said. "Otherwise he would have been an easy kill."

"Even so, your past two attempts caught Arthan out in the open," Arasemis said. "Not holed up in a castle. Not protected by an army." Arasemis put his face in his hands. "So be it . . ."

Marlan looked at the parchment-strewn floor of the library. He was ashamed to argue with the master, but at least the newer trainees were not around to hear it. "If Arthan travels back to Eglamour then we'll have another chance on the road."

"No, we'll let him go for now. His days are still numbered, but there are other things we need to focus on here at Thorendor. Then we'll go to Eglamour."

"I thought we needed to remove the lord minsters before overthrowing the king?" Marlan asked.

"I finished translating my grandfather's work. Remember that I said there was something under Thorendor? I'm certain of it now. Thorendor was built to hide and protect an ancient Candlestone shrine."

"A shrine? What did Erwold write?"

"He wrote that Enildir, son of Rildning, always intended to move Candlestone back to the Ashlands, where the greatest Gallerlander forest once stood, but that he never had the opportunity. It was only generations later that they went back."

Marlan squinted, not following what the master was saying. But Arasemis, growing excited, did not slow down.

"Erwold wrote that he thought the tombs of Rildning and Enildir and others were moved to Thorendor, along with mysterious 'relics.' Treasures are evidently hidden below the foundations of the castle. We must gather Rodel and Fet—"

They were both surprised to see Fetzer step out from one of the thick curtains.

"What are you doing?" Arasemis asked.

"I was practicing what you've trained us to do."

"This was a private discussion," Marlan said. "The master did not train you to spy on him."

"There are no secrets between members of the Order of the Candlestone," Fetzer said with a grin.

"I am the master of this Order and this castle," Arasemis said. "You will not sneak around here unannounced again, is that clear?"

"Do you wish to hide something from me, your best student?"

"Best student!" Arasemis glared at him.

Marlan help up his hands. "There is no reason for this. Fetzer, you're offending the master. He is naturally secretive, given the events of his life. So make your amends and make yourself known in the future, because, you're right, we don't hide anything from each other."

"If I had been permitted to go, Arthan would be dead," Fetzer said.

"Perhaps," Marlan said. "But your training is important. If you want to be the best, you need to—"

"Fair enough," Fetzer said. "What is hidden beneath Thorendor? It won't delay our mission in Eglamour, will it?"

"I decide the timing of tasks," Arasemis said. "Fetch Rodel and Juhl, then everyone can—"

"Am I a servant?" Fetzer asked.

Arasemis stood from his table and reached inside his belt pouch.

Marlan held up his hands again. "Go, Fetzer. Before you're on your hands and knees struggling to breathe."

Fetzer glared at them, then slowly turned, taking a long time to exit the room.

"Still think he's the answer to a prophecy, do you?" Arasemis asked as he reseated himself.

Marlan sighed heavily but remained silent. After a few minutes Fetzer returned with Rodel and Juhl. She still looked sickly.

"As you all know," Arasemis began, "I've been neglecting my duties to teach because I've been working on my grandfather's secret papers. It seems there is much more to Thorendor beyond being the ancient capital of Candlestone."

Arasemis stood from his table and plucked up a leaf of parchment, which he began to read from.

> Descend into the deep roots,
> Where crafted stone meets cloven earth,
> Where the oldest blood spilled,
> And Nalembalen tunnels lie preserved.
>
> The sacred shrine of Candlestone
> Is not a stale chair or chapel
> But armory, treasury, and decision hall

For the waking of the chieftains.

Beware the last gasp of the tyrant kings.
Desperate, they will come a-hunting.
Delve farther into the vast waters,
Where Nalembalen's roots once drank.

"What does it mean?" Juhl asked.

"It means there's a whole world beneath Thorendor that we've never seen," Arasemis answered.

"The first part, about stones meeting the earth, must be the cellars," Marlan said.

"Very good, Marlan," Arasemis said. He snatched up a dry torch. "Let's go take a look."

Marlan and the others were familiar with the cellars. Those dimly lit chambers flanked the laboratory and small forge beneath the castle's ground level. The students often trained in the maze of vaults stuffed with dried staples, wine, and other supplies. Arasemis once told Marlan it was enough for Thorendor to survive a long siege.

"Erwold's clues make perfect sense to me now," Arasemis said as they entered the largest cellar chamber. "Thanks to Rildning's rough map and the detailed colonial charts, I've always known the ancient Gallerlander tree city of Nalembalen was located somewhere in Wallevet Ministry."

"It was destroyed and renamed the Ashlands," Marlan said.

"But," Arasemis said, pointing his finger upward, "the forest returned strong many years later. Colonists never settled there because they feared the ghosts of the heathen."

"So Candlestone returned here, when the new kingdoms arose during the time of King Thorendor of Aberynbane?" Juhl asked.

"Yes, you remembered," Arasemis said. "Now, recall the passage about the stones meeting the earth." He moved the torch close to the wall.

"There, at the bottom," Marlan said.

"The stone is different," Fetzer said.

"Cut stone above . . ." Arasemis said.

"*Cloven earth below,*" Marlan said. "*Where Nalembalen tunnels lie preserved.*"

"You can see here, these sections are earthen walls dug with stone implements," Arasemis said. "See the chipped markings here? The Gallerlanders would not have used metal tools. Now, if memory serves, there used to be a passage . . ."

Fetzer had been poking around and was now shoving kegs and crates aside. Marlan could see the decaying little door over his shoulder.

"Well done, Fetzer," Arasemis said.

When Fetzer had cleared the way he tugged on the door. The rusty iron handle pulled right out, so Fetzer took out a gold-clad knife and began prying at the rotten wood.

"Where did you get that?" Marlan asked.

"I stole it from the ship captain Candlestone hired for the Gottfried task," he answered, pulling open the door.

Arasemis brought the torch over, revealing a downward ramp. An old torch was sconced inside. Fetzer pulled it down and touched it to Arasemis's torch, then proceeded down the ramp.

"Look at the mixed composition of earths here," Arasemis said as they walked. "Layers of ash at the top, then ancient streambeds, and this—petrified wood."

"The tree root tunnels of Nalembalen?" Marlan asked.

"I believe it is," Arasemis said. "Look how this passage is curved and the stones are few."

They walked single file down through the tunnel until they came to a large room. Huge wine barrels lined the walls, some of them burst open and rotted long ago. The stone floor was brown with old spillage.

"I never bothered to explore down here because I simply thought Thorendor's foundations ended at these cellars," Arasemis said.

"Where is the Candlestone shrine?" Fetzer asked.

"Patience," Arasemis said. "You found the first door. Find another."

"Perhaps," Rodel said, scuffing his moccasin in the brown residue, "perhaps this is what Erwold meant when he wrote *where the oldest blood spilled.*"

"I interpreted the *oldest blood* to be the earliest generations of Candlestone," Marlan said.

"But recall Rildning's account of the Gallerlanders' last stand as being in the tree root tunnels," Arasemis said.

"Regardless of whose blood it was," Rodel said, "Erwold may have hidden his meaning to be this room."

"I don't see an armory or treasury," Fetzer said, tapping his foot on an intact barrel. "Is this wine any good?"

"Just a crust of vinegar by now," Arasemis said. "Walk the walls with the torches. Look for anything: a door, loose rubble, an etching. Anything at all."

They searched back and forth.

"What is this black stone?" Rodel asked, pointing to the keystone in an arch on the far wall.

"Wood that was charred before it was petrified," Arasemis said. "Definitely not original to the tunnel."

"There is something glittering in it," Rodel said.

Arasemis held his torch up. "Looks like electrum."

"Didn't the Gallerlanders hoard electrum at High Chief Gratgofa's tree, where the Graparins protected it?" Marlan asked.

"Yes," Arasemis said, "but they had underground electrum vaults hidden throughout their lands."

"None of the arches in this room have that black petrified wood," Rodel said.

"A clue to a false wall?" Juhl asked.

"We are currently at the lowest depth under Thorendor I've ever visited," Arasemis said. "I don't want to remove walls under the castle, but, if Erwold's writing sent us to this room, there must be a route through it to depths beyond."

"I have a vial of void varnish," Marlan said, holding it aloft.

"How many times have I told you to leave your belts in the laboratory?" Arasemis said, snatching the vial from Marlan. "Between you and Fetzer, you'll burn the castle down on all of us one day . . . This one vial won't be enough for this wall. We need some copper."

"Those wine taps have copper in them," Rodel said.

He and Fetzer kicked at two taps until they broke off from their empty barrels.

"Get all of them," Arasemis instructed.

The students stomped and pulled at each barrel. Thick black liquid rolled out of several barrels.

"Hurry, before that stuff gets in my moccasins," Arasemis said. "Now, pile up the brass next to this wall. Good." He gave his torch to Marlan, then took a second vial from his own belt.

"Master," Marlan said. "You have—"

"Don't," Arasemis said. "I know what can be safely kept on my person. Heat the brass."

Marlan and Fetzer put the torches to the taps and waited. Finally Arasemis waved them away and poured the void varnish on the wall and hot taps.

"Stand back by the tunnel," Arasemis said.

They stepped through the wine ooze, and Arasemis positioned himself behind a barrel. He threw his vial, shattering it against the wall. Purple and blue flames leaped up the wall. Marlan watched as the copper in the taps liquefied, sliding up the wall as if reaching for the void varnish. It soon chewed into the earth and petrified wood, hissing and filling the cellar with a white, sweet-smelling mist. The students covered their noses with their tunics.

"It is harmless to your lungs," Arasemis said. "It's essentially water vapor, extracted from inside the earth and stone. Just don't touch the copper scum. Rodel, that tapping hammer over by the first barrel, if you please. You'll have the honor, since you noticed the black keystone marker."

Rodel retrieved the small hammer from the wine ooze and carefully found his footing at the wall. The smoking earth looked porous like a sponge. With each swing of the hammer the earth shattered and the remaining flames died away. The hole was enough for them to squeeze through.

"Watch your step," Arasemis said. "The copper scum will desiccate your leg if you step in it."

One by one they stepped into the secret room beyond. Marlan's torchlight revealed Candlestone symbols carved into the black petrified wood floor tiles. An arcade of arched tunnels branched out ahead.

"Which one shall we take?" he asked.

"All of them," Arasemis said. "One at a time."

72

ROWAN

Countryside near Torgsbad Castle, Alpenon Ministry
Bloomfade, 3034

"My father *and* brother are dead, my lord." Rowan looked at the letter in his hand again, still finding it hard to believe Bardil was gone.

"Dark times, Rowan," Asteroth said, shifting in his saddle. "Dark, indeed . . . But if you leave your wardship now, when we're on the cusp of giving the Rugens what they deserve, you'll be missing out on the most momentous events on this continent in a generation."

Rowan stared into Asteroth's wide eyes, seeing excitement, hate, and death. The big man was not one for exaggerations. "Arthan says he needs me in Rachard," he said.

"He wants to protect you, of course. But you're nearly a man in your own right, Rowan. And already old enough to make your own decisions." Asteroth cocked his big square head. "Arthan cannot manage his own capital?"

"My brother's letter says the king has appointed him to a new post in Eglamour," Rowan said. "Marshal of Inquiry. Something about hunting down the assassins."

"Inquiry!" Asteroth laughed, startling Rowan's horse. "Erech's newest magistrate, then? That sounds too right to be a jest."

"My lord," shouted one of Asteroth's commanders. "Looks like they're coming out of the woods."

357

They looked ahead to see a band of riders crossing over from Rugenhav. Rowan could see it was a larger group than usual. Asteroth drew his massive sword and spurred his horse forward.

"Ride them down!"

Rowan hesitated. The borderlands were certainly exciting and he had learned much at Asteroth's side. But Rowan found it difficult to think what might happen if war came.

He stuffed Arthan's letter in his pocket, resentful of all his brother was accomplishing and experiencing. Rowan had not been there for the deaths of Maillard and Bardil, nor their funerals. His brother was now a lord minister and senior adviser to the king. Rowan wondered if he'd recognize Rachard.

He kicked his horse forward as the rear guard of Asteroth's cavalry formed up around him. He could not go back to Rachard now, not to be Arthan's steward. Here on the borderlands he was the ward of a fearsome if despotic lord. Asteroth was a man of conviction and action, and a brute. But Rowan had grown accustomed to his violence. And part of Rowan wanted to see the Rugens suffer.

There was also Etzel, the Rugen spy that Rowan had come to enjoy talking with. Asteroth had let him speak to her when they returned to Cantrileme Castle from their patrols, hoping she would give up something useful. Etzel was unfinished business for him.

Rowan had a purpose down here in Alpenon. He lifted his sword for the charge. He would not go back now.

73

WREDEGAR

Borel District of Eglamour, Toulon Ministry
Bloomfade, 3034

Unable to stay in Vesamune's cellar a moment longer, Wredegar put on local garb and departed from a back courtyard window—as befitted a Wosmok. He frequently reminded himself that he was a knight, not a widsemer, but the dark arts had become second nature for him after all this time.

It was dusk as he set out for the slums of the Borel District, as he often did. It was a place where things happened and interesting people passed through, and he enjoyed the food. He dared not enter the taverns known for Rugen fare, lest he be identified as a Rugen or let his speech slip. Tonight he aimed for the alley lined with Ovelian grills, hoping to find fresh catch wrapped in herbs that came by sail, then wagon once each month.

As he approached the alley, his training rang an alarm in his head. The dirt streets were different. Usually they were crowded with merchant wagons, riders, barking dogs—even after nightfall. But tonight they were deserted.

Wredegar considered going back to the ambassador's residence, but he was intrigued. He came to Borel enough to know how unusual this was. He pressed on toward the alley where the grills scarcely smoldered. As he drew closer he saw through the windows of the buildings that people were crowded within.

He approached the door to an Ovelian-style inn named Calza Aria, and it opened for him. Inside were all kinds of people, residents of Borel. He had little hope of reaching the innkeeper to buy a drink.

As he pushed through anyway, he picked up enough of the surrounding banter to realize what was happening. The merchants, tinkers, discharged soldiers, farmers, masons—everyone present was armed to the teeth. Swords, axes, shovels, picks, cudgels, and knives.

Wredegar had seen the riots in Eglamour since the king's proclamation. From a distance. They were ugly events that usually ended with soldiers bloodying the rioters. The whole thing was utterly foreign to him. Such disloyalty simply did not exist in the grand cities of the Rugen Empire, and certainly not in the capital. But Wredegar reminded himself that the Donovards were a people of inferior culture and laws.

The Eglamour riots had also always been during the day, sparked by the latest wave of soldier discharges, food confiscations, or tax collections. But something else was stirring.

"You with Fosset's group?" a short bald man asked him, poking his chest.

Wredegar hesitated.

"I say, you with Fosset?"

Wredegar nodded and prepared his best Donovar slum speech. "Course. What's it to you?"

"But you're not armed."

Wredegar felt for his knife. He usually avoided carrying his sword when he was dressed as a commoner, to avoid attention. "Only this," he said, pulling out the short blade.

The short man thrust a yew bow into his chest. "Shoot well? We need more archers. They'll be pickin' us off from the walls tonight."

Wredegar nodded. "They'll be the ones gettin' picked off."

The short man regarded him closely. "I don't remember seeing you last time . . ."

"Came recently, from the south."

"What's your name?

"Ricot," Wredegar said. "Carpenter apprentice from Gadolin."

"Well, you came for the right one. Keep your aim true." The short man gave him a quiver of arrows before clomping off.

Wredegar told himself to leave the inn at once, but his curiosity would not let go.

"Don't worry much about Cid," said a young man nearby. "Stout of stature and stout of heart, but short on brains, as we say. I'm Arnaut."

"Ricot," Wredegar said.

"You came to Borel just to join us?" Arnaut asked. Wredegar nodded. "I'm from Rachard in Delavon Ministry," Arnaut continued. "There are many here from Mordmerg, too. You may have heard of it. They know how to light a proper riot. Took the minister's army to break them, but they made their point well enough."

Wredegar was only half listening to the chatty youth, but the mention of Mordmerg caught his attention. "Who from Mordmerg?"

Arnaut pointed toward the large table in the middle of the inn. A burly man with a black hood draped on his back and shoulders was talking with other hard-faced men and women.

"That is Lunfrid, the one with the shaggy straw hair. He was one of the leaders of the Mordmerg revolt. He organized all this with Fosset, who is down the street at Fatneck Tavern."

"There are many more rioters making ready?"

Arnaut nodded. "Sun's down. Will be anytime now."

No sooner had Arnaut finished speaking than Lunfrid rose from his table. Someone slammed a mug on the table, and everyone turned to him.

"The time has come!" Lunfrid shouted to immediate cheering. "Tonight, we take Borel. Tomorrow, the palace!" Lunfrid let the crowd cheer a moment longer before silencing them. "We made the masters of Mordmerg quake, but we weren't as prepared as we should have been. Now preparations have been made. We have joined you followers of Fosset tonight, throughout the district, to help take back homes, livelihoods, and all that is rightfully ours. The time has come!"

Lunfrid pushed toward the door and the mass of angry folk surged after him. Wredegar was swept into the flow. It was the most exciting thing he'd seen for some time, and he'd finally be able to take aim at a Donovard soldier. He could hear Vesamune's condemnation of his behavior, but he pushed her voice from his mind.

They walked out into the street in the direction of the Borel alderman's keep, which was situated in the middle of the district. Columns of men and women, modestly armed and mostly unarmored, flooded out of taverns, inns, meeting halls, shops, and homes. The few Eglamour guards who patrolled the streets of Borel were nowhere to be seen.

Wredegar sang along with their chants, enjoying himself. He realized the peril of his situation when the crowd arrived at the central square and found Eglamour soldiers protecting the alderman's keep. He tried to angle out of the crowd of marching rioters, ostensibly to find a perch from which to shoot, but the crowd pushed him further toward the keep.

A horrifying melee ensued. Armored knights and soldiers skewered the commoners, but the mass of marchers pressed forward. Unable to escape, Wredegar gripped his knife with his left hand, leaving his thumb free to grip the bow staff. He drew an arrow with his right and notched an arrow, ready. The people ahead of him pressed into the soldiers and fell quickly.

His moment came when a soldier lunged for him. He feinted left, then stepped right, sinking his knife into the soldier's exposed neck. A knight rushed forward, sword lifted high. Wredegar aimed his bow like a crossbow, shooting the arrow through the knight's visor. Then he threw down the bow and picked up the fallen knight's sword, keeping the knife in his left hand.

Feeling death surge around him, Wredegar could not suppress his training. He fought as he had on many battlefields prior to being pressed into Wosmok service. For the first time in a long time he felt unchained. Free of the shadows. Savoring the honor of facing one's opponent face to face. He tore through the guards and rallied the rioters around him.

After a short time he turned toward the orange light behind him. The rioters had broken through and set fire to the alderman's keep. Surviving soldiers scurried away if they could. Cid approached Wredegar.

"Ricot the carpenter, was it? Why didn't you ask for a sword from the start?"

"Guess I just . . ." Wredegar wiped the blood from his brow, unsure what to say as he tried to calm down.

"Doesn't matter," Cid said. "We'll take the guard posts throughout the district next. In the morning, they'll send the army in on us. But we'll be ready. Follow me, Ricot."

Cid ran across the square toward another street, with Wredegar and many others jogging behind. As they approached an alley he veered toward the wall and let his pace slow. He stopped and bent over, as if adjusting his boots, then he ducked into the darkness of the alley.

74

ARTHAN

Rachard Castle, Delavon Ministry
Bloomfade, 3034

"You've changed."

He kept his eyes on the ceiling. "Have I?"

Meriam snuggled closer on the bed. "You've always been confident, discerning. But now you're resolute, and you don't smile anymore."

"The House of Valient is in real danger," he said, turning his head to meet her eyes. "The kingdom is a shambles, and well-informed assassins travel freely through my lands. And the Rugens are on our doorstep. These are just a few of the obstacles to a smile."

Meriam blinked. "I know your burdens are many. I hoped being here with me would help you forget about them for a time."

Arthan closed his eyes. "It's difficult to forget."

She propped herself up on her pillow. "Your father, and Bardil, would be proud of what you're trying to do. You're honorably serving a king who doesn't deserve the throne. You're going to hunt down those assassins. And you'll defend Delavon."

"Perhaps not so honorable for long . . ."

She squinted at him. "What does that mean?"

He was not about to discuss his intention to negotiate with the Rugen ambassador, nor his intention to learn more about alchemy. "Nothing. Difficult, is all."

"I'm shaken too," she said. "Bellumet was like the father I never had. I hope I can serve you as chief engineer as well as he did, my lord."

"Don't call me that. You have my heart, Meriam."

"Do I?" She lay back down. "You'll be away in Eglamour for God knows how long. Again."

"My first journey was short, and here I am."

"But attacked twice since then," she said. "I liked Hullen. The gently sloped domes, in the old Brintilian style. And the arches and round keystones. Now as I supervise the repair I'll only be reminded of those assassins."

Arthan slid an arm under her pillow and hooked her waist with the other, pulling her toward him and looking her in the eyes. "I will come back. I'm doubly in the service of the king now, for how long I cannot know. But I love you, Meriam. I will come back."

Her skeptical eyes softened at his words, and they kissed. But Arthan could feel all the pressing issues in Eglamour creep back into his mind. He knew he wouldn't be spending as much time in Rachard as he had hoped. As she had hoped. He tried to push these thoughts away, to savor this moment with her. He brushed her hair from her cheek.

"And I love you," she said. "My heart is yours if you'll but take it."

"I desire it, all of you," he said. He held her close again. "I will come back."

"Then what will you do?"

"We'll be together."

"You know what I mean. Will you always love a low commoner?" she asked.

"I would love you if you were the lowest peasant."

"But would you wed me?" she asked. He hesitated. "What are you waiting for, Arthan? The world to fall apart around us?"

"I have my duties, Meriam . . ."

"Do men with duties lack proper wives?"

"Must we have such formalities? My heart belongs to you, and yours to me."

"I will be your mistress if nothing at all, but not gladly," she said. "I want you here, with me, in the safety of Rachard. As husband and wife."

"I am called to serve, Meriam."

"You have changed. I fear Eglamour will make you crave crowns and power above all else, if it has not already. How else might that corrupt court change you?"

"I am still Arthan Valient. We've known each other since we were children, Meriam. I'll never abandon you, or us. But I must do my duty. We are young still. Time is on our side."

"Time sides with no one," she said.

"Nevertheless, my father's duties have fallen to me, and I must not fail."

"I will be here," she said, turning her eyes back up to the ceiling.

✌

Arthan found Master Pelinaud where he always could be found, in the training hall of Rachard Castle. Arthan and his brothers had all learned the sword from him in this hall and in the courtyards. Pelinaud now spent his days teaching some of the sons and daughters of lesser nobles sworn to serve the Valients.

"My lord, wonderful to see you alive," Pelinaud said. "I heard about what happened at Hullen."

"Thank you, old friend. Can we speak privately?"

Pelinaud dismissed the trainees and proceeded to organize the weapons on the table as they talked.

"They got closer this time," Arthan said, "though there were only two of them. They became distracted, or frightened . . ."

"By what, my lord?"

"This." Arthan brought out Adrithayn.

Pelinaud raised his bushy silver eyebrows. "I've not seen this sword since—well, it has been a long time . . ."

"Father showed it to you?"

"Yes. Before you were born. I've not seen Adrithayn since, nor have I seen anything like it again."

"What can you tell me about it?"

Pelinaud took the sword in his grip and wielded it. "Light, well made, and designed to fit well into your Crusader swordcraft."

Arthan waited for more, but Pelinaud simply returned the sword to him. "What about . . . powers?"

Pelinaud sighed. "Your father asked me the same question. As I told him, a sword's power is in your own arms and shoulders and back. There is nothing mystical or unusual about it, despite its peculiar decoration and design."

"Have you heard of chemina arcana?" Arthan asked.

"Of course. Folklore is rife with such things."

"What if it's not just a story?"

Pelinaud silently shook his head.

"I carry Adrithayn now, and I used it at Hullen," Arthan said. "When the assassins threw their powder clouds, this sword absorbed it. Then, when I crossed swords with my opponents again, the cloud seeped out and sickened them."

"Impossible," Pelinaud said, still shaking his head.

"I choked a bit on the cloud myself. Father knew there was something special about this sword. He didn't understand chemina arcana, but he said—"

"Adrithayn is a beautiful, ancient sword with reflective properties given to it by exotic metals. But it is not a magical sword."

"I didn't claim it was the magic of folklore," Arthan said, "nor did Father. It was designed to do whatever it does naturally. Let me show you."

Arthan looked around and spotted a brazier. He piled on a few more small logs and ripped a cloth from a nearby table and put it atop the logs. When the cloth began to smolder, Arthan slowly sliced Adrithayn through the smoke. The blade blackened as the smoke vanished. Arthan drew the sword away and looked at Pelinaud, who blinked repeatedly.

"Pick up a sword," Arthan said, and the master did. When they crossed swords the smoke swirled about Pelinaud's face. "Do you believe me now?"

The old master coughed before clearing his throat. "I, well, there must be some—"

"Explanation, yes, that is what I seek. Chemina arcana, whatever that means, must be the explanation."

Pelinaud rubbed his whiskered chin. "There is an old folktale about the Smithy of Forlorn, or maybe the Forlorn Smithy—something like that. Long ago he crafted a sword and suit of armor that could absorb the color of nearby objects and thus could hide among common things. Magical nonsense, of course, but Adrithayn reminds me of it.

"Now, when I was a boy," Pelinaud continued, "there was another man who claimed to have found this smithy's gauntlets. People didn't believe him until, they say, he was seen one day without his hands. Then the next day, he had them again. I never saw this myself, mind you, and that crazy man is long since dead. But there was a historian who came all the way from Eglamour not too long ago just to hear the tale and search the man's derelict house and overgrown patch of land. The historian is probably still in Eglamour and might be able to tell you about this."

"What is his name?"

Pelinaud rubbed his whiskers again and squinted. "Danleri, that was it. Former rector of the Bredahade Academy in Wallevet. His name sounds Ovelian, but I recall his mother was a Donovard. Never mind that. If Danleri is still in Eglamour, you should speak with him."

"Thank you, Pelinaud. I will search for him. As for Adrithayn, and our discussion, I trust you'll keep it to yourself."

"Of course, my lord."

"One more thing, Pelinaud. My brothers and I are grown, and who can say when children will run the halls of Rachard Castle again? We are no longer in need of a trainer of swordcraft, but I do require worthy castellans to govern the new warcastles. I want you to lead at Hullen, under the command of Countess Iserenne of Sobel. If the worst comes, you will be Delavon's protector in the west. Will you accept?"

"It would be my honor."

"Go there as soon as Meriam says it can be garrisoned."

"I shall, my lord. God's speed and protection over you."

"And you."

75

FETZER

Fetzer was bored and frustrated. Arasemis and the students were wandering the ancient root tunnels, finding stores of stone-bladed weapons but little else—until finally they came to a great oaken door. Its front was eaten and bored through by worms and termites, the whole of it layered with spiderwebs.

"No lock," Marlan said.

Fetzer pushed the others out of the way. He was determined to find whatever was hidden under Thorendor sooner than later. He was done listening to Arasemis's analysis of the soil and petrified roots of a dead forest, and his endless stories about the early generations of Candlestone.

He went up to the door and pushed, then he gripped the worm-eaten holes and pulled. It would not budge. "Are you all just going to stand there?" he asked.

"Everyone on the door," Arasemis said.

They pulled with their combined weight until it edged open. Its long iron hinges sheared off layers of rust and grime with a metallic shriek. When the thick door was opened enough, they could see its inner surface was plated with electrum. Their torches made it shimmer, but it was the glint of what lay inside that made them squint.

The room was colossal, with many tiers that led down into farther depths. Electrum ingots, bars, plates, and bagged coins were stacked on stone tables and tall overloaded shelving built into the walls. The floor was inlaid with electrum panels of intricate design.

Fetzer gawked at the sight, certain no one had seen so much precious metal in one place since it was first set down. "Treasury," he muttered.

"Not to the ancients who built this place," Arasemis said. "Electrum was sacred to them. A gift from their god to be reforged into a sword that would defeat the great demon at the End of Days."

"That didn't stop the colonists from minting electrum coins from captured electrum," Marlan said.

"Hilsingor and his Frontier Corps stole quite a bit, it's true," Arasemis said. "The royal court in Eglamour still has many of the original electrum statues. But the variable content of gold, silver, and copper in the electrum frustrated merchants. That's why it fell out of use as coinage."

Fetzer was sick of the history lessons. "We can buy a kingdom with this wealth. How can we get it out of here?"

"We're not going to buy a kingdom," Arasemis said. "But we are going to remake Donovan. We'll not touch any of this, however. It was sacred to the Gallerlanders and was surely cursed against hands that would tear it from this vault."

Fetzer turned toward the master. "I don't believe in curses. We could pay several armies with this. Armies that would march on every king in western Pemonia."

"That is not the way of our Order," Arasemis said. "Now is not the proper time for us to have a large army. People will naturally flock to our side when their tyrants are gone. If we try to force an army together now, we'll be no better than the kings we intend to overthrow."

"That is why we work selectively and in secret," Marlan said, "so that the people will rise up and welcome a new era of elected chieftains, like the days of old."

"We respect and use the old ways of the Gallerlanders and the other original peoples of Pemonia," Arasemis continued. "And we'll respect their electrum."

Fetzer turned to Marlan. "Tell me you want to use this wealth to our immediate advantage?"

"The master has spoken, Fetzer," Marlan said.

Fetzer walked to a pillar where the Candlestone symbol was carved into an electrum plaque and pointed to it. "It does not say Gallerlandia, it says Candlestone. We represent a new era, not an ancient heathen horde. This wealth was destined to be used for our cause, today."

Arasemis and the other students watched him, unmoving.

"What do you need that I have not provided?" Arasemis asked. "Thorendor feeds and supplies you, and my personal wealth will sustain all our efforts. There can be nothing you need or want that we cannot purchase with my own gold when the time is right. Thus, it is no sacrifice to let the electrum sleep here."

Fetzer opened his mouth to protest further, but he knew they would not listen. Arasemis's antiquated thinking had power over everyone but him. He knew it was ludicrous to let this wealth sit idle when it could hire more mercenaries than Candlestone would ever need—but he knew he could not convince the others.

"I want to kill kings myself, but this could buy mercenary armies that could overthrow kingdoms faster," Fetzer said again. "I am tired of waiting."

"Candlestone has waited a long time," Marlan said. "We are on the edge of changing the world, be sure of that. But we mustn't rush the natural pace of events."

"It's time for us to explore a different tunnel," Arasemis said, exasperated. "We know this is here, but we still need to find the armory and decision hall that Erwold wrote about. Come along now."

ๆ

It was not long before one of the unexplored tunnels led them to another great door. It was equally old but less heavy, due to an inner surface of iron rather than electrum.

"Surely this cannot be the armory," Fetzer said.

They looked around the wide octagonal chamber. Each wall had a small platform that held a full suit of armor and multiple weapons. The visors of each helmet were like Naren-Dra masks, and the breastplates were etched with the Candlestone symbol.

"Eight suits of armor doesn't make an armory," Fetzer said.

He looked at Arasemis, who was in a daze. The students fanned out for a closer view of the equipment.

"Look, Fetzer," Marlan said. "There are no common suits. They're all unique."

Fetzer strolled up to one that shimmered like electrum but was darker and coarse. "Looks ancient and obsolete," he said.

Then something caught his eye. The armor had tiny channels cut into the metal. They ran along every surface, from the helmet to the gauntlets and greaves. A peculiar smell tickled his nose as he leaned in closer. Rodel suddenly pulled Fetzer's torch backward.

"What are you doing?" Fetzer asked.

"Smells like lamp oil," Rodel said. "It could be spilled everywhere."

"Oh my," Arasemis said, rushing over. "Erwold wrote of this . . ." He fumbled with a sheaf of parchments from his robe. "These are flame veins."

"Flaming armor?" Fetzer asked. "Well, let's see it!"

"No!" Arasemis's voice echoed off the walls.

Rodel snatched Fetzer's torch from him.

"They could be in need of repair first," Marlan said. "We mustn't damage any of them."

"Hands off, like the electrum treasury," Fetzer said. "What good are any of these secret things if we can't use any of them?"

"Silence!" Arasemis said, skimming his notes. "I know my grandfather masked his descriptions to protect these secret chambers, but give me a quiet moment to sort it out . . ."

Fetzer fixed his eyes on the veined armor. If Marlan got a flaming sword, he was determined to have the flaming armor.

"My God," Arasemis mumbled. "Mechans."

"What?" Marlan asked.

"Mechanical suits," Arasemis said. "They actually built them."

"It's just fancy-looking armor," Juhl said, tapping on the breastplate of another suit.

"Yes, well, our closest translation for the Gallerlander term is simply 'mechanized suit,' abbreviated as mechan. But it doesn't mean automaton, like those trifle birds and such that tinkerers make. A better translation might be moving armor."

"I'm confused," Juhl said.

"As am I," Rodel said. "All quality armor should move when you're in it, some more than others . . ."

Arasemis shook his head. "My apologies, but we've not yet delved into machina arcana. Suffice it to say that these eight armors have special properties that aid the wearer. For example, if these are flame veins in this one, there must be a reservoir that holds the lamp fuel that is made to course through the veins with a pump, probably linked to the legs or arms. Think of it as wearable alchemy controlled by the body's natural movements."

"What about this one?" Juhl asked.

They walked to the armor she was examining, and Arasemis smiled. "You see these small levers, and these holes? It's like a miniature crossbow fitted inside both arms. These rods on the thighs and torso must cock the device by harnessing the movements of walking or running."

"Machine armor," Marlan said. "How strange."

"They combined the arcanae," Rodel said.

"Precisely," Arasemis said. "But be warned. One who dons such armor must have mastered aerina to move in such complex and undoubtedly heavy armor. And without an expert grasp on chemina, this armor is dangerous to the wearer. And, of course, the mechanical design of the—"

Fetzer could not stifle a snicker when they noticed him. His hands were held up, showing the veined gauntlets he had put on his hands, and he had touched the torch held by Rodel. Fetzer smiled as a thin streak of red raced down his metal finger, spreading like a web of triangles across the back of his hand and to a series of larger veins on the forearm flanges.

Fetzer twirled his hand about, marveling at the flames that spurted here and there. He touched his fingers together, sharing the fire with his other hand. "Remarkable that I cannot feel any heat within . . ."

"I told you not to," Arasemis said in a grave voice.

But Fetzer could see the jealousy in the other students' eyes. "Be glad that I've tested its safety," he replied.

"Gauntlets must be easy enough," Marlan said. "You wouldn't get out of the plate and mail fast enough if something went wrong."

"Just look at it, Marlan," Fetzer said. He was unable to take his eyes off the gentle lines of flame. "Imagine what this could do . . ."

A moment later the veins blinked from fingertips to the flanges. The flames disappeared, leaving a faint smoke rising from the veins. Fetzer looked at Arasemis, bewildered.

"If you'd been listening, you would have heard me say they must be dependent on a reservoir and pumps. Take them off, now."

Fetzer took off the gauntlets and returned them to the suit. Curious, he touched the outer metal. It singed his bare finger, and he smiled.

"Now, as I was saying," Arasemis began anew, "according to these writings, the mechan that Juhl has asked about is called—my translation here—arrow armor. Like the other seven mechans, this one was designed by several of the founding Candlestone members and crafted by the Maluram smithy named Niberi. A Gallerlander princess wore this one."

"Niberi is the one who made Rildning's elinderum armor," Marlan said.

"Elinderum?" Rodel asked.

"An alloy of electrum and cinder," Marlan said.

"Unfortunately his armor is lost to us," Arasemis said. "But in this chamber we have armors that have been creatively crafted, repaired, and improved by generations of Candlestone."

"What's this one?" Rodel asked, pointing to a mechan without traditional gauntlets or gloves of any kind.

"Wheel armor," Arasemis said. "Look at the equipment. Rahlampian windrazor swords are built into flexible gauntlet-like devices, like a sword arm. And steel wheels extend from the heels and flip down from the toes, so the wearer could be a quick-moving whirlwind of blades. It was first worn by the Rahlampian chieftain named Mrigamad."

Arasemis lifted the parchment to his eyes. "Let me go through each suit. This one, fury armor, was made for the Bronhildi warrior Kemet, who lost his sight in battle. The visor is solid and the suit stoutly built. A mechanism fed furywine into his mouth to keep his other senses extraordinarily alert, similar to what Fetzer experienced in training.

"This one is called shroud armor, first worn by a Gallerlander chieftain named Owerdir. It also has exterior veins through which many alchemical liquids can flow, either to be used as a weapon or to change the appearance of the armor. It seems the wearer could even hide in plain sight."

"Like the fabled Hidden Eyes clan of the Naren-Dra," Juhl said.

"That's right, very good, Juhl. Over there is ship armor, worn by a Nyden captain named Bothrobim. The suit is watertight and buoyant, allowing the wearer to swim atop the water or use ballast to swim below the waves for a time. On that wall is bear armor, used by an ancient colonial who was a friend of Rildning's. The fur has probably been replaced several times, but the movable clawed gauntlets are said to draw strength from the leg rods when the wearer charges an opponent.

"Over here is forge armor, worn by Niberi herself. The cindersteel protects the wearer from all heat, whether acidic or by flame, and the spring-loaded mechanism on the back propels a hammer over the helmet to strike the head of the enemy, like a heavy third gauntlet.

"And finally, the mechan demonstrated by Fetzer is lamp armor, made to honor Rildning though never worn by him. Erwold noted that elinderum, an alloy of electrum and cinder, protects the wearer from the fire. He wrote that all eight mechans have been modified over hundreds of years, with new alloys mostly, and some he was unable to identify. Fascinating . . ."

"When can we wear the full suits?" Fetzer asked. "Let's see what they can do."

"Master, I support using them as well," Marlan said. "It's a pity that we've lost three of our members before finding this vault. We'd have used all but one of the mechans. But we'll make good use of what we can."

"From the looks of these, we'll be well protected," Rodel added.

"And perhaps more likely to finish the formidable tasks ahead," Juhl said.

"If they still work," Arasemis said. He turned to the students with a serious gaze. "To be blunt, none of you is ready for these. Mastery of aerina and chemina before machina."

"But the builders of these mechans surely hadn't mastered the first two arcanae," Marlan protested. "The arcane knowledge was not yet codified, nor complete."

"The arcanae are never complete," Arasemis said. "There is always more to discover."

Fetzer could read the indecision in the master's face. Arasemis seemed as eager to try on one of the suits as his students were. Fetzer gnashed his teeth at the thought of Arasemis claiming himself as the only one knowledgeable enough to wear a mechan—especially given his missing arm.

"It's not as if we're building the mechans ourselves, without mastery of the arcanae," Fetzer said. "They were safely made, as I've demonstrated."

"And we'll keep training," Marlan said. "With new tools that can help assure our success."

"Any of these mechans might kill any of you," Arasemis said, "or your companions beside you. It's one thing to wear flaming gauntlets, but walking with your whole body aflame cannot be taken lightly—to say nothing of wearing it in the chaos of battle. If all of you insist on this path, it will require strictest discipline, complete concentration, and more training with the little time we have to spare."

"I choose the lamp armor," Fetzer said.

"No, I will have it," Arasemis said. "It will be the hardest to tame, followed by the shroud armor, which will be Marlan's because of his skill in alchemy. Juhl, the wheel armor demands your speed and nimble frame. Rodel, you will wear the arrow armor. And, Fetzer, you will take the forge armor."

Fetzer became hot with frustration. "Shouldn't the one-armed man have the mechan with a third punch? I have no such handicap."

"He is your master," Marlan said.

Arasemis remained calm. "Your aggressiveness propels you, Fetzer. The hammer mechanism will aid you when your enemies surround you."

Fetzer kept his mouth shut. He was already plotting how to snatch the lamp armor.

"So we have training to do," Marlan said.

Arasemis sighed, then looked down at his parchment. "There is so much more to learn, and not only beneath Thorendor. There are tombs down here somewhere, and burial sites scattered across Pemonia that hide more relics and buried history. We could find the missing ingredients of the furywine of the Hrals.

"There is also the story, told in the colonial record and Enildir's book, about a mysterious shore in the Nake lands that killed men who merely walked upon it. And other tales about the volcanic forge under the Gilgalem Mountains, and the fabled airships, and the wildmen who still live in the Black Forest that Erwold thought could be tamed for Candlestone's ends. So much can now be revealed and revived . . ."

"We could spend a lifetime looking for all the Candlestone relics and secret places, Master," Marlan said. "Shouldn't we remain focused on our tasks?"

"It is a historic time," Arasemis said. "Donovan and Rugenhav are on the cusp of war, the perfect backdrop for what will be the Order's greatest performance since the killing of Hilsingor. And yet, at the same time, Erwold's writings and clues point to so much that we could use to complete our ultimate task."

"Airships, if they ever existed, would be the most wondrous weapons," Fetzer said. "But the mechans are right here, and our skills sufficiently sharp. We shouldn't waste time looking through dusty tombs for trinkets or machines that never were."

"I agree with Fetzer," Marlan said. "I want to find the secrets of Candlestone too, but it seems best to let that wait. We can set our plot in motion and always return to the relics later, to aid future efforts."

"We are meant to discover all of these tools to ensure our success," Arasemis said. "Erwold wrote that finding and employing the artifacts of the Order would lead to a widespread collapse of the kingdoms. Embarking on these pilgrimages, as he called them, to the hidden places was my grandfather's dream. He believed every tool should be gathered first."

"But the ancients and Erwold could not predict the momentous events of our times," Marlan said. "Now is the time to take advantage of the political upheaval to overthrow kings with what we have, as you have said."

"I agree with them, Master," Juhl said. "It's what we've trained for."

"And the mechans give us a new advantage," Rodel said.

"We've done well thus far, despite the loss of Bertwil, Morroy, and Garion," Marlan said. "We must finish what we've started so their sacrifice means something."

"You are right," Arasemis said. "The temptation of the relics is enormous for me, especially after seeing these mechans with my own eyes after decades of merely reading about them. I wish I had found Erwold's writings earlier, but we must look forward. We have momentum against the House of Avaleau and the high nobles."

"Once the kingdoms begin tearing themselves apart, perhaps we'll take time for the relic hunt to strengthen ourselves," Marlan said.

"Blood now. Relics later. Much blood after," Fetzer said.

"Everyone take down the mechans assigned to you," Arasemis said. "You must dedicate yourself to training with them before we go to Eglamour."

76

MILISEND

Eglamour Palace, Toulon Ministry
Bloomfade, 3034

Milisend eyed Serdot all evening, waiting for the right moment. He had not seemed to notice her watching. The king's court was packed with people eager to voice their growing complaints to the throne. Yet Erech was nowhere to be seen. Brugarn claimed he was resting and not taking visitors, so Brugarn presided over the court.

Milisend tried to watch Brugarn and Serdot at once, hating the one and placing her hope in the other. Brugarn had repeatedly denied her entry into the king's tower. She knew he was consolidating his power on the eve of war with Rugenhav. Her father had already retreated back into himself, content to let Brugarn and Chaultion make his decisions while he hid away.

As Milisend watched, she realized Serdot was not looking at Brugarn like the other courtiers. He was looking across the court, watching someone else. She tried to trace his gaze and guessed it was directed at Lord Reimvick. Deep down she knew Reimvick must have known about Garion, maybe harbored him. Looking back, his behavior was always different, loitering around court longer than others. There was more to it than his professed love of gossip. Serdot may have seen it before anyone else.

Milisend glanced back toward Serdot, but he was gone. Her eyes shot back to Reimvick, who was slowly making his way toward the door. Chaultion interrupted Brugarn's talk to whisper in his ear. Brugarn in turn whispered to Waldemar.

"Today's court is suspended until this afternoon," the steward announced. The courtiers collectively moaned with displeasure but dispersed. Brugarn had already hastened out of the room toward his private chambers.

Milisend searched the crowd for Serdot. Finally she caught sight of him, moving toward Reimvick. She picked her way through the crowd and snatched Serdot's arm.

"I need to speak with you," she whispered.

"Princess," he said with a curt bow. "Perhaps another time."

"Now, Serdot!"

He was clearly torn, glancing back and forth between Reimvick and her. His irritation was plain to see. "Remember when I saw your black leathers?" he whispered back. "I'm still working on that investigation, you see?" He jerked away from her, but she persisted.

"It is a matter of life and death," she said, not bothering to mask her desperation.

"Yes, my investigation certainly is," Serdot said as he turned away.

She grabbed his arm again, digging her nails into his forearm. "You will speak with me. Remember, if I am to wed Valient, he will no longer be your only master."

Serdot turned back to her, a faint look of surprise and respect on his face. "Very well, Princess."

They exited the hall. Still clutching him, she turned Serdot into the right-hand corridor after Reimvick turned left in front of them. She spoke softly.

"I'm sorry to break you off your hunt, Serdot, but I require your service."

"How may I help, Princess Milisend?"

She ignored his sharp tone. "When will Lord Valient return to Eglamour?"

"I expect him within two weeks."

"That's too long. You must help me directly then."

"I've not been informed of the problem, Princess."

"This is a delicate matter, Serdot. But since you've seen me thieving, I'm sure I can depend on your discretion once again. Chief Magistrate Tronchet currently holds a prisoner by the name of Regaume."

"Your lover in crime."

Milisend cut her eyes at him. "Yes, and I'm not surprised that you know. But you must also know that he is innocent. Release him, secretly if possible."

"That would put me in violation of my oath. The marshal is a lawkeeper. As his agent, so am I."

"Please, Serdot. Regaume is a thief, but he is special to me. And he has not committed the crimes the Ralmogard magistrate claims."

"How can you be sure?" Serdot asked. "Have you ever seen how he lives when he's not stealing into the palace to see you, or whisking you off to the woods?"

"I brought you into my personal matters for your help, not your advice. If you are acting on behalf of a lawkeeper and my future husband, then do me this service."

"As a royal, you can petition Tronchet directly."

"I've tried, with little effect. Tronchet has delayed sending Regaume to Ralmogard, but time is running out, Serdot. You must help me."

"Your father is the king and thus lord of all lawkeepers."

"Do I have a father? Have you seen the king? It has been weeks since I've been allowed to see him, Serdot. Brugarn sits on the throne even if the crown does not yet sit on his head. Please, I have no one else to turn to."

"I regret I cannot."

"Please!" She shamelessly let the tears spill from her eyes.

"You love this Regaume?"

She nodded. "If I'm fated to wed Valient, I will grow to love him. But a part of my heart will always belong to Regaume, whether he lives or dies. Should Regaume live, I will be a happier wife to your master."

Serdot regarded her cautiously. "Princess, when Lord Valient returns you should petition him directly. I cannot do this myself. I am sorry."

Milisend struggled to wrangle the rising anger and sadness inside her. "Will no one help me?"

"I'm sorry." Serdot spun away from her and disappeared into the crowd.

77

BRUGARN

Eglamour Palace, Toulon Ministry
Bloomfade, 3034

"You've got your war, my lord." General Chaultion tossed the dispatches on the table.

"Took longer than I planned," Brugarn said with a smile. "I didn't think the Alpenon rebels would take this long to erupt."

"Asteroth was heavy-handed, as you wanted." Chaultion absently twisted his white mustache.

"Perhaps not heavy-handed enough. Tell me exactly what happened."

"You recall the Rugens' answer to our intent to sell that damned Geras Vilarwef to the Austveedes?"

Brugarn nodded. "I wasted too much time negotiating with that insufferable Vesamune. Ransom at the border and so on."

"Well, Asteroth found a way to upset those tediously made plans. He sent the body of Geras in a wagon across the bridge, then tossed his head in the river. Your brother only got half the ransom, of course, but the Rugens got only half of Geras." Chaultion could not stifle a chuckle. "Even we could not think of a better way to spark a good war."

"Excellent! The Rugens immediately attacked Alpenon?"

"Soon thereafter. That bastard Graf, the Warden of Havelbern, organized a force quicker than Asteroth guessed he would. Your brother's letter says he was prepared for a flare-up of the Durgens rebels and the movement of Rugen

382

troops into his ministry, but Graf brought more soldiers than he expected. Asteroth requests reinforcements."

"I will reconvene the court this afternoon to announce that we are at war, as the city will undoubtedly be swirling with rumor. All lord ministers will be called to serve in the kingdom's defense." Brugarn could not stifle his own giddy chuckle. "This was well done, General. And it's only the beginning."

"And a fine beginning it is, my lord. You will inform the king?"

"I suppose, but not until after court. I'm sure Erech is still sleeping, aided by an extra dose of the queen's popaver. I've made sure they're both well stocked."

"The lord ministers will require the king's clear consent," Chaultion said.

"I'm the lord minister of Toulon. You needn't remind me of our traditions. Erech will support the defense of the kingdom, and most will believe it is an unprovoked Rugen invasion. In other matters, how is the suppression of the Borel District going?"

"The rioters are all but defeated," Chaultion answered. "One of their leaders, Fosset, was killed, but we couldn't find his deputy, Cid. Unfortunately, the news in the slum is that the Blackhoods from Mordmerg have come to help them."

"Crush these rebels before you go to Alpenon—no excuses. Send my regards to Asteroth when you see him."

"I do not plan to travel to the borderlands at this time, my lord. There is much still to do here to prepare the northern armies."

"You are the High General of the Armies of Donovan. The king would go to the border to defend his honor under normal circumstances. And I, well, I have you to fight and win my wars, General."

"Lord Asteroth asked that I stay in Eglamour, my lord, to arrange his reinforcements and supplies. He said he does not want, or need, my help."

"That is because my brother has always seen Alpenon Ministry as his own personal little kingdom. And if that's how he wants it, fine. So long as he destroys any Rugen army they send across the river."

"The Rugens will likely invade Gadolin as well, my lord."

"And Erath will stop them as well. The twins are big men with big swords and fierce hearts. I'm confident in their abilities, and we'll send them what they need. When Rugenhav is sufficiently drained of soldiers and gold, and when our nobles are properly aligned behind me, we'll make our move against Erech, and I'll take Rhunegeld into my hand. They'll crown me, and I will take a new army south, the savior of my brothers and my kingdom."

78

FETZER

Thorendor Castle, Wallevet Ministry
Bloomfade, 3034

After some time, Fetzer finally pulled his gaze from the candle's flame and began to write all that had been filling his head.

Mechan training has progressed well despite the endless cautions from Arasemis. He wears the lamp armor but doesn't actually use it. Ridiculous. Meanwhile, my forge armor is burdensome. It's too heavy for wall running, and the hammer perched between my shoulder blades disturbs my balance, especially when deployed against the practice targets. It crushes helmets well enough, but I'd rather torch them with flaming gauntlets. I've not given up hope of persuading Arasemis to give me the lamp armor.

Juhl, always deadly beautiful in combat, is stunning to watch in the wheel armor. It is light enough for her to run the walls, then deploy the steel wheels from her boots, quickening her speed further. I've never seen a Calbrian landship, but sailing on rocks must sound similar to her wheels on the stone tiles of Thorendor. As with all the mechans, her approach is no longer silent, but her speed denies an opponent any advantage. And replacing her hands with fingerless anchiclade blades completes her shocking form. Altogether she is nearly impossible to catch or disarm.

Rodel has settled into his arrow armor with a satisfaction I'm jealous of. Arasemis should have given that mechan to me, if not the lamp armor. The small crossbows hidden inside his bulky forearms can shoot four bolts or poison darts simultaneously. The mechanism that recocks the crossbows harnesses his walking movement. Revolutionary.

Only Marlan's shroud armor appears to use the ancient Naren-Dra preference for illusion over offensive action. He has tested the veins with many alchemical fluids. Once, he was all but invisible against a stone wall while using a mica cloaking solution. It seems anything we use in alchemical powder eggs can be liquefied to use in his mechan. Arasemis says even poisons could be used, making him unapproachable, but that it's too dangerous for us to test.

Everyone has superb mechans but me. Why couldn't Arasemis have given me the bear armor? Or even the fury armor? Anything would be better. I'm starting to wonder if the old man is trying to sabotage me. Marlan has privately urged me to be patient. But I can see my friend's patience with Arasemis is also beginning to wear.

When we were all down in the tree root tunnels, the students might have revolted against Arasemis if he had insisted on relic hunting over king killing. Even Rodel. The old man is simply too giddy about the dusty past, especially the ancient heathens. He's unfocused, aloof, and out of touch with the modern world. Marlan is hopeful that the importance of our next tasks will bring Arasemis back to the present and force him to focus. I'm not convinced.

Training continues to go well. I feel better in the forge armor but still not as nimble as I'm used to being. And wall running is still too difficult, though I can bound off the walls when I have to.

Arasemis says we will leave for Eglamour in two days. He has a safe house for us in the slums of the city where we will live until our tasks are complete. We will travel in two groups to reduce the risk of disruption.

Arasemis and Juhl and I will go together one day after Marlan and Rodel. We will take the direct route from Bredahade while they will go around through Lundwynland. Both groups will be disguised as wine merchants and will travel in wagons with our mechans and weapons hidden in the barrels.

Arasemis says we must go sooner than planned because of the war. We received news of the Rugen invasion he predicted and want to make the most of this opportunity. I cannot wait to begin.

79

ARTHAN

On the Road to Eglamour, Wallevet Ministry
Bloomfade, 3034

Arthan was frustrated. Livonier had insisted not only that he ride in his armored carriage but that a whole brigade of the Delavon Army escort him. With the deaths of Bardil, Bellumet, and others, Arthan found it hard to argue against the danger, and Livonier was unwilling to take any chances. Arthan knew his protector was right, but the arrangement slowed his journey. He had received a few short letters from Serdot while he was away from the capital, but he still felt blind and deaf without his spymaster nearby. He hoped Serdot had made more progress than he dared to describe in his letters. Serdot did not trust even his own handpicked messengers enough to include much detail.

The long time alone in the carriage gave Arthan lots of time to think. He hoped he was doing the right thing in recalling Rowan from his wardship under Lord Asteroth. The Alpenon borderlands were becoming dangerous, and Rowan would have Medoff and Alfrem to guide his leadership of Delavon while Arthan was in Eglamour.

Arthan wondered how long he would be away. He wondered whether Meriam would still wait for him if he were gone longer than they'd planned. He was not sure what he would do if she did not. He had complete confidence in her ability to supervise the rebuilding of the warcastles for Delavon's defense. He was less certain in his own ability to give her what she wanted, despite his own desire to be with her.

"What now?" Arthan muttered aloud as the carriage came to a stop. He leaned out the window for a look.

Livonier was spurring his horse forward. Arthan stepped out of the carriage to stretch his legs. He still wished to be on his own horse but knew what was expected of lord ministers. He looked up and down the convoy line. Most of the three thousand men of the brigade followed behind his carriage. Two companies scouted ahead for signs of danger and to clear the road of traffic. Arthan was satisfied with Livonier's tactics; he simply wanted to move faster.

Arthan looked forward again, hoping to see the two companies moving again. Soon they were, but slowly. Then he spotted Livonier riding back.

"My apologies, my lord. A merchant wagon was not eager to make way for us."

"A wagoner?" Arthan asked with a smile. "Our brigade halted by a wagon?"

"The merchant owner claimed to be the brother of Lord Reimvick," Livonier said. "By the name of Aratsemis, or something like that."

"Where is he?"

"Just up ahead, on the side of the road."

"I want to meet him," Arthan said. "Forward!" he called up to the carriage driver before ducking back inside. He waited at the window, watching until the covered wagon came into view. Livonier was already waiting with the wagon.

"Greetings, Arasemis," Arthan said as he stepped out. "My apologies for my large convoy. I'm afraid recent events have made it necessary in the eyes of my protectors."

"Think nothing of it," Arasemis replied. The big red-bearded man smiled warmly.

"And my condolences for your brother. Raymond was a good man."

"And mine for Maillard and your brother," Arasemis said. "I've heard about the attempts on your life," he continued. "Any chance you've bagged the scoundrels?"

Arthan thought it curious that such a friendly-looking brother of Lord Reimvick's would be a hermit. Then Arthan noticed his missing arm and reasoned that was the cause of his self-imposed isolation. Yet Arthan did not detect any shyness in his eyes—rather an unexpected eagerness.

"Not yet," Arthan said, wishing he could say the opposite. "But my duty takes me to Eglamour nonetheless. What brings you on the road?"

"This wagon of fine old wine," Arasemis said. "I spend my days tending the aging barrels. A few are a gift for my brother Edmond and the rest I'll sell in the Eglamour wine market."

Arthan thought his story peculiar. "It must be fine indeed to risk the long road and not trust an able merchant to deliver it for you." Arthan eyed Arasemis's companions, a young blond driver and a pale-faced woman who joined them on the bench. They were well armed to be servants and too few to be a proper guard.

"Only the best wines are aged in the cellars of Thorendor," Arasemis said. "I have old wines—some might say of ancient technique—that are sharp for but a moment, then quiet bliss forever after."

"Sounds . . . unique," Arthan said.

"May I offer you a barrel?" Arasemis said. "A gift to celebrate your new lord ministership."

"No, I must press on with my journey, but thank you."

"I insist, and you may have your pick," Arasemis said, standing from the bench and throwing back part of the canvas.

Arthan could see the wagon was full of neatly stacked barrels and kegs. He noticed Arasemis's movements startled the blond man. Arthan looked at the barrels again.

"Regrettably, I must press onward. But perhaps I will share a cup of your brother's gift in the capital. May I offer you the protection of my convoy? Many bandits have taken to the roads of Toulon, and they'll undoubtedly treasure your wine. You have need of more guards by my count."

"I will not be the cause of any delays for you, Lord Valient," Arasemis said. "And I do not fear the banditry. I look forward to seeing you again at the king's court."

"As do I. Godspeed."

"Farewell."

Arthan returned to his carriage and watched the peculiar man and his companions pass behind. Something about Arasemis turned his stomach. Perhaps it was his posture with a missing arm, or his formal and insincere way of speaking. Arthan could not put his finger on it.

And there was something odd about his companions as well, especially the behavior of the blond man. The trio seemed out of place, even in their home realm of Wallevet. And the transport of old fine wine when it was nearly Midsummer was odd.

Arthan made a mental note to ask Serdot about Arasemis again. Then he turned his thoughts to Eglamour.

80

THEUDAMER

Heingartmer, Ward of Havelbern
Bloomfade, 3034

"I don't care about the gold or Geras's head," Theudamer said. "This wasn't how I envisioned attacking Donovan, but Graf was right to take the army across the river in response to Asteroth's trickery."

"Graf's advance has already slowed," General Algus said. "I wish you had sent me, instead of the warden."

"Graf is not merely a warden but a general in his own right now," Theudamer said. "Besides, I want you here to coordinate Graf's advance with General Valk's push into Gadolin. And later the advances into Toulon, Austveeden, and Nore as well. I plan to join Graf in Durgensdil while you organize our reinforcements and supply trains from here."

"It will be my honor, Your Majesty," Algus said. "But you know I prefer to fight at the front."

"You're too old now, Algus, like Wardenlord Herzol here," Theudamer said. "When I go to lead the armies I cannot leave this pacifist here by himself. So the two old white-haired men will stay here in my stead."

"I wish to accompany you at the front," Herzol said.

"No, you'll stay, old friend. Someone must balance Algus. In youth this general plowed through any enemy. In old age he defeats Death daily. But Meliamour, you will travel with me."

"As you wish."

"Tell me, are the new Wosmoks ready? The time for training is over."

"Yes, Your Majesty," Meliamour said. "I've already sent half to accompany Valk's army in Gadolin and the other half will join Graf's."

"Excellent. Any word from Vesamune?"

"Nothing of high importance. The ambassador is still being held captive at her Eglamour residence. They are letting her send and receive letters, but the Donovards are reading her correspondence."

"Have no fear for her. The Avaleaus would be fools to murder my own niece, even now. Cutting the head off a ransomed rebel is one thing. Killing an emperor's blood is another."

"I'm not so certain," Meliamour said. "Duke Brugarn is vile. Wredegar is with her, though—perhaps he'll manage to help her escape."

"That is my hope," Theudamer said. "I do not want the Avaleaus using her as a hostage. But tell her to keep in touch with Lord Valient, in case he will still be of use to us. Keep me apprised of her situation."

"I will, Your Majesty."

"Algus, ensure my army is ready. I want to be on the march within three days. Graf will need reinforcements soon."

Algus nodded. "May you return victorious, Your Majesty."

"May you return alive and the differences between our people and theirs finally settled," Herzol said.

"I leave Heingartmer in your able hands, Algus and Herzol," Theudamer said. "But on imperial matters Empress Evorelune will be my voice while I am at war. She will lean on the wisdom of you both. Remember that she is with child and will delegate much to you. When my child is born you will notify me at once. Farewell."

81

MILISEND

Eglamour Palace, Toulon Ministry
Bloomfade, 3034

"I'm sorry, Princess," Tronchet said. "I'm no longer able to delay his transfer to Ralmogard. They will be collecting Regaume next week at the latest."

Milisend kept calm by staring at the floor and breathing deeply.

"There is nothing I can do," he said.

"May I see him?" she asked.

"Of course."

Milisend followed Tronchet up into the prison tower. There was so much she wanted to tell Regaume, yet she mainly yearned to hear his voice. The wrenching creak of his cell door was a welcome sound to her ears.

"My love," Regaume said, his face brightening as she entered. He shifted his shackles to stand.

She embraced him and did not let go until Tronchet excused himself, pulling the door closed behind him.

"How are you?" she asked. "Are you fed enough? I will have Rosellen bring something."

"Well enough," he said. "It's wonderful to see you, Mili."

"Tronchet says you will be transferred into the custody of the Ralmogard magistrate next week. Tell me what to do. I can smuggle anything into this cell or I can take the keys."

Regaume sat on his flimsy bed and stretched his legs with a grunt. The locks on his ankles silenced Milisend. They were large iron spheres missing a square bit on the inner sides.

"Double-hulled foot bearings," Regaume said. "They put them on me the other day. Impossible to pick the inner locks without the fittings that Tronchet keeps. So if you stole his keys they would be useless without the square fittings."

"Then I'll steal the fittings," she said.

"You'd never smuggle them in," he said. "They are heavy and bulky by design."

Milisend collapsed into his arms. "I must do something, let me do something," she murmured. "I walk the halls of the palace thinking only of you and escape. I asked Lord Valient's man, Serdot, for help. He shrugged me off, but I will petition Valient directly."

"You are a princess of the House of Avaleau," Regaume said. "Yet the lord minister will not make time to see you?"

"My father's royal line weakens by the day, replaced by Brugarn's influence. A war has begun, Regaume. Open war in Alpenon and Gadolin."

"War?"

"I'm afraid, Regaume. Father is locked away in his tower, downtrodden and endlessly brooding. Brugarn doesn't even let Mother see him. Not that she could. The queen lies in bed all day in a popaver stupor now. I have my sisters to commiserate with, since Henrey remains in the capital. But soon he'll take Avalane back to their home in Elmbrel, and I'll be alone . . ."

"Be brave, Mili. You are stronghearted, more than you give yourself credit for. These dark days will not last."

"You sound so certain."

He took her soft face in his gentle hands, his eyes shining bright and fearless. "You must be strong, Mili. Think of my travel to Ralmogard. Tronchet will demand they chain me with their own shackles so that he may keep these costly ones here. You know I'll find a way to escape on the road or in Ralmogard, and not for the first time. I'll not die on the gallows like my unfortunate fellows. I'll come back for you, Thimblegloves, and we'll leave this place together."

"Promise me, Regaume."

"I promise, Mili. I will come back for you."

82

FETZER

On the Road to Eglamour, Wallevet Ministry
Bloomfade, 3034

"But what possessed you to offer Arthan a wine barrel, and of his choosing?"

"Calm yourself, Fetzer." Arasemis paused to cough. "I knew he wouldn't accept any wine, and we needed to appear legitimate."

Fetzer stared at Arasemis.

"Let it be, Fetzer," Juhl said. "The master knows what risks to take."

"No one can accuse me of fearing risk," Fetzer said, cutting his eyes at her. Juhl was irritating him more lately. His private advances toward her over the past few weeks were consistently deflected. He began to dislike her outright but still hoped she would be drawn to his ascendancy.

"Fetzer, did you see the way Arthan eyed us?" Arasemis asked. "Especially when you carelessly revealed your surprise when I offered a barrel to him? Arthan suspects something is amiss. Clearly he hasn't figured us out, but he's starting to put things together in his head."

"We could have joined his convoy," Fetzer said. "Then I could have killed him at camp one night."

"If all of you had used your two prior chances, Arthan would already be dead," Arasemis said between coughs. "Attacking him and his thousands of protective soldiers on the open road is suicidal. We must preserve ourselves for our primary task. I'll not argue the point further."

Fetzer looked out into the countryside from his side of the wagon bench. If Arasemis would simply give him the lamp armor and Marlan's flaming sword, no amount of soldiers would be able to stop him.

"It won't matter anyway," Juhl said. "Arthan and the others will be dead soon enough."

Arasemis grunted in agreement and wiped his mouth with a handkerchief. Fetzer kept silent and looked forward again, watching the dust cloud of Arthan's convoy grow smaller and smaller in the distance.

Later, when the trio camped for the night, Fetzer poured his anger into his journal.

> I can see the light of their campfires in the hills ahead. Now would be the moment I would be making ready in the darkness, searching for his tent and finding him, as I did his squealing brother. Were it not for Arasemis's obsessive caution, Arthan would already be in my grasp, breathing his last. His death would be a final prelude to the pain-filled cries of a king. Then kings.
>
> Arasemis is probably right about one thing: Arthan's suspicion. Only a complete fool, blind and dumb, would fail to see what has happened around him. Perhaps Arthan does not wish to see his fate for what it is, even when it stares back at him. "Godspeed," he said, believing, like the masses, that God aids us. Arthan does not see God for what he is, does not know him as the Dark One, as I have come to. Playthings, all of us. Life is a game of brief survival, an entertainment. Nothing more. Few will have true glory, most will waste their time with false victories.
>
> We are on the eve of a darker dawn, and I must be its bringer. Down with kings and the highborn. Down with light and false glories. Only one thing is permanent, real, and wonderful: death. And I must be its bringer.

83

ARTHAN

Clonmel Estate in Eglamour, Toulon Ministry
Bloomfade, 3034

Arthan breathed a sigh of relief when the long road to Eglamour ended. His brigade escort was probably a decent deterrent against attacks, yet he felt a good bit of luck had befallen him, too. Either way, the whole brigade could not stay with him in the capital.

"But my lord," Livonier said, "when the time comes for you to return to Delavon, you'll need their protection."

"Send them home," Arthan said, stepping out of his carriage. "It's one thing to explain the necessity of a brigade as an escort to the king and Brugarn but quite another to garrison so many of my soldiers in Eglamour. I don't want Brugarn to accuse me of posting my own army in his city."

"What about keeping only two companies?" Livonier asked. "They can be barracked here at Clonmel."

"Clonmel doesn't have the space for them, especially with the kings' men that are already here as part of the inquiry office. We have space for only one troop of thirty additional men, but no more."

"Surely we can't trust the kings' men," Livonier said.

"I cannot turn them away without insulting the king. And they are choice veterans."

"Very well. And you're sure you don't want me to command them?"

"Livonier, you are my most trusted knight. But for now I must keep the Racharders separate from the king's men, ably led by Sir Dardanon. Once again, this will help me avoid Brugarn's accusations of undue influence."

Arthan turned to walk up the front steps of Clonmel just as Serdot appeared in the open doorway. Arthan was glad to see him, but Serdot's always-serious face looked especially dour.

"Are you not glad to see me in one piece?" Arthan asked.

"I'm sorry about Bardil and the others," Serdot said, meeting him on the steps. "Everyone here offers their condolences. I'm afraid I have more ill news for you, however, my lord. But first, a Rugen messenger is waiting for you inside."

"Tell him I'm not taking visitors. I've only just arrived and require some rest."

"He is insistent, my lord. And I recommend you meet with him, if only briefly. We are now at war with the Rugens."

Arthan caught his breath. "What has happened, Serdot?"

"Much, as I will tell you. But we need to move quickly. This messenger was sent by Vesamune. She has been under arrest at her residence by Duke Brugarn's order. He will not let her leave the city."

"Lead the way, Serdot."

Serdot brought Arthan and Livonier to the waiting Rugen.

"Greetings, Lord Valient," said the Rugen man in perfect Donovar. "I am Wredegar, an assistant to Ambassador Vesamune. She has been made a prisoner in Eglamour despite diplomatic assurances between our kingdoms."

"Unfortunate," Arthan said. "What do you want?"

"May we speak privately, my lord?" Wredegar asked.

Arthan looked at Serdot. "He is unarmed," Serdot said.

Arthan waved Livonier and the Clonmel guards out of the room, but indicated that Serdot would stay.

"Thank you," Wredegar said. "I have a message from Vesamune. On behalf of the Emperor of Rugenhav, she offers you her protection."

"From whom?"

"We heard about the attempts on your life," Wredegar said. "Vesamune sends her condolences. We wish to offer you our protection because we value your friendship."

"Are we friends, Wredegar?" Arthan asked. "A war has begun, if you haven't heard. How would you protect me, even if I required it?"

"The ambassador considers you to be the most reasonable high noble of Donovan, someone we can cooperate with to stop the war before it goes too far. The life of one Vilarwef rebel is not worth a war for us."

"I'm listening."

"My emperor is prepared to help remove your enemies so that you can better be of service to your kingdom, and the broader peace, in the footsteps of your father. My emperor respected Lord Maillard."

"Your emperor's envoy to the Empire Alliance Council was not so respectful. Tell me, Wredegar, who does Vesamune believe my enemies to be?"

"The king's brothers, of course. And those who would deny the House of Valient its rightful place on the throne of Donovan."

"You mean a House of Valient under Rugenhav's rule."

"In return for our assistance, my emperor would expect your partnership, yes."

"Your rulers are mistaken if they have pegged me as a traitor to my own people."

"Erech is a shadow of a king. You know, as do we, that it's only a matter of time before one of his brothers takes the throne. And all of them wanted this war. Will you not work with us to avert more bloodshed?"

Arthan thought about the vision of boldness he had had at Maillard's tomb. He looked at Serdot, who gave a quick nod. "Everything you've said is true, though I do not agree with or accept the terms as you've presented them. However, I'm willing to hear what Vesamune has in mind."

"An exchange of letters, couriered only by Serdot and myself to maintain utmost secrecy. We want to know about Erech's condition and be forewarned if his brothers make any attempt to crown themselves. From us you can expect to receive information about your enemies. We know Eglamour better than you do, including the mysterious killers."

"Are you saying you know the identities of the assassins?"

"We have our strong suspicions."

"Most people believe the Rugens are to blame," Arthan said.

"The people on the street regularly heckled and threatened Vesamune for that reason," Serdot said, "when she was still out in public."

"You must provide what you know about the assassins as part of this bargain," Arthan said. "Otherwise, I'm not interes—"

"Did you know that Lord Minister Edmond Reimvick of Wallevet recently visited the slums of the Borel District?" Wredegar interrupted.

"Reimvick is a close friend of mine and a high noble of Donovan," Arthan said. "He is not my enemy."

"You are clearly in need of our information," Wredegar said. "Why would a high noble, even a gossip-hungry one such as him, visit the place where the riots against the king have their roots?"

"Lord ministers go wherever they wish, and Reimvick is no rebel rouser. Borel has been a dangerous slum for many years. No one is surprised the riots began there after the Proclamation of Expediency."

"But Reimvick went alone and disguised. We've been watching him since he privately threatened Vesamune at court. He said her days were numbered and that our emperor would soon fall to ancient forces."

"That doesn't sound like the Reimvick I know," Arthan said. He noticed Serdot fidget, something his friend never did. "But I will consider what you've said."

Wredegar stood. "Thank you for your time, my lord. I shall leave you in peace. If you agree to speak with us, simply send a note to the ambassador."

After Wredegar had departed, Arthan turned to Serdot. "From the beginning, please."

"The Avaleaus reneged on ransoming the Durgensdil rebel leader, a man named Geras Vilarwef, to the Rugens. Lord Asteroth accepted some of the ransom money but gave a deceased Geras to the Rugen Warden of Havelbern. The Rugens responded by invading Donovan."

"The Rugens have been raiding border towns for weeks," Arthan said. "How is this any different?"

"They destroyed the city of Gardwerp, my lord, and took possession of the two border castles, Torgsbad and Sernpert. They were all short sieges. Asteroth fled to his capital at Cantrileme, from which he plans to counterattack."

"No word from Rowan?" Arthan asked.

"No, I'm sorry. What's more, Brugarn has announced a full-out war, claiming Erech demanded it."

"Did he?"

"No one has seen the king for some time, not even Waldemar. Erech has been locked away up in his tower, said to be drugged to sleep away his depression."

Arthan sighed. "I was gone too long . . ."

"My lord, regarding what Wredegar said about Reimvick, I fear he may be right. I cannot vouch for Reimvick going to the Borel District, but I found the remnants of an alchemical laboratory in his quarters here in the palace. I was able to secretly enter with Garion's key."

Arthan shook his head with confusion. "There must be some mistake . . ."

"The key only worked in his door. What's more, I spoke with someone who witnessed Reimvick destroy the laboratory after our discovery of Garion, probably to hide any evidence of his involvement."

"The House of Reimvick has been a staunch ally to the House of Valient for generations," Arthan said. "Raymond and Edmond were both friends of Father. Edmond Reimvick has been nothing but a trustworthy and wise friend to me."

"I spoke with him myself. He showed signs of deception when I spoke about Garion."

"Who is your witness who claimed to see his laboratory?"

"My lord, you know I prefer to closely guard—"

"You're accusing a high noble of being involved in multiple murders, Serdot. As Marshal of Inquiry, I'll not go after him unless I know the details."

Serdot reluctantly recounted finding Princess Milisend in Reimvick's apartment. Arthan listened intently. "So the rumors about her were true," he said. "Amusing . . ."

"I believe what she told me," Serdot said. "Regardless, several undeniable facts remain: Garion had a key to Reimvick's chambers, those chambers held a secret laboratory, and Reimvick destroyed the laboratory after we caught Garion. And Garion was also from Wallevet. He studied at Bredahade Academy before joining the Crownblades."

Arthan nodded. "Yet another link to Wallevet. Raymond was the first one assassinated . . . Serdot, did you ever find out anything on the youngest Reimvick sibling, Arasemis? I met him on the road to Eglamour."

"The hermit of Thorendor? No, I have—"

"Serdot! What did you say about Garion at Bredahade?"

"He previously studied at the academy there . . ."

"You once told me Arasemis had been kicked out of his professorship there many years ago," Arthan said. "Reimvick must have recruited Garion."

"Or Arasemis did . . ."

"How did I not see this earlier? Arasemis acted peculiar, telling me he was coming to Eglamour to sell wine. He must be involved, too. Now both brothers will be in the capital."

"Which means they are planning something big. The start of war with Rugenhav cannot be a coincidence."

"How do we proceed, Serdot?"

"I'll continue to watch Reimvick closely. I think he's been preparing a place for assassins to shelter in Borel because there's no good reason for him to go there. But I'll need to confirm that, in case the Rugens are part of this conspiracy."

"Conspiracy to do what?"

"My lord, I think it's clear. They've targeted the lord ministers at a time when the king is most vulnerable. Someone—the Reimvicks, the Rugens, Brugarn—is trying to overthrow Erech and take the crown."

"You don't think they are recruiting those skilled assassins from Borel?"

"Borel is a pit, my lord, and it's only gotten worse with the riots. It can be a haven for all types."

"Do you think the Rugens are involved?"

"It's possible. They've certainly been planning for war. Perhaps they were going to make an attempt on Erech's life before Asteroth forced their hand on the border. But if we're to take Wredegar's claims at face value, Reimvick's private harassment of Vesamune suggests they're not involved. But that may be what they want us to think. This is a complex game, but one you can play for your benefit—and the kingdom's—if you play it carefully."

"It's not a game, Serdot, but the future of our people. Watch Reimvick. I want to know every detail. I'll think about how to approach the king."

"My lord, I think you should be giving thought to how to do this yourself. The king's mind is so muddled and Brugarn has all but officially supplanted him. As Marshal of Inquiry, your authority is still significant as long as Erech is alive."

Arthan nodded solemnly. "I will think on it. What else have I missed since—"

"My lord!" Livonier said, returning to the room. "A messenger has arrived with word from Rowan."

Arthan took the letter and read aloud to Serdot.

> Dear Brother,
> I wish to apprise you of events here at the border. Things have moved quickly, and it's been difficult for me to discern where they are going next. So much is uncertain.
>
> The borderlands of Alpenon and Gadolin are now the scenes of daily fighting. The Rugens are slowly taking towns and cities. Lord Asteroth tries to be everywhere at once because he doesn't trust his commanders. But it's wearing on him, and we lack reinforcements.
>
> What's more, the Durgensdil rebels have become more daring with their attacks, and more effective. They recently took Gaton Castle, which had been Asteroth's primary base from which to raid rebel positions in the Brindthum Mountains. One loss among many, and for that, Asteroth blames a lack of support from the king and Brugarn.
>
> Finally, you'll recall my informing you earlier about Asteroth's catching of Rugen spies. The only one to survive his violence, a woman named Etzel, has come to view me as her only hope. I have visited her many times, hoping to learn

something of use. She confided that assassins traveled from Austveeden into Donovan, and that they will be gathering in Eglamour. If I free her, she has promised to tell me more. But she remains in Cantrileme, so I do not see her much now that we rove the borderlands.

I pray your newfound authority as a favorite of the king will help bring this growing chaos to an end, but not before we bloody the Rugens' noses a bit.

Rowan Valient
Melsard Town

"Assassins massing in Eglamour," Arthan said. "Too bad this Etzel is in Cantrileme. Regardless, I think it's clear the Rugens are part of what Reimvick and Arasemis are doing."

"But it's still odd," Serdot said. "If the Rugens were behind two attempts on your life, why would they go to so much effort to secure you as a potential partner?"

"I'm confused by it all too, Serdot. Remember the Blackhoods were in Mordmerg, and they seemed to clash with Father's assassin, that Marlan fellow. Those Blackhoods were Donovards. None of this makes sense . . ." Arthan rubbed his brow. "Perhaps I just need a rest after traveling."

"This is what I think, my lord. We've all but nailed down Reimvick's treachery, and I will seek further proof. The Rugens may be backing him, but none of the assassins have been Rugen, nor Blackhoods, as you pointed out. The assassins have all been wall-running alchemists, which does not fit Rugen methods. Once we get our hands on Reimvick, more of these pieces should fall into place."

"Keep at it, then, but we need answers soon. The king, if he's still coherent, will expect the Marshal of Inquiry to have answers. And I have another task to pile onto your plate."

Arthan drew Adrithayn, laid the sword on the table, and unfolded the letter Maillard had left for him about the alchemical sword. He let Serdot read it, then told Serdot how Adrithayn had absorbed the assassins' poisonous cloud during the ambush at Hullen.

"Remarkable," Serdot said as he studied the blade.

"You dabble in alchemy, don't you, as a widsemer?"

"Enough to supply myself with a few pouches of cloaking dust for quick escapes," Serdot said. "And, of course, a few acids and solutions for letter opening, resealing, lock picking, and, well . . ." Serdot smirked sheepishly.

"Go on."

"I've also used sleep candles on occasion to slip into rooms I wouldn't usually be welcomed into."

"You're more of an alchemist than you've ever let on, my friend. And it's perfectly fine. My father's letter has opened my eyes to an unseen world."

"A shamed world," Serdot said. "Alchemy is still widely perceived as dishonorable, underhanded work, even for widsemers."

"I've thought about it, Serdot. I count your secret skills to be among the most honorable, for they can spare many lives and grief when used properly. I wish to know more about this chemina arcana and this sword. I consulted Master Pelinaud back in Rachard, and he told me to find a respected historian here in the capital by the name of Danleri. Do you know of him?"

"I do not, my lord, but I shall find him."

"I want to better understand this blade and the things Father wrote about. As you read, he believed it would be in my best interests to do so."

"And I agree," Serdot said. "I'll bring this Danleri to Clonmel when I find him."

84

RODEL

Auch Tenoshun, Lundwynland Ministry
Bloomfade, 3034

"We should have gone around this city." Rodel wished he had spoken up sooner. He liked Marlan and trusted his judgment, but he should have listened to his own instincts this time.

"We have to look the part. It would have looked suspicious for two wine merchants to avoid Auch Tenoshun," Marlan said. "It's a major exchange for the trade to Almeria, via Quayrond."

"But then we wouldn't be in this situation," Rodel said.

They watched as the guard came back. "I relayed your request, and the magistrate denied it," said the guard. "You'll have to leave your goods here and take your case to the magistrate yourself, if you wish."

"Our lord will be displeased," Marlan said. "This is no time for—"

"There's a war in the south, and the king's new proclamation also demands the tax on such goods," the soldier interrupted. "Take it up with the magistrate."

Rodel and Marlan exchanged a look. Rodel knew Marlan was not about to give up the barrels with their mechan armor hidden inside.

"Give us a moment to collect our papers," Marlan said to the guard.

Rodel followed Marlan off the bench and into the canvas-covered wagon. They scrambled across the tops of the barrels looking for the ones marked M and R.

"Do we have time?" Rodel asked.

"We have a few moments before they get suspicious," Marlan said.

"I'll need more than moments to affix my thigh rods and levers," Rodel said.

"Get your mask helmet on first," Marlan said.

The pair hurriedly pried off the barrel lids and brushed away the packing cloth. Piece by piece they donned their mechans. Marlan's shroud armor was the easier fit and he had already loaded the alchemical cartridges in his arms and breastplate back at Thorendor. Rodel finished clasping one of his internal crossbow mechanisms in his arm before reaching for his helmet.

"The guards are talking," Marlan said. "Almost time."

"Where are we going to run to?" Rodel asked.

"We'll escape the city. Back through the gate we entered."

"We can't run all the way to Eglamour, Marlan. Certainly not in these suits."

"We'll have to find a boat. The river from the north of the city empties into the Torfnabruk. From there we can sail up to the Orbruk. It's a tributary that will take us most of the way. We'll make for land at Aughreim, just a day's walk from the capital. We know Arasemis and the others were going to Borel District. We'll be late, but we'll get there."

"You in there!" a guard shouted. They could hear him walk to the rear of the wagon. "Finding papers or drinking wine?"

"You finish up and I'll stall them," Marlan said, pulling a lever on his arm. A blue liquid coursed through the external veins of his armor. Then he drew his alchemical sword.

Rodel nodded as he worked to affix his thigh rods, peering at Marlan through the crystal-lensed slits of his mask helmet.

"Meet you in the grove outside the gate," Marlan said. He threw open the canvas. Blue-gray smoke was already seeping from the veins into the air around him. The guard did not have time to blink. Marlan's sword opened his mail and half-plate armor, sending sparks in all directions as his sword flamed brightly.

Rodel struggled to close the clasps of the second mechanism on his forearm. The fit was perfect but the fingers of his gauntlets were still crusted with a stubborn rust. The fighting outside intensified as he stood up in the wagon and attached the final cocking rods from his thighs to his torso, then up to his shoulders.

Rodel's arms stiffened as the whole mechanism engaged. He lifted his legs repeatedly, hearing the clicks as each miniature crossbow was loaded with bolts. When it would click no more he flexed his arms and neck, then reached up and tore down the canvas.

Marlan was a whirl of flame dimmed by the blue-gray smoke. The soldiers that flooded toward them hesitated when they saw him. Rodel aimed his hands, then pulled the thumb loops. The thwack of the crossbow cords vibrated up into his helmet as the bolts shot into the soldiers. Rodel jumped down from the wagon and ran toward the gate, shooting every soldier who approached him. Rodel knew from the metal-searing sound of Marlan's sword that he was close behind.

The gatekeepers responded quickly. The last crack of light between the doors darkened. Rodel turned and loosed another round of bolts into the pursuing soldiers. The blue smoke trail behind Marlan was thickening, and the soldiers who passed through it coughed violently.

Marlan plowed past Rodel toward the gate. Rodel watched but kept moving to reload his armbows. Marlan hacked at each set of hinges on the great doors, then the middle lock. The entry area was filled with flying sparks amid the smoke. The ground shook when one of the doors crashed down.

A moment later Marlan tore into the portcullis outside. His sword became white-hot as molten iron piled up like slag on the ground. Rodel could feel the radiating heat, even inside his mechan. Few soldiers braved the smoke, fearing what they had seen. They offered no help to their screaming brethren in the gatehouse. Rodel watched as the flames of the door crept up into their floor. Water dripped down into the gateway as they struggled to put it out, adding steam to the smoky, sparking mix swirling around Marlan.

At last Marlan vanished. Rodel followed, stepping through the hole in the portcullis. He ran into the clear air outside, following the blue smoke trail into the grove.

"Magnificent!" Rodel shouted through his helmet. "I've never seen such a thing!" Then Rodel became worried.

Marlan had thrown his sword down. It was lying in scorched grass, still white-hot, and Marlan was stripping off his gauntlets as quickly as he could. His bare hands were red with blisters. "I'll be fine," he said. "I brought a salve. We must get to the river port. They'll be after us."

"Quench your veins," Rodel said.

"I already added water. It needs time to clear out."

As they caught their breath Rodel watched as the blue residue in the veins of the shroud armor drained and the smoke faded.

"Your arrow armor still works well enough," Marlan said.

Rodel kicked a leg to reload an armbow. "I like this."

Marlan put salve on his hands, wrapped them in linen, then put his gauntlets back on. He gingerly sheathed his sword, which still glowed red. "Ready?"

They darted from the grove. Soldiers were trickling out of the destroyed gate, but a few shots from Rodel sent them diving to the ground. The soldiers on the wall simply watched them go.

Rodel had presumed the river port was close by, but they had to run across a lumpy field. He wanted to rip off the mask and the mechan and its stilted rods and squeaky, greasy wheels and pulleys. Rodel wondered whether Marlan's suit was more flexible or if his agility was due to his mastery of aerina arcana. Rodel now understood why Arasemis had been hesitant to teach them machina so soon.

By the time Rodel caught up, Marlan had already taken command of a small boat on the docks. He had forced off the crew and was prodding the captain toward the helm with his red sword. Rodel frightened away the gawking crew and passersby, then lifted the boat lines from the dock.

Rodel hopped aboard and they were underway, two big sails billowing freely above them.

85

FETZER

Borel District of Eglamour, Toulon Ministry
Midsummer, 3034

"Could your scribbles betray us if they were found by the enemy?" Juhl asked.

"Arasemis's behavior on the road was riskier than anything I could write to myself." Fetzer glared at her as he dipped the quill. "Besides, my writings shouldn't concern a Lambic princess. Do they teach princesses to read in your country?"

Juhl studied his face for a moment. "I think you are a risk to all of us. Arasemis always seems to know what he's doing, but I don't know why he hasn't put you in your proper place."

"Pick up a sword when you're ready," Fetzer said, turning to his journal. "Then you'll know," he mumbled to himself as she walked away.

> We arrived at Eglamour with little further trouble. My dreams have been awash in Arthan's blood since seeing him on the road. So close, so close . . .
>
> Our safe house in the Borel District is comfortable enough. Arasemis knew precisely where to go, saying close friends had set it up for us. I'm uncomfortable not knowing who these supporters are, but Arasemis is guarded about it. The house is fully stocked with food and supplies

and a small laboratory. Juhl asked if our housekeepers are members of the Order. Arasemis simply said "they should be."

Marlan and Rodel should have been here by now. I hope Rodel hasn't done something foolish, or turned on us. I've distrusted him from the start. Marlan is too accepting of Rodel, Juhl is infatuated with him, and Arasemis . . . well, I cannot make any excuse for him.

Arasemis says if they are delayed another day we will proceed with our task without them. We've already spent too long pacing this house. Tonight we will prepare and scout our route to the palace.

My only concern is Arasemis's coughing. He became ill on the road. It may ruin our efforts to be silent . . .

86

ARTHAN

"None of you, nor the lord ministers cowering in their capitals, have done enough to support my brothers in the south," Brugarn said to the court. "Does the war fall on the shoulders of the Avaleaus alone, or does Donovan still have high nobles who have courage, grit, and honor?"

Arthan listened and watched Brugarn sitting confidently on the king's throne. Then he turned to whisper to Serdot. "The Duke speaks well enough but doesn't go to the borderlands to fight. Is this not what he wanted?"

Serdot nodded. "And General Chaultion still stands at his right hand instead of leading in the south. The duke is content to let others do the dying. He has regularly harangued the nobles like this since you left for Rachard."

"Where are the lord ministers of Hanovel and Barres?" Brugarn shouted as he searched the court with his eyes. "Are they still pretending to have problems with Calbrians and Almerians? With islands they should never have ceded to the enemy in the first place?" Brugarn pointed to Arthan. "As for you, I would think the king's Marshal of Inquiry would be here protecting the king, not spending so much time in Delavon."

"I traveled at the king's urging," Arthan said, "to prepare my lands for my extended work here in the capital. Yet I do not find the king on his throne upon my return."

"Selfishness is a base evil, especially in times of war when unity is critical for the kingdom," Brugarn said, turning back to the court. "This man spends lavishly on rebuilding ancient warcastles so that he may defend his own realm at the expense of our kingdom."

Arthan felt anger rise within him.

"Yet this so-called marshal cannot protect himself, despite his selfish efforts," Brugarn continued. "Death lurks at his heels, as evidenced by the bodies of the House of Valient that are piling up. How can Lord Valient protect the king if he cannot protect himself? How can he serve the king's needs if he withholds his gold for his own use while our people in the borderlands are slaughtered by the Rugens?"

"This is your war," Arthan said, ignoring Serdot's hand on his arm. "You wanted it, you provoked the Rugens, and now you sit on a throne that is not yours."

"I am the Duke of Toulon and the king's right hand! I serve him while he is ill. This man is the Lord Minister of Delavon, accuser of falsities. Spreading lies is easier than answering for the truth, it seems. Are you not fortifying Delavon at the expense of the king's treasury?"

"Rebuilding derelict defenses is no crime. Defending my lands is my right. As for the treasury, I have sent more coin than any—"

"So you admit to working to save your own skin, despite the great distance between Delavon and the borderlands. War is far from you, yet always too close, Lord Valient? Securing your post as marshal guarantees your presence in Eglamour, not on the war front, just as you've planned it. Yet there is nothing to show for it. I shall inform Asteroth and Erath that they cannot depend on the nobles of this court, especially this one. Reinforcements and supplies will be delayed until Delavon strengthens—"

"Their blood is on your hands!" Arthan shouted. "Where is the king? Let him come and see what you've made. Let him pass judgment on you, me, and anyone else."

"Sir Hamelin, bring your Crownblades closer," Brugarn said. "Lord Valient has become vicious, jealous of his luxuries, and resentful of my wisdom. Now all can see that he only cares for himself."

Arthan took in a breath to shout again but finally relented to Serdot's squeeze on his arm.

"He'll goad you into doing something foolish," Serdot whispered. "He's done it to everyone else."

Arthan looked around. The nobles and other courtiers were watching him as Brugarn continued his rant. Their eyes were glaring—not hateful, but disappointed. Arthan was embarrassed. He felt reckless, not bold. He looked at Hamelin, who stepped near to the throne and rested his hand on his sword hilt.

"Why are the Crownblades here and not with the king?" Arthan asked Hamelin, unable to resist. Hamelin remained silent, but the look on his face told Arthan he had shamed the knight. Arthan turned to leave the court.

"Witness but a taste of how the Valients retreat when they are called to serve," Brugarn called after him. "Maillard failed the king, and so have his sons."

Arthan turned to look at Brugarn. He bit his tongue and departed.

⁓

Back at Clonmel, Arthan and Serdot sat together. Arthan lifted his face from his hands. "I let him provoke me."

"You spoke the truth and defended yourself," Serdot said. "The nobles know those truths but are ashamed of them. Everyone is ashamed that they have watched idly as Brugarn slowly took power. Your impassioned defense reminded them of that."

"This has happened so quickly . . . Should I have stood there and listened to the duke's rubbish like everyone else?"

"The court expected Maillard's cool, calm demeanor. They expect viciousness from Brugarn, but they expect the firm mildness of your father."

"Father would not have allowed Brugarn to manipulate him, or the king, for that matter."

Serdot shook his head. "Your father did not face what you do. Erech was still a functioning king. There was no upheaval in the cities. No war. Only the shadow of it."

Arthan rubbed his face. "What hope is there if the Rugens plow through the borderlands and we have no true king to lead us?"

"You have a channel to the Rugen emperor via Vesamune," Serdot said. "Send a letter."

"I originally agreed to talk with them when it was still possible to avert or limit the war. But now both sides are committed and both want me dead."

"Brugarn may wish you into the grave, my lord, but I'm still uncertain the Rugens are behind the assassinations."

"Have you learned anything new?"

"Unfortunately not. Lord Reimvick has not traveled to Borel District, nor is he preparing to return to Wallevet. He spends his time as he always does: in jovial banter and entertainment. It's like he's waiting for something."

"Perhaps the Rugens' march into Eglamour."

"Use your channel with Vesamune," Serdot said. "They are looking for puppets in Eglamour. If you can't convince them to pull back their armies, then let them believe you can be a worthy partner, come what may. If the Rugens are behind the assassinations, perhaps it will buy you time. If they're not involved, as Wredegar claimed, then perhaps you'll be in a more advantageous position than the other nobles."

"A more advantageous position for what, Serdot?"

"The crown, my lord."

"I will not owe my crown to the Rugens."

"Of course not, but they are invading our kingdom at its weakest. You saw the look on the nobles' faces. We are without a king and have usurpers aplenty. Someone must lead, and they are looking to you as they looked to Maillard. Even Reimvick told you that."

"But what can I do while Brugarn and Chaultion control the armies of Donovan?"

"Keep Delavon fortified. Use your powers as marshal to uncover the assassins, thereby increasing your standing in the court. And use your channel to the Rugens to manipulate them for your own benefit and the kingdom's benefit, namely the crown."

"I have nothing to make the Rugens pull back their armies. And the south may already be lost if Brugarn is failing to support Asteroth and Erath as Rowan described."

Serdot nodded. "Brugarn may lose his war before it goes too far. He has been trying to scrape together enough gold and soldiers and supplies, but the effects of his Proclamation of Expedience have frustrated his efforts."

"I think you're right, Serdot. Even with Chaultion making his strategic decisions, they can't win the war they've started."

"If you don't secretly work with the Rugens, and if they defeat Brugarn and his brothers, they will have no incentive to work with you. They'll install a new puppet king. If you try to work with them, you could achieve the crown—especially if you prove your worth as marshal."

"There must be another way, Serdot. I grow less and less comfortable with the idea of talking with the Rugens as this war unfolds, regardless of my chances for the crown. And as long as Erech is alive, detached as he is, I become like Brugarn if I turn against him."

"The nobles are looking to you to do something. Maillard would have understood."

"There must be a third way . . ."

Serdot leaned back in his chair. "I don't see one, my lord. And time is running out to decide."

87

BRUGARN

Eddal Estate in Eglamour, Toulon Ministry
Midsummer, 3034

"More importantly, I demand your unflinching loyalty," Brugarn said.

"But Erech is my father-in-law," Henrey said. "I did not make the journey all the way from Elmbrel Ministry to be strong-armed into such an arrangement."

"Silence! If you think you'll rule Donovan instead of me because you wed Princess Avalane, I'll send you to the Alpenon front to die. A glorious death for the lord minister of Elmbrel, of course. Support me or leave southward tomorrow. I'll tell Avalane you volunteered to help Asteroth."

Henrey looked away, shaking his head. "Erech is not fit to be king, I agree with you. But this should be done the proper way. I guarantee you that most lord ministers—myself included—would support dethroning him if we follow the old customs. And the Patriarch of Donovan will need to be involved. The Church has long had a right to—"

"Then I shall inform General Chaultion that you'll be leading the next convoy down to Alpenon. Asteroth will be glad to have you."

"I don't want to be part of your war, Brugarn."

"You'll address me as Duke or Lord Minister, you coward. Or, live long enough, and I'll let you bow to me as king. You can be part of my war and die in glory, or you can serve me here with greater glory. This is your last chance, Henrey. I'll not offer you my hand again."

Brugarn watched the young man carefully. He knew what was going through his mind. Thoughts of his young wife, Avalane, and their little son. His lands in Elmbrel. Brugarn smiled to himself as Henrey fidgeted.

Brugarn stood abruptly from the courtyard bench. "Well, that's settled, then. Enjoy this last view of your peaceful gardens. I will let Avalane continue to live here awhile after you're dead before confiscating this estate for the treasury. Or perhaps I'll keep it for myself. I like that it's close to the palace yet feels removed. A beautiful respite."

Henrey did not respond, so Brugarn strutted toward the portico. He touched one of the columns as Henrey spoke behind him.

"You have my loyalty, Lord Brugarn."

"Good," he said, turning with a smile. "On my way out I will tell one of your servants to bring . . ." Brugarn looked past where Henrey was seated in the garden. A figure was running across the far gardens, and it appeared to have long blades in place of hands. He tried to call out, but his voice failed him.

Gray smoke, similar to what he had seen Garion throw, suddenly burst all around Henrey and billowed toward the portico. Another figure dropped down into the courtyard from the roof. Brugarn snapped back around, pressing his body against the back side of the column. He gritted his teeth as Henrey screamed out. He closed his eyes as the smell of sooty smoke enveloped him.

A few guards ran out into the gardens. A whirl of blades and more screams followed. Brugarn peeked an eye, but it was dark smoke all around. He pressed his back into the column, holding his breath for dear life.

The blades and screams soon ended. It became quiet. He waited until the summer breeze began to carry the smoke away. Only when more soldiers ventured out did he peel himself from the column to have a look into the courtyard. Henrey and his guards were a heap of red. There was no sign of the assassins.

Brugarn caught his breath with difficulty. He clutched a column for support. When he brought his hand away it was red with spattered blood.

"My lord, are you all right?" a soldier asked.

It took Brugarn a moment to realize it was one of his Crownblades.

"Where were you?" Brugarn said. "When I say a private meeting I mean out of earshot. They nearly killed me, you fool."

"Apologies, my lord. Which way did they go?"

"Never mind that. Get me to the palace at once."

88

ARTHAN

Eglamour Palace, Toulon Ministry
Midsummer, 3034

"The king's health is very poor, both mind and body," Waldemar said. "Hamelin finally permitted me to go up into the tower to see him, without Brugarn knowing. I'm not even sure Erech recognized me."

Arthan looked at the tree limbs bobbing in the breeze as they walked the path through a little wooded courtyard. "What can be done?"

"I spend most of my waking hours considering that question, Lord Valient. I'm not sure anything can be done. I'm a patient man ripe in years, but my hope has worn thin. If only your father were alive."

Arthan knew Waldemar did not evoke Maillard as an insult, but it still stung. The old steward and others had relied on his father for so long to overcome a myriad of problems, from the royal court to foreign lands. Arthan grasped how difficult that was to imitate.

"What can I do?" he asked.

Waldemar stopped walking. "No one should compare you to Maillard, but you cannot blame us for trying. Your behavior with Brugarn the other day at court . . . Well, you won the trust of many nobles, and you spoke the truth. But I know Brugarn, and he cannot be dealt with so directly."

"Serdot told me as much."

"Perhaps it was wrong of me to demand so much from you so quickly. You are still so young, and our reliance is due to our own failings. Do not misunderstand me, Lord Valient. You can become the great uniter your father was, a great leader of our kingdom. You have that potential. But your wisdom must be grown with time and care."

"They say time is a quick fish with constant change in its wake," Arthan said.

Waldemar smiled. "A wise observation, indeed."

"May I ask a question regarding a more personal matter?"

"Of course."

"When you met with the king, did he mention his intention for me to wed his middle daughter, Princess Milisend?"

"A royal wedding is no personal matter," Waldemar said. "I would be most happy to witness such a merger of the houses of Avaleau and Valient, the sooner the better. It would drain the legitimacy that Brugarn has gathered around himself to be the next king. Alas, Erech did not speak of it to me."

"Before I left for Rachard, he asked me to consider wedding her. I would do so, for the good of the kingdom, but that time may have passed."

"I'm sure the king's intent was genuine," Waldemar said. "But his mind has deteriorated so quickly. Was anyone else aware of his intent for you to wed her?"

"Duke Brugarn was the only witness, unfortunately. He was as surprised as I was."

Waldemar turned glum again. "Then there is your answer. It's certain Brugarn has dissuaded Erech from the notion of joining the houses. Such an arrangement would destroy his position."

"I thought as much," Arthan said. "Then it's not to be."

Arthan and Waldemar turned at the sound of soldiers shouting, then Brugarn's booming voice.

"There you are!" The duke stomped into the wooded courtyard, smacking the branches out of his way like a child in a tantrum. "They almost killed me and you're shading yourself in leisure!"

"My lord?" Arthan asked, looking at the blood smudged on Brugarn's hands and tunic. The duke was clearly shaken.

"Are you all right?" Waldemar asked.

"Do I look all right, you old fool? Lord Valient has failed in his duties as marshal. Lord Henrey was slain this time, but it will be you who will explain it to Princess Avalane."

"Me?" Arthan wanted to curse him, but he tried to keep calm, mild, diplomatic. He was determined to channel the wisdom and patience Waldemar spoke of.

"You're a disgrace," Brugarn continued. "What good is a Marshal of Inquiry if you cannot track down these assassins? We'll all be dead before you—"

"Are these not the Crownblades behind you?" Arthan asked calmly. "You'll recall the king charged me with investigating, not protecting. Perhaps you'd care to describe what you saw? Did they come toward the palace?"

Brugarn sniffed. "I'm not part of your office. What have your investigations found, then?"

"That is privileged information," Arthan said. "I cannot divulge it prematurely, in fear of losing—"

"I've heard enough," Brugarn said. "I'll speak to the king about it. Marshal of Insolence!"

Brugarn stomped off with his Crownblades in tow. Arthan glanced at Waldemar.

"That was better," the steward said. "Don't provoke him, let him spout his nonsense, and don't give him anything to latch on to."

"Henrey dead . . . I must get back to my duties."

"Find these people, whoever they are," Waldemar said. "The Rugens will have no one left in Eglamour to conquer."

89

MARLAN

Torfnabruk River, Lundwynland Ministry
Midsummer, 3034

"I know what you're thinking," the captain said, "and you won't have any need to, I swear. I've worked with high banditry before and kept my mouth shut. I'll get you to Aughreim safe and quick, then be on my way. Won't say anything, I swear."

Marlan glanced at the captain as he finished replacing the bandages on his hands. He had not said anything to the old sailor about what might happen to him once they arrived in Aughreim. He wondered if the captain had overheard Marlan talking with Rodel last night. Rodel was in favor of letting the captain go, something Marlan knew Arasemis would never allow. The Order of the Candlestone had long kept its secrets by silencing witnesses who could prove dangerous later.

Marlan's eyes met Rodel's as he replied. "You'll do as we say, Captain, regardless. Do it right, and I'll consider your keeping your life."

"Of course, Master."

Marlan had watched him. The captain simply could not help staring at their mechans and Marlan's sword. Marlan had no doubt the old man would talk about what he had seen and describe their faces to the lawkeepers. They were not going to keep their masks on throughout the voyage, given their limited supply of gill fern fronds. The captain could also probably guess their ultimate destination. He simply knew too much.

Marlan tried to put thoughts of what would have to be done out of his mind for now. He had considered trying to steer the riverboat himself, but he'd never been on the Orbruk before. Marlan tested the flexibility of his bandaged hand before winking at Rodel and walking to the prow. Rodel met him there, and they whispered.

"You know how I feel about letting him go," Rodel said. "Even if he talks, it won't stop us."

"Part of me agrees with you. But surely your training, whatever it was for, tells you to silence him to avoid the risk."

Rodel nodded. "But will it matter this time? If we're successful in Eglamour, everyone will know the name Candlestone."

"Only if Arasemis and the others have had better luck than we've had. If something worse happened to them, everything could be up to you and me. It's not worth the risk."

Rodel looked out onto the darkening mirror of the river, then down at the gentle swell where the prow cut through the water. "My training did require killing for security, but we were taught that we had already failed if our security was compromised in the first place. I know we had no choice, I just . . ."

"You were a Wosmok, weren't you?" Marlan asked. Discomfort flickered in Rodel's eyes. "Juhl didn't tell me. I weaseled a hint out of her and, with Arasemis's tale of your prison carriage falling into the river, could make a guess. Not many Rugen widsemers roaming around Donovan."

"There were few, but now likely more, given the war."

"We're brothers now, Rodel. When you took the Candlestone oath we became family, regardless of where you came from. The war means nothing between members of the Order, except that it's an opportunity, as Arasemis said." Marlan paused to smile. "Well, Fetzer has his own views, but he's still bound by the oath."

Rodel nodded. "He is a singular individual."

"Driven like no other," Marlan agreed. "As you've heard me say before, I do think he is prophetic for the Order, a bringer of the change we need to fulfill our ancient task."

Marlan watched Rodel watching the water. "Aside from him, Juhl likes you, quite a lot."

"Is it forbidden within the Order?"

"No, as long as it doesn't interfere with our tasks. Fetzer also favors Juhl, so that could be a problem given his jealous temperament. How do you feel? I know many Lambics and Rugens wed."

"I have no such aims. My duty is to complete our tasks."

Marlan regarded him with curiosity. "You quit the Wosmoks and became our brother. A hardened Rugen assassin, willing to kill a foreign king yet wishing to spare the life of a boatman. As a man of few words, you offer fewer answers."

"I've always been a wanderer, Marlan. Being a Wosmok was good for a while because we were left to ourselves for long stretches of time. But I tired of it. It was killing without purpose." He turned to Marlan. "Candlestone has given me purpose."

Marlan looked out across the river to the lands in front of them. "Let me tell you about the history of this realm, Lundwynland. It was settled by a people cursed to wander. You can read about them in Arasemis's library. After the ancient Bronhildi tribe joined the Brintilian Empire, they intermarried with the imperials. Most stayed in their native lands, but some traveled west to where the conquered Goyn clan of the Gallerlanders dwelled. They intermarried again with the Goyns, so three quarters of their blood was heathen.

"These are the Lundwyn people of today," he continued. "They were displaced several times by the empire but finally were granted these lands by the first kings of Donovan. In return, the Lundwyns were banned from using their whisper alchemy, which they developed from the old heathen ways."

"Whisper alchemy?"

"Arasemis is not certain whether it existed or whether it was just an ancient tall tale. The notion came from embellished Brintilian imperial dispatches during the colonial era. They claimed native alchemists could slather concoctions on their tongues and whisper in people's ears to drug and influence them. Whatever the case, it was enough for the early Kingdom of Donovan to outlaw it. Alas, the

Lundwyns returned to their home after generations of wandering. Candlestone is the home you've been searching for, Rodel. You've felt it. We will remake the world."

Rodel nodded, returning his eyes to the darkening water. "How much farther?"

"Shouldn't be more than a few days to Aughreim. We'll find some horses and make our way to the capital in a short time. Hopefully Arasemis will not begin without us."

"And our boat captain?"

"I'll use the sleeping powder first," Marlan said. "He'll pass easy."

PART IV

BITTER TRUTHS

90

TRONCHET

Eglamour Palace, Toulon Ministry
Midsummer, 3034

"Hamelin, you previously said that the king has often been awake at these late hours," Tronchet said. "That is why I've come now."

Hamelin shook his head. "It's useless, Tronchet. The king's mind is not healthy. He will not hear your plea about your prisoner."

"It's not just about the prisoner. I also want to discuss Henrey's death."

"Duke Brugarn already has," Hamelin said.

"How did the king react?"

"I have watched Brugarn bring many matters of great importance to the king, yet the king does not answer. Brugarn's visits only serve to keep up the appearance that he counsels with the king."

Tronchet nodded. "I suppose I also hoped to see Erech for myself. If he is so far gone, what keeps Brugarn from taking his crown?"

"I'm commander of the Crownblades, not a political prognosticator."

Tronchet frowned. "Very well, if I cannot go up I shall find my own bed for what's left of the night."

"I'm sorry, Tronchet. Brugarn is strict about who goes up into the tower. He has even forbidden me from going up without him."

"Then who protects the king?"

"Is there a king who needs protection?"

Tronchet could plainly see Hamelin's frustration and shame for posing the question. "He is still our king . . ." he said. "Good night, Sir Hamelin."

Tronchet stifled a yawn as he trudged through the palace back to his quarters in the prison tower. He passed through the corridor leading to the apartments for visiting dignitaries. He spotted movement in the shadows. A large dark form was pushing a wheelbarrow.

Tronchet stepped to the wall and peered around a column, watching as the figure stopped in front of Lord Reimvick's quarters. The figure opened Reimvick's door and picked up what looked like a small keg from the wheelbarrow and placed it inside. Then he closed the door and departed with the wheelbarrow.

When all was quiet and still again, Tronchet approached the door. He listened but detected no sound, though he smelled what reminded him of spiced cake. He thought it odd for anyone in the palace to receive such a secretive late-night delivery but did not knock. He resolved to return the next morning to see if he could catch Reimvick.

91

SERDOT

Eglamour Palace, Toulon Ministry
Midsummer, 3034

Serdot commenced his routine of watching for Reimvick's exit from his palace apartment early each morning, then following him to the gardens where he enjoyed some fresh air before meeting other nobles to break his fast and gossip. Serdot always made note of who Reimvick talked to and where he went thereafter. Still no travel to Borel.

Serdot often acted as if he were busy walking here or there or talking to someone. But today he chose to keep out of the apartments' corridor. He waited behind a column in an adjacent room, within view of Reimvick's door. The lord minister had not emerged at his usual time.

Serdot waited and watched. He became anxious as time passed. More servants would be up and about soon. He would become unable to simply wait behind the column without looking suspicious. At the sound of footsteps, he walked into the corridor and paused at a side table, where he acted as though he were writing a letter.

Serdot soon noticed someone else loitering at the far end of the corridor. Serdot acted as if he had not noticed the figure for a time, then grew too curious not to look. Serdot pocketed his mock letter and walked over, careful to keep an ear bent toward Reimvick's door.

"Good morning, Chief Magistrate," Serdot said.

Tronchet looked puzzled. "Ah, good morning, Serdot. What brings the right hand of the Marshal of Inquiry into the palace today?"

"I'm always here," Serdot said.

"And everywhere, I'm sure."

Serdot noted that Tronchet did not move on, as was the lawkeeper's habit when he ran into Serdot. "What are you waiting here for, if I may ask?"

Tronchet became visibly uncomfortable. "I, well . . . I wanted to make sure everything in this wing of the palace was . . . in order, given what happened to Henrey." Tronchet glanced twice at Reimvick's door as he spoke.

"Do you suspect something is amiss?" Serdot asked.

"Well, I . . ."

Tronchet trailed off as Reimvick's door opened. They both turned to watch the lord minister exit. He seemed his usual self. Tronchet hesitated with a half step.

"Am I keeping you from an appointment with the Lord Minister of Wallevet?" Serdot asked.

"Yes—no, I . . ."

Serdot waited for Reimvick to leave before grabbing Tronchet's arm. "Will you walk with me, Chief Magistrate? I have something importa—"

"Let go of me, you scaly widsemer," Tronchet said too loudly.

"Please, Sir Tronchet. It is about Reimvick . . ."

Tronchet jerked his arm out of Serdot's grasp before settling himself. "Why don't you speak plainly instead of being so opaque and secretive? What is it, then?"

Serdot ushered him toward a door that led to a balcony, and Tronchet relented. They spoke while overlooking the city.

"I know you were waiting for Reimvick," Serdot began.

"What of it?"

"So was I."

"Why?" Tronchet asked.

"Why are you interested in him?"

"I'm the head lawkeeper of the realm, don't forget. You tell me what you're doing."

"Did you see something?" Serdot asked. "Anything out of the ordinary?"

"Maybe I did. Why should I tell you?"

"Lord Valient is charged by the king to investigate threats to the Crown. And we suspect Reimvick is involved. You must keep that to yourself."

Tronchet became less ornery. "Why do you suspect him?"

"What did you see, Tronchet?"

Tronchet puffed up his chest with a deep breath. "I can investigate anything, you know . . ." Serdot's blank stare deflated his pride. "Fine, well, I don't even know what I saw."

"But it interested you enough to keep watching him."

Tronchet sighed. "I saw someone bring a keg to Reimvick's door in the middle of the night. I was on an errand when I spotted—whoever it was. I couldn't see much, and the person left."

"Did this person speak to anyone?"

"No one was around. He left as quick as he came. It could be nothing."

"It could be everything," Serdot said. "Who else has a key to Reimvick's quarters?"

"These are dignitaries' apartments," Tronchet said. "Only I have additional keys."

"Then it must have been Reimvick, unless someone stole yours."

"Don't be ridiculous." Tronchet fished a ring of keys from his belt. "These are the skeleton keys for the whole palace. None are missing."

"Let's have a look in his rooms, shall we?"

"Absolutely not. He is a lord minister and worthy of respect. I will simply ask him about the keg."

"Don't do that," Serdot said. "It may be dangerous for you."

"Is that a threat?"

Serdot pulled Garion's key from his pocket. "If you won't open his door, then I will."

"What is that? You can't bluff me. These are the only skeleton keys . . ."

Serdot turned for the door. This time it was Tronchet who grabbed his arm.

"What is going on? If you don't tell me about Reimvick I'll go to him myself."

"You'll be endangering Lord Valient's investigation, and perhaps more lives, if you do. Or we can work together. But you must be strictly silent about it." Tronchet nodded, so Serdot returned to the balcony. "Good. This key *will* open Reimvick's door. We found it on Garion's body."

"The assassin? How did he—? Why is Reimvick . . . ?"

"I've been in his rooms once already. Nothing definitive, but that's why I've been watching him. We simply don't know enough. Now you know and must keep silent."

Tronchet nodded. "I will."

"Shall we enter his quarters?" Serdot asked.

They returned to the door and waited until the corridor was empty. Tronchet watched the corridor entrances, while Serdot turned the lock. Then they entered.

"I can't believe Garion had a key," Tronchet said. "I can't believe it. What does that mean?"

"Quiet, please, Sir Tronchet. Help me look for the keg."

They glanced around the main room. A presence candle on the table was unlit, but the layered wax around the base suggested that Reimvick had been paranoid enough to light several.

"Looks like he's grown more comfortable, but why?" Serdot mumbled.

"What?"

"Never mind. Keep looking."

Tronchet approached the wardroom door. "Locked." He pulled out his skeleton key before Serdot could come over. The magistrate walked in with Serdot close behind him. Everything seemed ordinary. Then Tronchet unlocked the privy door and gasped. Serdot peered around him, catching a glimpse of the open keg. It was packed with glass vials, liquid-filled flasks, and powder pouches.

"What in God's name . . . ?"

"It's a secret alchemical laboratory," Serdot said. "Just as before."

"Alchemy? The diabolical arts here, in the palace? Disgusting! He will be arrested at once."

Serdot stood in the doorway. "It's not time for that yet."

"What do you mean? Get out of my way!"

Serdot held up his hand. "You'll not arrest Reimvick yet. We must learn more about what he's up to and discover who else is involved. Then let Lord Valient decide."

"I've been a lawkeeper longer than Valient has been alive," Tronchet said. "You think I'm going to wait for his decision before locking up this dabbler in the dark arts? Garion must have been in league with Reimvick, don't you see? I must question him myself."

Serdot rolled his eyes. "You promised to cooperate, Sir Tronchet."

"Don't give me that nonsense. I'll have—"

"I know snaring Reimvick would be good for you. Perhaps the king would see you, perhaps Brugarn would like you more—though that's unlikely. And that's if you're able to prove Reimvick did more than practice alchemy. It may be distasteful to you, but it's unlikely to justify arrest. They'll make a mockery of you."

"Don't talk to me like some schoolboy. I'll have—"

"Sir Tronchet, Sir Tronchet, if you'll not work with me and Arthan on this, I will lock you in this lab and let Reimvick find you. If he is part of the assassins then he'll kill you in here and stuff you down the privy."

"You have Garion's key, but I've got—"

"These?" Serdot held up the magistrate's key ring.

"Dirty widsemer trickster!"

"Now, are we on the same side yet?" Serdot asked. "You forced me to tell you about Reimvick, now I'm forcing you to be quiet about it. Do we have an understanding?"

Tronchet glanced at the alchemy bottles and ingredients strewn all over the little room. "Fine."

"I have your word on it, as an honest lawkeeper in honorable service to king and Crown?"

"Yes, yes. But you have a week to find out what you need to know. He'll be arrested thereafter, since he's a threat to everyone in the palace."

"Fair enough," Serdot said. "But from the looks of things, we may not have that much time anyway. Destroying a laboratory to hide evidence made sense. Rebuilding a lab at great risk is ominous indeed."

92

THEUDAMER

Torgsbad Castle, Alpenon Ministry
Midsummer, 3034

"My apologies, Your Majesty," Graf said. "We were overwhelmed and Asteroth's army burned the forests and farms, so we could not forage. We had no choice but to fall back here for supplies. I ordered immediate repairs to the castle."

"Graf, you have the distinction of invading Donovan and causing wonderful problems for Asteroth," Theudamer said. "You've done more with a single brigade than many do with three."

Theudamer looked down from the castle wall, watching his newly arrived army file across the stone bridge where Graf had been tricked by Asteroth. Soldiers, knights, wagons of corn and beer, equipment, everything his army needed.

"We'll be more than twelve thousand strong on this front," Theudamer continued. "And well supplied. General Valk has half our number marching into Gadolin as we speak. He should be able to move through the plains quickly. Tell me about Asteroth and his men. What have you seen?"

Graf cleared his throat. "We got within view of his capital, Cantrileme, before they turned us back. We clearly took them by surprise. Asteroth tried to use his soldiers conscripted from the rebel-held areas in the west, but, of course, half of them deserted or joined our ranks. Asteroth retreated to regroup with his Donovards and forced us back the next day with a vicious counterattack. Obviously they didn't pursue us for long. Overall it seems Asteroth has abandoned the borderlands."

"Or wants us to think he has," Meliamour said.

"What about the rebels?" Theudamer asked. He turned to face the high Brindthum Mountains in the west. Their snow-covered peaks glistened in the midday sun.

"The rebels now control the Orringholm River Valley," Graf said, "all the way to Orringholm on the coast. The Almerians still own the port city, but only because they continue to sell arms and supplies to the rebels."

"Make sure the rebels get rid of the Almerians," Theudamer said. "We will supply them, no one else."

"The Almerians make a lot of gold from their trade at Orringholm," Meliamour said. "They'll not give it up freely. The rebels won't like losing Almerian support either."

"Who leads the rebels now that Geras is dead?" Theudamer asked.

"Ardis Vilarwef, Gothal's sister," Graf said.

"Gothal must have anointed her while we marched here," Meliamour said.

"Ardis is currently in the Brindthum Mountains at the rebel stronghold of Thumtorf," Graf said. "She's gathering her new command."

"Now that we're in Durgensdil, I want the Almerians out," Theudamer said, turning to Meliamour. "Send your new Wosmoks to do it. Graf, go and fetch the new commander Meliamour sent to you earlier."

"Your Majesty," Meliamour said when Graf had gone, "the new Wosmoks are better used to penetrate Asteroth's fortifications. To swiftly take all of Durgensdil, we'll need them to weaken his defenses and help pave the way through Toulon to Eglamour. The Almerians are of little threat and can be dealt with later."

Theudamer turned to her, unable to hide his smirk. "Don't be afraid of losing your influence within Graf's army just because I'm temporarily reassigning your Wosmoks. Whether in Heingartmer or on a campaign, I will always have need of your services."

"Thank you, Your Majesty."

"We will strike the Donovards so hard and so quickly that they will be sure to go crawling to anyone who might help them—even the Almerians. If we let the Almerians keep Orringholm for now, it provides them an avenue from which to disturb our supply lines. It also gives the rebels another option instead of being dependent solely on us."

"Here he is," Graf said. "Sir Hedger, the emperor has a task for you."

"Get rid of the Almerians in Orringholm," Theudamer said. "Do it quickly, using any means Meliamour gives you. Do not tell the rebels unless you must. How many under your command?"

"Three, Your Majesty," Hedger said.

"I want all of you to return to the army within a week, in time for us to lay siege to Asteroth's capital," Theudamer said.

"Your Majesty," Graf said, "Orringholm is a two-and-a-half-day ride from here. And Asteroth's men are likely to slow our approach to Cantrileme."

"Then leave now and ride it in two days, Hedger," Theudamer said. The emperor turned to Graf. "We'll not be slowed down. Look at the army I have brought. We're going to crush them."

"Yes, Your Majesty."

"I tolerated your excuses for retreating earlier, but no excuses this time," Theudamer continued. "Cantrileme will be under siege within seven days or you will be sent back to Havelbern and stripped of your general's cape and wardenship."

Theudamer glanced at the steady march of his soldiers across the bridge before turning his eyes north, toward Eglamour. "I want the Avaleaus to panic. I want Erech and Brugarn and the others to lose all faith in the ability of Asteroth and Erath to defend them. I want their castles to burn and their people to submit. And I want to be sitting on the throne of Donovan before winter."

93

FETZER

Borel District of Eglamour, Toulon Ministry
Midsummer, 3034

etzer stared at the candle. Every flame and fire reminded him of his destiny to lead the great change. The very name of Candlestone proved it. He wished Arasemis would act. He wished to be let lose against the Avaleaus all at once. He hated the halting nature of the master's tactics.

We've been waiting too long. The killing of Henrey was flawless. We were initially confused by the rumors that Duke Brugarn had been killed. If we had known Brugarn had been there moments before, we would have killed him too. He was lucky this time.

Henrey's death also proved to Arasemis that I can complete a task with ease, with some help from Juhl and despite the ridiculous forge armor. Arasemis came with us but mercly watched from the rooftops, rightly fearing that his worsening cough would give away our surprise attack. He didn't light up his lamp armor. Didn't even use it! Not that we needed his help.

But that hasn't stopped him from critiquing us. I think he has grown restless, too, waiting as we are for Marlan and Rodel to arrive. We expected their roundabout path to take longer, but not this long. Arasemis is also anxious because a letter he was expecting from a supporter in the palace has not come. He says he still trusts the supporter—whoever it is—so we will give our companions and the letter more time.

Meanwhile we sit around this dingy house, forced to breathe the stench of the slum and listen to Arasemis's hacking. Seeing this place, living in it, makes me wonder why Arasemis is so eager to put the power he intends for us to take from the kings into the hands of chieftains chosen by the masses. The filth that walk the gutters of Borel can hardly be any different than the ancient heathen hordes Arasemis idolizes.

I'm not interested in Candlestone's dusty prophesies and lofty ends. Instead, I see the Order as a tool for me to craft my own realm, with speed and strength unmatched. I will help Arasemis kill kings, but for myself. Not for him and his dusty books.

In the meantime, we continue to wait . . .

94

ARTHAN

Clonmel Estate in Eglamour, Toulon Ministry
Midsummer, 3034

"I respectfully disagree, my lord," Serdot said. "I think we should wait a bit longer. We don't know who killed Lord Henrey. We got lucky with Garion, so all we have is Reimvick. We must let him lead us to the others."

"I understand, Serdot," Arthan said. "But time has run out. These assassins come out of nowhere, and I'm speaking from experience. It's anyone's guess who will be next. We must act in the hopes that Reimvick can tell us something. If someone else is killed, Brugarn will also have cause to depose me as marshal. It's more urgent now that Tronchet knows."

"I had no choice but to tell him," Serdot said. "You know I prefer to work differently."

"I know, but Tronchet has every incentive to do all of this himself."

"He will cooperate, I'm sure of that."

"What makes you so confident?"

"I threatened to lock him in Reimvick's privy laboratory, and I stole his palace keys. I gave them back, of course . . ."

Arthan sighed. "Well, these are not your usual methods, but no matter. As long as the chief magistrate cooperates." Arthan picked up his quill and wrote out a quick note. "Give this to Tronchet. It's a request for Reimvick's immediate arrest. I want it done as quietly as possible."

"As a lawkeeper, you have the power to arrest him yourself. Why do you need Tronchet?"

"I'm giving Tronchet the gift of arrest in return for his cooperation. He is to bring Reimvick here to Clonmel so that we may question him, given our knowledge of the other assassinations. When the time is right, we'll share the glory with Tronchet, so far as the Avaleaus recognize it."

"Very well, my lord." Serdot took the letter and smiled. "I think that's how your father would have done it, too."

"Quickly, now," Arthan said.

When Serdot had departed, Arthan leaned back in his chair. He had not taken enough time to prepare himself for this. He had no doubt Reimvick would come peacefully, though he might try to deny it all for a while and play the part of Maillard's old friend. Arthan was unsure how they would get Reimvick to confess, given the lack of hard evidence.

He steeled his mind for what he knew must be done. The methodical assassination of the royal family and high nobles would continue if he did not take action. He stood from his table and made certain all the windows of the room were latched and the curtains drawn tight, remembering that Garion had chosen to throw himself from the window rather than face more questioning. If Reimvick's secrets were equally precious, Arthan must not give him that option.

❧

It was not long before Serdot and Tronchet arrived with Reimvick, escorted by Livonier and a few guards. He was not shackled and appeared confused.

"Lord Valient, there has been a grave mistake," Reimvick said with an awkward smile. "The chief magistrate claims you've ordered my arrest."

"Yes, please sit down. Sir Tronchet, a word, please."

The chief magistrate eagerly joined Arthan in a quiet aside while Serdot showed Reimvick to a chair in front of the table. Arthan spoke softly.

"Tronchet, I must thank you for your timely cooperation. I know my appointment as Marshal of Inquiry may have stepped a bit into your domain as the king's head lawkeeper, but I assure you no insult was intended. Now, as a valuable addition to our investigation, I invite you to stay for Reimvick's questioning. But you must understand that any information gleaned from him must be kept confidential until this conspiracy is unraveled."

Tronchet nodded. "I respected your father, Lord Valient, and I see you beginning to follow in his footsteps. I do not wish to be an obstacle for you, so long as the king's law is upheld. And one other thing: tell Serdot to keep his fingers out of my pockets."

"Consider it done," Arthan said with a smile. "I will lead the questioning, given my experience with this conspiracy. You may participate as needed. Fair enough?"

Tronchet agreed, and they returned to the prisoner.

"I must say, I've never been arrested by the king's men or another lord minister," Reimvick said.

"The chief magistrate arrested you, my lord, but I will question you as marshal, not your fellow lord minister," Arthan said.

"What in heavens for?"

"Tell me about your relationship with Garion," Arthan said, taking a seat behind the table.

"The assassin? Why, I never spoke to the man. He was one of the Crownblades. Betrayed us all."

"My lord, you'll recall my exposing of Garion at court," Arthan said. "Garion's mask and the letter we found among his belongings?"

"Yes, of course. Thank God you discovered him."

Arthan gestured to Serdot, who unfolded the letter and placed it on the table in front of Reimvick. "As you can see, the letter ordered Garion to kill Duke Brugarn. The orders were signed simply 'E.'"

Reimvick stared blankly at the note, then looked up expectantly. "Yes, I see it."

Arthan leveled his eyes at him. "Your given name is Edmond."

"Well, how many given names, surnames, and other names begin with that letter?" Reimvick asked. "It could also be a title or God knows what."

"My original thoughts as well," Arthan said. "But then we found this in Garion's pocket."

Serdot placed the key on the table. Reimvick glanced at it and shrugged. "A key to what?"

"You tell me."

"A key . . . Is it marked with an 'E' as well, perhaps in the blood of my fictitious victims?"

"It opens the door to your quarters," Tronchet said.

Reimvick snorted. "Nonsense. I have my key right here." Reimvick pulled the key from his pocket, and Serdot took it from him to compare.

"A perfect match," Serdot said.

"So Garion made a copy of my key," Reimvick said. "I cannot say why he would do that, except to deflect attention from—"

Arthan turned to the magistrate. "Are spare keys to the dignitaries' apartments regularly made available to the Crownblades or anyone else?"

"No. I'm always informed of the smithy's key making, for the protection of the highborn and the ambassadors."

Arthan returned to Reimvick. "How did you manage a separate key for Garion?"

"Wait a moment," Reimvick said. "You can't believe I let that filth into my chambers. Why would any of us do such a thing?"

"Perhaps for the use of your alchemical laboratory," Arthan said. For the first time he noticed genuine discomfort in Reimvick's blanched face.

"This is ridiculous!"

"Serdot has already seen it, my lord, so it will do you no good to deny it," Arthan said, glancing at the widsemer.

"Twice," Serdot said. "I saw the remnants of the one you destroyed after Garion's capture and suicide. And also the one you've set up since then. A brandy keg, I believe?"

"Ridiculous! I can't—"

"I saw the keg as you wheelbarrowed it to your chambers," Tronchet said. "The little barrel stuffed with vials, flasks, and pouches for your privy laboratory!"

Reimvick shifted uneasily in his chair.

"Not to mention the alchemical candles you've been burning," Serdot said. "Presence candles. Have you suspected you were being watched?"

"Confess," Arthan said, leaning forward on the table. "The letter, the key, the laboratory. The timing of it all."

"Circumstantial nonsense," Reimvick said, his voice hardening. "I see you all enjoy prying into the lives of lords behind closed doors. I'm especially disappointed in you, Lord Valient. The reputation your father built, the legacy he left for you. Look at you, reduced to questioning like a petty jailor while the kingdom struggles on every front. Very well, hear what you've won.

"I confess to my laboratory. Alchemy being shunned as it is, I naturally kept it a secret. But the medications I prepare help ease my gout and bladder stones. I'll not apologize for it, even if you were to expose my alchemy to the court as part of this absurd investigation."

"Medicine?" Arthan asked as doubt trickled into his mind. Had he made a mistake? "Then why did you destroy the laboratory?"

"Like everyone else, I saw the alchemy Garion used. His cloaking cloud and all. I feared my medicinal alchemy would be found out and blamed for what you're accusing me of now. I panicked. But I succumbed to the need for more medication, hence the new laboratory."

"In the middle of the night?" Tronchet asked.

Reimvick scowled at him. "Stop your chittering, you keyhole-peeper. Alchemy would bring great disrespect to my house. Of course I wheeled it in under darkness."

Arthan leaned back in his chair, the doubt growing in his mind. He looked at Serdot, who slowly shook his head. Serdot's eyes seemed to say *don't believe him*, but Arthan couldn't shake the doubt.

"And the presence candles?" Serdot asked.

Reimvick shrugged. "An assassin makes it into court and nearly kills the king's brother. Forgive me for using my alchemical knowledge for my own protection."

"You haven't explained why Garion had a key to your chambers," Serdot said.

"Because I can offer no explanation," Reimvick said. "If Tronchet says he knows of every key to highborn chambers then he's either lying or fooling himself. You want an explanation? Maybe, as skilled as Garion appears to have been, maybe he sniffed out my laboratory and acquired a key to access it. If one of these assassins can infiltrate the Crownblades, it's not a stretch to say he found a way into my privy. Maybe he bribed a blacksmith." Reimvick turned to glance at Tronchet. "Or the chief magistrate."

Arthan stared at Reimvick, trying to read the stare that reflected back at him. He now feared he had made a terrible mistake. He glanced at Serdot again, and Serdot again shook his head. Tronchet was equally disarmed. Reimvick filled the silence.

"You know it, don't you?" he asked calmly. "You arrested the wrong man. As your fellow lord minister and the longtime friend of your father, I am compelled to forgive all. I'm only glad Maillard is not here to witness this. And Raymond as well. My older brother would have been appalled that the king's officer in charge of rooting out his murderers wasted so much time on the wrong man."

A light gleamed in Arthan's mind. "Raymond . . ." he said. Arthan cleared his throat and leaned forward again. "Raymond was the first victim."

"He had that distinction, yes."

"How hard did you look for his killers?"

Reimvick fumbled his words for a moment. "Well, isn't that your sworn duty?"

"I was only appointed marshal after Garion's discovery. Well after the deaths of Raymond, my father, and Gottfried."

"The conspiracy began in Wallevet," Serdot said. "And you replaced Raymond as lord minister."

"You can't suggest I had Raymond killed to take his seat." Reimvick looked at Arthan. "If you'd been killed, Rowan would have replaced you as lord minister. It's tradition, subject to confirmation by the king."

"Garion was also from Wallevet, wasn't he?" Arthan asked.

"Bredahade Academy," Serdot said. "Went missing for a year before joining the Crownblades. Doesn't that sound peculiar?"

"I suppose . . ." Reimvick said. Arthan noticed sweat break on his brow. "But many people are from—"

"Arasemis is on his way, did you know?" Arthan asked.

"Arasemis . . . ?"

"Your brother."

"His name is Osmond. He calls himself Arasemis because it's a nickname our grandfather gave him."

"I spoke with him on the road. He was going to bring you a gift of wine, he said, then sell the rest."

"I thought he was a hermit," Serdot said. "Has wine truly brought him out of Thorendor to make the journey to the capital?"

"Why are you still in Eglamour?" Arthan asked.

"I—now just a moment. I came to pay tribute to the king, same as you, and attend the Lord Ministers Council."

"Most of the ministers departed long ago," Tronchet said.

"You, me, Henrey, and Voufon remain," Reimvick said. "Well, Henrey no longer . . ."

"Voufon is helping to look after her sister, the queen," Serdot said.

"And Henrey was staying in hopes of seeing the king before he was killed," Arthan said. "My reason for being in the capital is clear. So I'll ask again, why are you still in Eglamour? What are you waiting for?"

"I have able aldermen and generals to look after Wallevet, same as you."

"I didn't ask about them. I asked about you."

"I, well . . . I want to know what is happening at court. And now we have the war and—"

"All the lord ministers have their representatives at court," Arthan said. "You're able to explain everything away except for your presence in the capital—and your brother's."

"I am a lord minister, free to travel and stay in the palace for as long as the king will have me in his service." Reimvick stood abruptly. "I expect to be left in peace for the remainder of my stay, and I expect to—"

"Sit down," Arthan said, standing up. "Who will be targeted next, Edmond? Will Arasemis draw the knife?"

Reimvick ignored him and stepped toward the door. Tronchet reached out, but Reimvick slapped the magistrate's hands away. "Ridiculous!" Reimvick shouted, again lunging for the door.

Serdot called the guards, and together they restrained the shouting, cursing lord minister.

Reimvick struggled. "Release me! I've had enough of this foolishness . . . I will take my case to the king, or Brugarn if necessary!"

"You're not going anywhere," Arthan said. "Tronchet, have the guards take him to the cells downstairs."

"Pompous prick!" Reimvick shouted. "I never forgive—you'll be done in Eglamour, done, I say! You cannot accuse me of anything!"

Arthan turned away and returned to his seat. Serdot sat down in Reimvick's chair when everyone had left. "I almost let him go," Arthan said.

"These things are rarely clear," Serdot said. "But his reaction says enough. He had prepared for this, with the exception of the question of why he is still here in Eglamour. And he probably didn't count on you seeing Arasemis on the road."

"Reimvick is somehow orchestrating all of this, isn't he?"

"Appears so," Serdot said. "But in the Garion letter, 'E' seemed to have a master."

"His younger brother? Arasemis, or Osmond—whatever his name is."

"Possibly. Suspicious, but we don't know enough about the brother."

"Find Arasemis," Arthan said. "As for Reimvick, you searched his chambers when you arrested him?"

Serdot nodded. "The laboratory was still there. But nothing else of note."

"Go back and search it again. Every cupboard, nook, and crevice. Cut every pillow and curtain, and search the privy. Unless he decides to confess, we'll need more than an assassin's key and a tantrum."

95

MILISEND

Clonmel Estate in Eglamour, Toulon Ministry
Midsummer, 3034

"Take your hands off me at once!"

Livonier released her arm. "Princess, I'm very sorry. Lord Valient is too busy with—"

"I don't care what he's doing. You will take me to him."

"But I—"

"I've had enough of trying to corner Serdot," Milisend continued. "I will speak to Lord Valient directly, with or without your help."

"You'll listen to her if you know what's good for you," Rosellen said.

Livonier pursed his lips before answering. "Follow me, please."

Milisend had never been to Arthan's city estate. Despite the circumstances, she allowed herself to appreciate Clonmel's beauty. The facade was the same weathered white marble that could be seen anywhere in the old core of Eglamour, but the interior was anything but typical.

As Livonier led them through, Milisend noticed that each room was paneled with dark wood and deep gray slabs of stone. The azure-and-violet flag with the lion of the House of Valient adorned every room, and statues of fine stone, electrum, and bronze portraying the heroes of ancient Donovan watched over each corridor. It was a fortified house fit for the Valients, and she was sure it merely hinted at their wealth. She wondered what had kept Brugarn from seizing all of it to alleviate the empty treasury.

"Please, wait here one moment," Livonier said. The knight knocked on the door to the chamber that Milisend guessed was Arthan's office. "My lord?" Livonier said as he poked his head inside.

Milisend shoved Livonier aside and slipped through the door, pulling Rosellen behind her. At the far end of the room Arthan was seated at a writing table. Serdot and another man she recognized as Sir Debanor, the knight captain of the marshal's guards, were seated in front of him.

All of them stood when she entered. In the silence Milisend felt slightly embarrassed, even ashamed for her impatience. But she reminded herself of Regaume's plight and regained her confidence.

"Pardon my interruption," she began, pulling Rosellen to her side. "But I have an urgent matter to discuss with you, Lord Valient. I assure you I will not consume too much of your precious time."

"Princess Milisend, please come in," Arthan said. "No apology necessary, and please call me Arthan." He glanced at Serdot and Debanor, who promptly arranged chairs for her and Rosellen.

"It's a private matter," Milisend said.

Arthan nodded, and his men departed the room. Milisend could not resist cutting her eyes at Serdot, but the widsemer paid her no attention. Milisend and Rosellen took their chairs. The princess moved gracefully, keeping her back straight and her eyes fixed on Arthan. He was a bit uncomfortable but kept a small, warm smile on his face.

"It has been some time since Clonmel hosted a royal," Arthan said. "Would you care for refreshment?"

"No," she said, not expecting this politeness. It was disarming and irritating.

"To what do I owe this honor?" he asked.

"I have repeatedly requested your assistance with a personal, delicate matter. Through Serdot. Several times."

"Yes . . . a friend of yours was arrested, correct?"

She glared at him.

"I must apologize," he continued. "The responsibilities your father bestowed upon me have not let me rest since I returned from Rachard. Forgive me for asking you to repeat the details of the situation."

"Regaume is his name," Milisend said. "He is more than a friend to me. He will be taken away by the magistrate of Ralmogard unless you order his release."

Arthan nodded. "I remember. He is a thief, is he not? I've heard about his crimes and those of his band of bandits."

"He is precious to me. And he's never murdered anyone."

"Princess, I regret that I cannot simply order his release."

"You are a lawkeeper."

"But I'm not the Lord Minister of Toulon, or the Chief Magistrate of Eglamour. My lawkeeping is focused on these assassins, not common criminals." Milisend looked down at her hands as he spoke. "I'm sorry, Princess. I can see he means a great deal to you. Alas, I can only speak with Tronchet."

"He has delayed Regaume's transfer but claims he cannot do more."

"Then he's certainly done more than is in my power to do."

"What does it matter, if the result is the same?" Milisend felt her eyes well up. She shook her head, determined not to let despair take her yet. "Could you free him secretly? Tronchet might turn a blind eye if it were you. The Ralmogard magistrate would never know what happened."

"I'm afraid such an effort would undermine the authority your father gave me, Princess."

"What authority does my father have to give? I've not seen him, have you? My uncle Brugarn is destined to do as he wants. Will you not save one life before his reign takes many?"

"I mustn't give Brugarn a chance to undermine me. I must focus on the assassins so our kingdom can better defend and rebuild itself."

Milisend looked away. The window framed her father's tower.

"I'm sorry for everything that has happened," Arthan continued. "You and your sisters are the strength of the

Avaleaus now. My advice, hard as it is, would be to forget about Regaume and focus on the preservation of your house."

"Isn't that what you're here for? You didn't save Henrey, but I suppose you are no Maillard. You are only concerned with yourself."

Milisend stood and turned for the door, Rosellen in tow. Arthan stood behind her.

"Princess, truly, I am sorry for your troubles."

"I don't need your pity," she said over her shoulder. "I needed your help."

Rosellen opened the door, and Livonier stepped out of the way. Milisend resolved never to return to Clonmel again. She held back her tears until she was safely in her carriage with Rosellen.

96

WREDEGAR

Eglamour, Toulon Ministry
Midsummer, 3034

"No, Wredegar. You're not going anywhere."

"You are not my commander, Ambassador."

"Look out these windows," Vesamune said, snapping open the curtains. "That Donovard rabble would tear me apart if not for the king's guards. I'll not have you wandering around the capital again."

"I blend in far better than you."

"You're cocky because the Borel rioters didn't sniff you out, but you were lucky. What if someone had followed you back here? This house would be a bonfire like the Borel alderman's keep. If you continue this way, you'll blend in as a dead rioter."

"I told you, I met some of the leaders of this upheaval," Wredegar said. "Including one who helped lead the Mordmerg revolt. I can learn a lot from them, and learn how to harness them for the empire. If I don't go back to them soon, they'll think Ricot has abandoned them."

"The time for those games is over. I'm an ambassador, not a warrior, held hostage in a kingdom we're at war with. I shouldn't be here. As the emperor's representative, you must protect me. Is that understood?"

Wredegar glared at her, knowing he did not have to comply. Ultimately he answered to her sister, Meliamour, who also took orders directly from the emperor.

"Vesamune, if I can liaise with these riot leaders, we could turn them into proper rebels—as we did in Durgensdil. We can use them to cause problems for the Donovards, maybe enough to topple the Avaleaus and save the lives of our own soldiers."

"That is for Emperor Theudamer to decide once we're back in Heingartmer."

Wredegar noticed her hands shaking. He knew she was not trained for this environment. He did feel responsible for not being there when she was last attacked on the street by a mob, before she was put under house arrest for her own protection. And she was probably right that the rioters would sniff him out at some point, or that he would have been killed.

"I suppose you're right," Wredegar said, "but if I had my Wosmoks, things would be different. You'd be safely out of here and we'd have the rioters in our pocket."

"We must not do anything else to provoke the Donovards," Vesamune said. "In time, they'll ransom me back to Rugenhav."

Wredegar's first thought was what he had heard about how the Donovards ransomed Geras Vilarwef, but he did not mention it to her. He truly hoped Vesamune would be ransomed so he could make his escape and return to his honorable knighthood.

"Very well. I'll not pursue the riot leaders at this time," he said. "I'll stay until they ransom you, but I can't stay in this house day and night. It's too confining for my peace of mind."

"An unnecessary risk. Still, I'm glad you finally see things my way," she said with a smug grin.

97

ARTHAN

Clonmel Estate in Eglamour, Toulon Ministry
Midsummer, 3034

"Where did you find all of that?" Arthan asked through a mouthful of eggs and bread.

Serdot set the bag of papers on Arthan's table. "When I was searching his chambers again, I thought it odd that Reimvick did not have much correspondence lying about, as any gossip-hungry nobleman would. I found a few drips of ink on the stone under his table and found a floor tile with new mortar around it. I pried it up and found this trove underneath."

"Excellent," Arthan said, shoving his plate aside. "Was there anything else?"

Serdot shook his head as he dumped the letters from the sack. "Just more alchemical ingredients."

"Let's start reading, then," Arthan said as he picked through the pile. "Did Tronchet see you?"

"No. I went in last night and was out again before the magistrate made his rounds."

"Let's keep him out of this until we have something to show. So far I see letters to his mistress, a page from a ledger, not much of use."

"All of it is useful," Serdot said. "Together it paints a portrait of his life. What's this, a letter to 'E' signed by 'O.'"

Serdot skimmed it wide-eyed before Arthan plucked it from his hands.

> E,
>
> My students completed the Lord Gottfried task. Unfortunately, not all of them returned to Thorendor. You may remember Morroy, the Calbrian. He died of his wounds. But we gained a new student whom I judge to be well suited for our work—if he will submit to my authority.
>
> O

"He mentioned Thorendor," Serdot said.

"So 'O' must be Osmond," Arthan said, "meaning Arasemis . . . Good of Reimvick to have clarified that yesterday. What further proof do we need that he's involved in the assassinations?"

"This letter establishes Arasemis's involvement, but not Edmond Reimvick's."

"But this is his correspondence," Arthan said.

"When you accuse him at court there must be no question."

"At least the Rugens don't seem to be involved. You were right, Serdot."

"There could still be another layer to this onion, my lord. They could be working on behalf of the Rugens. We only know what is written, not what's not. We must be open to other possibilities."

"Look, here is another one," Arthan said, holding up another letter.

> E,
>
> We leave Thorendor in three days for your location. Thank you for arranging everything in Borel, and for your preliminary details about the palace. I look forward to more information on the best route from Borel to the palace.
>
> As for us, we've made the discovery of a lifetime: arcanae relics that will aid our tasks like nothing else before. Modern Candlestone will never be the same. I will show you once we are in Borel.
>
> O

"My God," Arthan muttered. "He is supporting them . . ."

"That's what we need."

"What are the arcanae relics, Serdot?"

"When I spoke to Henrey's guards, they said the assassins wore queer-looking armor. One of them had boots with wheels and blades affixed to gauntlets."

"We must find where they are hiding in Borel before they kill again."

"Borel is a dangerous place. Brugarn's men are still fighting pockets of rioters. Here is another one . . ."

> E,
>
> Not only has our latest task against Valient failed, but he has an alchemical sword. When he arrives in the capital get a good look at it. Juhl didn't expect it, of course, but she is all right. This is very worrying. Reply soon.
>
> O

"So Arasemis is afraid of Adrithayn," Arthan said. "Father was right about the sword."

"Perhaps Arasemis is more surprised than anything. None of his other targets defended themselves with alchemy."

"I know you haven't had time to find that historian, Danleri, but if Arasemis fears my father's sword, I need to understand it."

"Don't worry, my lord. I'll find Danleri."

Arthan nodded. "So, why did Reimvick keep all of these letters? Why not toss them in his fireplace?"

"Not everyone is careful, even conspirators. Reimvick's hiding of his correspondence tells me he valued keeping it enough to risk its discovery. Hard to say why . . . Look, here is an unweathered and unsealed parchment. Reimvick never had the chance to send it."

> O,
>
> I will be unable to meet you in Borel. That bastard Valient and his pesky widsemer are determined, and they're getting closer. I must limit myself to

risks that are absolutely necessary, if we are to succeed. If the relics that you found are truly revolutionary, then my hope is that the following instructions will be unnecessary.

The king is still holed up in his tower, as I've written before. I don't expect him to change his location. Duke Brugarn has posted Crownblades at the tower's main stairwell. Brugarn himself moves about the palace and the city frequently, and he keeps more Crownblades with him.

The queen can be found in her bed with her sister, Lord Ministeress Voufon, nearby. The chambers of princesses Milisend and Brielle are in the northeast wing of the palace, near the prison tower. Brugarn's bedchamber is one floor above in the northwest wing. Do not confuse the northern prison tower with the king's south tower. They appear similar but the king's tower will have fewer lit windows at night.

Remember what I told you about the gates and the other lord ministers. I agree with your plans to shelter in Wallevet for a while when this phase of our work is over. I look forward to hearing about the next phase of your plans.

I hope my assistance proves my loyalty for the cause you ably lead, even if I never formally joined it in the way you had wished. At least I was not like Raymond or Father. I think Grandfather Erwold would be proud of us.

E

"We have him now, Serdot. Damned by his own hand."

Serdot sighed. "I owe you an apology, my lord. When we first came to Eglamour I told you that Reimvick was a persistent gossip and occasional annoyance, but nothing more. I couldn't have been more wrong."

"He deceived all of us, Serdot."

"But it is my business to see through such things. I will remember this lesson . . . We must move quickly. Arasemis did not receive this letter, but he'll soon hear about

Reimvick's capture. He'll try to complete his work at an accelerated pace."

"Let's delay announcing Reimvick's treachery at court. I'll go at once to Hamelin and Tronchet so the royals can be warned. They will have to secure the palace and search for any assassins who may already be inside."

"I will go downstairs to question Reimvick about Arasemis's location in Borel," Serdot said, "and what other instructions he already sent to Arasemis."

"Find out about his students, too. Names, descriptions, anything. And whatever Candlestone is."

"My lord, Reimvick is unlikely to give up these details freely. As these letters show, he is clearly committed to their plot."

"You're a widsemer. Surely you have methods to elicit these details from him."

"Elicitation takes time, my lord. And we have no time. But there are quicker, harsher methods . . ."

Arthan blinked and turned away, thinking of the lives at stake, his father, and the boldness he had adopted. "Do what you must, Serdot. We are besieged by the Rugens without and by Candlestone within. The future of our kingdom depends on us."

98

RODEL

Rodel peeked around the corner of the alley, then motioned behind him. Marlan promptly crossed the street into the next alley. Rodel liked traveling with Marlan. They understood each other and Marlan had quickly learned Rodel's Wosmok hand signals for moving quickly through a city or at night.

Infiltrating Eglamour's outer wall was as easy as at Aughreim, even while wearing their mechans. They abandoned their stolen Aughreim horses in a nearby forest, then ran up the walls while careful to avoid the guards. They knew Borel was in the outer city, and it did not take long for them to learn where.

Borel was a nasty place, the worst slum Rodel had ever seen. Despite the riots, it was overcrowded with newcomers looking for a home, out-of-work artisans, and former soldiers turned mercenaries. Beggars and bandits were everywhere. And those were just the areas recaptured by the king's men. Rodel and Marlan took care to avoid the areas of fighting.

When night fell they approached the southern edge of Borel.

"What are we looking for?" Rodel asked when he joined Marlan in the next alley.

"Arasemis said to meet them at a well near the gate that leads to the Genthus District, toward the southwest."

Rodel leaned against the grimy wall of the alley and looked up at the stars, shaded as they were by the haze of hearth fires, summer dust, and sewer stench. "The noise and smell of this place . . . No wonder they riot. What soldier is willing to patrol here?"

"That's why so many underground alchemists live in Borel, shunned as they are from the other districts," Marlan said. "Machinists are even said to be here, though Arasemis doubts their skill."

They pushed on, sprinting over rooftops when the shanty-stuffed alleys got crowded. Soon they found the gate to the Genthus District and the nearby well. They waited around the corner until the single gate guard paced by.

"What are we looking for?" Rodel whispered.

"They were supposed to be waiting for us, but of course we were delayed. Arasemis would have left some clue for us if they had to leave, however."

"Maybe a hidden note with directions to the safe house?"

Marlan shook his head. "Too risky. But let's go have a look before the sentry returns."

They trotted to the well and looked around all the stones for a bit of parchment. They lifted the bucket, looked inside and at the bottom, and inspected the winch. Nothing. As they prepared to give up, a voice came from a bench hidden in the moon shadows.

"Have you lost something?"

Marlan swiftly rushed toward the voice, drawing his belt knife.

"No need—" the man tried to say, but Marlan put his hand over his mouth and the knife to his throat.

Rodel gently lifted Marlan's knife, fearing he would kill the man. "Look at him," Rodel said.

Marlan pulled the man from his bench and into the moonlight. A thin, ragged scarf was tied around the man's eyes. But he was young like them.

"Who are you?" Marlan asked, removing his hand but pointing the knife at him.

"The watcher of the well," the man said. "And someone who can maybe help you . . ."

"Why do I need a blind man's help?" Marlan asked, lowering the knife.

"My sight is black but my hearing is like that of a black adder. You came to the well, searching, but not for water. And only when the guard's footsteps faded. None who come to this well move as you've moved, ever."

"What can you offer us?" Rodel asked.

"Are you seeking a path?" the man asked. "I know of secret paths. Paths your eyes cannot see."

Rodel glanced at Marlan. He was still unconvinced.

"Has someone hired you to help us?" Marlan asked.

The man nodded. "He who has the strength of two men in his one arm."

Rodel glanced at Marlan again. He nodded.

"Tell us the path," Rodel said.

"It cannot be told, only walked. And only at night." The man smiled. "Not that it makes a difference for me. Follow, please."

Rodel and Marlan gave him space to move. The man felt for his bench and gathered a small sack that held his provisions. He walked down the alley next to the district wall, feeling his way with the tips of his fingers.

Around the corner the man opened an unlocked door in the wall. It was completely dark inside. Marlan pushed Rodel in front of him. Rodel reached into the darkness and grabbed the man's shoulder, and Marlan did the same with him. They shuffled forward, squeezing through narrow passages and ducking beneath beams. Up stairs and then down again. On the other side of the walls they could hear people talking, laughing, shouting, and snoring. There were the scents of smoked meat, beer, and vomit. Then sweet perfume.

After a few moments the path became quiet again and light gradually appeared. Rodel squinted, seeing candlelight beaming through the gaps around a closed door in front of the blind man.

"We are here," said the man. He plucked a key from his pocket. The lock turned, and they stepped into the light. It was an empty cellar, with a small table in the middle with a lone candle. "I will go no farther," the man said. "Farewell."

Rodel and Marlan watched him depart back into the darkness, pulling the door behind him. He locked the door, then shuffled away. They looked at each other before ascending the stairs at the end of the cellar. When they opened the door at the top of the stairs, a familiar voice called out.

"Well done, my apprentices," Arasemis said, smiling from a chair by the hearth. "A fine stew is still on the fire."

"My apologies for the delay, Master," Marlan said.

"It's of no consequence," Arasemis said. "You and Rodel have arrived safely."

"Courtesy of the well watcher," Rodel said.

"Juhl and Fetzer?" Marlan asked.

"Resting, as you soon should be." Arasemis held a handkerchief to his mouth and coughed harshly.

"Who was the blind man?" Rodel asked.

Arasemis cleared his throat. "Our supporter in the palace found him for us—" He stopped to lean forward and cough again.

"Are you all right, Master?" Marlan asked.

"Just a foul air from the road exacerbated by the stench of Borel. Now, that's all the talk for tonight. Eat and rest yourselves. The eve of a great chance has come."

99

THEUDAMER

Nairnbern Castle, Alpenon Ministry
Midsummer, 3034

"I think we should order Wredegar to escort Vesamune out of Eglamour, Your Majesty," Meliamour said, standing with Theudamer outside his tent.

Theudamer looked at Nairnbern Castle lit by the glow of the predawn sky. The distant thud of wood and iron echoed repetitively as the Donovards tried to fight off the battering ram at their door.

"I know they suspect Vesamune of orchestrating the assassinations," Theudamer said, "but I value the information she continues to send about Eglamour." He lifted Vesamune's letter to his eyes again.

> . . . and if it were not for the additional guards
> Brugarn has posted around my residence, I'm sure
> the common rabble would have sacked the house
> and dragged me out into the streets. Only
> Wredegar can get in and out without being seen,
> but it's only a matter of time before Brugarn's
> men are posted inside my home. I'm under no
> illusions that his "protective" guards are doing
> anything but waiting for his order to . . .

"I understand her peril," Theudamer continued, "but as an ambassador to my enemies, she knew the risks."

"She is your niece, Your Majesty. Like me, she will always obey you. But the Donovards will eventually be unsatisfied with her house arrest. The death of Lord Henrey will demonstrate that the assassins—whoever they are—acted despite her arrest. If the Donovards persist in thinking she is behind the killings, they'll kill her. As she said, it's only a matter of time."

"Her dispatches are valuable, Meliamour, and will only be more so as we march toward the capital. More than any of my advisers, you understand the value of unique information."

"Your army is still several months from the capital," Meliamour said. "Will you permit me to send Hedger and the other Wosmoks to Eglamour to extract her? Wredegar could stay and continue to send dispatches about the city."

"I don't want to send the Wosmoks north until Asteroth capitulates down here."

"She is my sister, Your Majesty. She has been a loyal servant."

Theudamer resumed watching the Donovards on the ramparts. "So be it. Order Wredegar to escort Vesamune out if she so desires."

The distant thudding ended with a crunching sound. General Graf rushed up to them a moment later. "Your Majesty, the siege ram has burst through Nairnbern's second gate!"

"Excellent!" He turned to Meliamour as he put on his helmet. "You have my orders. In your letter to Vesamune tell her about the imminent fall of Nairnbern, the last bastion before Asteroth's Cantrileme. Tell her we'll be in Eglamour sooner than the Donovards will expect, but that she is relieved of her duties if she wishes."

"Thank you, Your Majesty. May today's victory be swift."

"It will be," Theudamer said as she hurried away. The emperor strolled to his horse with Graf. "What is the situation, General?"

"I've just given the order for the first wave to attack the inner gatehouse. Your cavalry is ready for the charge."

Theudamer mounted his warhorse, towering over his attendants as the ballistae and trebuchets began to pelt the castle walls again. Graf mounted, and they rode to the front of the waiting cavalry. The emperor looked up and down the lines as the fighting at the gate grew louder. The Rugen banners, bearing the four gold crowns and black wolf head on a field of deep blue, fluttered in the breeze.

"The Donovards were not prepared for our swift march from Torgsbad," Graf continued. "That, or Asteroth is hoarding his better knights at Cantrileme."

"Where are Ardis Vilarwef and her rebels?"

"In the forest beyond Nairnbern, ready to intercept any that try to flee, as you ordered."

Theudamer drew his great sword. "Sound the charge!"

The trumpets blew as the cavalry moved forward with Theudamer in front. He kept his eyes on the inner gatehouse, its tower partially destroyed by his catapults. As he rode he saw the assaulters rally and push into the outer courtyard. A few moments later the emperor and his cavalry channeled into the gateway under a hail of arrows from the archers on the wall.

He did not slow down, yet some of his knights surged ahead of him. They burst into the courtyard, close behind the initial assaulters. Theudamer could see the panic on the faces of every Donovard inside. The cavalry kept its momentum despite the spear-spiked barricades and lines of crossbowmen.

Theudamer followed his knights as they jumped a barricade, punched a hole in the defenses, and rushed into the stunned defenders. He swept through the Donovards, hacking down on them and deflecting their spears with his long shield.

"Your Majesty!" Graf shouted, blood splattered on half his face. "The enemy cavalry!" He pointed his sword toward the far side of the long courtyard. The Donovards had already begun their surprise charge.

Theudamer held his sword aloft. "To me!" he shouted to his knights.

They regrouped and charged forward. Spears, swords, and shields splintered. The leader of the Donovards was unhorsed and killed. The Rugen soldiers who continued to pour into the courtyard soon swept over the rest.

When the battle around him subsided, Theudamer turned to Graf. "Order the riders down every alley. Eliminate everyone. Requisition supplies and post a small garrison. We will march to Cantrileme at once."

"Perhaps tomorrow, Your Majesty? The men could use a rest and time to secure the—"

"If you insist on having me repeat myself, I'll strip you of your general's cloak myself."

"Prepare to march!"

100

FETZER

Borel District of Eglamour, Toulon Ministry
Midsummer, 3034

"I didn't plan it this way," Arasemis said, "but this will have to do."

Fetzer noticed his voice was hoarser than yesterday.

"What happened to our palace supporter?" Marlan asked.

"We don't know," Arasemis said between coughs. He dabbed his lips with a handkerchief. "I know him like a brother. He would not abandon us. Something must have happened to him, so we'll not use our plan to smuggle into the palace as wine merchants."

"But how will we get our mechans inside?" Juhl asked.

"We can still use the barrels . . ." Arasemis paused to hack into his handkerchief.

Fetzer watched him closely, hoping he would fall over dead or announce he would not go with them to the palace. Fetzer had thought of a way to lay his hands on the lamp armor, but it would be easier if Arasemis did not join them.

"As I was saying . . . we can still use the barrels. Instead of smuggling them in ourselves with help from our supporter, we'll simply pay someone else to do it."

"And risk them finding the mechans?" Marlan said.

"Not worth it," Rodel said.

"I agree," Juhl said.

"The right merchant can be paid enough not to peek," Arasemis said, "and position the barrels right where we need them to be."

"Can't we just go over the walls with our mechans on, like we did for the Henrey task?" Juhl asked.

"Unlike how it was with Henrey," Arasemis said, "the palace guards are now on alert. And if something happened to our supporter, they may expect us to come over the walls. Since I never received the supporter's final instructions, we'll need time to scout around to locate the chambers used by the royal family. The king's tower is the only certain place. So we need a quiet entry and time inside."

"Perhaps only one of us should scout the interior, then report back," Marlan said.

Arasemis shook his head as he coughed. "I've made the decision. I will have Nidlade recommend a merchant who will not ask questions and who can get into the palace. Today or tonight, if possible. Make sure your barrels are ready."

"Who is Nidlade?" Marlan asked.

"The blind one. He is not yet a member of our Order but should be. He has assisted Candlestone and various other causes against the crown since he was a boy."

When Arasemis paused to cough, Fetzer caught a glimpse of red on his handkerchief.

"When Nidlade has found someone suitable," Arasemis continued, "Fetzer will lead everyone since he has done most of the scouting to the palace."

"You won't be coming?" Rodel asked.

"My illness . . . At least I was able to watch Henrey's assassination. This time I would only be a burden. I very much wished to use my lamp armor for this grand event, but I'll have to wait."

℘

> All this waiting gave me time to finalize a plan to acquire the lamp armor. The old fool hasn't bothered to check his barrel since the Henrey task. I've switched his lid for mine. Since he's not going to the palace, he won't know until it's too late. Then I'll wear it like a second skin for the rest of my days . . .

101

ARTHAN

Clonmel Estate in Eglamour, Toulon Ministry
Midsummer, 3034

"Hamelin and Tronchet are taking appropriate action," Serdot said. "The royal family has been informed, and Brugarn wants Reimvick's head. I assured him we would turn him over to Tronchet once we learn as much as we can from him. Brugarn insisted on telling Erech about the threat himself."

Arthan took note of Serdot's face as he listened. For once the alert widsemer looked tired. Arthan knew he had been up all night with Reimvick.

"You interrogated him yourself?" Arthan asked.

"I had one of Tronchet's jailors assist."

"Did Reimvick say anything useful?"

"A few things," Serdot said. "He agreed to tell you directly, and claims he'll tell you more. But so far we have nothing to help us pinpoint where Arasemis is."

"Tronchet said he was going to send his men into the slums of Borel now that the rioting has all but ceased. They're probably sweeping through it now."

Serdot sat down and called to the guards, "Bring the prisoner up."

"He's still a lord," Arthan said, but he was unsure why. Perhaps it was because he knew his father had always respected the enemy. He took a deep breath as they brought Reimvick into the room. His eyes were tired and sunken, his hair disheveled. His face was puffy but otherwise unmarked. He smelled of sweat and vomit.

"Get him some water," Arthan said, trying to casually sort the documents on his table. The cup of water came and Reimvick drank, his eyes shifting silently between the stack of correspondence and Arthan.

"As you can see, we found your stash of letters under the floor of your quarters," Arthan said. "Is there anything you wish to say before we begin?"

"Only that . . . you are a coward."

"Serdot said you were willing to tell me something."

"Shall I repeat it?" Reimvick asked.

"Were I a coward, I wouldn't have accepted this post. And you're the one who paid someone to murder your own brother."

"I did no such thing."

"And my father," Arthan said. "And Gottfried and Bardil and Henrey and many more."

Reimvick looked past Arthan, staring at the wall behind him.

"All right, I'll start. What about this letter?" Arthan held it up for him to see. "Addressed to 'E,' it says Arasemis and his followers are leaving Thorendor for Eglamour . . . thanks to 'E' for arranging everything in Borel . . . thanks for sending preliminary instructions."

Reimvick stayed locked in his stare.

"Or this one," Arthan continued, "written in your hand. Let's see . . . You're unable to meet them in Borel . . . Unkind things about me and my 'pesky widsemer' . . . Then you give the locations and movements of the royal family. Thank you, by the way, for not mentioning Clonmel . . . Ah, here it is. You wrote that you looked forward to hearing about the next phase of Arasemis's plans, and you hoped that your assistance proved your loyalty to the cause. You go on to disparage your deceased brother and father. Shall I read the whole thing to jog your memory?"

Reimvick's sullen eyes shifted to Arthan's, but he kept silent.

"Pity you didn't have a chance to send that letter to Arasemis," Arthan continued. "Perhaps it's too late anyhow, seeing as the king's men are already sweeping through Borel. Why did you keep all of this damning correspondence, anyway? A proper conspirator would have burned them after reading."

Reimvick could not hold back a guttural, chilling chuckle. "When the new history of the world is written, it will draw on the pivotal events preserved in my letters."

"That won't be happening, but we will certainly draw on them for your trial," Arthan said. "And the trial of Arasemis and his adherents. Who are they?"

Reimvick smirked. "They are the end of you, all of this."

"Let's start with Marlan, then," Arthan said, picking up Marlan's mask from his desk. "We found this after Marlan killed my father. It matches Garion's, so we know Marlan is with you and Arasemis. Did Arasemis send Marlan to work with Blackhood thugs in Mordmerg? Or did you?"

Reimvick shook his head. "You cannot stop them."

"We will. Tronchet is reconquering Borel as we speak."

"Tronchet." Reimvick snickered again. "I thought you were more intelligent, young Arthan. Not the quality of your father, but not a fool. No one can stop what we've revived. Our Order has survived nearly a thousand years of war, vile kings and emperors, earth-ripping storms and famines . . ."

"Order? You mean this Candlestone. What is it exactly?"

"As I told Serdot, Candlestone is the new light shining across the world. A hard, piercing light for those who would veil it. Change is afoot."

"How much are the Rugens paying you?"

Reimvick laughed aloud. "You think the Rugens are capable of this? Perhaps you are a fool! Even if they were so capable, you should welcome it. Do you really think Erech and the House of Avaleau is worth saving? Do you look at men like Brugarn as worthy of protecting?"

"Not all the Avaleaus are like them," Arthan said. "Duke Henrey was a good man. Are Erech's young daughters so vile as to justify your treachery?"

Reimvick shrugged. "Sacrifices must be made when change of this magnitude is required."

"And what change is that? Did you intend to crown yourself, or put Arasemis on the throne?"

Reimvick shook his head slowly and gave Arthan a look of pity. "This is not about who gets a throne. It's about denying thrones to all."

"Go on."

Reimvick held up his hands. "You are like them, incapable of comprehending this revolution."

"We can help you find a clear way to speak," Serdot interrupted.

"Take me back to your jailor, young widsemer. You'll get no more from me, however much you pinch, twist, stretch, or brand my flesh. And I'll not seek Garion's window. I live only to hear of the success of Arasemis. I will wait for it, come what may, then release my soul in peaceful satisfaction."

"That's not what I want for you," Arthan said. "If Arasemis is so unstoppable, then you should be confident enough to talk about his plans."

"All of you will drown in the waves that will surge out from Eglamour in every direction. Donovan will never rise as a kingdom again. And it will only be the beginning."

Arthan slammed his fist on the table, letting his frustration spill out. "Where is Arasemis?"

Reimvick smiled. "He is here, as you well know."

"The arcanae relics mentioned in Arasemis's letter," Serdot said. "What did he find?"

"Anyone's guess, but I can't wait to see what he does with them."

Arthan and Serdot exchanged a frustrated glance, then Arthan stood and motioned for the guards to take Reimvick away. He noticed the lord minister's gaze and followed it to the alchemical sword on his belt. "Do you like it?" Arthan asked. "Arasemis is afraid of it. In his letter he asked you about it."

"If I were able to write him back, I would say he has no cause for worry. For the young, haughty nobleman wearing it knows nothing of its history or how to use it."

"Arasemis's adherents know better," Arthan said with more confidence than he felt. "They tasted Adrithayn at Hullen. Now, you'll remain in chains here until your trial at court. At any time, you can agree to tell us about Arasemis and his followers. If you do, I will petition the king to spare your life. Brugarn will likely preside over the trial, so you'll need all the help you can get."

The guards pulled Reimvick up from his chair as an out-of-breath palace soldier rushed into the room.

"Lord Minister! Marshal, sir!"

"Calm yourself," Serdot said.

"Sir, the palace is under attack! Some evil—they came from nowhere, sir."

"Who? Rugens, rioters, assassins?"

The soldier shook his head as he tried to regain his breath. "Many, few . . . Difficult to see, my lord. They used colored smoke, foul . . . Moved so fast . . . They say it's like what happened to Lord Henrey."

Reimvick chuckled happily as the guards pulled him out of the room. "The utter joys of alchemy!" he shouted. "The days of hiding chemina will be over as you struggle to keep up!"

Arthan rushed to the window and threw open the curtains and shutters. Smoke of various colors hung over the palace. Several black columns of smoke were also rising from inside the complex.

"Serdot, have Livonier make our men ready at once. All archers and mounted knights."

102

MILISEND

Eglamour Palace, Toulon Ministry
Midsummer, 3034

"Again, I apologize for the inconvenience, but it's for your own protection," Tronchet said.

"You could have taken these precautions sooner," Princess Avalane said with tears in her eyes. "Perhaps my Henrey would still be alive . . ."

Tronchet hung his head. "I'm sorry, Princess."

"How many, then?" Milisend asked.

"Thirty extra soldiers for each princess, with your permission," Tronchet replied. "They are now under Sir Hamelin's command and are waiting in the corridor."

"More of these men in my chambers?" Princess Brielle asked.

Tronchet nodded. "Women soldiers also."

"For how long?" Milisend asked.

"Until the assassins are caught. Last night I told you about Lord Valient's discovery of Lord Reimvick. We are getting closer to ending this, I assure you."

"Have you gotten closer to freeing Regaume?"

"Mili," Avalane said, "we are surrounded by war, death, and soldiers. And you still worry for the thief? Tronchet, how soon before they take him away to Ralmogard?"

The magistrate looked at Milisend, searching for a way to say it. "I'm afraid I'm the bearer of all the bad news . . ."

"How soon?" Milisend demanded.

"They are due this morning, Princess. I'm sorry."

Avalane turned to Milisend. "Then you can finally put him behind you."

"How long since Henrey was butchered?" Milisend asked. "Have you put it behind you?"

Avalane put her hands over her face and cried.

"Henrey was her husband," Brielle said with a scowl. "One day, when I'm old enough to wed, I hope you'll not say such things to me, Mili."

Milisend glared at Tronchet but could not find any words.

"If I have your permission, I will inform the soldiers," he said. "Each of the ten is led by a Crownblade, of course. All of them are under your orders, but keep them nearby. Before I leave, there are a few other rules Duke Brugarn wanted me to relay about leaving the palace grounds."

Milisend turned her back to him and walked to the window. She felt remorse for how she had spoken to Avalane. She had loved Henrey like a brother. The palace was quickly feeling like a prison, more than it ever had before. Everyone could see Brugarn's paranoia. News of Reimvick's arrest was already spreading.

Tronchet droned on. If he was not going to speak about Regaume's release, she wanted him gone. She racked her brain for ideas but had tried everything she could think of. Except one . . .

She left the common room as her sisters continued listening to Tronchet. Rosellen followed her into her private chambers.

"What are you doing, Princess? Avalane will not be happy that you've walked away like that."

"Please, Rosellen. The time has come for me to do this myself."

"Do what yourself?"

Rosellen followed her into her wardrobe. Milisend unlocked the little drawer that held the black leathers, mask, and climbing slippers that Regaume had given her. She assembled her accessories, then began taking off her dress.

"It's too dangerous in the daylight, Mili. We should have thought of this last night."

"We didn't know the Ralmogard magistrate's men would be here in the morning, Rosellen."

"What about the assassins? They could be anywhere. And with all the additional guards posted everywhere, it will be impossible for you to free Regaume. And the guards may mistake you for an assassin!"

Milisend turned to her. "My dear friend, you know me better than anyone, even Regaume. And so you know why I must try. I will never be happy if I sit by while they take him to the gallows."

"Even if you save him, where will you go? And think of your mother, your sisters . . ."

"If I'm with Regaume, I will go anywhere. Mother and Father are no longer the people they once were. My sisters will understand. You can tell them about all of this." Milisend held up her mask. "They will understand. Or they won't, it makes no difference to me anymore." She put on the mask.

Rosellen could not help but smile. "They would never understand this . . ."

Milisend put on the slippers.

"I will miss hearing about your adventures," Rosellen continued.

"I will miss your care and love," Milisend said. "Your companionship, advice, good gossip, and helping me sneak out of the palace to see Regaume all those times . . . I've never known a better friend. You've always been by my side, Rosellen. Since we were girls."

"I'll be here still, should you ever sneak back in to visit."

Rosellen handed her the black dagger for her belt. Milisend took it and gave her a long hug, then pulled the hood over her head.

"Regaume will be saved for sure," Rosellen said, adjusting the hood.

"He saved me first," Milisend said. "I was never meant to wed any lord."

"I suppose not. I hope that you—"

They were startled by the fierce shouts of men in the corridor. The clash of steel was sudden and loud. Rosellen gasped and they hugged.

"They are here!"

"Hide!" Milisend said. She pulled the dagger from her belt and moved toward her closed door. Her hand trembled in front of her as the screaming grew louder. The stone floor shuddered with the fall of armored bodies. She forced herself to reach for the door, dagger ready.

She jerked it open and stepped into the corridor. Soldiers lay scattered and broken, red with burns and deep gashes in their armor. Her heart leaped into her throat as she stepped around them. An orange light glowed from around the corner. She quickened her pace as she realized the assassins were circling around toward the princesses' common room.

She neared the corner and smelled the burning of lamp oil and flesh. She turned the corner and felt the heat through her leathers. She saw two smoke-shrouded figures enter the common room at the end of the corridor. One had long, shining blades for hands. The other was on fire, yet not in pain.

Milisend rushed forward, fearing for her sisters. She felt a certain inevitability grip her, yet the screams of her sisters propelled her forward. As she neared the burning door a body was thrown out into the corridor. It was Tronchet, the robe lapels on his chest aflame. He hit the wall and fell, silent. Milisend took the sword from his hand and stepped into the doorway.

Avalane and Brielle were already dead. The figure with the blades, a woman, was approaching the last Crownblade in the room. She skated into the Crownblade using wheels that flipped down from her boot toes and from the heels. The Crownblade broke his sword on her armor, and she killed him swiftly.

Then the other figure drew Milisend's gaze. He walked in armor that blazed like a hearthfire. He was busy deliberately touching everything with flaming fingers. Curtains, furniture, anything that would take the fire. Black smoke collected quickly in the high ceiling. Then the burning man walked to Brielle's personal chambers, dispatching a wounded soldier who had been hiding.

The woman seemed to be resting, or waiting. Milisend surged in toward her, eyeing what looked like a gap in the armor on her back, just under her shoulder. The woman noticed her at the last moment and turned, but it was too late. Milisend plunged the dagger into the gap.

The woman screamed and pulled away, taking her dagger. She struggled to reach the blade in her back. Milisend raised Tronchet's sword, but Rosellen's scream distracted her. Then the burning man appeared in Brielle's doorway. Rosellen was alive for the moment, held fast in the man's burning hands.

Milisend lowered her sword as the woman struggled to remove the dagger. But the burning man did not demand she throw down her sword. He was happy to wait. Rosellen screamed as his fire leaped onto her dress and into her hair. Milisend looked at the blank, unfeeling mask covering his face. His armor shimmered golden bright.

Milisend charged at him, and he tossed Rosellen aside. She brought her sword high as the burning man stepped toward her. He moved a bit but let her strike him on his shoulder. Sparks erupted, and Milisend felt an intense heat. The burning man reached for her sword. She nimbly skipped around him, looking for a weak point in his armor as Regaume had taught her to do. The burning man appeared amused as she became frustrated.

The blade-handed woman had positioned herself at the exit. Milisend felt tears wet the inside of her mask and the cold grip of death again. The faces of the Crownblades, Tronchet, the lord ministers, and others better with a sword than she flashed through her mind.

Walking slowly, the burning man maneuvered Milisend into a corner. She was summoning her courage for a final charge at him when his head suddenly bent forward. He turned around, and the spear that had jabbed the back of his helmet fell to the floor. Rosellen tried to recover the spear for another jab, but he smacked the weapon away and took hold of Rosellen's head. She struggled and screamed out before falling limp.

Milisend picked up the spear and whacked the burning man in the head and ran past him toward the door. The woman was bent over, her white hand out of the bladed gauntlet and still reaching for the dagger in her back. Milisend jabbed at her, but the armor deflected and broke the spear tip. The woman repositioned herself in the doorway and slashed out at Milisend.

Milisend gave up on the door and jumped through the shattered window to a rooftop close below. She looked up after landing, seeing the burning man looking down at her briefly before disappearing.

She got up and ran across the rooftops, her heart heavy with grief.

103

BRUGARN

Eglamour Palace, Toulon Ministry
Midsummer, 3034

"The time for dithering is over, Voufon," Brugarn said. "As Lord Minister of Laume, your lands lie north of Alpenon. Asteroth requires your immediate aid to prevent the Rugens from marching on Eglamour."

"Toulon is the greatest realm of Donovan," she said. "Laume has a fraction of your soldiers and resources, and I'd have to cross my army through mountains if the Laume River Valley is taken. My ministry would be left undefended."

"If Laume must be sacrificed to save the kingdom, then we should accept that," Meltres said.

"Who is this whom I've neither asked for nor have need of his advice?" Voufon asked.

"You must remember Meltres," Brugarn said. "He was our ambassador to Maillard's ill-fated Empire Alliance Council. I've chosen Meltres to organize the defenses of southern Toulon."

"You're jesting," Voufon said. "He looks like a sickly scribe. Has he ever ridden a horse?"

"Actually, I served in Alpenon years ago with my cousin, General Chaultion," Meltres said.

Voufon shook her head in disbelief.

"I neither asked for nor have need of your advice on such matters," Brugarn said to her. "What I want from you, Voufon, is your army. You may think it small, but if the Rugens break past Asteroth and march toward Eglamour, your army's attack on the Rugen flank would slow them down until I receive Henrey's forces from Elmbrel and other armies from the east. Your soldiers will buy time for the rest of us."

"At what cost?" Voufon asked. "Is Laume to be destroyed because you and your underlings did not prepare?"

"I require your complete loyalty."

"You are not the king."

"He is sitting on the throne," Meltres said.

"You have no crown and you do not wield the Rhunegeld," Voufon said. "Sit where you like, but you are no king."

Brugarn smacked her, and she stumbled to the floor. "Not yet," he said. "This conversation is over, Voufon. Go say farewell to your sister, if the queen still recognizes you and anyone else through her popaver fog. Then return to Laume to gather your forces. One of Chaultion's commanders will accompany you to make sure you do it right."

Voufon came to her feet, shaking but with defiance in her eyes. Brugarn was still uncertain whether she would submit to him. He would never know. As Voufon opened her mouth to speak, a peculiar gurgling sound came from Meltres. He fell forward, landing facedown on the floor. Two tiny crossbow bolts protruded from the back of his head. More shots came from behind the throne, one sinking into Voufon's thigh.

Brugarn hopped from the throne and ran toward the middle of the floor to shield himself behind Voufon as the Crownblades reacted. He turned to see a masked, armored man running out from behind the throne, his bulky forearms shooting bolts at the Crownblades that encircled Brugarn.

Brugarn dove to the floor, catching a glimpse of another masked assassin coming through a window. Voufon screamed as the crossbow bolts ricocheted off the columns and walls. Brugarn felt one bite into his shoulder, then his neck. Then his legs. Voufon's body fell on top of him, her blood spilling on him.

He screamed out as orange smoke engulfed him and the Crownblades. A glowing red sword swept through the cloud, cutting down Crownblades left and right. Wounded and pinned, Brugarn reached for the hem of Voufon's red-soaked robes. He pulled the fabric over his face as the orange smoke thickened. He felt the taste of vomit in his mouth but pressed the fabric into his face, trying to breathe as sparingly as his racing heart would allow.

The screams of his guards filled his ears, and the stench of the smoke burned his nose. He squeezed his eyes and mouth shut and felt his mind fog as the blood drained out of him.

&

When Brugarn awoke he found himself in his comfortable bed. Two blurry faces hovered over him. When his eyes cleared he saw his physician and Arthan.

"Where . . . are they?"

"They escaped," Arthan said.

"My lord, you must rest," the physician said.

Brugarn's head was spinning. He felt weak, and his body hurt all over. A heap of bloody rags and crossbow bolts were stacked on a table near his bed. But for once he was glad to see Arthan. "Tell me . . ." Brugarn whispered.

"I was at Clonmel when we heard the attacks," Arthan said. "I brought my men, but we were too late for the king's daughters. We found their charred bodies . . . When we came to your chambers the two assassins were still fighting the Crownblades. We flooded in, and they disappeared. In addition to most of your guard force, Lord Minister Voufon and Sir Meltres perished."

"Reimvick?" Brugarn whispered.

"We still have him. And we're still searching in Borel for Arasemis."

Brugarn cleared his throat. "Arrest Vesamune . . . I will have my revenge . . ."

"We don't think the Rugens are behind this anymore."

Brugarn shook his head on his pillow. "It's war . . ."

"I will arrest her," Arthan said. "The king, in case you were concerned, is safe. And we've moved the queen into the lower chambers of the king's tower, so we could consolidate the remaining Crownblades. Hamelin says he has less than fifty, plus the regular palace guards. My Racharders are also on patrol inside and around the palace."

Brugarn nodded, then they stared at each other for a moment. Brugarn recognized that he was in a vulnerable position. If Arthan wished, he could quietly end Brugarn's life. Brugarn could see those thoughts bubbling behind the lord minister's eyes.

"I must thank . . . you for saving me . . . from them. A second time . . ."

"It is my duty."

"Yes . . ."

He was confident the son of Maillard would let him live. He lifted his hand with his wist ring. Arthan hesitated but finally grasped his hand. Brugarn smiled, but Arthan did not. He turned and departed. Brugarn looked at his physician.

"Popaver . . . Make me sleep."

104

MARLAN

Cellars of Eglamour Palace, Toulon Ministry
Midsummer, 3034

"Who was the black-masked woman?" Marlan asked, rolling a keg away from the cellar wall for a seat. "And how did she know where we would be?" Rodel asked.

"Maybe she was just lucky," Fetzer said, staring at the candle. "She moved quickly though, like she'd been trained in aerina arcana. And she wore black leathers head to foot, like a dark widsemer."

"I'm not sure it was her intent to be there to fight us," Juhl said, lifting her arm as Rodel finished wrapping her torso. "Except for stabbing my shoulder blade, she was completely defensive. And she escaped as soon as she had the chance, so unlikely a bodyguard."

"I suppose it doesn't matter, since you succeeded in killing the princesses." Marlan said. "We can report this mystery woman to Arasemis when we return to Borel. He may have ideas about her."

"You didn't have trouble with Brugarn and Voufon?" Fetzer asked.

Marlan sighed. "So we thought. Rodel filled them with bolts, and I used the poison clouds. We couldn't confirm the bodies because Arthan and more Crownblades flooded in."

"Did you kill him?" Fetzer asked.

"He had that sword, the one that absorbed alchemical clouds at the warcastle ruin and made Juhl sick. This time it absorbed the heat from my sword. It was harmless against my armor, of course, but not Rodel's."

Rodel held up his left arm. "Melted the cocking rods on my side here, rendering my left arm crossbows useless. I ran first, fearing I had been wounded."

"We hid in various rooms before coming here," Marlan said. "On the way we heard guards describing Brugarn as still clinging to life."

"So are we to deviate from the plan, to make another attempt on him?" Fetzer asked.

"No, we must move forward," Marlan said. "If he is mortally wounded like he must be, we would be wasting our time breaking through his guards. If he lives, we'll have another opportunity after we finish the king."

"So what next?" Juhl asked.

"From what we can tell, the king's tower must be the northern one," Marlan said.

"The merchant brought us in over there," Fetzer said. "It cannot be the king's tower. Not enough Crownblades standing guard. It must be the southern tower."

Marlan shook his head. "Wish we had that final letter Arasemis was expecting from our palace supporter. If we only knew who he was, and where he was . . ."

"One of the master's many failures," Fetzer said. "Which reminds me, would Arasemis fake illness to avoid the danger of this task?"

"You've gloated about stealing his lamp armor," Juhl said. "Now you dare to accuse the master of cowardice?"

"Only the most daring members of this Order will survive these tasks," Fetzer said, glaring at her.

"Fetzer also took his time burning those women," Juhl said to Marlan. "He enjoyed it too much, in my opinion. And he endangered us by starting those fires."

"Their deaths were supposed to be quick and clean," Marlan said. "And fire-setting is not part of the plan, not until the task is done."

"These are cruel rulers of multitudes," Fetzer said. "They deserve much worse than brief suffering at death. And look what that fire has bought us: more soldiers distracted with putting it out than looking for us."

"The youngest princess was just a girl," Juhl said. "I don't love any of them. But Candlestone is meant to be quick and clean. Deaths are meant to be precise and with little suffering."

"I'm still disappointed that you stole Arasemis's armor," Marlan said, "but I won't force it off you. I'm only using an obscurant in my mechan veins because I don't want to risk poisoning any of you. Your fire must be similarly controlled, or it will cut out your lamp oil reservoir. We must work together to finish this."

"The south tower is the king's tower," Fetzer said.

"I think it's the northern one," Marlan said.

"We cannot split up this time," Rodel said. "It will take all of us to reach the king."

"South tower, Marlan," Fetzer said.

Marlan stared at him, knowing they could not take the time or the risk to scout the towers again. Part of Marlan was glad Fetzer was wearing the lamp armor. It was fearsome and would make torching the palace easier at the end. And Marlan's faith that Fetzer was a prophetic leader of Candlestone was strengthened by seeing him in the mechan that Arasemis had chosen for himself.

But Arasemis was still the master, and disobeying the master was disloyal to the ancient Order. Yet Marlan's conviction that Fetzer would come around was not shaken. He knew he would learn to respect Arasemis and properly prepare to succeed him as master when the time was right. Marlan knew Fetzer would lead Candlestone well when he learned self-control.

"Fine, south tower," Marlan said. "If you're right, we'll kill the king, then escape the way we came, and you can torch everything. If you're wrong, we may not make it to the north tower. Juhl, are you patched up enough to continue?"

Juhl nodded. "I'm going to keep that woman's dagger for the next time I see her."

"Rodel?"

"I transferred the left side bolt cartridges into my right. It's awkward to run with the rods engaged only on one side, but it's minor. And I have the candle alchemy bag right here. I'm ready."

"Fetzer?"

"I want to be the one to kill Erech."

Marlan knew that the honor of killing the king was his, as Arasemis's designated leader of the task. "We must get to him first. Then whoever has the best opportunity will take his life," he said simply.

105

ARTHAN

Eglamour Palace, Toulon Ministry
Midsummer, 3034

When Arthan left Brugarn's bedside, he found Serdot waiting for him outside the door.

"Will he live?" Serdot asked.

"His physician says he shouldn't have survived the attack."

"Pity he did. If he lives through the night, I could slip something into his popaver."

"I'll hear no more of that, Serdot. If God takes the wretched man we'll all be the better for it, but it won't be by our hands. Tell me about the situation in the palace."

"The assassins are hiding somewhere. Hamelin's Crownblades are searching everywhere. General Chaultion has summoned additional soldiers from the outlaying garrisons. There are still fires burning in the northeast wing and creeping up the prison tower. Tronchet is still alive, but barely. He lost his keys, or the soldiers dropped them when they helped him out of there—both unlikely. The assassins probably stole them, which means they can go wherever they please."

"Will our favorite magistrate live?" Arthan asked as they briskly rounded a corner.

"I think so. He's burned on his hands and face, and will be foggy in the head for a while. Ugly gash on the back of his head. He's in and out of sleep, so we can't get him to tell us anything. I thought about Milisend's thief, but without Tronchet's keys . . ."

"Well, now that Milisend is dead . . . We have more important things to do than save a condemned thief."

"The separate attacks that killed the princesses and Voufon tell me we're dealing with a group, maybe a dozen assassins or more," Serdot said.

"There were only two that attacked Voufon and Brugarn. Regardless of their number, my God—almost the entire Avaleau monarchy is wiped out."

"Erech, his brothers, and the queen are the only ones left of the direct line," Serdot agreed.

"We must find these killers, Serdot. We've never seen anything like them, their armor and weapons, the way they move and run walls. Even the Crownblades are far outmatched."

"I saw how your alchemical sword reacted to their flaming sword. Unless Hamelin has an armory of arcanae weaponry hidden away, you may be the only one who can stop them."

"Where are you leading me?" Arthan asked.

"Hamelin asked me to bring you to one of the passages in the southwest wing. Remember how most doors there were reported to be blocked, locked from the inside since the attacks?"

"Yes. With strong sleep candles littering the floors."

"Right, and tripwires that shot orange powder. Those two Crownblades died, by the way. Well, Hamelin found a corridor unlocked and without traps. A single unlit candle, but his men are too frightened to approach. They've all heard about your sword and want you to see it first."

Arthan looked at Serdot. "The Crownblades are waiting on me to investigate a candle, Serdot? Brugarn may have Hamelin's head over these attacks—maybe mine, too—yet Hamelin is worried about an unlit candle?"

"The tactics of these assassins have frightened the knights, my lord. You recently embraced the ancient arts crafted into Adrithayn, as Maillard intended. But the knights are unaccustomed to such things."

"Adrithayn is a mystery to me as well. I know you've not had time to find that historian, Danleri."

"I did make inquiries before the latest attacks. I confirmed what Pelinaud said, that Danleri lives here in the capital, over in the Genthus District. Also, Danleri once taught at Bredahade Academy, where Garion and Arasemis once were. I planned to send a letter summoning Danleri to Clonmel."

"Send it today. I need to know how Adrithayn works, and about the arcanae in general. These assassins clearly have a grasp of the ancient arts, leaving us at a great disadvantage."

"Just as your father warned in his letter. I will have Danleri come to Clonmel as soon as possible."

"Come, we don't want to keep Hamelin waiting, worried over a candle."

❧

When they arrived at the corridor they found Hamelin pacing back and forth. Arthan's Marshal of Inquiry soldiers, led by Sir Debanor, and a contingent of Racharders led by Livonier were also waiting.

"A candle?" Arthan asked.

"Don't mock me," Hamelin said. "I've lost more than a few Crownblades to these tricks. As if the superior armor of the assassins weren't trouble enough."

Arthan glanced at the many knights who watched him intently. He knew they were brave men and women simply caught off guard by strange methods. "Let's have a look, then," he said, stepping toward the door.

A knight opened it for him, and it was just as they had said. The corridor was dark, with only moonlight shining through the windows. A single, abnormally tall candle sat in the middle.

"Careful," Livonier said. "If this is the least obstructed corridor, it must be a trap."

"Or a diversion," Serdot said, "since this is not the way to the king's tower."

"Perhaps they move in roundabout ways," Hamelin said.

"They're just buying time for themselves," Arthan said.

"For what?" Hamelin asked. "They go anywhere whenever they want."

"For the final assault on the king's tower. How long before the smithies break through the south corridor obstacles?"

"An hour at most," Hamelin said. "Then we'll have to deal with the poison traps they've likely set there."

Arthan stepped into the corridor, keeping his eye on the unlit candle. He felt a hand on his shoulder. It was Livonier.

"My lord, let one of the Racharders go first."

Arthan drew Adrithayn from his belt. "This is my duty."

Serdot followed him into the corridor. "Here is Marlan's mask, my lord. I have Garion's." Arthan took the mask, keeping his eyes fixed. "I don't have any gill fern fronds to refresh these," Serdot continued, "so breathe sparingly if you can."

"Better than nothing," Arthan said, watching the candle. It was white and normal, except for being about knee-high. It was sitting on a pewter plate, which appeared to be full of water.

"Serdot," Arthan whispered. "Can presence candles light themselves?"

"None that I'm familiar with."

As they moved forward Arthan thought he saw a faint ember float up from the wick. He stopped and nothing happened. When he took another step he was sure he saw an ember.

"Did you see that, Serdot?"

"Yes, my lord."

"We're about to become familiar with a self-lighting one." He kept his sword out front.

"Look, the ember grows," Serdot said.

Arthan saw it. The wick reddened as they crept closer. Within seconds the wick burst into flame. The white candle turned red, and its fire beamed. It burned quickly. Spent wax beaded in the water and spilled over the plate onto the floor, but instead of pooling it kept rolling—toward them—like rivulets of burning oil. When they stopped walking it stopped rolling.

They stayed still as a scarlet cloud formed around the flame, spinning like a miniature whirlwind that gained strength as the candle burned down. The cloud brightened as it expanded. Arthan lunged forward and swiped through the cloud. He smelled sulfur through his mask as the edge of the cloud bubbled outward. Then it shrank and Adrithayn's blade turned scarlet.

Arthan stepped back from the cloud, but the candle continued to pump out the gas. He stepped forward again and swiped at the candle itself. The top half was cast off and extinguished itself when it hit the ground.

Arthan breathed out and straightened. "Well, that was not as bad as—"

He saw a flash through his mask as the candle stump relit and the remainder of the scarlet cloud ignited. Arthan hacked at the candle and plate until it was a heap of fragments with rising embers. He placed his hand over his heart, feeling it stutter. It made him think of Meriam.

"Your robes are singed," Serdot said.

"So is your mask," Arthan said.

"What was that evil magic?" Hamelin said.

Arthan turned to see the knights walking down the corridor. "Careful, residue of that foul air may linger."

"It's not magic," Serdot said. "Just clever alchemy."

"Your sword," Debanor said, pointing to Adrithayn's scarlet hue.

"I think as long as it does not strike metal, the poison will stay in the blade," Arthan said. "I think."

"We must make haste for the king's tower," Hamelin said.

106

FETZER

"Ready?" Marlan asked. Everyone nodded. He led the charge around the corner, with Fetzer close behind him. The Crownblades guarding the stairs to the king's tower saw them coming and sounded the alarm.

Fetzer smiled under his mask. He would do as Marlan asked him not to do. He knew Marlan and the others would stay out of his way.

As he jogged, Fetzer reached to his left side and opened the metal flap above his hip. He found the knob and pulled it outward, then rammed it back in again. The air escaped as the lamp oil surged through the veins in his armor and up into his helmet. He veered toward the wall and smacked at a torch sconce with his hands.

The fire snaked down his arms and across the mechan. He felt the suit expand and tighten around his body at the heat. Juhl and Rodel cursed behind him. Marlan did not turn, but the bright light and heat was impossible to mistake.

Marlan crashed into the Crownblades, his flaming sword parting their ranks. But most of the knights were distracted by Fetzer. Their eyes widened with fear, and he relished it. He threw himself into them, slashing and reaching out for them with flaming fists. Rodel's crossbow bolts pelted through the smoke and into the knights, and Juhl skated in with her tornadic blades. Of the two dozen Crownblades and guards, half fell in those first moments.

Fetzer pushed through to the door to the stairs and found it locked. He let his fire leap onto its wooden planks, but it would not catch for long. There were too many iron studs and plates. He turned back to the fight.

"The door is locked solid!"

Marlan dispatched a knight and came over, jabbing his red-hot sword into the great lock. It melted out of the door like pudding. He and Fetzer charged into it, forcing it ajar. But obstacles had been positioned behind it. Spearmen stabbed out at them from the inside. Marlan melted down the door's hinges, freeing it from the wall and falling inward, contributing to the blockage.

"Put the poison in your mechan veins!" Fetzer shouted. "If not now, when?"

He knew Marlan was irritated with him. He stood there with his arm shielding his face from Fetzer's heat as the others finished the guards. Finally, Marlan opened his flap and pumped the knob, sending a purple liquid through his mechan veins. The misty gas soon whispered out. Marlan continued to hack at the fortified door as the mist seeped through to the spearmen.

Fetzer and Rodel dispatched the last of the Crownblades. Juhl was standing awkwardly against the wall for support. Rodel went to her as Fetzer looked on.

"It's nothing," she said through her mask, swatting Rodel's hand away.

Fetzer knew her shoulder still pained her, raw as it was. She should have been more careful.

Marlan finally broke the door in half after several spearmen succumbed to the poison. Fetzer and the others followed him through the debris and finished off the guards.

"Fetzer, Rodel," Marlan said as he pointed to an open door with the Avaleau coat of arms on the lintel. "The queen's new room should be down this hallway. Do it quickly."

Fetzer looked toward the broad spiral staircase. He did not want to waste time with a bedridden queen. Without hesitation he ran toward the stairs.

"Fetzer!" Marlan shouted.

Fetzer pressed on. Let them kill her, he told himself. He was destined for something greater.

He felt a new vigor flow into his own veins under the mechan. He did not stop for the guards who came down the spiraling steps, tossing or slashing at them. He charged upward until he reached a large anteroom. It was full of guards, and they were ready to defend, but not ready for his walking fire.

He charged into them, finding a few knights brave enough to confront him. But none rivaled his swordsmanship, and all withered from the heat. All of them perished or fled. He left the wounded ones to struggle with their unquenchable burns, charging up the next spiral staircase.

107

ARTHAN

Eglamour Palace, Toulon Ministry
Midsummer, 3034

"We're too late!" Serdot shouted.

Arthan sprinted past the fallen Crownblades. It was only the mangled wreck of the heavy door that gave him pause. It looked as though it had been chewed by the fabled volcanoes of the Far East. And a peculiar stench hung in the air with the smoke. Something poisonous. Inside the anteroom was more carnage.

"Hamelin, go to the queen's quarters with half the men," Arthan said. "I'll take the rest upstairs."

Hamelin rushed down the corridor as Arthan mounted the broad spiral stairs. Screams and heavy thuds echoed down, and the putrid smell became stronger.

Arthan paused, looking at the scarlet hue of Adrithayn. "Serdot, I think it's time for the Candlestone masks again. We're getting closer." Serdot complied and Arthan turned to Livonier and Debanor. "Regretfully, we only have two. Stay back if they use poison clouds."

They pressed forward until they reached another anteroom. Dead and wounded soldiers lay littered about. Arthan crouched next to one of the Crownblades.

"How many?"

"Four assassins . . . I think," the knight said. "A burning man . . . purple mist, wheeled blades . . . and a crossbow-armed one . . ."

Another knight lying next to the first was struggling to speak. Arthan went to him and held his hand.

"F-five . . ." the knight whispered as blood trickled from his mouth. Then his eyes rolled skyward and his mouth dropped. Arthan thought he had passed, until he noticed the dying knight's eyes tracking something above them.

Arthan looked up into the rafters and saw the edge of a dark form fall behind him. Serdot was knocked to the floor, his small crossbow taken from him as he fell. Then the slender figure disappeared up the next set of spiral stairs.

"Stop him!" Arthan shouted, but the figure was gone.

108

MILISEND

Eglamour Palace, Toulon Ministry
Midsummer, 3034

Milisend told herself her next encounter with the assassins would be different. She knew they would kill her father, but she would not stop now, and she'd certainly not waste time explaining herself to Arthan. In the end, it would not matter. She would stop one of them, preferably the burning man, even if it killed her.

Milisend saw a shadow move on the curved wall of the spiral stairs. The figure raced toward her, with wheeled boots tearing down the wall. The assassin's bladed hands scraped at the center column of the stairs. Milisend ducked low as the assassin passed, then she turned as the assassin's masked face looked at her from below. Milisend pointed Serdot's crossbow at the eye slits of the mask. She hesitated, and the assassin vanished down the stairs. It was her only shot, and she would need the bolt.

Milisend pushed up from the stairs as the assassin's metal wheels echoed up the stairwell. Then she sprinted forward, taking three steps at a time.

109

MARLAN

Eglamour Palace, Toulon Ministry
Midsummer, 3034

It was easy to see where Fetzer had been. New fires danced on tapestries and furniture. Marlan knew Fetzer would not listen, so he did not try to stop him. They were breaking through the layers of guards faster than Marlan or Arasemis had planned. He hoped that once the task was done, Fetzer would calm down and submit to orders again. Marlan turned to Rodel after the last guard on the landing was finished off.

"Post yourself here, Rodel," he said. "If Valient's men make it past Juhl, don't let them get past you. You have to hold them off until we're done."

Rodel nodded. "And after?"

"You and Juhl escape to Borel. Make sure you're not followed. Fetzer and I will arrive separately. Then we'll follow Arasemis's lead, probably back to Thorendor."

Marlan left Rodel at the top of the spiral stairs and looked for Fetzer's golden light. He let Fetzer stay ahead of him, like a hunting dog chasing down game. The king's tower chambers were like a small maze, with many sitting and entertaining rooms, a solar, bathhouse, and kitchen.

110

MILISEND

Eglamour Palace, Toulon Ministry
Midsummer, 3034

Expecting another wall runner, Milisend cautiously watched the curved wall of the stairs for more fast-moving shadows. But she did not slow down until she reached the top. Fire and bodies were everywhere.

She stepped toward the sound of fighting ahead but paused at a clicking sound, like the turning of several locks or wheels. She dove to the ground and rolled amid the whip of a crossbow and the ricochet of bolts. When the shooting stopped she sprinted toward the man hiding in the shadows behind the landing.

The assassin was shaking one of his arms frantically. Milisend pounced on him, repeatedly stabbing at the seams of his armor. But he was quick. His fist caught her in the mouth, and she tumbled away. He tried to pull at a crossbow bolt jammed in his bulky arm, but it would not clear. He seemed more concerned with watching the stairwell than fighting her.

Milisend took a step backward, and he did not follow. She turned and sprinted for the balcony.

111

MARLAN

Eglamour Palace, Toulon Ministry
Midsummer, 3034

A waste, Marlan thought to himself. The Crownblades had little hope but had died bravely. They were the last to die for this king. Finally Marlan found Fetzer taking down a few soldiers guarding a locked door. Marlan stabbed through the lock with his flaming sword, quickly melting it.

"Are you ready?" he asked Fetzer.

Fetzer did not even look at him. He kicked open the door, and they pushed into Erech's bedchamber. The king was out on his balcony, staring up into the first glimmer of the predawn sky. Fetzer ran straight for him.

At the last moment Erech turned and swept the ancient Rhunegeld sword across Fetzer's breastplate. The surprise blow knocked Fetzer off balance, and he fell. Erech was initially stunned to see Rhunegeld pull flames from Fetzer's mechan, but he raised the blade to strike Fetzer where he lay.

Marlan could not get there in time. Erech slammed Rhunegeld down onto Fetzer as he tried to stand. Erech's sword burned bright. Flames continued to leap from the lamp armor to Rhunegeld. Marlan realized the sword was like Arthan's. Fetzer rolled away from Erech's next slash.

Marlan charged, raising his own flaming sword, and the king squared himself. Marlan did not expect the vigor displayed by Erech as their swords clashed. The king was still strong despite his weakened mind. Marlan was startled to see

Erech's sword now shining as white-hot as his own but without searing the king's ungloved hands. Marlan feared that Erech would be able to melt open his mechan.

Fetzer finally found his feet. The two fought Erech along the balcony, which looped around the tower. Marlan could hear Fetzer's fury as he shouted with every blow, slashing and lunging recklessly. Marlan had to avoid Fetzer more than once, which eased the pressure on the king. Erech backpedaled to rest, but they turned the corner and kept on.

A slender black figure appeared on the balcony behind Erech, like the one Fetzer and Juhl had described in the princesses' wing. The black-clothed woman was still. It took Marlan a moment to realize she was aiming a small crossbow. The next instant he saw a glint of light. Marlan instinctively looked away, but not soon enough.

The bolt punched diagonally through the mask's crystal lens, shearing off the outside corner of his eyebrow, taking some bone with it. The lens lodged into Marlan's cheek. His skull quaked with pain, and he shrieked. He backed away from Erech and Fetzer's engagement and turned back around the corner to avoid another shot.

Marlan took a deep breath and carefully pulled off the mask. He released the pressure on the mechan's poison reservoir but knew it would take the veins a moment to empty. He pulled the lens from his cheek and tossed it from the balcony. The winds quickly dissipated the residual cloud, so he allowed himself to breathe. Then he charged back around the corner.

He dodged around Erech and Fetzer, their combined heat now warming the stones of the tower like a hearth. He ran past them toward her. He felt the blood gush from his face, but he saw her well enough. She raised her sword.

Marlan's sword melted straight through her blade, leaving her with a shard. She jabbed at his wounded face with her fist. Marlan fell to the ground, expecting a blow to the back of his head with the shard. But it did not come. He paused on his knees, his head throbbing and robbing him of his balance.

112

ARTHAN

Eglamour Palace, Toulon Ministry
Midsummer, 3034

Arthan found moving with the Candlestone mask to be awkward. The narrow, crystal-lensed eye slits did not allow for much visibility. He wondered how the assassins, nimble and quick as they were, could do anything with the masks on.

As he climbed the stairwell behind Serdot, he noticed a peculiar sweet scent inside the mask. He remembered Serdot explaining how the gill ferns layered inside the mask provided fresh air. The scent was refreshing.

"Down!" Serdot shouted.

Arthan crouched as best as he could in his armor amid the squeak and scrape of metal wheels on stone. He caught a glimpse of the figure as she spiraled down the wall, bladed hands extended. One of the knights behind Arthan did not duck quickly enough. His headless body fell onto the soldiers coming up the stairs. There was more shouting below as the attacker spiraled down.

"Where do they get such exotic weapons and armor?" Arthan yelled out in frustration.

"Arcanae . . ." Serdot said as they pushed forward.

"We need that Danleri fellow to explain it all," Arthan said.

"I sent a summons before we left Clonmel," Serdot said. "Hurry, my lord, we're nearly at the top."

113

RODEL

Eglamour Palace, Toulon Ministry
Midsummer, 3034

odel watched the black-leathered woman go. He guessed that Fetzer and Marlan could deal easily enough with her, whoever she was. Rodel was more concerned with Juhl's plowing down the stairwell, knowing the Donovards would be too numerous for her and desperate to save their king.

Rodel waited at the top of the stairs, cursing his mechan. The jammed bolt would not dislodge, so his whole arm mechanism would not turn and recock for the next shot. He disengaged the cocking rod on his thigh and walked a bit easier.

The scraping echo of Juhl's wheels finally faded, now replaced by the shouts and footfalls of the Donovards. He picked up a sword from one of the fallen Crownblades but had no intention of confronting all of them. He knew Fetzer and Marlan would not need him to delay them, and he certainly would not die to buy them a few moments. He was more concerned about Juhl.

When the shouting grew louder Rodel reached into his pouch. He tossed his last two poison eggs down the stairs. He waited for the orange smoke to drift up and heard the coughing and vomiting. He was surprised to see two masked figures turn the corner and charge up despite the smoke. Was it Arasemis and Nidlade, or other supporters? He hesitated until he saw the second one had a scarlet-hued sword that absorbed some of the orange gas.

Rodel pulled out a couple cloaking eggs and threw them at the top of the stairs. Black smoke engulfed the landing as he ran behind the stairwell, breaking more cloaking eggs as he went. The Donovards stumbled up into the room. He waited flat against the smoke-shrouded wall as the soldiers ascended and rushed toward the tower balcony. When the stairwell was quiet again he hopped over the side and spiraled down the stairs.

It took time to leap over the bodies. When he reached the bottom he heard Juhl struggling. She was at the end of the corridor by the broken doors, crossing blades with a determined Crownblade. Blood trickled out of her mechan where the black-leathered woman had stabbed her. Juhl moved slow, but fast enough to block the knight's attack.

Rodel rushed to engage the Crownblade. Juhl used the opening to slash at the Crownblade's legs and Rodel quickly finished him off.

"Juhl, you are not well."

She collapsed, and he caught her. "Is . . . the task . . . ?" she whispered.

"Fetzer and Marlan will finish it, if they haven't already," he said as he pushed up her mask. He pulled his up as well. "Now it's time for us to leave."

Juhl shook her head. "Leave me . . . Make sure it's done."

"We've done our part, Juhl. We'll meet them in Borel. Can you walk?" He stood her up and pulled the lever on her thigh to disengage her boot wheels, then the levers that retracted the blades. "I've got enough cloaking eggs to get us out," he continued, "but you must take off this mechan."

She scowled at him. "I'll not abandon it . . . We are Candlestone."

Rodel summoned his strength and threw her heavy arm over his shoulder, pressing his gauntlet over her wound. Then he hurried her onward.

114

MILISEND

Eglamour Palace, Toulon Ministry
Midsummer, 3034

She ran to them. "Father, it's me!" Milisend yelled as she joined the fight against the burning man. The king paid her little attention. If he recognized her voice he did not show it, but neither did he attack her.

Milisend flung her sword shard at the man's mask, then kicked and punched at him as Regaume had taught her. The assassin's flames soon danced onto her gloves and arm leathers, forcing her to back away and smack them out. But it was no use. Only her father's sword kept the hellish assassin from killing them both.

Weaponless, she ran back toward the tower door to claim a sword from the slain. She ran straight into Arthan as he stepped onto the balcony. When he instinctively raised his sword, she hacked at the side of his neck with the ball of her hand, where a curved metal plate was stitched into her glove. He fell back into the room and she backpedaled to the balcony, still without a weapon.

Erech struck the burning man across his ribs. A burning liquid burst out, spraying the assassin and her father with bright oil. The flames on the man quickly died down, while those on the king grew on his robes. Erech screamed in pain and his next swipe at the assassin missed.

Milisend tried to distract the assassin, but he would not let her get close. He quickly disarmed her father and punched the king with a red-hot gauntlet, his flames having faded away. The assassin kept Milisend at a distance with his sword, then took hold of the king with his other hand.

Milisend disarmed the assassin as he looked into Erech's eyes, but he kicked her when she bent for the sword. She looked up and saw him pull a golden knife from his belt. He plunged it into Erech's neck. She screamed as the assassin shoved her father over the balcony. She ran to the side and caught a glimpse of him before he disappeared into the smoky darkness.

Milisend snatched Rhunegeld from the ground as the assassin approached toward his wounded friend. She felt the clench of a hand on her shoulder before she could turn.

"It's you!" Serdot cried.

Milisend wrestled free and chased after the assassins.

115

FETZER

Fetzer scooped up Marlan and his sword. He pushed Marlan toward the far side of the balcony.

"I have the hook if you can wall run," he told Marlan.

Marlan nodded as he wiped the blood from his face. Fetzer opened the hatch on his leg where the spare lamp oil cartridge was stored. He lit the top with the dying fire in his arm veins, then tossed the cartridge behind him, knowing the black-leathered woman would follow. The cartridge burst on the stones, scattering flames and buying them time.

Fetzer reached into the hatch on his other leg and pulled out a grappling hook. Marlan unwound the steel cable from his pouch, and Fetzer connected it to the hook.

"It's not long enough by far," Marlan said.

"Should get us halfway, then we'll run the rest."

Fetzer secured the hook around a crenel on the balcony. "You first."

Marlan hesitated. Fetzer knew the pain in his head was great. He expected Marlan to fall. But with the weight of their mechans, there was no way to carry him down.

Marlan grabbed the cable and jumped. The cable snapped taut, and he swung toward the tower wall. His boots found a grip in the wall, and he ran diagonally downward. But his wall run was too fast. Fetzer watched as Marlan spiraled around the tower once. When he came around again his feet lost the wall and he fell into the smoke that still billowed from the palace fires.

Fetzer took hold of the loose cable and jumped. Fear flashed through his mind as he fell toward the billowing gray, but his training told him that his momentum would keep him on the wall. His feet connected to the wall and he let go of the cable, running harder than he had all night. He spiraled down around the tower's column with ease.

On the second turn his view became obscured by the smoke, and he was disoriented. He felt his feet leave the wall, and he too fell. A moment later he crashed into the slate tiles of a roof. He laughed wickedly as he sat up. Then he felt a hot hand on his shoulder and knew it was Marlan's gauntlet. His friend was coughing bitterly.

Fetzer took his hand and pulled him to his feet. Then he pulled Marlan behind him, smiling behind the mask. He was a king killer now. He could not wait to gloat in Arasemis's face.

116

MILISEND

Eglamour Palace, Toulon Ministry
Midsummer, 3034

ere flames could not slow her now. She jumped the burning oil as the smoking man jumped the balcony ledge. She rushed to the side and frantically tried to use Rhunegeld to pry the grappling hook from its catch. Only when the cable swung loose could she angrily toss it down into the smoke.

Milisend looked out into the pale darkness of the predawn sky. For an instant she thought the dawn had come. But the bright light in the corner of her eye was the prison tower. It was engulfed in flame and smoke, as was the entire eastern wing of the palace. Beams collapsed and stones burst.

She watched the prison tower, heartbroken. She wished she had chosen to die with Regaume. Her tears blurred her sight, and she screamed at the darkness over and over again. Her whole body suddenly drained of stamina, ready to collapse with Regaume's tower. She wanted to join her family in the ashes, join her beloved. Rhunegeld slid from her fingers to the stone.

Milisend stepped up onto the balcony ledge and fixed her eyes on the burning tower.

117

ARTHAN

Eglamour Palace, Toulon Ministry
Midsummer, 3034

Every step Arthan took created stabbing pain where the dark slender figure had struck him in his neck. He put his hand to his neck to support his head.

"She went this way," Serdot said as he guided him. "It was Milisend for sure."

Arthan thought he saw a figure floating in the sky up ahead. When they stepped through the dying flames on the ground he realized she was on the edge of the balcony, looking out. She did not turn to them.

"You're certain it's not another assassin?" Arthan asked.

Serdot nodded. "Just like when I saw her in Reimvick's quarters."

Arthan approached cautiously and lowered Adrithayn's scarlet and orange blade. "Princess Milisend?" He took another step. "Come down from there. We are not enemies."

She said nothing. She did not move. Arthan looked beyond her at the burning prison tower. He remembered her plea for Regaume. Could he suggest that Regaume escaped, or that the Ralmogard magistrate took him in time? Would mentioning Erech's intention for them to wed bring her down? Nothing seemed appropriate.

"Please . . ." he said, but before he could say more she moved.

Milisend stretched out her arms, her palms down and fingers pointed, like wings. Her head tilted back.

"Princess! Please, come—"

She dove off the balcony in perfect form, soundless and graceful. Arthan rushed to the side. There was nothing to see in the billowing gray and black. And nothing to be said. His eyes welled, and his heart sank. For her, the king and queen, their other daughters. Everyone. And his failures.

Arthan pressed his eyes closed for a time, willing his pains and troubles to the back of his mind. He felt warmth on his brow and opened his eyes to see the sun peeking above the horizon.

"It is a new day," Serdot whispered shakily as they watched the sun's ascent. "There will be much to do."

Arthan took a deep breath and nodded. Then he picked up Rhunegeld.

118

ARTHAN

Eglamour Palace, Toulon Ministry
Midsummer, 3034

"I don't believe it," Arthan whispered to Serdot. "Brugarn must have gone mad from his wounds."

"Desperate and afraid, I think," Serdot said.

They watched as guards walked the duke into the grand hall and seated him on Erech's throne. Half his face was red with burns and boils. Most of his body was wrapped in linen gauze and padding. His attendants had thrown a soot-stained robe on him in a vain attempt to hide his injuries.

Brugarn sat uncomfortably on the throne, hunched and holding his side. His breathing was labored and hoarse. But his eyes swelled with anger, shifting among the faces of the courtiers. Arthan was surprised that so many had answered the duke's summons to court. Parts of the palace still smoldered. About half was reduced to ruins, including both of the high towers.

Steward Waldemar and General Chaultion took their places beside the throne, with Sir Hamelin nearby. Tronchet, his neck and head bandaged, was also at hand and leaning on a walking staff.

"Where is he?" Brugarn muttered to no one in particular.

"My lord?" Waldemar asked.

"The Lord Minister of Delavon . . . My marshal."

"Your marshal?" Chaultion asked, leaning in to speak more. But Brugarn waved him away.

Waldemar looked warily at Arthan, but Arthan stepped forward before the steward had to ask.

"I am here," he said.

Brugarn's tense face relaxed and his eyes were more at ease. But his eye contact drifted and it was apparent to Arthan that he could not see well.

"Let it be known," Brugarn said, "that Lord Valient chased the assassins away with . . . unorthodox methods." Brugarn glanced toward Adrithayn sheathed on Arthan's belt. "But successful nonetheless."

Arthan bowed low. "I'm unworthy of this praise. The king is dead . . ."

"But I live," Brugarn said, raising a shaky hand to dismiss his words. "Erech's death could be foreseen. What could the Crownblades do against such evil?" Brugarn cut his eyes toward Hamelin. "Though the assassins were so few . . . Alas, Erech has three brothers. I've summoned Asteroth and Erath for a council . . . to confirm me as king, with consultation with the church, of course . . ."

Brugarn hunched to cough, and Chaultion handed him another handkerchief. When he sat back up blood was already seeping from the fresh bandages around his torso.

"As I was saying," the duke continued, "despite this calamity, we are not without a worthy head to be crowned. This was the second time you saved me from those killers. Tell me about our enemy."

"They seem to be an ancient order of assassins," Arthan said. "We believe there are at least five of them."

"And a sixth, clad in all black," Hamelin said.

Brugarn glared at him. "Keep your silence. Do not interrupt the marshal again."

Arthan knew Hamelin was referring to Milisend, but only he and Serdot knew it had been her. After watching her jump from the tower, Arthan and Serdot had agreed to keep her activities and her suicide a secret, to honor her memory, since everyone believed she had perished with her sisters.

"Perhaps Sir Hamelin is correct," Arthan said. "They moved so quickly and often in the shadows."

"And their unique armor and weapons," Brugarn said. "What evil magic has visited us from the Depths of Memelos?"

"We don't believe them to have wielded magic, my lord. It was alchemy and other shunned arts."

"Alchemy . . ." Brugarn spat the word out like rotten food. "Alchemy was supposed to have been the obsolete puttering of old men who spend more time dabbling in evil and not enough time at the cathedral."

"We don't know how they turned this ancient art into a weapon against the monarchy," Arthan said.

"Where did they come from, Heingartmer?" Brugarn asked. "Or one of the southern wards of foul Rugenhav?"

Arthan braced himself for the answer he knew he had to give. "We don't think the Rugens were behind this, my lord. We think—"

"Rubbish! Complete rub—" Brugarn shouted himself into another coughing fit. "I'm . . . I'm quite sure Ambassador Vesamune would agree with you. Unfortunately for her, she is sweating out there on the headman's chopping block, alongside Reimvick."

Arthan had seen her when he had escorted Reimvick to the palace square from Clonmel, and had been surprised that Brugarn had ordered her arrest.

"Reimvick admitted that the Rugens were not involved," Arthan said. "We believe Reimvick's younger brother, Arasemis, is behind all of this. He resides at the family's ancestral estate at Thorendor Castle, outside Bredahade."

"Then the Reimvicks must be in league with the Rugens!" Brugarn shouted. "What other cause would lord ministers have to turn against the Avaleaus?"

Arthan shook his head. "Their reasons are still hidden from us."

"I'll tell you what it is: the overthrow of my house and kingdom," Brugarn said. "As the only royal still alive in Eglamour, I hereby appoint Arthan to be Lord Protector of the Realm. He shall have his duties as marshal, Tronchet's duties as chief magistrate, and Hamelin's duties as commander of the Crownblades—what is left of them." Brugarn bent to cough again.

"My lord," Waldemar began, but Brugarn threw his handkerchief at him.

"For permitting the death of the king and his line," Brugarn said, glaring at Hamelin, "you are hereby banished from Toulon Ministry. Leave your sword and be gone by sunrise tomorrow."

Hamelin clenched his jaw but forced himself to bow.

"My lord, Sir Hamelin fought bravely at my side," Arthan said. "Let me keep him under my command."

"I have spoken. And as for you, Tronchet, you are hereby stripped of your authorities as a lawkeeper. Henceforth you shall be called law-failing and a villain. Live in what hole you like, but do not show your face to me again lest you want a noose around it."

Tronchet did his best to bow. Arthan opened his mouth in the magistrate's defense but closed it again, knowing there was nothing he could say to convince Brugarn. He watched as soldiers escorted Hamelin and Tronchet out of the chamber, their heads hung in disgrace.

As Brugarn coughed, Arthan wondered what his role as lord protector would entail. It was clear to him that Brugarn was intent on gaining his protection and probably his wealth. He knew what Serdot would say, that Brugarn would bring Arthan close to him but that the duke would betray Arthan after he won the crown.

"As for the Wallevet Ministry," Brugarn continued, "Arthan, you will also rule it until a new lord minister is chosen. My decision is natural, given Wallevet's proximity to Delavon." Arthan bowed again, hardly believing his ears. "Your first task as Protector is to use your army against Thorendor. Then I want that hermit's castle leveled and everyone in it put to the sword. I want every stone of its foundation pulled up from the ground. When Thorendor no longer exists, prepare Wallevet for war with the Rugens."

Arthan supposed it was only the beginning of Brugarn's special requests, or perhaps the end. Brugarn doubled over, coughing up blood. The red seeping through his bandages had grown larger. Chaultion tried to whisper something in the duke's ear but was waved away.

"It is time . . . to witness . . ." Brugarn said when he had recovered. "The due payment for those . . . who plot against us . . ."

A group of soldiers helped Brugarn from the throne and slowly ushered him toward the royal balcony. Arthan and the others followed. Brugarn took his seat overlooking the large square. He held up a shaky hand to greet the crowd that had gathered, as if he were already king. The reaction from the people was muted but curious.

Arthan looked out and saw a platform where the executioner and his attendants had prepared the spectacle. Reimvick and Vesamune were standing there, shackled. The executioner looked to Brugarn's balcony and was given the nod to proceed. He wasted no time in fetching Reimvick first.

A lower magistrate read from a parchment as Reimvick was made to kneel in front of the block. "And so, for serving as an agent of the enemy during war, and for your role in the conspiracy to kill King Erech and destroy his house, for the killing of five lord ministers, for the killing of His Majesty's soldiers and personal guards, and the killing of many commoners besides, for all of which he has confessed, Lord Edmond Reimvick of Wallevet is hereby sentenced to death by beheading. Does the guilty wish to speak his last words before the people and God as witnesses?"

Reimvick cleared his throat. "My only regret is that the House of Avaleau still looks down from the palace, ever hungry to spill more blood. Not only mine, but yours, in time. Revolt! Change is afoot! Take up arms and the guidance of the ancients! Candlestone lives! Candlestone li—"

The headsman jerked his chains, pulling Reimvick's neck to the block. Reimvick tried to keep speaking but they handled him roughly. Arthan held his breath, touched by memories of all the times he had seen Maillard confer or laugh with Reimvick. But he shuddered at the cold-blooded duplicity, and how close the assassins had come to killing him. They had robbed him of his father and brother, and Reimvick was steadfastly unrepentant. He knew Maillard would approve of this end for Reimvick after his bitter betrayal, but it was still difficult to stomach.

The executioner swung the sword. The death tremors shook Reimvick's body as his head fell into a basket. The attendants were already pulling Vesamune to the second block. Brugarn chuckled softly.

"And so," began the magistrate, "for conspiring against our king and kingdom, and for the murders and destruction described, Vesamune Theudamer is sentenced to death by beheading. Does the guilty wish to—"

"Silence!" Vesamune shouted, her head held high. She looked at the crowd. "On the honor of my emperor, I swear this: we had no role in your pathetic politics. Alas, you have no king, nor men worthy to inherit the crown of the Donovards. My emperor will take your kingdom and avenge my wrongful death. Mark these words well: Donovan will never stand again!"

Arthan watched as she willingly laid her neck on the block. He knew she represented a dangerous enemy, but Serdot had been right about the Rugens and Candlestone. It was an injustice, one utterly unknown to the crowd and ignored by Brugarn. Arthan's thoughts were broken by Brugarn jolting up from his chair to lean over the balcony. The executioner paused at the sound of his strangled voice.

"Damn you and all Rugen filth!" the duke shouted, unable to avoid answering her speech. "The Rugens will never—" The duke coughed violently, his body struck with tremors. He tried again but only gurgles came out of him. Blood rolled freely from his bandages and his mouth. Arthan watched as the soldiers edged his chair toward him, but his legs fell from under him, and the soldiers laid him on the floor of the balcony. His physician came to him, and Waldemar cradled his head. Chaultion held his hand.

"Kill . . ." Brugarn muttered, "kill her, the Rugens . . . Kill them all . . ."

"We shall, my lord," Chaultion said.

Arthan crouched before Brugarn. The duke gasped for breath as his eyes fixed on Arthan. He reached out and tried to speak. Arthan could not bring himself to catch his hand. The duke's eyes drilled into Arthan before rolling back into his head.

Arthan stood, looking down at Brugarn's body. Chaultion quickly stood as well.

"Under these circumstances," the general said, "without a king in a time of war, tradition holds that—"

"That you stand aside and take the guidance of the lord ministers," Arthan said. Chaultion fumed, but Arthan turned toward the crowd that watched silently below. "As Lord Protector, I will preside in the palace and be the custodian of Rhunegeld until a regent is chosen or until Asteroth or Erath come to claim the crown."

Chaultion took a step toward Arthan "You cannot ma—"

Waldemar blocked him and hissed. "Let him speak!"

"As Lord Protector, I order the postponement of Ambassador Vesamune's execution," he continued. "She is the niece of the Rugen Emperor, and therefore a hostage in wartime and under my direct authority. Return her to the prison at once!"

The soldiers hesitated but obeyed. The crowd began to protest his intervention, and he heard shouts about assassins.

"We have nothing to gain by her death," he continued. "Our investigations show a mysterious group of assassins is behind the king's death. But make no mistake, it is the Rugens who threaten to overrun our kingdom. We will deal with the assassins, but we must not confuse them with vast armies marching to Eglamour. Take heart and prepare for the return of Lords Asteroth and Erath."

Arthan turned to Waldemar. "Lord Steward, please recall Sir Hamelin and Sir Tronchet and inform them that they are pardoned. I hereby annul Hamelin's banishment and restore his position, until the future king decides his fate. As for Tronchet, he shall remain my deputy and Chief Magistrate of Eglamour. Tell him to make sure Vesamune is well protected in a different, more comfortable cell befitting of her rank."

"You cannot make yourself king," Chaultion said. "Who are you but a young, untested whelp from a broken house?"

Arthan stepped close to Chaultion, close enough to see his white mustache twitch with discomfort, and lowered his voice. "If you are so certain of your statements, then I shall accept the forfeiture of your generalship, if you wish. I'm quite certain we can find another general willing to lead us out of a war you too easily welcomed."

Chaultion gave him a dark look but calmed himself. "I look forward to hearing from Lord Asteroth and Lord Erath."

"As do I," Arthan said.

The confrontation was interrupted by the hurried arrival of Sir Debanor, the knight captain of the Marshal of Inquiry's knights. "Lord Valient, my apologies, but I have an urgent message." Debanor glanced at Serdot as well. "The historian is waiting at Clonmel."

"Danleri," Arthan whispered to himself. The man he hoped held the keys to his many questions. "Thank you, Debanor. Tell him I am on my way. And tell Livonier to send a messenger to General Medoff. Have him prepare an army to march on Thorendor. I will meet him in Bredahade as soon as I'm able."

Arthan noticed that Chaultion had stomped away as he was speaking with Debanor. Waldemar came up to Arthan.

"I see Maillard in you now," the steward said. "Do not rush off to Wallevet too soon, and do not spend too much time at Clonmel. You will be needed here in the palace constantly until Asteroth or Erath arrive. Given that they are fighting to hold the Rugens back, that time may be long in coming."

"I must attend to some business at Clonmel. I leave the palace in your hands until I return."

"Know that I will consult with the Patriarch at once," Waldemar continued. "He will want to see you."

"Me? The Patriarch?"

"In the absence of Erech's brothers, there is no greater voice in the choice of a regent than the Patriarch of the Messengian Church. It is my hope that the Patriarch will choose you as regent."

"It is my hope that Asteroth or Erath arrive in Eglamour to claim the crown first," Arthan said, unsure why. He dreaded one of the violent twins taking the throne, but it was the proper thing to say.

Waldemar smiled. "True enough, no one hopes for such a heavy burden in these times. But you *are* Maillard's son."

119

MARLAN

Borel District of Eglamour, Toulon Ministry
Midsummer, 3034

"There must be a good explanation," Marlan said, pressing a bandage into his wounded brow.

"There is," Fetzer said, "but you won't accept it. Arasemis abandoned us."

"He was ill, Fetzer. All that coughing. He must have journeyed back to Thorendor early."

"Or perhaps he was captured," Rodel said as he changed Juhl's bandages.

Fetzer shook his head. "There is no sign of a struggle here, and few knew about this safe house, yet the forge armor is gone. Probably because Arasemis took it with him. Everything else is as we left it. If he was so ill, he wouldn't have traveled on the road. He faked illness, abandoned us, then left us for dead."

"But the food and supplies are still here," Marlan said. "Clearly Arasemis expected us to return."

"Then why didn't he leave a message with the blind well watcher?"

"If we could find Nidlade we could ask him," Marlan said.

Fetzer paced around a bit more. "I think we've waited long enough. Arasemis is not coming back. We risk being discovered if we stay here."

"We're not traveling until Juhl is able," Rodel said.

"She let that black-leathered woman get her. And she shouldn't have let her wound fester. We should go."

524

Rodel stood, squaring himself with Fetzer. "She put the task before herself, as you've so often said we should . . . as if you were our master."

"I've mastered more than you ever will, except for being a shifty Rugen. Tell me, Rodel, why did you not come out to the tower balcony? Were you afraid of heights, or just the Donovards?"

"I slowed them down enough for you to escape. Then I went back for Juhl."

"You let that woman get past you," Fetzer said. "You saw her, Marlan. How could she have so easily gotten past Rodel and his mechan? She's probably hunting us now."

"Are you afraid of her, Fetzer?" Rodel asked.

"Fetzer, you know that Rodel's bow arms jammed," Marlan said.

"Convenient timing," Fetzer said. "Is she a Rugen, Rodel? An old Wosmok friend you let in on our little task?"

"That's enough," Marlan said, wincing and holding his head.

"The Rugens would want the king dead, too, of course," Fetzer continued. "Invade from the south. Have us do their killing in the capital for them. Pave the way for their conquest of the kingdom . . ."

"The Rugens have nothing to do with Candlestone's work," Marlan said. "You know that."

"The Donovards don't agree. You heard the people talking on the street about Vesamune and her agent, Lord Reimvick."

"Reimvick was Arasemis's brother, our supporter in the palace," Marlan said. "Don't you see? Arasemis let me read some of their letters. Reimvick set up this safe house and arranged our entry into the palace. He supported Garion. He was no Rugen agent. He was one of us."

Fetzer was silent for a moment. "But if Arasemis kept Reimvick from us, what else is he hiding?"

"You're impossible," Rodel said, returning to Juhl's bandages.

"Why are you so angry with Arasemis?" Marlan asked. "Why are you always challenging his reasons? If it weren't for him, the Order of the Candlestone would have died out."

"What's it good for anyway, besides mechans and poison eggs?" Fetzer asked. "We don't need his rules and dusty books. We can overthrow kings ourselves. Why do we have to listen to Arasemis?"

"We work together, Fetzer," Marlan said as Rodel helped him wrap the bandage around his head. "Without unity of action and unity of purpose, we'd be no different than bandits, mercenaries, or political assassins. We are bound by an ancient oath to change the world, one dead king at a time. You used to believe in that."

"Did I?"

"We were not abandoned, Fetzer. They may have abandoned you at Perilune, but Candlestone will not. We swore oaths to each other."

"Make this Rugen prove it," Fetzer said. "Let's make Emperor Theudamer our next target."

"Arasemis will decide our next task," Marlan said. "We'll leave here, not because he abandoned us but because it's no longer safe. We'll seek the master's guidance at Thorendor, but I doubt he'll send us to Heingartmer this soon. The Donovards will be choosing a new king because Asteroth and Erath still live. Arasemis will have a plan."

"You go listen to his plans," Fetzer said. "Take the Rugen and the wounded with you. I'll stay here and make certain the next crowned heads don't last."

"Arasemis has not given you that task," Rodel said.

"I'll not waste more time with books and lectures," Fetzer said. "I'll stay and repair my mechan, then do as I wish. Someone needs to finish off the Avaleaus."

"The lamp armor is not your mechan, Fetzer," Marlan said.

"No? Who will take it from me? Arasemis? You?"

Marlan regarded Fetzer carefully. "You're tired. We all are. We did well, but we need to rest and plan. Your aerina arcana lessons were abbreviated, Fetzer, but self-control is fundamental. You want to stay in these slums? All right. I'll tell Arasemis you were too dedicated to leave. We'll overlook your disloyalty to the master, won't we, Rodel?"

Rodel nodded.

"Regarding the lamp armor," Marlan continued, "keep it if you dare. The master has been patient, but there is a limit. He will reclaim what he believes is rightfully his. You know that he is more capable than all of us combined."

"We'll see," Fetzer said.

"You wouldn't fight Arasemis for a mechan, would you?" Rodel asked.

"Arasemis doesn't have to make that mistake," Fetzer said.

Marlan shook his head and turned to Rodel. "How long before Juhl is well enough to travel?"

"Two days," he said, watching her sleep. "The stiches should hold after two days."

Marlan turned back to Fetzer. "You have two days to change your mind and come with us."

"That's two days you're wasting," he answered.

120

WREDEGAR

Wredegar had watched Vesamune come close to execution from a distance, wearing the local garb of his Ricot persona. He could not hear much of Vesamune's final speech but he was relieved that Lord Valient had spared her, despite leading her away in chains. He knew the Donovards would not release such a valuable bargaining chip.

He had always disliked Vesamune, but he had never wished this fate upon her. He touched his neck frequently now, thinking about Lord Reimvick's head. His would have been in the basket as well if he had not disobeyed her orders to remain at her residence. He knew the Donovards would have arrested him too. They would have suspected who and what he was, and he would not have been as lucky as she was.

He racked his brain as he left the square. It would be impossible to rescue her, so he needed to decide whether to flee or stay to monitor the situation. All his gold was at her residence, but it would be foolish to return there. Even if he had money, traveling southward in hopes of rejoining the Rugens would be dangerous, given that he was well behind enemy lines. All of it was a reminder that he wished to be back with the regular army. A Wosmok unit under his command in the capital would have made his predicament more tolerable, but now he was alone.

He reasoned that he was trapped in Eglamour for now. He was still a servant of the empire and a knight of the House of Auftengardin. He resolved to do whatever he could to make the capture of the capital easier for the Rugens. He would start by returning to the Calza Aria inn of the Borel District to find Cid.

Even if the rebel leader had perished in the recent army sweeps through the slums, he might be able to find others like Lunfrid or the young Arnaut. Anyone whom he could harness in the service of the empire against the Donovards. Perhaps, if he was successful in assisting the Rugen capture of the city, he would be transferred out of the Wosmok Legion and back into the army as a reward.

121

ARTHAN

Clonmel Estate in Eglamour, Toulon Ministry
Midsummer, 3034

"You must be careful with General Chaultion," Serdot said as they walked from the palace to Clonmel. "He still has the loyalty of the army despite what Brugarn did to the soldiers with the Proclamation of Expediency."

"The general meddles in political affairs too much for a man in charge of waging a war," Arthan said.

"He is steeped in war and politics," Serdot said. "Asteroth and Erath both favor the general more than they ever did Brugarn or Erech. Before the war, and especially now, no one has done more to get the twins more reinforcements and supplies than Chaultion."

"So when one of them is crowned king, they'll keep him despite his longtime service as Brugarn's right hand?"

"That is certain," Serdot said. "His power may rival yours, or eclipse it. Everything depends on the whim of the new king. But you have gained great respect among the nobles and the people, my lord. And you have the wealth of Delavon. Asteroth and Erath will try to contain your power while remaining dependent on your support."

"How soon will the remaining lord ministers arrive to consult about a new king?"

"They are all wary, given the assassinations. But Sigbert and Eperude are already on the road. Henrey's brother, the steward of Elmbrel, should be here by next month. Lord Ferin is still fighting with the Calbrians over the channel islands. And Lord Halevane is traveling abroad, in Austveeden, but he will likely come eventually."

"Barely a quorum for the council," Arthan said.

"At least you'll have some time to get things in order here," Serdot said. "I for one am eager to talk with Danleri."

"As am I."

When they arrived at Clonmel, Sir Debanor led them inside. A peculiar-looking gray-haired man was seated near Arthan's table. His robe was a modest honey-and-brown weave, a pattern distinctly foreign. His features looked like a Donovard except for his thick mustache, which reminded Arthan of the Ovelians.

"Lord Valient," Debanor said, "I present to you the ex-rector Danleri."

Arthan extended his hand to the old man. "Welcome, thank you for coming so quickly."

"Of course, my lord. I hope I can be of assistance in these dire times."

"I'm sure you will be," Arthan said, seating himself. "Serdot, please fetch Sir Livonier. And, Debanor, please stay as well. All of my top officers should be present for this discussion."

Arthan noted that Danleri was not surprised at the attention. Arthan looked down at a stack of unopened letters on his table, including ones from Rowan and Meriam. They would have to wait. Livonier soon joined the group.

"You already know why I summoned you here?" Arthan began.

Danleri nodded confidently. "Candlestone."

"What can you tell us about them?"

"I know little about the assassins of today. But I've studied their long history."

"This was your work at Bredahade Academy in Wallevet?"

"More of a personal fascination," Danleri said with a smile. "As a youth, I attended the academy, and Raymond Reimvick was my friend and classmate. I also knew his younger brothers, Edmond and Arasemis, very well. All of this killing has been Arasemis's work, hasn't it?"

"Yes, and Edmond supported him."

Danleri nodded solemnly. "I always worried this could happen . . . I stayed at the academy to teach, as did Arasemis, while Raymond and Edmond joined the court of their lord minister father. Arasemis's academic interests were an embarrassment to his father. But he was gifted not only in his studies, but also with the sword. If not for his becoming an expert in multiple schools of swordcraft, Arasemis's father would never have let him stay at the academy."

"What were these studies?" Arthan asked.

"I'll get to that," Danleri said. "You need to understand how Arasemis's mind evolved in those early days. He was quirky and awkward, and both Raymond and Edmond had nothing but contempt for him. But the Burgbud War changed him."

Serdot nodded. "The conflict between the Reimvicks and the Ganymyds."

"That's right. Before Eperude was appointed lord minister of Lundwynland, that ministry was still in the hands of the Lundwyn folk. Gaerte Ganymyd was their leader and believed he could take old ancestral lands from the Reimvicks. It was a short war, but the cadets and instructors at the academy participated.

"Having seen the slaughtering of whole Lundwyn villages, Arasemis openly spoke ill of his own father. He had always been adverse to authority, but now his attitude sharpened. Before Arasemis returned to the academy, he spent a lot of time with his grandfather, who was also a family pariah, shunted away at Thorendor.

"Once back at the academy, Arasemis twisted what I originally taught him about the ancient history of Pemonia. Gradually he introduced his own version of events to the cadets, including controversial stories about the Pemonian natives and their struggle against the Brintilian colonists. Many troubled years passed for Arasemis, but his status as the son—and later brother—of the lord minister of Wallevet assured his place. Eventually the rector asked Raymond's permission to dismiss Arasemis from the academy. Arasemis then exiled himself to Thorendor."

"I'm guessing that by this time his grandfather was dead?" Arthan asked.

Danleri nodded. "I continued to visit Arasemis at Thorendor after I became rector of the academy. We still had many of the same scholarly interests, and I never gave up hope that he would change. Naive, of course."

"So he planned all of this after his exile to Thorendor?" Arthan asked. "Were you not aware of what he was doing?"

"You could say Arasemis and I were two sides of the same coin. I believed studying the ancient arts of the natives informed us of our past, its lessons to be learned and evils to be avoided. Arasemis believed the ancient Pemonian ways were something to revive, something to be harnessed as a tool against tyranny and injustice. But he twisted it all, you see? His views are disturbed, mangled. He read what he wanted to in those ancient texts, then romanticized and glorified it all."

"Did he reveal his plans to you?" Serdot asked.

"Never. Eventually he no longer welcomed our debates and became hostile. So I went to Raymond. He was aware of Arasemis's fantasies but could not believe anything would come of them as long as Arasemis remained a hermit at Thorendor. I believe this was when Arasemis began recruiting cadets from the academy to train as his assassins."

"So Raymond was glad to have Arasemis holed away at Thorendor," Serdot said.

"Like their father, Raymond was ashamed of Arasemis. He preferred that Arasemis stay in the dark and quiet hills outside Bredahade. Raymond's failure to understand what Arasemis was capable of—and my failure to convey that—led to Raymond being Arasemis's first victim. I'm convinced of that."

"Tell us about the cadets he recruited," Arthan said.

"Looking back, when I was still visiting Arasemis at Thorendor, he was sharpening his knowledge of the arcanae but also experimenting. Even as rector of the academy I was, admittedly, jealous of his discoveries. He built a large alchemy laboratory, he refurbished the telescope atop the castle, and he converted a dining hall into what I later realized was a mechanically equipped training hall.

"Later, when two of our cadets, Garion and Marlan, disappeared from the academy, my gut told me that Arasemis had lured them to Thorendor. Both young men had been his students and were attracted to his controversial views. I knew Arasemis intended to train them, but I never guessed it would be for something like this . . ."

"That's when you left the academy?" Serdot asked.

Danleri nodded. "Knowing trouble was brewing at Thorendor, I convinced myself that I was the only one who could—or would—do something about it. I left the academy to focus on my own research. Barred from the best texts kept at Thorendor, I came to Eglamour to sift through the archives of the royal academy and other places where few can still read the old books."

"I heard from Pelinaud, my old instructor at Rachard who gave me your name, that you went looking for the Forlorn Smithy's disappearing gauntlets. Was that part of your research? And did you find them?"

Danleri shifted in his seat. "That was part of my research, yes. But I prefer not to discuss that matter at this time . . ."

"All right . . . What about Arasemis? Why do you think he killed the royal family?"

"Simply put, he believes the divine right of kings is a method of control created by evil men. Arasemis believes the chieftaincies of ancient natives, such as the Gallerlanders, Rahlampians, and others, are preferable and even holy. And so he has armed himself with their political and war-making methods, melded those with the swordcraft he learned at Bredahade Academy, and warped young minds to believe in a world he intends to create: a rejection of modern ways and a return to ancient Pemonia. Overthrowing kings is the first step."

"Why would you think that?" Arthan asked.

"It's not what I think, it's what I know. I debated him countless times. I just never thought he'd seek to make his ideas reality."

"The ancient heathens were conquered by the Brintilian colonists," Serdot said. "Why would he seek to reverse that?"

"Arasemis believes the arcanae was imbalanced between the Old and New Worlds at the time. The Pemonians experienced a fate that should never have been. He seeks to correct history. To correct the imbalance of arcanae."

"What exactly is the arcanae?" Arthan asked.

"Simply a modern term for the abilities of ancient peoples—Old and New World—that are combined, honed, and mastered. The term was originally used by scholars and followers of specific schools of swordcraft as a method of organizing and teaching students. But Candlestone adopted it as dogma. A philosophy of knowledge and training toward self-perfection for the sole purpose of overthrowing kingdoms and empires."

"The candle alchemy, wall running, and mechanical armor," Arthan said. "All of this is arcanae?"

"Unorthodox, to be sure," Danleri said with a nod. "More conventional are things like swordcraft, metallurgy, and shipbuilding. But combining and advancing these skills in creative ways yields new surprises. Anything unorthodox is now shunned in our society, though this has not always been so." Danleri paused and cocked his head. "I'm surprised you're not more familiar with the arcanae, given the sword on your belt."

Arthan unsheathed the blade and laid it on the table for Danleri to examine. Danleri was startled and looked at it anew. "I thought you weren't surprised by it?" Arthan asked.

"I thought this was an imitation, either gladed or treated. These original alchemical swords were supposedly lost long ago . . ." Danleri traced the symbols in the blade with his finger. "Too worn to read . . ." he muttered.

"There is more than one of these?"

"Eight, in fact, collectively known as glyphblades. Well, there used to be eight. Some were confirmed destroyed when such things fell out of favor and alchemy became a concealed endeavor."

"My father secretly willed this to me," Arthan said. "Can you tell me about it?"

Danleri raised his eyebrows. "Your father owned this? Oh my, that is interesting . . . The glyphblades were made for the eight original petty kings of what later became Donovan. After the strength of the Brintilian Empire faded, its provinces and colonies in Pemonia became independent. At the time, alchemical metallurgy was not shunned. It was valued and controlled by the powerful. These swords became a symbol of the petty kings' unity against their enemies."

"My father wrote in a letter that this one was made for the House of Valient when we ruled Delavon Kingdom."

Danleri nodded. "That confirms unequivocally that it's one of the eight."

"Can you explain how it works? When I sweep the blade through smoke or heat it seems to absorb those elements until I cross swords."

"Yes, that was an attribute of the eight. I'm not a practicing alchemist, but I do know a lot of the theory behind chemina arcana. That's why Arasemis and I initially worked so well together. I knew the books and could speculate about reactions, whereas he would actually experiment. Now, let me see . . ."

Danleri picked up the sword, feeling its weight and balance. He pinched the blade and rubbed it. He gave it a scratch with his nail, then flicked it to hear the ting. He held the blade close to his eyes, then slowly pulled it away. "Aha, I see . . ."

"What?"

"The grooves are worn. On this sword they are called veins, but obviously they still work. You can see them here."

Danleri put the glyphblade back on the table. From his robe pocket he pulled a convex lens and slid it up and down the blade. Arthan leaned in for a look.

"I see them," he said. "They look like ivy, with tiny pinholes."

"Made by forgotten masters," Danleri said. "The absorptive nature of the Eigenark alloy is enhanced with alchemical and metallurgical processing, then folded into the steel. Then a skilled etchingsmith with a steady hand made the veins and reservoir holes, which are coated with serpent varnish. This keeps the absorbed material in the reservoir until a metallic vibration triggers release. A sword is referred to as *charged* when it has absorbed material. In truth, these swords are always charged with common air, but obviously without noticeable effect."

"The king used this one," Serdot said, laying Rhunegeld next to Adrithayn. "We recovered it from his tower. We saw it charged with fire."

Danleri nodded. "I'd always suspected that Rhunegeld was one of the eight, but I knew the Avaleaus would never let me inspect the royal relic. Of course, the Avaleaus have no idea how to use it. They've simply used it as a symbol of their power and lineage without really knowing why. It never left the palace, and rarely left its scabbard. Marvelously preserved," he said, leaning over the blade with his lens.

"I intend to restore it to them, once Asteroth or Erath become king," Arthan said. "Should I tell them of its hidden worth?"

"Arasemis had always hoped to find a glyphblade. If you make Rhunegeld's secret known, Arasemis will probably come for it."

"His assassins know about Adrithayn and are afraid of it."

"That may be," Danleri said, "but I know how his mind works. He has tried to make his own. He's no blacksmith, and I doubt he's been able to make Eigenark alloy, but he seems to have been successful with some metallurgical methods, probably treating or glading—or both. I heard about the one assassin with the flaming sword. But those who wield such weapons pay a price, namely burned hands and accidental fires."

"Surely you've heard of the exotic armor used by the assassins," Arthan said. "The burning man's had glowing veins of fire."

"Yes." Danleri nodded. "I believe Arasemis found—or, less likely, built—wearable contraptions called mechans. They are special armors that were used by Candlestone warriors for centuries. They combine all aspects of aerina, chemina, and machina, which was the great goal of the Candlestone masters—including Arasemis. He must have found them somewhere, but where I could not guess. He had many treasure hunts planned."

"What else is Arasemis looking for?"

Danleri's tone grew dour. "Alchemical swords, shroud eggs, mechans . . . these are only the beginning. Arasemis will not be satisfied, indeed, he'll need other Candlestone relics to keep ahead of his enemies. He will strike to unearth more powerful relics, always reaching for new advantages over the traditional methods of war."

"What relics? What methods?" Debanor asked.

Danleri arched his eyebrows. "Unimaginable things . . ."

"Magic?" Livonier asked.

"Magic is a fairy tale for children," Danleri said. "More powerful and dangerous is the mind of man, twisting and cajoling the nature of the world. Breaking the natural boundaries in which we are meant to be set . . ."

"Wall running?" Arthan asked.

"Similar. That breaks the bounds on us that keep our feet on the earth. But think bigger. Imagine ships of the air. Stones that move themselves. Metals that transform the air into a flash of searching starlight."

"Do such things exist?" Serdot asked.

"I do not know, but old texts speak of them . . . These are things that people will readily say are impossible or magical, because the truth behind these methods is meant to be hidden to them. Arasemis will try to find these relics and use them to overthrow kingdoms. This war with the Rugens will buy him the time and opportunity that he needs."

"I will stop him," Arthan said.

Danleri could not stifle a small chuckle. "I once thought as you do, that I would be Arasemis's foil, the other side of his coin. But he has surpassed me, by far. He went from books to action. I remain in my books . . ."

"Not anymore," Arthan said. "You are now conscripted into the Office of the Marshal of Inquiry. Serdot will help you arrange for any and all books at the royal academy and other archives to be brought here to Clonmel. You will build a library, laboratory, and anything else you require. Hire whomever you need. All my resources are at your disposal."

Danleri blinked. "I am but one man, my lord, an old man."

"We will revive the arcanae for an army of Donovards. Arasemis will not be ahead for long. In fact, we should hunt for the relics ourselves."

"Arasemis has decades of research behind him and the best books," Danleri said. "And our modern society will reject your efforts as bowing to an ancient evil. It may be too late . . ."

"Then we shall do our best. Alchemy and the rest of it will no longer be shunned. As Lord Protector, I will convince Asteroth and Erath of this necessity, for the survival of our kingdom."

Danleri stood from his chair, his tone most serious. "You do not realize the danger you would release upon the world, and neither does Arasemis. He would use the arcanae to set up new dominions modeled on the ancient Pemonian natives he idolizes. He blinded himself to the reasons many of these methods were buried in the first place.

"Furthermore, you would soon adopt his methods to stop him. But regardless of who wins, the rapid evolution of the arcanae will be uncontainable. Your new army will make the arcanae widespread and accepted. Ever more novel ways of inflicting death and suffering on more people than ever before will follow."

Arthan leaned back in his chair. He understood Danleri's concern despite not understanding everything the old man was saying. "Then we will proceed with utmost caution. What else can be done otherwise?"

Danleri was clearly embarrassed and returned to his chair. "My apologies, my lord. You summoned me for assistance and answers, not a speech about how impossible this all is. The truth is that I don't know what the alternative should be. If I could travel back in time to those early years, I know exactly what I would do. But that opportunity has passed . . ."

"So Arasemis has opened a door that cannot be shut," Serdot said.

"I believe what you're telling me," Arthan told Danleri, "but I cannot hope to understand it all the way you do. Which is reason enough for you to join us. Perhaps there is still time to stop Arasemis and close the door."

"Unlikely."

"What can we do?"

"The arcanae should remain shunned," Danleri said. "Alchemical swords must not be put into the hands of every knight. All of your agents must not be taught to run walls. Any relics we find—if we find them—must remain secret.

We should find them only to deny them to Arasemis, not to use them ourselves. In fact we should destroy them."

Arthan nodded. "We will use only what is necessary and destroy the rest, and nothing will be shared outside this circle of officers without my consent." Arthan looked in turn at Serdot, Livonier, and Debanor. "Understood?"

All nodded in agreement.

"Well, ex-rector," Arthan said, "will you help us hunt down Candlestone and destroy them once and for all?"

Danleri sat silent for a moment. "Atonement for what I should have done long ago. What choice do I have?"

"What choice do any of us have?" Arthan said. "Destiny has put this burden on us, and we must rise to meet it."

A soldier burst into the room. "Apologies, my lord. Urgent message from Rowan. The messenger reports that Asteroth's armies are overrun by the Rugens."

Arthan jumped from his chair and snapped open the letter, wishing he had taken time to read the earlier note from Rowan waiting on his table.

> Brother,
> Our fallback position at Ambardil is lost. Asteroth
> intends for us to break out of the siege. We are
> sending our last messenger. I will do my duty.
>
> > Rowan

Arthan rushed to his table and reached for the earlier letter, cursing himself. "Rowan says they're being pushed from Ambardil, which means they lost Asteroth's capital," he said as he ripped open the earlier letter. He read it aloud.

> Brother,
> The city of Cantrileme fell quickly to the Rugens.
> Lord Asteroth's soldiers say the Rugen emperor is
> leading his army. We evacuated to Ambardil Free
> City, where we are working to prepare the
> defenses. But the people here hate Asteroth for
> what he did this past spring.
> Asteroth is angry that Duke Brugarn has not
> sent more reinforcements. The troops that did

arrive in Alpenon from Toulon were ambushed by the Durgensdil rebels, their supplies stolen. Please convey our urgent need to Brugarn.

Asteroth is determined not to flee to Gadolin or Toulon but to make his stand for Alpenon. Lord Erath's army is already preoccupied with the Rugens in Gadolin. Asteroth also says he will not retreat north because he's confident Brugarn will lead an army south, guided by General Chaultion.

If you know of such plans, please hasten them and send word. Asteroth hasn't received a letter from Brugarn or Chaultion for some time. Perhaps the rebels are gradually picking away at our messengers' routes.

As I finish writing, the Rugen army has been spotted on the horizon. If the worst should come, I will give my life in defense of the kingdom, as Father would have expected and as Asteroth demands. Do not grieve for me, but know my efforts served a greater purpose. If I die, I know you will serve well as the last of our line.

Please forgive me for resenting your accomplishments and disobeying your letter for me to return to Rachard.

Rowan Valient
Ambardil

"My God, if Lord Asteroth falls, the underbelly of Toulon is open for attack," Livonier said. "Eglamour will be next."

"Go and inform Chaultion at once," Arthan said. "And send word to Medoff: our plans to attack Thorendor will have to wait."

"Must we delay Thorendor?" Danleri asked. "Arasemis is counting on us being distracted."

"We have no choice," Arthan said. "Arasemis can kill us one by one, but the Rugens will take our kingdom sooner than he will overturn it. Go, Livonier!"

"Asteroth cannot defeat Emperor Theudamer," Serdot said. "Even if Erath could come to his aid from Gadolin, they are both outmatched."

"Asteroth and Erath were supposed to be the militarily competent ones," Arthan said, exasperated.

"They've long spent their gold on feasts and festivals," Serdot said. "They can't blame the state of their army on Brugarn alone."

"Will Chaultion turn the tide?" Arthan asked.

"He must," Serdot said.

"Arcanae could turn them back," Debanor said.

Arthan glanced at Danleri before answering. "We've just agreed not to revive the arcanae on a grand scale to defeat Candlestone. Neither will we revive it to defeat the Rugens. They use traditional methods, as we do. We simply must outwit and outfight them."

Another soldier rushed into the room. "My lord, you are summoned to the palace by Steward Waldemar. The Patriarch awaits."

Arthan turned to Serdot. "Is this the life of a Lord Protector, to be pulled in so many directions at once?"

"Yes, my lord. But you were born for it."

122

ROWAN

Ambardil Free City, Alpenon Ministry
Midsummer, 3034

Rowan looked up from the hoof-beaten grass at the Rugen soldiers standing above him. Behind them were the crumbling outer walls of the once beautiful Ambardil. The strong, regal stone walls and battlements were smoldering and broken. The central castle that had long been Lord Asteroth's home now had a Rugen flag raised above it. It had been Rowan's home as well.

He sighed with a heavy heart. Death was all around, poised to strike him at any moment. Lord Asteroth's body was not far away, and his best knights littered the ground. The final charge had broken through the Rugen siegeworks that ringed the city, but the Donovards were simply too few. Rowan glanced at the other survivors, lowborn knights and a few of Asteroth's nobles. Rowan could see the shame of defeat and the guilt of survival in their eyes—and the dishonor of losing their lord.

Rowan felt it too. But with Asteroth suddenly gone, he no longer felt any attachment to Alpenon. It was a land long torn by rebellion in the western mountains and coasts, and the rest of it was now conquered by the Rugens. He yearned for Delavon, and part of him wished he'd left sooner. The excitement and adventure of Alpenon had faded, and the brutal reality of war had set in.

"Our fates are sealed now," came a scraggly voice nearby. Rowan turned to see Mierbiot, one of Asteroth's barons. "If the lord minister had lived, they might have ransomed us," he continued, "but not now."

"What are they waiting for, then?" Rowan whispered. Mierbiot simply shook his head. Rowan liked the baron. He had been one of Asteroth's few decent men.

A group of riders approached. As soon as Rowan caught a glimpse of them he knew Emperor Theudamer was among them. It had been said that the emperor was a giant, and Rowan could see that he towered above everyone else. The grotesque skystone crown he wore on his head was unmistakable. It was said to be ancient, fashioned by the Raffen heathen ancestors of the Rugens. It was also said to make him a demigod of war.

Theudamer and his party rode up near the prisoners. At the emperor's side was Warden Graf, whom Rowan had seen kill Asteroth during the final charge. Two women were also with Theudamer. He was surprised to recognize one of them, Etzel, whom he had spent many hours talking with.

Etzel whispered with Graf. She looked haggard, worse than when he'd seen her last. Her hair was burned away and her scalp red. Her eyes were dark and sunken, her hastily bandaged arms hiding some cruelty. He realized that Asteroth's jailors had tried everything to get her to talk. He was glad to see her alive and free, but uncertain of what it would mean for him.

The emperor and his party eyed Rowan and the others and spoke among themselves in Rugen. Graf said something to Etzel, and her eyes searched the prisoners' muddied, bloodied faces. Rowan tried to hide his face from her. When he peeked to see if her searching eyes had passed, he found her staring at him. Then she pointed.

Theudamer and the others watched as Graf ordered the soldiers to pull Rowan up from the grass. Fear gripped him but he tried to keep calm. He glanced at Mierbiot and the other survivors, who watched as if he were walking to his execution.

"You are of the House of Valient?" Graf asked in accented Donovar.

Rowan nodded. His pride in his family improved his courage. He glanced warily at Etzel, but her stare was empty.

Graf looked down from his horse. "Your brother is the right hand of King Erech?" Rowan nodded again. "Then you will come with us. Pick someone to come with you."

Rowan hesitated, then slowly turned to the survivors. A frail hope lit in their eyes as they stared at Rowan. He suddenly felt sick in his gut, much worse than when he was sitting in the grass with them. He avoided their eyes.

"Quickly!" Etzel shouted.

Rowan looked at Mierbiot, who raised his eyebrows. Rowan nodded and Mierbiot slowly came to his feet. Rowan forced himself to look at the others, hoping they could forgive him.

"We're either the lucky ones or the first to die," the baron whispered as he stood beside Rowan.

Rugen soldiers escorted the pair behind the emperor and his party. Rowan was able to steal another look at the other woman. She looked similar to Vesamune, but younger. He looked at Etzel again, searching for any hint of their fate, but her eyes did not meet his. Rowan and Mierbiot were marched to a small collection of tents near the emperor's pavilion. Only Etzel dismounted to join the two prisoners into the tent, with guards posted outside.

Rowan entered first. He saw a quill, inkpot, and stack of parchment on a little table. "I'm sorry for what they did to you," he said as he took a chair.

Etzel's dark eyes flared. "Not sorry enough to prevent them from wrenching information from me . . ."

"You did not provide anything to Asteroth that gave him victory," Rowan said. "And I am sorry that I couldn't help you. You heard me ask Asteroth to let me talk with you more, instead of his jailors."

"What difference did it make?"

"None, I suppose. Despite being Asteroth's ward, I'm still a Valient. We respect our enemies."

Etzel nodded. "Then perhaps your brother will respect our demands, especially as they'll be written by your own hand." She gestured to the blank parchment on the table.

Rowan and Mierbiot glanced at each other.

"You will inform Lord Valient that you are our hostage," Etzel continued. "Along with the others. Your brother must convince the king to surrender the kingdom, or forfeit your lives. Additionally, we'll not spare him when we take Eglamour. Mierbiot will carry your letter with a contingent of our fastest scouts, to witness your situation to your brother."

"And if I refuse?"

Etzel touched a shiny new dagger in her belt. "Mierbiot will die slow in this tent. Then you, if you're still unconvinced. And, as I said, your brother will not be spared when we do march on Eglamour."

Rowan looked at Mierbiot.

"Don't let them scare you, Rowan," the baron said. "I'll give this dungeon rat a fair fight, and so will you. Keep your honor and spare your brother the decision he will have to make."

Etzel drew her dagger and pointed it at Mierbiot. "This is my preference as well," she whispered.

Rowan held up his hands to stay the rage in her eyes. "Etzel . . . I will write the letter to save the lives of my companions. But Arthan will not give in to your demands."

Graf entered the tent as Mierbiot began to protest. The warden looked at Etzel and her extended dagger, then spoke in Donovar. "I thought this would be finished by now. Does he need additional convincing?"

"I'll write to my brother," Rowan repeated. "But neither he nor the king will yield to your unreasonable demands. You've all but taken the whole of Alpenon. But attempting Toulon will be the end of your adventure."

Graf swiftly pulled out the sword strapped across his back and in one great motion crushed the table with a single blow. Rowan and the others shielded their eyes from the wood shards and splashing ink.

"Next will be your companion's head," Graf said. "Pick up the quill."

Rowan reached a shaky hand, pinching the quill from the middle of the wreck. He grabbed a parchment and knelt beside his chair, placing the parchment on it. "What . . . what shall I write?"

"You already know what should be written," Graf said. The warden turned to Etzel. "When it's finished, bring

Mierbiot. Then you can have rest before beginning your new assignment with Wredegar."

Graf left the tent. Etzel stared at Rowan. He glanced at Mierbiot.

"You don't have to," the baron said.

Rowan looked into Etzel's dark eyes before turning to the parchment. "I must."

> Brother,
> I am compelled under Rugen swords to relay their demands to you. Ambardil has fallen, and Alpenon with it. Lord Asteroth is dead. A few of his vassals survived. The Rugen emperor demands Donovan's surrender. If King Erech cannot be persuaded, I and the others will perish, and the Rugens will march on Eglamour. They say they'll not spare you either.
>
> I hope that better fortune has befallen you in the capital. Know that I fought well and, until this letter, kept my honor and

Etzel snatched the parchment from Rowan. The quill scraped a black slash across the page.

"Shall I sign it?" Rowan asked.

"Give your wist ring to Mierbiot."

He took off his ring and handed it to him.

"I am sorry to be the one to do this, my boy," Mierbiot said. "I will tell Lord Valient of your courage."

Etzel prodded Mierbiot toward the tent exit.

"Ride hard . . ." Rowan said.

123

ARTHAN

Eglamour Palace, Toulon Ministry
Midsummer, 3034

Arthan found Waldemar, Chaultion, Hamelin, and Patriarch Bavernon waiting for him in the great hall. The throne was empty, save for a symbolic black silk draped across it. Arthan was flanked by Serdot and Livonier.

"Your holiness," Waldemar began, "may I present Lord Arthan Valient of Delavon and Wallevet, Lord Protector of the Realm and Marshal of Inquiry."

Arthan bowed and kissed the wist ring of the Patriarch. "Your holiness, it is my honor . . ." Then he stepped back and looked upon the ancient face of Bavernon.

Heavy wrinkles creased with worry on his hairless brow, and his eyes were foggy. Arthan had met him only once, as a boy, and this was how he remembered him. The man seemed perpetually old yet undying. And yet he still functioned as the Patriarch of the Messengian Church of Donovan, the personal representative of the Martinus himself.

"That so many burdensome titles have been thrust upon your shoulders is a sign of these dire times," Bavernon said slowly.

Arthan was uncertain how to respond so he kept silent. He noticed Chaultion's white mustache twitch.

"And a sign of the stamina of the Valients," Waldemar added.

"So many have fallen," Bavernon said. "We wanted to discuss with you the potential for—"

"My lords!"

Everyone turned toward the opening great doors of the hall. Sir Debanor ran across the empty hall toward them, an opened message in his hand.

"I apologize, your holiness," Waldemar said to the Patriarch. "I told the guards this was to be a private meeting."

"Forgive me, my lords. And forgive me, Lord Valient, for opening it. I had to know if I needed to interrupt, given the letter you had just received from Rowan. This one must have been written on the same day."

Arthan took the letter and read. "I'm sorry. It seems . . ." Arthan tore his eyes from the letter and looked at them. "Ambardil has fallen. My brother has been taken captive by the Rugens, and . . . Lord Asteroth is dead."

"God in Heaven . . ." murmured Waldemar.

"May God rest him," Bavernon said, "Now Lord Erath is the last of his house."

"Damn the Rugens," Chaultion said.

"The letter was delivered by a low vassal of Asteroth, Baron Mierbiot," Debanor continued. "He relays his regrets for your brother, whom he knows well."

"I will speak with Mierbiot later," Arthan said. "Thank you. You are dismissed."

Debanor departed, and the group stood in silence for a moment.

"This changes things," Bavernon said. "We cannot wait for the Lord Ministers' Council to convene. Lord Erath must be escorted to Eglamour at once to take his crown."

"I will fetch him," Chaultion said.

"Then who will lead the defense of Toulon?" Waldemar said. "There is nothing to stop the Rugens from pressing north now."

"Send me," Arthan said. "The general is the most capable in preparing Toulon."

"I oppose that idea," Bavernon said. "Chaultion should escort Erath."

"The general is responsible for Toulon," Waldemar said.

The patriarch shook his head. "Erath is the last of the Avaleaus, and the Rugens are pressing him as well. We cannot risk sending Arthan. If we lost Erath and Arthan . . . Well, we've already discussed it."

"Discussed what?" Chaultion said.

"The Church will support Arthan as regent if Erath is killed," Bavernon said.

Chaultion's face twisted in disgust. "Him?"

"Me, your holiness? What have I—?"

"Tentatively," Bavernon said, holding up a gnarled hand. "As Maillard's son, Erech's marshal, and Brugarn's Lord Protector, you are already like a steward of Donovan. The Church will support you as regent until the Lord Ministers' Council can convene. That is, if Erath is lost."

"That is not what Duke Brugarn intended," Chaultion said.

"Brugarn was not the king," Waldemar said, turning to Arthan. "If you go to Erath, you'll be placing yourself in great danger. We cannot afford to lose you and Erath while the Rugens are on our doorstep."

"And with the assassins still at large," Serdot added.

"I insist," Arthan said. "As Lord Protector, it is my responsibility. I have my knights, led by Sir Livonier here, and I will take Sir Hamelin and his Crownblades to Erath. I will bring our new king back to Eglamour." Arthan turned to Chaultion. "I'm confident the general will better prepare Toulon than I would. Upon my return, we'll all join together to push the Rugens out."

Waldemar and the Patriarch exchanged looks. Bavernon gave a reluctant little nod. Waldemar looked at Chaultion. "General?"

"May God protect his journey," Chaultion said.

Arthan knew the general was happy to be rid of him for a while, perhaps pleased with the prospect of he and Erath dying. There would be no serious obstacles to seizing the crown himself, should he wish it. But Arthan wagered that as long as Erath was alive, Chaultion would not crown himself. He also knew this task was for him.

"Very well, Lord Valient," Waldemar said. "But if while on the road you receive word of Erath's death, return at once."

"I will bring Erath back," Arthan said, then turned to Hamelin, Livonier, and Serdot. "Prepare the knights at once."

124

FETZER

Borel District of Eglamour, Toulon Ministry
Midsummer, 3034

etzer dipped the quill hastily, dappling ink on the page. He needed to finish this part because he was determined to move forward with his plan.

The rioters were foolish to have tried to face the army in the capital, even in Borel. Not only did they not get beyond the district, they invited the army to crush them. They've learned nothing from Mordmerg. The Blackhoods in particular should have known better.

Since Marlan and the others departed for Thorendor, I've wandered Borel and much of the capital, learning its rhythms and watching the rioters. I keep this journal at the safe house, which I doubt will be discovered by the authorities. They are too preoccupied with the downfall of the Avaleaus. But I cannot sit idle, as a great opportunity has arrived. I met a rebel captain named Cid who agreed to introduce me to a Blackhood leader named Lunfrid.

People say that Duke Brugarn succumbed to his wounds and that Arthan is Lord Protector. I can't help but wonder where the rulers of the kingdom would be if we had killed Arthan back when we had the chance. I want to convince

Lunfrid and his Blackhoods to attack Arthan's estate at Clonmel. With his guards busy, I could sneak inside and kill him once and for all . . .

❧

Fetzer walked from the safe house to the Calza Aria inn at sundown, as prearranged with Cid. He was disappointed when he walked in and found Cid sitting alone at a corner table with several fresh mugs of beer.

"Where is he?" Fetzer asked without greeting Cid.

The short man took his time finishing a gulp. "Sit down and have a drink."

"I'm not interested in wasting my time with anyone but your leader."

"He'll be here," Cid said. "It's you who better not waste Lunfrid's time."

Before Fetzer could insult Cid further, Lunfrid entered the tavern. He pushed back his black hood and approached the table.

"Lunfrid, this is the man I told you about," Cid said. "His name is Fetzer."

Lunfrid regarded Fetzer cautiously. "You're a noble."

"Are you the leader of these poorly planned riots?" Fetzer asked.

Lunfrid squinted at Fetzer before turning to Cid. "You brought a discourteous nobleman into our circle?"

"Both of you sit down, please," Cid said. He gestured to the fresh mugs of beer. Fetzer and Lunfrid relented and joined him. Cid looked at Lunfrid. "I wouldn't bring someone like this to you if I didn't think he was worth your time. I met Fetzer just before the big riot."

"Just before the soldiers tore your band apart," Fetzer said. "And Borel with it."

Lunfrid glared at him. "Have you joined us, or are you all talk?"

"Of course not," Fetzer said. "You won't have anyone left if you keep your poor tactics up. Now, are you the top leader, or am I wasting my time?" Lunfrid's eyes flared.

Cid held up his hands. "Just a damn smidge of patience. I'm taking a risk by letting you meet Lunfrid. He's in charge of our group ever since Fosset died at the keep, and he helped lead the rebels at Mordmerg. He'll decide if you can meet Navarron. Now, Lunfrid, I met Fetzer earlier, but he hasn't joined us yet. He's offered to help us, however, if we help him."

"Who are you and why do we need your help?" Lunfrid asked Fetzer.

"He's the burning man," Cid said. "From the tower."

"You?" Lunfrid mocked. "This little nobleman is the king killer, with his opulent sapphire wist ring and boyish face? He belongs in a posh court somewhere, not among my ranks."

Fetzer looked at Lunfrid's muscular neck, choosing the place where his fist could neatly impact the artery and stun him long enough for Fetzer to open his throat with the nearby table knife. Lunfrid noticed Fetzer's calm, dangerous gaze and stopped talking.

"Tell him, Fetzer," Cid said.

Fetzer regarded them both. If his plan did not work, if they did not accept what he proposed, he would kill them both. "I've gone this far, so I'll give you one more chance," he said. He pulled his tunic open, exposing the breastplate of the lamp armor underneath. Lunfrid studied the veined etchings. Fetzer knew he would not understand what he was seeing, and he was not going to explain it. The sight of the unusual armor should be enough.

"Are you with the Rugens?" Lunfrid asked.

"I'm with myself," Fetzer said. "And you're going to help me."

"Why should we?"

"Because I can teach you how to overthrow kings properly."

"You killed all the ministers and the royals yourself?"

Fetzer nodded.

"But they caught one of them," Lunfrid said. "The one who tried to kill Duke Brugarn at court. Garion was his name. And they beheaded Reimvick and arrested the Rugen ambassador."

"I'm the one that's left," Fetzer said. He reveled in the lie, not bothering to hide his smile.

"Now," Cid said, "Fetzer wants our help with his scheme. In return, he'll help train and lead our rebels."

"But I want to meet Navarron," Fetzer said.

"What scheme?" Lunfrid asked.

"Your next riot will be at Arthan's Clonmel Estate," Fetzer said. "You'll serve as a distraction to keep his guards busy, so I can kill him."

"You killed the king and fought your way through all the Crownblades, but now you need us?" Lunfrid asked. "Cid, this smells to me . . ."

"Arthan has survived two of my attempts on his life," Fetzer said. "Most embarrassing, so I prefer that my third attempt succeeds. I've heard that he is Lord Protector now, and thus the best-guarded man in the kingdom."

"Then perhaps you've also heard that Arthan is no longer in the capital," Lunfrid said.

Fetzer set his jaw and squinted.

"He departed yesterday," Lunfrid continued. "Word is that he's gone to retrieve Lord Erath from Gadolin, to bring him back as the new king. The Rugens slew Asteroth."

Fetzer stood abruptly, knocking his untouched beer onto the floor. He bumped into another man.

"Watch yourself," said the man, looking down at his beer-splashed boots. "Now you'll have to buy me—"

Fetzer grabbed the man by the lapels and raised a fist to strike him.

"Fetzer!" Cid yelled. "Let go of him. Ricot! Where have you been?"

"This is Ricot?" Lunfrid asked. "The one who helped us at the alderman's keep?"

Fetzer shoved Ricot out of his way before he could answer.

"Fetzer, wait," Cid said. "We want to make a deal."

Fetzer was already plotting his route to Gadolin. Arthan would likely avoid the Rugen-infested roads through Alpenon. And traveling east to Wallevet, then south into Gadolin would take too long. The remaining option was the road around the black forest of Onderhem, through the Eldinbane Moors, and eventually to Rethsrond.

And even if Arthan trimmed down his guards for quicker travel, he would still be slower than Fetzer. Fetzer was certain he could reach Arthan before he reached Rethsrond, maybe sooner. He realized he was surpassing his boast to Marlan about continuing to target the Avaleaus. He could kill Arthan and Erath. Deprived of lord protector and future king, Donovan would fall apart, freeing Candlestone for the next task: Emperor Theudamer. Fetzer simply had to find the right place on the road and wait for Arthan to return with Erath, instead of beating Arthan to Erath.

"Fetzer!" Cid shouted, shattering his thoughts as he neared the door. "Did you hear what I said?"

Fetzer turned and walked back to the table where Ricot had taken his seat beside Lunfrid. "I must go. If you value your lives, you'll not speak of me. When I return, we will accomplish more than you've dreamed."

125

MARLAN

Thorendor Castle, Wallevet Ministry
Luminebb, 3034

"I'm sorry, Marlan," Arasemis said. "I had a good reason to leave in the manner that I did."

"May I hear it?" Marlan said. "Because Fetzer thinks you abandoned us. That's why he stayed in Eglamour."

"Come and sit," Arasemis said, gesturing to a chair near his book-strewn table. "You are tired from the journey. Juhl and Rodel are well?"

"Juhl's injuries are healing, but she needs rest. Rodel is tending to her. Please don't think them rude for not coming with me. They went straight to their quarters."

"It's quite all right," Arasemis said. "The night is for sleep—except for me." Arasemis smiled warmly.

"I wouldn't be able to sleep without talking with you," Marlan said. "We completed the task well, but when we returned to Borel you were gone. No warning, no message, no Nidlade."

"I hope Fetzer hasn't whispered in your ear too much. As I said, I had good reason for leaving. That reason may make little sense to you at first, and it certainly won't placate Fetzer, but listen to what I have to say."

Marlan nodded.

"You and Garion were not exactly my first students. The first to be well trained and focused, to be sure. But there was another, a young Austveede noblewoman named Anureen."

"I remember her from the academy . . . She was your student?"

"For a short time. She had been admitted to the academy as a ward to Count Atilon. Part of the count's effort to expand his merchants' trade with Austveeden. She showed the right interests and potential, so I began to teach her about Candlestone. Unfortunately she was recalled to Austveeden after the death of her father. I never heard from her again, until a message arrived to me at the Borel safe house."

"How did she find you in Borel?"

"She didn't. Our loyal servant Yorand sent a messenger to Borel with the letter. After I read it, I knew I had to return to Thorendor as soon as possible. Anureen told me that she had found a way to assassinate the king of Austveeden, and asked for my guidance."

"Wonderful!" Marlan said. "What did you tell her?"

"I was writing my reply when she suddenly arrived at Thorendor. Luckily her access to the Austveede king is not fleeting. We have time to plan it right."

"She is here?"

Arasemis nodded. "Already asleep. You will meet her tomorrow, and we'll integrate her plans into ours. This is the best of Candlestone. Our common passion never dies."

Marlan tamped his excitement. "But you could have left us a message, Master. Or one with Nidlade. What happened to him?"

"You'll remember my bitter cough," Arasemis said. "Despite my condition, I knew I needed to harness Anureen before she tried to do things by herself, since she lacks the benefit of your training. So I took Nidlade with me on the road. Since Nidlade is blind, we hired a wagoner, and Nidlade administered my medicines.

"As for not leaving a message for you, I feared exposing all of us if the authorities discovered the safe house. I'm sorry, Marlan, but you must understand. I'm extremely proud of our accomplishments. Departing like that without talking with you was difficult, but in the best interests of Candlestone."

Marlan nodded. "I understand. Were you in the capital long enough to hear about Edmond?"

"Yes, and I expected execution to be my brother's end, as did he. His position in the palace as our supporter was obviously risky, a secret I had to keep close. I wish he had come around to Candlestone sooner than he did. But at least he wasn't as feckless as Raymond."

"As master, we remain loyal to you," Marlan said. "But the others will appreciate knowing about Anureen and what you had to do. And about your brother's sacrifice. Fetzer will . . . he will be himself. I don't know . . ."

"We'll have time to discuss him. Get some sleep. Nidlade and Anureen will join our Order tomorrow."

☞

Marlan, Rodel, and Juhl listened as Nidlade and Anureen take the oath. Then Arasemis stood from the table and spoke.

"Nidlade, as your reward for your assistance to my brother Edmond and in the service of our ultimate task, you will be given the fury armor mechan, first created for the ancient Bronhildi, Kemet, who was also blind. And for you, Anureen, as a reward for your loyalty to our cause despite having been so far away, you will be given the ship armor, first worn by a Rahlampian chieftain."

Marlan watched and listened to their thanks while thinking about the rate of loss within Candlestone. Garion, Morroy, Bertwil, and Edmond. Maybe Fetzer, too, if he grew too reckless and impatient. Marlan was glad Arasemis was keen to recruit new members. They would be critical if Candlestone was to tackle more kings and emperors.

"I'm sorry that all of our Order is not here to welcome you both," Arasemis said, taking his seat. "Nidlade has already met Fetzer and knows of his stubbornness."

Nidlade smirked.

"I wish I could have convinced him to return with us to Thorendor," Marlan said.

"Fetzer did well at the palace," Juhl said.

"Don't waste your breath complimenting him," Rodel said. "He wouldn't appreciate it even if he were here."

"Fetzer is like a wild horse," Marlan said, "with great potential but requiring great care and training."

"He's uncontrollable," Arasemis said. "I have long given him too much room, hoping, like you, that he would mature into his role."

"I still believe he is prophetic," Marlan said. "Harnessing his energies will take time."

"He is a growing fissure within our Order," Arasemis said.

"Then we must adjust," Marlan said. "The king and most of the royals are dead. Should we evacuate Thorendor and move elsewhere, to ready ourselves for the next task?"

"We will stay at Thorendor," Arasemis said.

"They probably know from Edmond that Thorendor is linked to the assassinations," Rodel said. "They will come for us."

"Who will come?" Arasemis asked. "The Rugens are on the doorstep of Toulon, and Lord Valient is too busy in the capital to march the Army of Delavon into Wallevet. We will stay and continue our studies and training, especially now that Nidlade and Anureen require it."

"What about our next tasks?" Juhl asked.

Marlan nodded appreciatively. "Strike while the iron is hot."

"Our next task is study and training," Arasemis repeated. "The Donovard nobles will soon be at each other's throats, driven by the Rugen march and their lack of a king."

"They still have a king in Lord Erath," Rodel said.

"For how long?" Arasemis countered. "He will inherit a smoldering palace and a crumbling kingdom. We will wait in Thorendor, safe behind our forests and the eyes we pay to watch the roads. If an army comes, we'll flee into the woods and mountains. But rest assured, we have nothing to fear yet. Donovan is on its knees, which means we are running walls."

"Then shall we attack the Rugen or Calbrian monarchs?" Juhl asked.

"Or the Austveede king?" Anureen asked.

"At the right time, yes. But first let us watch how the war progresses, how it weakens both sides. Then we'll strike when a winner arises, weak from battle and drunk with victory. In the meantime we have much to do to prepare."

Marlan rubbed his face, half-wishing he was still in Eglamour. "I'm weary of books, Master . . ."

"Not books this time. Maps. We will study the locations of the Candlestone relics. We could use them for our next tasks. Mechans are only the beginning . . ."

Marlan nodded. Then he remembered his friend. "Will we go back to Eglamour to fetch Fetzer?"

"We'll let him stew there for a while," Arasemis said. "He can't spoil our plans there now, and we'll not bore him with our ancient texts and maps. Besides, he knows where we are when he's ready to come back."

126

ARTHAN

Near Eldinbane Moors, Toulon Ministry
Luminebb, 3034

"As king, this will be my policy!" Erath shouted.

Arthan cringed at the bellowing voice that filled the carriage. Erath had been belligerent since Arthan escorted him from Rethsrond.

"My lord, replacing the Proclamation of Expediency with a harsher edict will not win your people over, nor would it help much against the Rugens who already have a foothold in the kingdom."

"Don't mistake me," Erath said, "I'm grateful that you came to Rethsrond. But I do not need the advice of your house. I will show you how a king should lead. The House of Avaleau will be more feared than ever!"

Arthan glanced out the window into the dusky light. Beyond Serdot, mounted on his horse beside the carriage, dark rain clouds threatened to burst with the fading of the sun. Part of him wished he had let Chaultion retrieve Erath. Arthan had heard nothing but rage and rants since turning back for Eglamour. Given his own losses, he could understand Erath's anger, but he could also see Erath making matters worse.

"I still find it difficult to swallow that Brugarn named you Lord Protector," Erath continued. "A man of your youth. You'd gain experience if I sent you back to Gadolin to defend my ministry from General Valk and his veteran Rugens."

"Your brother appointed me despite our political rivalry. I will serve until I am discharged as you see fit."

"And what need do I have of a marshal of inquiry?" Erath asked. "You did not prevent the slaughter of my brothers by those shadowy folk. Have you nothing to contribute except carriage rides and unsolicited advice?"

"We've learned much about the assassins, my lord. They call themselves the Order of the Candlestone. We believe they are based at Thorendor Castle in Wallevet Ministry. They are skilled at—"

"Then why haven't you toppled every stone of that cursed place?"

"I came for you, my lord, as soon as we heard about Asteroth. Chaultion is preparing to defend Toulon against the Rugens but will spare a force for Thorendor when we're able."

"This is why my new policies are needed," Erath said. "Those assassins, the Rugens, our own people—all of them only respond to the sword. Everyone and everything must be mobilized against our enemies. Donovan will not fall as long as an Avaleau is at the helm. When that crown is on my head, your Lord Ministers' Council will cease to—are you listening to me, Arthan?"

Arthan was looking out the window again as the last rays of light were blocked by passing woods. With his carriage near a bend in the road, he could see that the convoy was stopped just inside the woods.

"Why are we stopping!" Erath shouted.

"Looks like a tree is down," Arthan said, trying to see through the limbs.

Erath opened the carriage door.

"My lord," Arthan said, "I urge you to stay inside. It's safer—my lord!"

Erath hopped down to the ground. "Nonsense! That's the difference between you cautious Valients and the bold Avaleaus. Kingdoms are ruled by the bold, young Arthan."

For a moment Arthan struggled between his desire to be bold or cautious, remembering his inspiration at Maillard's tomb and also Candlestone's unpredictable methods. Against his better judgment, he hopped out after Erath, who was strutting toward the fallen tree.

"My lord, please," Arthan said to Erath, waving Serdot away. "Having survived a few Candlestone assassination attempts myself, this is a time for vigilance."

"Enough! We are far from their playground at Eglamour and their nest at Thorendor."

They approached the soldiers trying to move the tree.

"Stop wasting my time!" Erath shouted at them. "Rope it to the horses and pull it out of my way. Make haste!"

Hamelin and Livonier rode up to them.

"My lord," Hamelin said, "I beg you, return to your carriage."

"And you, my lord," Livonier told Arthan.

"The armored carriage is the safest place," Serdot said.

"Your Crownblades and my men agree with me," Arthan said. "Let us—"

"I said enough of all your whining!" Erath thundered. "I'll not be cowed by our enemies and certainly not a fallen tree. Move it at once, or I'll have all your necks on the block!"

Arthan watched as the soldiers lashed the trunk of the tree to a pair of horses, glancing warily at the woods around them. As the tree began to move, Arthan noticed that the severed trunk was fairly flat, not a jumble of broken shards, as a naturally fallen tree would be.

"Do you see that?" he said to Serdot.

"Odd discoloration," Serdot said. "And chewed, or maybe dissolved. Like an acid."

Arthan turned to Erath, but before he could speak a soldier picked up a second rope from the grass. As he lifted it they saw one end was tethered to a branch above them, and the other was tied to a branch in the fallen tree. The soldier moved to jerk it down.

"Don't!" Arthan shouted.

"Stop the horses!" Serdot yelled.

But it was too late; the trap had engaged. Hewn branches swept down from the trees above, swinging from either end with bound ivy. Dozens of eggs were fastened along these beams, and they shattered into the sides of a wagon full of

Crownblades and other mounted soldiers. Clouds of orange, green, and purple burst into the damp air.

Arthan reached into his robes and pulled out the two Candlestone masks. He fitted one to his face and tried to pick his way through the fast-growing clouds to give the other to Erath. But he became disoriented amid the screaming soldiers, unable to see beyond his reach. He called out for Erath and Serdot but could not hear them. Then an orange light appeared, faint at first. The light grew brighter and darted about. Arthan knew what it was.

The burning man swept through the clouds, mercilessly chopping through the panicked soldiers who were vomiting, scratching, and struggling to breathe. Arthan drew Adrithayn and carefully paced toward the light. The burning man was here, then there and gone again, sprinting between the soldiers, wagons, and horses.

Arthan expected to hear Erath's bellowing voice, but he could not find him or any of his own men in the chaos. He resolved to withdraw from the confusion and ran hard out of the clouds. He found Serdot crouched and coughing on the edge of the woods.

"Are you all right?"

"My mask was bumped off for a moment," Serdot said, holding his mask up to show he still had it.

"Put it back on. We must find Erath. When we do, escort him away. My blade will take the fire from the assassin's armor."

Serdot nodded as he refitted his mask. Then they charged back into the fray. The clouds had turned brown and faded with the onset of rain. Bodies tripped them at every step. Erath's voice boomed out from across the road. As they came closer they saw the burning man crossing swords with Erath and Hamelin, both of them weakened from the poison.

The burning man seemed startled to see two Candlestone masks coming toward him. It was enough hesitation for them to surround him, but he quickly refocused and seemed to relish the challenge. He twirled like a storm of flame, engaging all four of them effortlessly with his single sword. Arthan tried to be defensive while keeping the assassin contained, wary of flinging Adrithayn's absorbed poison and flame onto the others.

The burning man's flames dampened with the rain. His golden glow slowly faded, and steam swirled around his quick movements. He scored a strike on Serdot's helmet, sending him to the ground. Erath, his head unprotected, leaned in to take a swipe with his broad blade. The assassin punched him with his hot gauntlet, then angled his sword down on him.

Hamelin parried the strike as Livonier joined the fight. The assassin plucked an egg from his pouch and aimed it at Hamelin's visor. Hamelin ducked, but the assassin struck him down. When Hamelin fell wounded, Erath swiped again at the burning man, who abruptly turned and ran. Erath and Arthan gave chase. With his armor now putting out more steam than fire, the assassin bounded up the side of a tree, then somersaulted out above his pursuers. The assassin cut down at them as he flipped, opening the top of Erath's head and striking Arthan's helmet.

Erath's blood sprayed onto Arthan, coating the lenses of his mask. He wrenched the mask off as the assassin's fiery armor completely snuffed out. Arthan looked down at Erath's writhing body. He stooped, hoping to save him. But Erath was gone.

Arthan stood in time to parry the assassin's next attack. Livonier and Serdot came to his defense, and the assassin ran into the woods. They chased him, following the steam and scent of scalded metal. But he was quick. Arthan jerked on Livonier's arm as the dark forest in front of them became awash in fresh poison clouds.

Arthan came to a stop, since he was without a mask. Serdot stopped as well.

"Let me chase him!" Livonier shouted.

Arthan shook his head, his jaw clenched. He wiped Erath's blood from his face as it trickled down with the rain from his hair. Then he placed his hand over his chest as he felt his heart lurch and skip. He knelt and took a moment to calm his breathing.

Livonier cursed as they watched the poison clouds swirl silently among the trees and bushes ahead of them, the sound of the assassin's running long since faded.

"We must escort him back to Eglamour," Serdot said.

Livonier finally nodded and took Arthan's hand, pulling him to his feet.

Arthan's heart settled and he sighed, staring into the dark forest ahead. "I am regent . . ."

EPILOGUE

Eglamour, Toulon Ministry
Midsummer, 3034

The choking burn of the black smoke seeped into her lungs. The heat of the charred palace stones swept over her. Voices called to her amid the crackle and popping of the roof beams. Something screamed inside her head as the earth rose up to meet her tumbling body. Visions of Regaume, aflame and pulling at stubborn bars of iron, played over and over in her mind.

The darkness slowly faded into an orange light. It was distant at first but drew closer. She saw a man aflame, but it was not Regaume. He was armored, his face masked. There was evil in his wake, like a long cape. As she looked upon him she drew strength from somewhere, perhaps from the flaming man himself. She heard a voice that said his death was inevitable. She believed it, but, strangely, did not want him to die yet. She craved the dark strength that she was somehow siphoning from him.

The man came closer. So close now. She felt the evil heat, smelled his footsteps in the seared earth. She could see inside the mask, through the tiny eye slits. His face hid a skull that quivered with hate, fear, and bloodlust. The light around him grew bright, forcing her eyes closed. But still the light pierced, beckoning.

She gave her eyes to the light, opening them slowly. The sun beamed in through passing clouds and remnants of smoke. Her eyes shifted right to see the looming hulk of a burned tower. She remembered. That was where Milisend died. Where she jumped. The pain and sorrow and hopelessness had pushed her. Milisend had been weak, not yet tasting the dark strength of the burning man.

She sat up with the sound of crunching roof tiles. A growl rolled in her stomach. The leathers on her legs and arms were burned away here and there but could be mended. She touched her face and found the familiar leather mask that Milisend had worn. She reached around to her aching back, feeling the spinal plates so deftly sewn into the suit still intact. Regaume had commissioned the very best for Mili.

She remembered that Mili had not been fond of what he called her. Thimblegloves. It had not sounded like a real name until now. Thimblegloves now had a dark strength that Mili lacked. Thimblegloves had danced with the burning man, jumped into the abyss, and wandered in the mist-shrouded puzzle forest of a dying mind.

Thimblegloves felt a hunger in her mouth and stomach. A grievous hunger rooted in her mind, perhaps her very soul. A strange hunger that could not be sated with any nourishment. Her parched lips quivered with the thought of it. *Revenge.*

APPENDIX

HOUSE OF VALIENT

MAILLARD VALIENT: Lord Minister of Delavon Ministry, Count of Bram. Resided in Rachard.

His Children
ARTHAN VALIENT: Eldest living son.
ROWAN VALIENT: Ward to Lord Minister Asteroth Avaleau of Alpenon.
BARDIL VALIENT: Youngest son.

His Household
MEDOFF CORMIER: General of the armies of Delavon.
LIVONIER: Knight commander and Medoff's deputy.
SERDOT TREMEY: Master widsemer.
ALFREM: Alderman of Rachard, political counselor.
PELINAUD: Crusader swordcraft master, instructor.
BELLUMET: Chief engineer.
MERIAM: Engineer's assistant.

His Vassals
ISERENNE: Countess of Sobel County. Resided in Wilsmar.
DARDANON: Count of Imvorlon County. Resided in Oradrond.
GOLBANE VALIENT: Count of Caval County. Resided in Brambard.

Others
NESTORATH: Bishop of Rachard.
HURMANT: Alderman of Mordmerg.
CUERN: Knight.
ERBOLN: Knight.
ALDON: Knight.
DANLERI: Former rector of Bredahade Academy. Resided in Eglamour.

THE ORDER OF THE CANDLESTONE

ARASEMIS: Ruler of Thorendor, arcanae expert. Resided in Thorendor Castle.

His Students
>MARLAN: Former Bredahade Academy cadet.
GARION: Former Bredahade Academy cadet.
BERTWIL: Almerian swordsman, former sailor.
MORROY: Calbrian swordsman, former drifter.
JUHL: Lambic princess in exile.
FETZER: Former Perilune Academy cadet.
ANUREEN: Austveede of noble birth.

His Supporters
>YORAND: Mute servant.
ADALANE: Deaf servant.
NIDLADE: Blind safe house keeper.

Associates
>RILRANEF: Chief of a smuggler ring based in Eddengard, Donovan.
RENAUD: Smuggler captain of the *Meurden*.
GREFFID: Ship's cook aboard the *Meurden*.

HOUSE OF WACHOT

SIGBERT WACHOT: Lord Minister of Barres Ministry. Resided in Gradhild.

His Vassals
    ATILON: Count of Perilune. Resided at Perilune.
    -- RENZ: Administrator under Atilon.

Perilune Academy
    CABOT: Headmaster.
    GADE: Cadet.

The Sember Family
    ARCHAVAL SEMBER: Baron and knight commander who served Count Atilon.
    EDWORA SEMBER: Deceased wife of Archaval.
    FERNON SEMBER: Eldest son of Archaval, knight in Atilon's army.
    FETZER SEMBER: Youngest son of Archaval, cadet at Perilune Academy.
    LAVAL SEMBER: Brother of Archaval.

HOUSE OF REIMVICK

RAYMOND REIMVICK: Lord Minister of Wallevet Ministry.
Resided at Bredahade.

His Siblings
EDMOND REIMVICK: Senior royal courtier.
OSMOND REIMVICK: Also known as ARASEMIS.

His Family
VERNON REIMVICK: Deceased father of Raymond,
Edmond, and Osmond.
ERWOLD REIMVICK: Deceased father of Vernon.

BLACKHOODS

NAVARRON: Leader of the Blackhood rebels.

Members
LUNFRID: Second in command at Mordmerg.
ADKINTUDE: Lunfrid's lieutenant.
FOSSET: Eglamour rebel.
CID: Deputy to Fosset.
ARNAUT: Rioter in Eglamour.
RICOT: Donovard alias for Wredegar disguised as a
rebel from Gadolin.

HOUSE OF AVALEAU

ERECH AVALEAU: King of Donovan. Resided in Eglamour.

His Wife
    ANDRILENNE AVALEAU: Queen of Donovan.
    -- MARIELLE: Head handmaiden to the queen.

Their Children
    AVALANE AVALEAU: Eldest princess of Donovan, Lord Ministeress of Elmbrel Ministry.
    MILISEND AVALEAU: Middle princess of Donovan.
    -- REGAUME: Milisend's lover, a master jewel thief.
    -- ROSELLEN: Milisend's handmaiden.
    BRIELLE AVALEAU: Youngest princess of Donovan.

His Siblings
    BRUGARN AVALEAU: Duke of Donovan, Lord Minister of Toulon Ministry, resided in Eglamour.
    -- BALVENE: Baron.
    -- FRUM: Baron.
    ASTEROTH AVALEAU: Duke of Donovan, Lord Minister of Alpenon Ministry, Erath's twin, resided in Cantrileme.
    -- HAMON: Knight commander.
    -- MIERBIOT: Baron.
    ERATH AVALEAU: Duke of Donovan, Lord Minister of Gadolin Ministry, Asteroth's twin, resided in Rethsrond.

His Household
    CHAULTION: High General of the Armies of Donovan.
    TRONCHET: Chief Magistrate of Eglamour.
    HAMELIN: General of the Crownblades.

WALDEMAR: Steward of Eglamour Palace, Deputy
    Alderman of Eglamour.
-- DEBANOR: Waldemar's son, palace guard knight.
GEROLD: Trusted royal courier.
MELTRES: Political counselor.

His Vassals

    MAILLARD VALIENT: Lord Minister of Delavon
        Ministry.
    RAYMOND REIMVICK: Lord Minister of Wallevet
        Ministry.
    SIGBERT WACHOT: Lord Minister of Barres
        Ministry.
    GOTTFRIED: Lord Minister of Leauvenna Ministry.
    HENREY: Lord Minister of Elmbrel Ministry,
        husband of Avalane Avaleau.
    RAND HALEVANE: Lord Minister of Merbredel
        Ministry.
    EPERUDE: Lord Ministeress of Lundwynland
        Ministry.
    VOUFON: Lord Ministeress of Laume Ministry, ruler
        of Nore Territory, sister of Queen Andrilenne.
    FERIN: Lord Minister of Hanovel Ministry.

Other

    BAVERNON: Patriarch of the Messengian Church of
        Donovan.

HOUSE OF THEUDAMER

INGOTHER THEUDAMER: Emperor of the Rugenhav Empire, resided in Heingartmer.
EVORELUNE: Empress of the Rugenhav Empire.

His Household
ALGUS: Chief General of the Rugen Imperial Armies.
VESAMUNE THEUDAMER: His niece, Ambassador to Donovan, elder sister of Meliamour.
MELIAMOUR THEUDAMER: His niece, master widsemer, Master of the Wosmok Legion.

His Vassals
HERZOL AUFTENGARDIN: Wardenlord, adviser.
RITHERMELK AUFTENGARDIN: Warden of Auftengardin, younger brother of Herzol.
GRAF AMESNER: Warden of Havelbern.
VALK HOLGARD: General.
GOTHAL VILARWEF: Head of the House of Vilarwef, titular head of the Durgensdil Rebellion. Exiled in Rugenhav.
-- GERAS VILARWEF: Gothal's younger brother and leader of the Durgensdil Rebellion.
-- ARDIS VILARWEF: Gothal's younger sister and a senior rebel leader.

Wosmoks
GARENTORF: Deceased commander of Donovan Wosmoks.
WREDEGAR AUFTENGARDIN: New commander of Donovan Wosmoks, son of Herzol.
ETZEL: Commander of Austveeden Wosmoks.
HEDGER: Wosmok.

GLOSSARY

Aberynbane: A former petty kingdom ruled by King Thorendor, whose death cleared the way for the unification of the Kingdom of Donovan.

acrobatics: One of the two divisions of aerina arcana focused on the sole use of the body and mind for defensive and offensive maneuvers. Acrobatics also includes specialized tactics such as evasion and tree and wall running. See also *swordcraft* and *aerina arcana*.

Adrithayn: An heirloom sword long held by the House of Valient. See also *glyphblades*.

aerina arcana: The first of the three arcanae, aerina comprises knowledge of oneself, body, and mind. Aerina encompasses two divisions, acrobatics and swordcraft.

aglanrit: Twisted, stunted trees that grow only in the snow-clad Narendra Mountains of eastern Donovan and southwestern Calbria. The extreme toughness of the wood was valued by the Naren-Dra people for making masks and other items to protect themselves from the cold.

Agnesci: In Messengian religious tradition, the Agnesci were one of the two original peoples created by God. They originally inhabited the southern continent. See also *Almerics*.

alchemy: One of the two divisions of chemina arcana focused on the mixing of ingredients for medicinal, illusory, offensive, and other specialized purposes. See also *metallurgy* and *chemina arcana*.

alderman: Leader of cities and towns in Donovan.

Almeria: The continent to the north of Pemonia. Also known as the Old World. The collective inhabitants of Almeria are known as Almerians.

Almerian Confederation: A confederation of kingdoms that dominate Almeria; successor of the Brintilian Empire.

Almeric Empire: The first unification of the Almeric peoples. Founded by Lord Wilhargant in the year 1, marking the beginning of the Second Era.

Almerics: In Messengian religious tradition, the Almerics were one of the two original peoples created by God.

They originally inhabited the northern continent of Almeria and later founded the Almeric Empire. See also *Agnesci*.

Alpenon Ministry: A southwestern territory of Donovan. The Rugens and separatist rebels of western Alpenon call it Durgensdil.

alterlocum: A metallurgical method of promoting specific properties within alloys used for weapons and armor. The dissolving solution removes impurities in the metals and replaces them with desirable materials that fuse in the voids left by the impurities.

Ambardil: A free city in Alpenon Ministry, Donovan.

anchiclade: An ore named after the Anchiclade Mountains of southwestern Calbria from which it was mined. The ancient Rahlampians alloyed the ore with bog iron to forge windrazor swords, which were exceptionally thin, light, strong, and resistant to rust.

Anchiclade Mountains: A mountain range in southwestern Calbria.

arcanae: The plural of arcana. Used to refer collectively to the three ancient arts: aerina, chemina, and machina.

Arcodum: A shrine island on the coast of Arukia that was converted into a prison tower where many Arukans were imprisoned after being defeated by Marshal Hilsingor during the First Crusade.

Armagnon the Pocked: An ancient king of Donovan long considered by many Donovards to be their weakest king, until the reign of Erech Avaleau.

Arukia: A region of Almeria that was home to the Arukan peoples and kingdoms.

Auch Tenoshun: The capital city of Lundwynland Ministry, Donovan.

Auftengardin: A northeastern ward of Rugenhav.

Auftengardin, House of: A powerful Rugen family and rulers of the Ward of Auftengardin who were longtime partners of the House of Theudamer, emperors of Rugenhav.

Aughreim: An inland port city in Toulon Ministry, Donovan.

Austveeden: A small kingdom in western Pemonia wedged between Donovan and Calbria that was formerly part of Vaynland and includes the Gilgalem Mountains. The people of Austveeden are known as Austveedes.

Avaleau, House of: A powerful Donovard family and longtime kings of Donovan.

Banebrand: Marlan's alchemical flaming sword.

Barres Ministry: A northeastern territory of Donovan.

beast lore: A branch of alchemy pioneered by the Arukan people.

Beldmerg: A city in western Delavon Ministry, Donovan.

Benrollen Company: Donovan's wealthiest and oldest royally chartered group of maritime merchants.

Bevil Ahrazmis: An ancient scribe to a senior general of the Wartemur Army during the Brintilian colonization of Pemonia.

black adder: Giant snake of the Black Forest of Ondirhar in central Gallerlandia known for its potent venom. The adder's venom and antivenom blood were two ingredients used by the Hrals to create a tonic that caused their turserkgyn fighting trance.

Black Forest: See *Onderhem Forest*.

Blackhoods: A group of criminals in Mordmerg led by Navarron.

bloon(e): The square-shaped gold coins of Austveeden.

Bomlofoss Mountains: A mountain range in western Donovan.

Borel District: A large slum in Eglamour, capital of Donovan.

Bothrobim: An ancient Nyden ship captain.

Bram: A county in Delavon Ministry, Donovan.

Brambard: The capital of Caval County in Delavon Ministry, Donovan.

Bredahade: The capital of Wallevet Ministry, Donovan, and the location of the lord minister's castle and academy.

Brindthum Mountains: A mountain range in western Alpenon Ministry, Donovan, occupied by the separatist Durgensdil rebellion.

Brintilian Empire: An Old World empire that began its rise to power around the year 2010. The Brintilians oversaw the first restoration of Old World civilization after the tumultuous periods following the collapse of the Almeric Empire. After the Brintilians reconsolidated the Old World kingdoms they led the Age of Exploration to the New World of Pemonia.

broadblade swordcraft: A school of swordcraft originating from northern Calbria and emphasizing crushing attacks with an unusually broad-bladed sword that must be strapped across the user's back when not in use.

Bronhildia: An ancient tribal realm in modern Hanovel Ministry, Donovan previously inhabited by the Bronhildi.

Burgbud War: A brief conflict in central Donovan between the Houses of Reimvick and Ganymyd sparked by the latter's attempt to reacquire ancestral lands in Wallevet Ministry. The Ganymyds' defeat marked the end of their rule of Lundwynland Ministry.

Calbria: A large kingdom in central Pemonia. The people of Calbria are known as Calbrians.

Calbrian Sea: A large sea in northern Pemonia nearly completely bounded by Calbria and Donovan but connected to the Edinon Sea via the Strait of Delnollen.

Candlestone, Order of the: A secretive order founded in 2270 by rebellious Brintilians and natives from across western Pemonia. The Order sought to undermine the expansion of the Brintilian Empire into the New World.

Cantrileme: The capital of Alpenon Ministry, Donovan.

castellan: The governor or captain of a castle or fortified town.

Caval: A county in Delavon Ministry, Donovan.

chemina arcana: The second of the three arcanae, chemina comprises knowledge of materials and the methods of extracting essences to use hidden attributes. Chemina encompasses two divisions, alchemy and metallurgy.

cinder: A rough, porous volcanic rock originally mined by ancient Gallerlanders beneath the mountains of Gilgalem. Smiths have long used cinder to make heat-resistant armor and tough weapons.

cindersteel: A very light alloy of cinder and steel primarily used for expensive broadswords and heat-resistant armor that also provides excellent protection against many steel weapons.

Clonmel: An urban estate in Eglamour owned by the House of Valient.

Congregantism: A splinter sect from the Messengianism religion. Congregants do not recognize the authority of the Martinus, have differing roles for their patriarchs, and believe Azra to have been the fourth of God's Holy Messengers.

Crownblades: The knights dedicated to protecting the king of Donovan and the royal family at Eglamour Palace.

crusader: An honorary title originally given to nobles and knights who joined the First Crusade in Arukia and the Second Crusade in Pemonia. The title was later used to describe knights trained in the Crusader school of swordcraft.

crusader swordcraft: A school of swordcraft that originated in Almeria and was refined in Pemonia. The school emphasizes fighting in coordinated pairs or groups to better withstand the charges of desperate Arukans and native hordes in Pemonia.

Delavon Kingdom: A former kingdom ruled by the House of Valient prior to the unification of Donovan. Most of the kingdom's old territory survives as Delavon Ministry.

Delavon Ministry: An eastern territory of Donovan.

Delnollen: An island located in the Strait of Delnollen claimed by Donovan, Calbria, and the Almerian Confederation.

devices: One of the two divisions of machina arcana focused on the design and construction of large machines such as cranes, watermills, and windmills, as well as small machines such as pumps and pulleys. See also *mechanics* and *machina arcana*.

Dimanus: An Arukan member of the seventh generation of the Order of the Candlestone.

Donovan: A kingdom in western Pemonia. Donovan was originally the second New World colony founded by the Brintilian Empire, after New Lorin Colony. The people of Donovan are known as Donovards.

Durgensdil: The original name of a Brintilian colony that later became Alpenon Ministry. The inhabitants are primarily ethnic Rugens who support independence from Donovan.

Durrow: Northeastern district of Calbria.

Ebronin the Elder: An ancestor of Rugen Emperor Ingother Theudamer.

Eddengard: An inland port on the Elme River in southwestern Barres Ministry, Donovan.

Edinon Sea: The sea northwest of Pemonia.

Eglamour: The capital city of the Kingdom of Donovan.

Eldinbane Moors: The uplands in southern Toulon Ministry, Donovan.

Eldreim: A port city in eastern Barres Ministry, Donovan.

electrum: A natural alloy of gold and silver with traces of copper, it was considered sacred by the ancient Gallerlander peoples and later minted by the Brintilian Empire.

elinderum: An alloy of electrum and cinder developed by the ancient Maluram smithies of Gilgalem Mountain.

Elmbrel Ministry: A northwestern territory of Donovan.

Elme River: A major river in Donovan that serves as the border between Wallevet and Barres Ministries.

Empire Alliance: A treaty that helped prevent major wars between the Almerian Confederation and the kingdoms of western and central Pemonia, and coordinated trade rules. It was signed in the year 2889.

Eniri: An ancient Gallerlander princess.

Enthiri: A member of the fourth generation of the Order of the Candlestone and a great-granddaughter of Rildning and Eniri.

fait(s): The copper coins of Donovan.

Fanedor: A city in eastern Alpenon Ministry, Donovan.

Far East: The eastern realms of the continent of Pemonia, known for volcanic lands, high mountains, acidic seas, and isolated peoples.

Faukshal: The main island of the Faukshal Island District of northern Calbria.

First Crusade: The Martinus of the Messengian Church declared the First Crusade in 2253 to counter the Arukan Rebellion. Marshal Hilsingor led the Rivercross Corps to defeat the Arukans and imprison many of them in Arcodum.

flashoak: A species of oak tree native to Torxil Island east of Barres Ministry, Donovan. The tree completes its lifecycle in two years. The wood, when dried and powdered, is prized by alchemists for various uses.

Forlorn Smithy: A member of the thirty-fifth generation of the Order of the Candlestone.

free city: City-states and small islands in western Pemonia that were once ruled directly by the Almerian Empire. These enclaves later became self-ruled to avoid seizure by the Pemonian kingdoms, but they retained Almerian garrisons to guarantee their protection. The free cities are major hubs for trade between the continents.

Frontier Corps: The first united army of Old World crusaders and provincial legions formed during the colonization of Pemonia to defeat the native tribes. Led by Marshal Hilsingor as the Second Crusade, the Frontier Corps later garrisoned castles across the frontier and were responsible for carving out many new imperial provinces from tribal lands.

furywine: An alchemical drink that causes uncontrollable rage. A stronger version that included black adder blood and other lost ingredients was used by ancient

Hral warriors prior to battle. They fought to the death or died from drinking the tonic.

Gaerte Ganymyd: The leader of the Lundwyns and Lundwynland Ministry prior to the Burgbud War.

Gallerlandia: An ancient tribal realm in modern Donovan and Austveeden previously inhabited by the Gallerlanders.

Gardwerp: A city in southern Alpenon Ministry, Donovan.

Garnault: A river in Delavon Ministry plentiful in tuning stones.

Gaton Castle: A fortress in the Brindthum Mountains of western Alpenon Ministry, Donovan.

Genthus District: A district of Eglamour City in Toulon Ministry, Donovan.

Gidemond Kingdom: A former petty kingdom ruled by the House of Reimvick prior to the unification of Donovan.

Gilgalem Mountains: A mountain range in southern Austveeden that served as a sanctuary for the ancient Gallerlander tribe.

glading: A metallurgical method of infusing specific properties into weapons and armor by folding special materials into alloys as they are made.

glyphblades: Eight alchemical swords crafted for the original petty kings of the lands that later became Donovan. Adrithayn and Rhunegeld are two surviving glyphblades.

gode: A rust- and corrosion-resistant metal originally mined in ancient Bronhildia for primitive swordsmithing.

gode steel: A hard alloy of iron and gode first made by the ancient Bronhildi tribe.

Goyngard: A city in northern Toulon Ministry, Donovan.

Gromanese: Inhabitants of Groman Island, part of the Faukshal Island District of northern Calbria, who are known for their export of fine wines.

guldir(s): The gold coins of Donovan.

Hanovel Ministry: A northwestern territory of Donovan.

Harkarom Mountains: A mountain range in Barres Ministry named after an ancient highchief of the Bronhildi tribe that resided in the area during the colonial period.

Havelbern: A northern ward of Rugenhav.

Heingartmer: The capital city of the Rugen Empire.

Hidden Eyes: An ancient order of Naren-Dra shroud alchemists sent to secretly watch and sometimes kill the leaders of rival tribes. Also known as the Clan of the Hidden Eyes.

Hildegad: The main island of the Hildegad Island District of northern Calbria.

Hilrond: A town in Toulon Ministry, Donovan.

Hilsingor: Marshal Hilsingor was the ancient Brintilian commander of the Rivercross Corps during the First Crusade in Arukia, and commander of the Frontier Corps during the Second Crusade in Pemonia.

Hrallandia: An ancient tribal realm in modern Donovan previously inhabited by the Hrals.

Hullen: A ruined warcastle built in Sobel County of Delavon Ministry, Donovan. Built by the Frontier Corps during the colonization of western Pemonia.

Imvorlon: A county in eastern Delavon Ministry, Donovan.

Kemet: An ancient Bronhildi warrior.

Lambochardy: Island kingdom south of the continent of Pemonia. The people of Lambochardy are known as Lambics.

landship: Large six-wheeled ships originally built by the Rahlampians to sail across land, lakes, rivers, ditches, etc., and later adopted by the Calbrians. Landships are often equipped with catapults and archers.

Laume Ministry: A western territory of Donovan.

lawkeeper: The magistrates and lesser officers responsible for keeping the king's peace throughout Donovan.

Leauvenna Ministry: A northern island territory of Donovan.

lord minister(ess): The high noblemen and noblewomen charged with governing the land ministries of Donovan. They are senior vassals who answer directly to the king.

Lord Ministers' Council: The body of all lord ministers of Donovan with responsibility for providing counsel to the king, raising armies, levying taxes, and other administrative duties. The council also confirms the selection of new kings jointly with the Messengian Church of Donovan.

lorin(s): The silver coins of Donovan.

Lundwynland Ministry: A northern territory of Donovan.

Lyonseln: The capital and largest port of Leauvenna Ministry, Donovan.

machina arcana: The third of the three arcanae, machina comprises knowledge of natural physical and theoretical forces. Machina encompasses two divisions, mechanics and devices.

Maluram: A minor subtribe of ancient Gallerlanders who were master smiths that lived primarily in the Gilgalem Mountains of modern Austveeden.

Martinus: The title used by the head of the Messengian Church. Named after God's first Messenger, Martinus Arnabin. The Martinus dwells in the Cryphanic Temple of the Holy Messengers in Almeria and is advised by the Temple Curia. The Martinus is also referred to as Temple Father or Holy Father.

mechan: The ancient suits of mechanized armor crafted by the first generation of the Order of the Candlestone. The first eight mechans were arrow armor, bear armor, forge armor, fury armor, lamp armor, ship armor, shroud armor, and wheel armor.

mechanics: One of the two divisions of machina arcana focused on the movement and properties of machines. Physical mechanics encompasses simple machines such as pendulums, screws, rudders, and sails, while theoretical mechanics studies buoyancy, radiants, gravity, and other fields. See also *devices* and *machina arcana*.

Melsard: A town near the Rugen borderlands in Alpenon Ministry, Donovan.

Memelos: The name of the devil in the Messengian and Congregant religious traditions.

Merbredel Ministry: An eastern territory of Donovan.

Merbredel Mountains: A mountain range in Merbredel Ministry, Donovan, still inhabited by wildermen believed to be the descendants of the Nake people of ancient Pemonia.

Merl: A town in eastern Alpenon Ministry, Donovan.

Messengianism: The dominant religion of Almeria and about a third of Pemonians. The religion was named after the Messengers, the great teachers believed to have been sent by God.

metallurgy: One of the two divisions of chemina arcana comprising the extraction and study of metals and stones, the crafting of stone, the making of alloys and amalgams, and the mixing of aggregates. See also *alchemy* and *chemina arcana*.

Meurden: A smuggler ship owned by Rilranef the Round.

Middlesea: Archipelago clusters and isolated volcanic islands between the northern continent of Almeria and the southern continent of Pemonia.

Mollering: An island in the Strait of Delnollen.

Mordmerg: A free city in Delavon Ministry, Donovan.

Mrigamad: An ancient Rahlampian chieftain.

Nairnbern Castle: A fortress in central Alpenon Ministry that protected the approach to Cantrileme.

Nakeland: Brintilian name for an eastern peninsula of modern Donovan now known as Merbredel Ministry, previously inhabited by the ancient Nake people.

Narendra Mountains: An ancient tribal realm in the high mountains of modern Calbria previously inhabited by the Naren-Dra people.

Narendrabruk: A river valley that serves as a border between Calbria and Delavon Ministry of Donovan.

Niberi: An ancient Gallerlander Maluram blacksmith.

Nore: An island territory split between Donovan in the northeast and Rugenhav in the southwest.

Nothild: A Bronhildi member of the seventh generation of the Order of the Candlestone.

Oladet: A town in Elmbrel Ministry, Donovan.

Onderhem Forest: The remaining core of the ancient Black Forest of Ondirhar in central Donovan that was once the territory of the Gallerlander tribe.

Oradrond: The port and capital city of Imvorlon County of Delavon Ministry.

Orbruk: River in northern Donovan.

Orringholm: A free city in Alpenon Ministry, Donovan. Located in the Orringholm River Valley, which serves as the border between Rugenhav and the Alpenon Ministry of Donovan.

Ovelia: A kingdom of southern Pemonia. The people of Ovelia are known as Ovelians.

Owerdir: An ancient Gallerlander chieftain.

Patriarch of Donovan: The leader of the Messengian Church of Donovan and subordinate to the Martinus.

Pemonia: The continent to the south of Almeria. Also known as the New World. The collective inhabitants of Pemonia are known as Pemonians.

Perilune: A county in Barres Ministry, Donovan.

popaver: A medicinal drug derived from a plant of the same name, used as a pain reliever and cough suppressant. It was also used to make the laudanum tincture beloved by Ovelians.

Quayrond: The primary coastal port of Lundwynland Ministry, Donovan.

quillshades: The adherents of the Order of the Shady Leaf who believe they can use writing to summon spirits from the earth, trees, stones, and other natural objects to do the bidding of men. The Order's roots lay in the stone-worshiping traditions of the Nake tribe in modern Merbredel Ministry, Donovan, but quillshades were gradually outlawed and arrested in most Pemonian kingdoms for their use of alchemical tricks to steal money or to intimidate or for their heretical religious beliefs.

Rachard: The capital city of Delavon Ministry and the original seat of the House of Valient.

Raffenia: An ancient tribal realm in modern Rugenhav previously inhabited by the Raffen people.

Rahlampia: An ancient tribal realm in the lowlands of modern Calbria and previously inhabited by the Rahlampian people.

Ralmogard: A free city in Toulon Ministry, Donovan.

Rampilar: A ruined warcastle built in the Caval Moors in Caval County of Delavon Ministry, Donovan. It was built by the Frontier Corps during the colonization of western Pemonia.

Reimvick, House of: A powerful Donovard family and rulers of Wallevet Ministry.

Rethsrond: The capital of Gadolin Ministry, Donovan.

Rhunegeld: An heirloom sword long held by the House of Avaleau. See also *glyphblades*.

Riddertin: A ruined warcastle built in Gadolin Ministry, Donovan, by the Frontier Corps during the colonization of western Pemonia.

Rilhammor: A large port city in Elmbrel Ministry, Donovan, and one of the first major ports to be established in Pemonia by the Brintilian Empire.

Rugen Empire: The realm dominated by the Kingdom of Rugenhav, encompassing the mainland Rugen wards, the island ward of Nydenbern, half of the island of Nore, mining colonies in Lambochardy, and far-flung islands in the Sepacian Sea.

Rugen Wars of Unification: A series of conflicts that consolidated many Rugen petty kingdoms.

Rugenhav: A kingdom in western Pemonia and the core of the Rugen Empire. The people of Rugenhav are known as Rugens.

Sea of Pemonia: The body of water between the islands of Leauvenna Ministry and the northern coastlines of continental Donovan.

Second Crusade: The Martinus of the Messengian Church declared the Second Crusade in 2262 to encourage Old World noble families and commoners to establish more colonies and subdue the natives of the New World. Marshal Hilsingor's sailing to Pemonia to lead the Frontier Corps signaled the height of the Second Crusade.

Sember Family: Barons who served under Count Atilon and the Lord Minister of Barres Ministry, Donovan.

Seralin: The last Exarch of Pemonia of the Brintilian Empire.

Sernpert: A Donovard border castle in southern Alpenon Ministry.

sickness of the southern winds: A Lambic term for frostbite that creeps into the head and neck via the ears, nose, and mouth.

Sobel: A county in western Delavon Ministry, Donovan.

Strait of Delnollen: The channels between the Calbria and Donovan coastlines of the Calbrian Sea.

swordcraft: One of the two divisions of aerina arcana focused on swordsmanship and unit tactics. See also *acrobatics* and *aerina arcana*.

synthic: A rare condition characterized by the merging of the senses in ways only apparent to the synthic, such as seeing written letters and numbers in various colors, tasting shapes viewed with the eyes, and envisaging music and sounds in color and shapes.

Taranoga: An Ovelian merchant ship used by the Order of Candlestone for travel.

Temeszal: A kingdom in eastern Pemonia. The people of Temeszal are known as Temaris.

temple knight: The senior knights of the Messengian Church who protect the Martinus, Patriarchs, and basilicas, and other special tasks.

temple swordcraft: A school of swordcraft originating from Almeria and emphasizing high-held guards and strikes.

Theudamer, House of: A powerful Rugen family and rulers of the Rugen Empire.

Thimblegloves: The thieving name given to Milisend by Regaume.

Thorendor Castle: An isolated fortress with peculiar architectural features located near Bredahade, the capital of Wallevet Ministry, Donovan.

Thorendor, King: A petty king whose lands were absorbed into Wallevet during the unification of the Kingdom of Donovan.

Tiberon: The capital of the Kingdom of Calbria.

Toninbern: An eastern ward of Rugenhav.

Torfnabruk: A large border river in central Donovan between Toulon and Lundwynland Ministries.

Torgsbad Castle: A Donovard border castle in southern Alpenon Ministry.

Toulon Ministry: A central territory of Donovan and location of the kingdom's capital of Eglamour.

Toulon River Valley: A large river system in northern Toulon Ministry, Donovan, in which the capital of Eglamour was founded.

treating: A metallurgical method of transferring specific properties onto the surfaces of finished weapons and armor by soaking them in prepared solutions.

tuning stones: Stones that naturally preserve the acoustics of earthquakes and originally used in Almeria to tune musical instruments. During the colonization of Pemonia, they were used as catapult ammunition to deafen, disorient, and frighten tribal warriors.

Valient, House of: A powerful Donovard family and rulers of Delavon Ministry that were longtime partners of the House of Avaleau kings of Donovan.

Vaudreuil Mountains: A mountain range west of Bredahade that forms the western border of Wallevet Ministry.

Vorrault: A free city in Wallevet Ministry, Donovan.

Wachot, House of: A powerful Donovard family and rulers of Barres Ministry.

Wallevet Ministry: A central territory of Donovan.

Wallon Arazmis: A member of the fifth generation of the Order of the Candlestone who assassinated Seralin the last Exarch of Pemonia in 2356. An ancestor of Arasemis.

wardenlord: The chief counselor to the emperor of the Rugen Empire who also serves as the ceremonial head of the wardens who govern the regions of Rugenhav on behalf of the emperor.

War of All Kingdoms: The final series of battles prophesied by the Order of the Candlestone to mark the end of the misguided modern era and the return to small, tribal societies ruled by elected chieftains.

Wartemur Army: An army that formed after the dissolution of the Frontier Corps in 2371 in what later became Donovan.

widsemer: A special scout trained in the ranger arts of spycraft, tracking, physical endurance, and poison-making established by the ancient master ranger Widsem. Adherents attend formal training at the Widsemer School of Rangerhood in Karnool, Austveeden, or one of a handful of training outposts across Pemonia.

wildermen: The modern Pemonian term for a variety of forest- or mountain-dwelling peoples believed to be the descendants of ancient native tribes.

wist: A gray-blue metal alloyed with gold, silver, iron, and copper to craft the signet rings of Donovard nobility used to authenticate documents.

Wosmok: An elite widsemer soldier of the Rugen Army used for subversion, sabotage, and assassination. The name is derived from the ancient Raffen word for *ghost*.

Zulgauet: A ruined warcastle sunken into a bog in Imvorlon County of Delavon Ministry, Donovan. It was built by the Frontier Corps during the colonization of western Pemonia.

ACKNOWLEDGMENTS

Thanks and appreciation to many for lending an ear, providing encouragement, and mending my scribbles. To my mother, who taught me to love books and to explore the art of writing. To my father, who taught me hard work and perseverance. And to my editors Anne McPeak and Tricia Callahan, for their talents and guidance.

ABOUT THE AUTHOR

CHRISTOPHER C. FUCHS writes the Earthpillar epic adventure novels and half-tales, with flavors of historical fiction, fantasy, and steampunk. *Lords of Deception* is his debut novel. He is also the author of *The Depths of Redemption*, *A Light in the Depths*, *The Revolution Machine*, *The Fourth Messenger*, *Arcodum*, and *The Feuding Tower*.

To stay informed of upcoming books and receive discount codes, subscribe to the Earthpillar mailing list at EarthpillarBooks.com.

ৎ

Save money, shun pirates, and support this author by buying direct from the Loremark storefront at Gumroad, where books often cost less for Earthpillar subscribers.

https://gumroad.com/loremark

SNEAK PEEK

The story of Arthan, Arasemis, Milisend and the others will continue. But for now, go back in time, nearly eight hundred years before Arasemis revives Candlestone, to witness the very beginning by reading the double-prequel to *Lords of Deception*. The first book is a journal written by Rildning himself, then step out of the journal and into an age of conquest and exodus across the New World that would set the stage for *Lords of Deception*...and what comes next.

The Depths of Redemption

Craving the adventures of his past life as a colonial knight, Rildning joins an expedition to seek allies among the natives of the New World of Pemonia. When the mission goes awry, Rildning learns the true objectives—gold and blood. Feeling betrayed by the empire and haunted by his past, he pushes onward in search of a lost companion.

Rildning struggles to survive the wilderness only to be taken captive by natives. By abandoning his old life and enduring the natives' trials, he earns their respect and finds a new purpose—and even love. As the imperial legions threaten the natives' capital, Rildning discovers an ancient prophecy that could bring the Old and New Worlds together, or forever keep them at war.

A Light in the Depths

Suffering heavy losses in a widening war, Rildning and his Gallerlander companions fan out across the continent to persuade other tribes to join in a common defense against the Brintilian Empire. But Rildning discovers that ancient tribal rivalries die hard and many still suspect him of spying for the empire.

And Rildning has another problem: his journal now lies in the hands of Marshal Hilsingor, imperial commander of the Frontier Corps. Knowing his enemy well, Hilsingor is determined to undermine Rildning's efforts and eradicate the remaining tribal enclaves.